Where the Dead Walk

By John Bowen

For Caroline, Henry and Freya

'Spirituality can mean something that I'm very sympathetic to, which is a sort of sense of wonder at the beauty of the universe, the complexity of life, the magnitude of space, the magnitude of geological time. All those things create a sort of frisson in the breast, which you could call spirituality. But I would be very concerned that it shouldn't be confused with supernaturalism.'

- Richard Dawkins.

'We don't really understand most of what's happening in the cosmos. Is there any afterlife? Who knows?'

- David Eagleman.

Chapter 1

The staircase sways in shot as the camera tracks the small group climbing its narrow wooden steps. The image is grainy, green-tinted monochrome, low light amplified 'night vision', a style of video familiar to regular viewers of TV paranormal investigation show *Where the Dead Walk*.

The group gathers at the head of the landing before a door. One after another they step through it into the void beyond. The camera follows, crossing the threshold to reveal a large attic space cluttered with bric-a-brac, disused furniture, crates and boxes. It seeks out a slim woman and a heavyset rural-looking man sporting beefy muttonchop sideburns. The night vision's idiosyncrasies conspire to transform the two into an otherworldly-looking duo, the man resembling some sort of Tolkienesque troll, the woman an ethereal albino creature with luminous eyes and a dark seam snaking up the left side of her neck.

In reality their appearance is somewhat less exotic. The man is the landlord of the public house in whose attic the group presently huddles, the woman is Kate Bennett, *Where the Dead Walk*'s principal presenter. When not rendered via night vision her eyes are a simple, sober, mahogany brown and the dark seam climbing her neck is easily identifiable as a burn scar.

She places a hand on the landlord's arm. "This is where most sightings of the apparition have occurred?"

"S'right," the landlord responds. "Majority of the staff won't come up here alone anymore."

"How many people claim to have witnessed the Pale Lady?"

"Over the years? Loads."

"You mentioned objects being moved, knocked over, sometimes even appearing to have been thrown?"

The landlord nods. "That's not all. Few weeks ago I was shifting some stuff over there and the door slammed shut for no reason. BANG! Just like someone had given it a good shove. I'm not easily spooked, but even so I tend not to hang around up here any longer than need be."

Kate nods sympathetically. "Can we stay for a while?" She looks to check with the rest of the crew. "Is that alright with everyone?"

The crew mumbles their consent.

Kate calls forth one of the group, a short, neat-looking, middle-aged man in a dark suit. "Charles? Can you sense anything here with us?"

The man nods. "I certainly can, Kate. There's a good deal of energy concentrated in this space. I'm certain at least one presence is..." He pauses, his face registering surprise. "Goodness me. Did anyone else feel the temperature drop?"

There are vague mumbles of agreement.

The man, Charles, looks around, as though trying to track something travelling among the cobwebbed rafters. "I feel very strongly there's some manner of unfinished business connected to..." He closes his eyes, cocks his head to one side as if hearing something the others cannot. "*Ah*..." he sighs decisively, "the spirit belongs to a woman, one burdened with a terrible anguish, a feeling of unforgivable betrayal. *How could he have?* she thinks. *How could he have—*"

The man breaks off abruptly, startled by a loud crash.

The camera spins around, wobbles uncertainly for a moment before pulling focus on the shattered remains of a vase on the floor. The attic erupts in a jumble of screams, swears, and frantic movement...

The view lurches back up, captures everyone scrambling for the doorway, until a female voice calls out apologetically.

"Ah, sorry everyone, I think I may have caught that with my elbow."

"For Pete's sake, Claire," exhales a man's voice from behind the camera, and then a moment later, "My poor heart's going like the clappers..."

"Your heart?" another male voice chirps. "Never mind your heart. What am I going to do about my bloody pants?"

And just like that the tension is punctured. Everyone laughs.

—

Kate turned to Keith, who was perched in front of the MacBook Pro's screen.

"Okay, skip back approximately six seconds and cut as everyone's bolting for the door."

"Eh?" Keith twisted from the display, running a rough assembly of the previous night's footage on Final Cut Pro. He had honed what he dubbed his 'flash edit' down to a fine art. In just a few hours now he was able to put together a collection of the most promising sequences captured from the previous twenty-four hours filming while still at whichever local hotel the crew happened to be using. It was a great way to gauge how well a location had played, or in this case hadn't.

Kate pointed to a spot on the thumbnail timeline at the top of the screen. "There. After the shot moves to the broken vase and everyone's freaking out and scrambling for the door, but before Claire speaks."

"Um... Kate, won't that make it look like..."

"Like what?"

"Like the vase could have been broken by, you know..."

"What?" she asked innocently.

"Well, a ghost or poltergeist or something."

She shrugged. "Who's to say it wasn't?"

"Erm, well, Claire? She said she knocked the vase over?"

"No," Kate corrected him. "Claire said she *may* have caught the vase with her elbow. Maybe she didn't?"

Keith leaned back. His paunch pulled against his t-shirt; it bore a graphic of Mr T's face and underneath it the legend, 'Quit your jibber-jabber, fool!' He had an eyebrow raised and an expression that said *really?*

Kate looked him square in the eye.

"Look, Keith," she said. "The 'Bale of Hay' episode was a duffer. Pretty much the entire night was a washout. We could really use at least one juicy incident..."

"I don't know, Kate... What happened to the show's mission statement? I thought it wasn't supposed to be about 'juicy incidents', you know?"

Kate steeled herself. There was a line to walk here, and not just with Keith, but the show itself. They had set out with the finest of intentions—firmly committed to the rigorous investigation of the paranormal, without any manufactured flash, and mostly they had followed through. Mostly.

At the outset they had even drafted a mission statement detailing the spirit in which they would carry out their investigations. They agreed the credibility of the show hinged upon securing the viewer's trust. You had to be seen to be serious, or at least reasonably sober. If there was a bump, you raised the possibility of dodgy plumbing first. If there were claims of ghostly figures wafting about, you first ruled out things like light from passing traffic refracting through window panes and so forth. This was how you established and built up your credibility, then when you did encounter stuff that wasn't so easy to explain away it had greater impact. If your audience viewed you as a bunch of gullible ninnies who thought every creak was a restless spirit that was impossible. On the other hand, put out too many shows without an unexplainable bump, strange shadow or such and you ran the risk of serving up some perilously dull viewing...

As admirable as the whole 'staunchly objective stance' thing was, circumstances had changed since the show's inception. The 'Bale of Hay' provided a case in point. In an ideal world they would just drop it and do another location. Unfortunately the ideal world wasn't the one they inhabited. They existed in a world metered by time and budgetary constraints, under the beady eye of a new commissioning editor Kate suspected would like nothing more than to ditch their show entirely. Tight on money and short on time, they had to get season two in the bag, and make it look worth the effort. As a result the 'Bale of Hay' was going to have to pull its weight.

She shifted her chair around, faced Keith head on and addressed him earnestly.

"Can I ask you something, Keith?"

"Sure, Kate."

"Why do you think people watch our show?"

"They're interested in ghosts, paranormal activity, all that stuff."

"I agree. Absolutely. Our viewers sit themselves down on their sofas hoping to catch a glimpse of the paranormal. They want to see us brush up against the 'other side'. They're hoping to see ghosts, tables tremble, light bulbs flicker, watch Charles converse with poor souls unable or unwilling to 'cross over'. There's an audience for that, Keith." She paused. "Now—and feel free to be as candid as you like with me here—do you think there's a similar sized audience hungry to watch a show about Claire destroying pottery? Do you think that show, let's call it 'Spatially Challenged with Claire Montgomery', would pull in as many viewers?"

"No, Kate," Keith sighed dryly. "I don't expect it would, but aren't we supposed to be committed to investigating *real* incidents of paranormal activity?"

Kate deliberately didn't respond.

Keith frowned uncertainly. "Aren't we?"

"Yes. Of course we are. Absolutely," Kate said after a second or two. "But, maybe, we can offer more than just that."

"We can?"

"I think so," Kate said. "Let me ask you something else. You ever camp out as a kid, or have a sleepover with a friend?"

"Yeah..."

"You and your friend ever swap spooky stories? Ghost stories, urban myths, that kind of thing?"

Doubtless beginning to wonder where Kate's line of inquiry was heading, Keith nevertheless nodded.

"Of course you did. Me too, and you know what? I loved those stories; still do love them in fact. One of my favourites featured a husband and wife house-hunting with their young daughter. They've seen a wonderful place with an unbelievable asking price in their local property paper and arranged a viewing... You familiar with this one?"

Keith shook his head.

She continued, "Well, when they arrive the place looks stunning, even better than it had in the property rag. Not only is it in a prime location, it's in immaculate condition. The garden's incredible too, big and beautiful with a charming old oak tree at the bottom, complete with a swing hanging from one of the boughs. Maybe because it's so easy for them to imagine their little girl playing happily outside they suggest she does just that while they take a look around inside. The house doesn't disappoint. Practically falling over themselves to make an offer, they go have a chat with the agent, at which point their interest abruptly cools...

"Driving home, their daughter asks them if they're going to buy the house. The mum and dad share a glance, and say the house was okay, but maybe not for them. In the back seat, the girl shrugs. After a beat, she tells them she enjoyed playing in the garden, but thought the big girl was mean to not let her have a go on the swing.

"The couple, who checked on their daughter from every one of the house's rear facing windows and saw no girl, suddenly go deathly pale as the conversation they had with the agent replays in their heads. When they enquired why such an amazing property was on the market for such an attractive price, a little reluctantly, the agent had explained. The owners were seeking a quick sale because they couldn't handle living there any longer following a tragedy they suffered the previous summer," Kate paused before giving up the punch-line with a wicked grin, "when their teenage daughter fell from the swing in the garden and broke her neck!"

Despite himself, Keith started to smile.

Smiling right along with him, Kate kept rolling. "Okay, okay, please, one more? And I swear this one's actually true—my next-door-neighbour's sister's aunt actually worked with someone who was friends with the couple it happened to.

"It's a dark, foggy night, right? And this couple are driving home through some country lanes when a woman suddenly appears in their headlights waving her arms. The guy hits the brakes and they screech to a halt.

"The woman's white as a sheet and shaking badly. Clearly distraught, she begs for their help. The car she was in slid off the road and crashed; her little boy is still trapped in the backseat. The guy immediately jumps out and leaves his girlfriend to take care of the woman and call an ambulance while he goes to rescue the kid. He comes upon the wreck a short stretch up the road and, sure enough, hears crying coming from the back seat. Wrenching open the crumpled door he finds the woman's son, a toddler, bawling but, thankfully, uninjured.

"In the front of the wreck it's a different story; the figure in the driving seat is ominously still. Reaching forward he checks their neck for a pulse, only to confirm the worst; the driver's dead. He takes the boy and carries him back to where his girlfriend's waiting with the woman, except when he gets there he finds his girlfriend alone.

"'Where's the woman?' he asks.

"'She took off after you,' the girlfriend says, arguing she thought it best she stayed put for the ambulance.

"The guy unloads the toddler on her and sprints back through the fog to the site of the crash. He calls out to the woman, but there's no answer. Fearing she was more injured than she appeared, he begins to search for her, circling the wreck. As he moves around to the front of the vehicle he glances through the broken windscreen. The corpse behind the wheel stares dead-eyed back at him, freezing him in his tracks, because she is…"

"The same woman who flagged him down," Keith finished, his smile broadening into a wide grin.

"Pretty good, eh?" Kate said, grinning along with him, but quickly she added, "You know what's really funny, though? Even as we both shared those stories, Keith, in tents with our pals in our back gardens or sleeping bags on our bedroom floors, I'm willing to bet we were both ninety-nine-point-nine percent sure they were complete rubbish—but we didn't really care."

Keith's smile faltered suddenly. "I guess so…"

"Why do you think that is?"

Before he could respond, Kate deftly supplied the answer for him.

"I think it was because that last zero-point-one percent of doubt was enough," she said. "Enough to make our hearts thump a bit quicker, enough to raise the goose-bumps a little, enough to let us wonder if there might not be more to it all, more than we think we know about life and death. And that's another reason I believe people watch our show, Keith. They're still open to that zero-point-one-percent. They're hoping they might just catch a glimpse of that dead woman in the driver's seat or the ghostly teenager haunting that back garden."

"But—" Keith started.

Kate cut him off. "Hey, don't get me wrong, I'm not for one instant suggesting we fabricate anything. I'm no cheat, and I'm no dyed-in-the-wool cynic, either. I've always been open-minded to the existence of the paranormal. I honestly do believe things happen which can't be readily explained, and one day I dearly hope to capture something like that on camera, but until then... I don't think it hurts to toss our audience the odd bone. I mean, really, is that so bad?"

"I... suppose not," said Keith, uncertainly. He glanced at the MacBook Pro's screen. "Well, I suppose Claire *did* say she may have caught the vase with her elbow..."

"Exactly," said Kate. "So... we cut just after the vase breaks and everyone goes nuts?"

"I guess..."

Before he had time to reconsider, Kate shot him a smile, gave him a squeeze on the shoulder and got moving. Out in the hotel corridor the smile immediately wilted. Despite the spiel she had just delivered, her conscience felt the uncomfortable pinch of compromise.

15

She and her business partner, Henry White, had expected producing season two of the show to be easier. They had, quite reasonably, assumed everything would run smoother thanks to the experience they had gained putting together the first. If anything, though, it had proved to be even harder, and that was without factoring in the whole business with Viva TV's new commissioning editor, John Dickinson. From their very first meeting his interest in the show had come across as distinctly lukewarm. He had intimated if season two didn't deliver Viva might want to reconsider picking up a third.

Keith's reaction was understandable, like the rest of the crew he was blissfully ignorant of Dickinson's grumblings. The reality was, however, that season two needed to get bums on seats. From this perspective, high-minded 'mission statements' started to look like something of a luxury.

–

It was a dour morning. The weather was being almost aggressively sullen. For her part, Kate tried to count the positives and be thankful the drizzle had let up for a spell, rather than focus upon the wind which was blowing stiff enough to steal hats and toupees.

Henry White, her co-presenter, co-producer, and business partner, bounded over. Athletic and disgustingly fresh-faced for his thirty-six years, Henry was one of those enviable people who seem to possess endless reserves of energy.

"Good to go?" he asked.

Kate belted her coat tighter. "Whenever you're ready."

She took a second and attempted to compose herself in front of the Bale of Hay's wonderfully imposing

Tudor entrance, clawing a handful of hair from her face, only for a surly gust of wind to blow it right back an instant later.

Mark, the camera operator, was hunkered down, peering into his viewfinder. He had set the camera up at ground level to better capture the building against the backdrop of the pewter grey sky. He made a couple of final adjustments and indicated he was good to go. Keith dashed over, fussing with Kate's mic yet again, grumbling about the wind. Kate told him not to fret. If it picked up on the audio too much they would just have to dub over it later. Finally, Henry readied the clapperboard in front of Mark, smartly brought it down. Kate took her cue.

She stared back at the Bale of Hay for a few seconds, as though contemplating the edifice, and then turned, directing her gaze straight into the camera's eye.

"The night we spent in the Bale of Hay did not pass without incident," she began. "Henry and Keith both witnessed what appeared to be a strange shape moving through the cellar. Was this the same restless spirit others have reported seeing here, the wife of the building's very first landlord, the so-called Pale Lady, rumoured to have taken her life after finding her husband in the arms of another woman, or perhaps some other troubled entity? And what of the potential poltergeist activity we witnessed, the swinging lampshade on the upper landing and the vase dashed to pieces on the attic room's floor?"

She paused momentarily, adjusting her features into a picture of consternation. "We've encountered many strange things during the course of our investigations. For many of them, one may be able to suggest entirely reasonable, scientific, explanations. And yet, just because a rational explanation *can* be put forward, that doesn't necessarily rule out a supernatural one. More and more often I find myself wondering how thin the line is that separates the gullible from the open-minded, the rational from the hopelessly blinkered? Because if we're to find incontrovertible proof of the paranormal this is the line we must tread. We hope you'll continue to join us on our journey as we venture into places—" pause for dramatic effect—"*where the dead walk.*"

Henry brought down the clapperboard. "That was great Kate. We can do another take if you like, but I honestly think we—"

Henry was silenced mid-sentence by an anxious cry of, "Kate!" The show's production assistant, Claire, was sprinting over. The look on her face alone was enough to tell Kate something was terribly wrong.

"I just got a call from the office," Claire said, stricken. "They've been trying to reach you. It's your dad, Kate. He's been taken to hospital. They think he's had a heart attack."

Chapter 2

Henry insisted on driving her to the hospital. Kate felt sick, her head swarming with grim scenarios; like a cloud of angry hornets these thoughts bumped and buzzed, stopping only to sting. Part of her refused to believe it was happening. Her father didn't have a weak heart; he was strong as an ox. There had never been even so much as a hint there was anything wrong with his heart...

"Not long now."

Kate realised Henry was talking to her.

"The hospital, Kate, we're almost there," he said kindly.

Shaken from her thoughts, Kate suddenly became aware of just how rapidly they were travelling. Had they been going this fast the whole time? Watching the world blur past from the passenger seat of Henry's immaculate and beloved seven-year-old Aston Martin, she was forced to concede there were times when a sports car was good for more than just looking flash. She resolved never to tease Henry about his pride and joy again.

They hit traffic on the way into the city. Henry was forced to slow down and thread his way through it until finally they reached the hospital. He got her as near to the front entrance as he could and she jumped out.

"You okay?" he asked.

"No," she admitted, "not really."

"I'll park up and be right with you."

She shook her head. "You don't need to stay. I've no idea how long I might be here. Go home. I'll call you as soon as I find out..." *How bad things are?* "...what the situation is."

"Are you sure? I can—"

19

"Go home, Henry. Please."

—

Reception, lift, brisk walk. When Kate got to the Coronary Care Unit she found a couple of police officers waiting for her near the friends and relatives room.

"Aggravated burglary?" she echoed, in response to the female PC's summary.

"It looks that way, Miss Bennett. From what we can gather your father arrived home and disturbed the thief. One of his neighbours—" the PC checked her notepad— "a Janette Holloway, saw a bearded male fleeing the scene. Suspicious, she crossed the road to check things out and found your father lying in his hallway. It was Ms Holloway who called for the ambulance. Your father was very lucky, Miss Bennett."

"Lucky?" Kate repeated. Her dad had been robbed and suffered a heart attack in the same morning.

The PC caught her expression and quickly added, "Perhaps lucky was the wrong way to put it. What I meant was he was lucky to be discovered so quickly, lucky his neighbour, Ms Holloway, was proficient in first aid and lucky the ambulance was on the scene in minutes. These things can make all the difference."

—

Kate followed the nurse through the Coronary Care Unit's sterile tranquillity to a side room where a doctor was studying a monitor, and beside him her father lay still, eyes closed with an oxygen mask covering his nose and mouth. Whether asleep or sedated, Kate wasn't sure. What she did know was he looked deathly pale and horribly fragile.

When she neared him he opened his eyes, saw her and tried to say something, except the oxygen mask reduced his words to an unintelligible mumble. Kate leaned over him, stroked his forehead and whispered into his ear, determined not to let her voice wobble.

"Shush, Dad. It's okay. Please, just relax okay?"

She tried to muster a smile, send the message everything was going to be fine, that being in CCU wasn't such a biggie, but while the corners of her mouth went through the motions she feared the result lacked conviction. Despite a number of professional acting gigs before settling into presenting, Kate knew her limits. Although to be fair, she reckoned there were Oscar winners who would struggle under similar circumstances. If you happen to find yourself lying in a hospital Coronary Care Unit breathing from an oxygen mask, there are likely few thespians capable of conjuring smiles potent enough to convince you you're not at least part way screwed.

The doctor introduced himself and began to outline her father's condition. He supplied the salient details slowly, with the practiced air of someone accustomed to imparting grave news. When he dared to pause, the question hovering on her lips bolted.

"Will he be okay?" she asked.

"It's early days. We're giving him oxygen to take the strain off his heart, drugs to thin his blood, and of course we're monitoring him closely. It's not clear yet if he was assaulted. It's possible he sustained the bruising you see on his face there when he collapsed..."

The doctor continued. Kate shut up and listened, and slowly, bit by bit, the information sank in. The long and short of it seemed to be that while her dad wasn't out of the woods yet if the next couple of days went well there was every chance of a full recovery. When the doctor

21

left, Kate drew a chair up beside her dad's bed and sat down. A realization dawned on her; she had been expecting this to happen, or something like it. It was like she was cursed to keep one ear forever open, listening, waiting for the other shoe to drop, as though it were inevitable sooner rather than later something bad was coming... Her world had felt brittle for so long now, as if the people she treasured had all been set on fault lines, each one straining to split into yawning fissures and swallow them whole. First it had been her mum, then Robert and Joel. Now it seemed there was a grinding fault line right beneath her dad, and—

She drew a deep breath, fought to collect herself, deny the thin shoots of despair that threatened to take root. Instead she turned her attention outward, studied her dad's face as he dozed, a face that presently looked pale, drawn, and bruised.

After a while he stirred and tried to speak again, and again she kissed his head, shushed him, urged him to rest and he soon fell back to sleep.

Her mum and dad had been in their mid-thirties when they had adopted her. Not exactly ancient, but hardly kids either. They were her family, her whole family. Their own parents had passed away in late middle age, and neither had brothers or sisters. As a consequence, Kate had no aunts, no uncles, and no cousins. There had just been the three of them, which in Kate's book had been just fine. She had never wanted for more. Her family had felt complete, and then, when she was fourteen, her mum had got sick. After much pestering she and her dad had finally persuaded her to see a doctor. There had been tests, and following these a diagnosis that was really closer to a sentence.

The cancer had taken her less than a year later, nine days after Kate's fifteenth birthday. Back then, the cracks snaking across her world had been mere hairlines, she reflected bitterly, all but invisible. She'd had no idea of what was to come... And now, if she lost her dad—

With some effort she shut down this train of thought and reached for his hand again, taking care to avoid the drip line that vanished into a vein beneath a swatch of micro-pore. She tried not to see how every minute, hour and day of his sixty-four years were laid bare, and failed. How could she not suddenly notice the hair tufting from the cuff of his hospital gown was coarse and grey, how prominent the veins were atop his hands, how the skin bunched at the knuckles? The sobering conclusion was that they looked dangerously like the hands of an old man. When exactly had this happened? When had her dad's big strong carpenter's hands become these old man's hands? Today? Last month? Last year? When?

She remained by his side through the afternoon into the evening, and then late into the night, until finally exhaustion, the doctors' sincere assurances they would contact her if there was any adverse change in his condition, and indeed her dad's own oxygen mask-muffled pleas had finally persuaded her to go home and get a few hours' sleep. When she left the CCU, she was surprised to find Henry waiting for her in the small family room outside. He spotted her through the large window, lifted his head from his jacket rolled up behind his neck, raised a hand and climbed stiffly to his feet.

As he emerged, Kate crossed the corridor to meet him. She was about to repeat how she had told him not to wait for her, that it really hadn't been necessary, but somewhere in the space of those few steps something else happened. She wound up in his arms.

He held her as she shook, her head buried under his jaw, tears sinking into the fabric of his shirt.

Chapter 3

Sebastian watched it again, skipping past the show's gothic opening sequence to the part where *she* appeared.

Kate Bennett stood before an old mill, her lips moving but silent. The sound on the television had been muted. Sebastian had watched the DVD countless times since obtaining season one of *Where the Dead Walk* and what Kate Bennett was saying wasn't important. His interest lay in what he could see. When she began to turn and gesture to the building behind her he hit pause. The image froze.

The burn scar that snaked up her neck was clearly visible, and quite distinctive. Her shirt collar was open, exposing a v-shaped area of chest converging in just a hint of cleavage. The pale scar tissue crested the apex of her shoulder, kinked, and curled upwards to disappear beneath her ear. On first sight he had been almost sure, tantalisingly sure, it was identical to the one he remembered, sure enough to begin making plans, sure enough to take action. Concrete proof was what he had required, and Renwick had just delivered it. He turned away from the television screen, began to sift through the series of digital stills spread out on the table.

The first was of a large manila envelope with a name and two words carefully handwritten on the front. The manila envelope simply read:

Kate
Adoption papers

Sebastian progressed to the next photograph. This one featured the first of several sheets of paper lying on the opened envelope. Sebastian re-read them in turn. He studied the information carefully, as he had done many times over the past few hours. There was no doubt about it; Kate Bennett was the girl. The scar had provided a spark of hope, the information Renwick had obtained this afternoon confirmed it. After years of searching, holding hard to faith, knowing she was out there somewhere, he had finally found her. What he could never have anticipated was how, through the medium of a cable television show, she had in truth found him. It seemed like nothing short of providence. He called back into the house and a woman, a fragile-looking dark-haired wraith, appeared in the doorway.

"Sebastian?" she enquired, her voice soft and eager.

"Go fetch Renwick. Tell him I have another errand for him."

Chapter 4

It was close to three a.m. when Henry drew up outside Kate's flat.

She had spoken little during the journey. Henry knew why. Kate was embarrassed. She was tough. Breaking down in front of him wouldn't sit easy with her. She was likely mortified about having, literally, cried on his shoulder, but he knew full well telling her this was daft would only make her feel worse.

She turned her face from the window where it had been directed pretty much since getting into the car and offered him a tired smile.

"Thanks, Henry."

"No problem."

She looked at him, seemed about to say something else, but didn't. The moment passed.

"Go get some rest," he said. "You won't be much use to your dad if you're exhausted, and don't dare worry about work. I'll take care of everything."

She studied him. The tired smile was back.

"You're not so bad Henry. Anyone ever tell you that?"

"I'm sure there are plenty who'd disagree."

"Would most of them be slim and blonde by any chance?"

He made a face at her. "What can I say? I'm often misunderstood."

"Hm. I'll bet."

"Come on," Henry prodded. "Get yourself inside, get some sleep. I'll stop by the office on the way home," he said, "see if there's anything urgent I need to attend to before tomorrow," his eyes went to the dashboard and caught the time, "...or to be more precise, later today." He ran a hand over a stubbly jaw and yawned.

"Why don't you come in for a minute, grab a quick cup of coffee? The last thing I need on my conscience is you falling asleep at the wheel and crashing into something. Nice car like this? It'd be a crime."

Henry considered giving her the face again, but then conceded she had a point. It had been a long day, on top of a very long night. A shot of caffeine wouldn't exactly hurt.

"Alright, a quick coffee and I'll leave you to grab some sleep."

—

It wasn't the first time Henry had been inside Kate's place. He had been before, mostly for work-related stuff, and then there had been that one night... The night that had started as a shared taxi home and ended with breakfast.

Kate dumped her bag on the dining table. "Sit down. I'll put the kettle on."

He strolled into the living area and obeyed, plonking himself down on one of the twin sofas. Quasi-open plan, clean and contemporary, Kate's flat was attractive and ordered, a lot like the woman herself. Henry sank back in the sofa and let his weary eyes fall shut. Uninvited, his unruly mind wandered and found itself back at *that* night, the night they had shared a taxi home following the season one wrap party at the office and Kate had told him to come in for a drink. He thought back to how they had tumbled through the doorway, sniggering at some joke Kate had cracked about the cab driver's aftershave, a scent she had dubbed *Kebab pour homme*. They had wobbled into the lounge, at which point things had taken a somewhat unexpected turn, to Henry at least. There had been a momentary, oddly-charged standoff and then they had practically lunged at one another. Lips, hips, zips, hands and buttons, hastily peeling off the other's clothes as they tumbled onto the sofa and—

"Henry?"

"Uh? What?" He opened his eyes, experiencing a half second of disorientation before looking up to find Kate standing over him, holding out a mug of steaming coffee.

"Penny for them?" she asked, head cocked as he relieved her of the mug.

"Pardon?"

"Your thoughts?" she prompted. "Wander off for a while there, did you?"

He recovered quickly. "Ah, no, just resting my eyes as my granddad used to say." He raised the coffee and took a sip. It was hot, and strong enough to rip a telephone directory in two. Just what he needed.

Kate dropped into the sofa opposite, and for a moment they both sat in silence, drinking their drinks, then out of the blue, Kate said, "So, do you think maybe Dickinson's got it in for us?"

John Dickinson was Viva TV's commissioning editor. Kate was alluding to Dickinson's veiled comments regarding where *Where the Dead Walk* fit, or perhaps no longer fit, into Viva's portfolio of original programming. Soon after being appointed he had summoned them for 'an informal meeting' to discuss the 'disappointing' ratings for the tail-end episodes of season one.

They had been surprised and unsettled by Dickinson's perspective. To begin with, the ratings toward the end of the season one's run hadn't been poor, just not as good as they had been for the opening half, the strength of which had been considered

28

something of a pleasant surprise by Dickinson's predecessor. In their view, the show was still finding its feet, finding its audience, and compared to Viva's other home-grown shows, even taking into account the tail off, the figures were decent enough.

"It's possible," Henry mused, "but I think he's more likely just blowing smoke. He knows they'd be daft to rely on the U.S. stuff too much. If the channel's going to build any kind of identity it needs domestic productions. Perhaps he's just trying to make sure we keep our foot on the gas?"

"You think? I'm not so sure. I wonder if he doesn't like our deal predating him. Maybe he's one of those guys who need to have their fingerprints on everything?"

"Look, he came in promising the brass better ratings. He's just pushing some of the pressure down, that's all."

"I don't know," Kate yawned. "Maybe it's—" She yawned again.

"Okay," Henry said, "enough shop talk. *You* need some sleep, and I should be going, right after I take a quick trip to your bathroom?"

Kate waved a hand toward the hallway. "Knock yourself out."

"Cheers."

When he returned a few minutes later he found her curled up on the sofa. Her eyes were closed and she was snoring quietly. Sheer exhaustion had triumphed. He stood for a moment, just looking at her. Asleep, the armour was gone. She looked peaceful, vulnerable. It made him feel protective toward her. She'd had more than most people's share of bad luck. For her sake, he hoped her father's heart attack was a passing shadow and nothing more.

Their little 'thing' following the season one wrap party slipped unbidden into his mind again. He recalled lying still beside her the following morning, trying not to disturb the tender insides of his skull, feeling curiously content, even entertaining thoughts of what kind of couple they might make. For about twenty or thirty minutes it had been easy to ignore his complete inability to achieve anything resembling a monogamous relationship, easy to overlook Kate's... well, own particular baggage. The daydream actually began to seem plausible, and then Kate had woken up—and wasted no time establishing what happened had been a... mishap. He could relax, she reassured him. No harm, no foul. What else could he do but echo her sentiments? They agreed it had been an accident, caused by high spirits and/or strong spirits. It didn't have to mean anything. There was absolutely no reason why their private and professional friendship shouldn't just carry on exactly as it had before.

And the surprising thing was it had.

Things did just carry on as they had before, sort of.

Henry collected the two empty coffee mugs and returned them to the kitchen. Back in the lounge, he pulled the throw off the sofa, draped it carefully over her, and deftly slipped a cushion beneath her head. She stirred momentarily, mumbled something, but didn't wake.

Finally, before letting himself out, once he was absolutely certain she was fast asleep, he bent and kissed her forehead.

Chapter 5

The house stood at the top of the hill, alone.

Beyond, the cliff edge dropped away to a tar black sea that shone darkly under the night sky. The house was not as old as it appeared, having actually been built around a decade previously. Despite this it looked like it had been perched on the rise for a century or more. The Victorian style architecture contributed greatly to this false impression, but so equally did the years of neglect it had suffered. The house had effectively been vacant since the day it had been built, and not a shred of maintenance had been carried out in the intervening years. Creepers had been allowed to scale its walls unchecked, moss to grow in thick clumps over its tiles and brickwork, and a decade of accumulated grime and the glare of a dispassionate sun had bleached its once white-washed rendered walls a bleak tombstone grey.

It was in the small hours that Renwick ground to a halt, parking his Land Rover beside the rough track leading to the rise. Stiff from hours of driving, he elected to get straight to work rather than idle in the car until sunrise. Torch in hand, he unstrapped the ladder from the Land Rover's roof, collected the large steel toolbox from the boot, squeezed through the weed-choked gate and set off up the hill, wading through the knee-high wild grass to where the house brooded in silhouette.

He put the ladder to one side for the time being and set the toolbox on the front porch. He knelt, popped the catch, flipped the lid and removed a steel crowbar. The tool in hand, he began to circle the house, sizing up the job. Halfway around, he chose a window and began to lever off the wooden boards. When he was done, he moved along to the next one, and the next. With every additional one an indefinable unease seeped into him. Whether it was the crowbar in his hands, or the hour, or the near silence broken only by the gurgling whisper of the sea beyond the cliff, Renwick felt like a trespasser, which was foolish. The house not only belonged to Sebastian, it was Sebastian who had sent him here to prepare it. He told himself this several times, but reason proved a poor remedy. The feeling persisted.

Once all the ground floor windows had been seen to, Renwick returned to the Land Rover, fetched the ladder and began to tackle the upper ones. Around an hour later every black-eyed window was done. Only the front door remained boarded up. Warm from his exertions, despite the chill of the night air carried off the ocean, Renwick climbed the steps to the front porch to finish the job.

With a grunt, he prised free the last of the boards sealing the door and set them aside with the rest at the back of the property.

He fetched the house keys from his pocket and sorted through them until he located the one labelled *front door*. It slotted easily enough into the lock, but turned with a dry grinding scrape.

Renwick pushed the door wide and peered inside the house's interior. It was pitch black. He retrieved his torch and swept its beam through the large entrance hall. The circle of light skittered about, illuminating several doors, and a large staircase, all liberally draped in a heavy array of cobwebs. Renwick took a single step inside, and stopped.

A shiver ran through him. He swept the torchlight around some more, wondering why he felt so reluctant to enter. It was just a house, after all.

No.

It wasn't just a house. It was Sebastian's house.

He lifted his foot, set it back behind the threshold. It would be light soon enough, an hour at most.

32

He turned and stared back down the rise, just making out the Land Rover's roof beyond the tall grass and wild bushes. There was no reason to go stumbling around in the house right now, none at all. He pulled the door closed.

Far better to wait, wait for the light.

Chapter 6

Daylight cut through the window blinds. Kate blinked, disoriented, until she realised she was lying on one of her lounge sofas. Her eyes wandered to the wall clock. It was twenty past six in the morning.

She took note of the throw covering her and the cushion under her head.

Henry, she thought, and then, right on the heels of this, the hospital. She had to call the hospital, find out how her dad was. She reached for the phone, but just before her fingers made contact she hesitated. Someone from the hospital would have called if anything bad had happened, surely, wouldn't they?

She looked toward the window where the day was already underway, as yet untainted by news of either skew. She left the phone in its cradle and climbed to her feet, went to the bedroom. The wardrobe door slid sideways on its runner with scarcely a nudge. The top shelf was above her eye line, so a little rummaging was required before she found what she was looking for. The box was buried beneath some old blankets. Her fingers located its sides and tickled it forward until she got a proper hold. She brought it down and set it on the bed, but she didn't open it, not yet. It had been a while since she had last taken the box out, and she was wary of her motives.

Kate couldn't say if the things inside helped, she only knew that part of her needed them, needed to see them sometimes, touch them, to know they were there. She had got rid of nearly everything else, excised all the unintentional reminders, but had kept this small collection. Were someone to ask, she would probably tell them they were keepsakes, and while this was true in a way, it wasn't the whole truth.

She took the lid from the box and set it on the bed.

Inside a man's plaid shirt was roughly folded into a square. Upon it were two other items: a small black box, and a grey knitted rabbit. Kate reached for the small box first. She thumbed it open and looked at the pair of wedding bands inside. Next she removed the shirt and the knitted rabbit. She stared at them for a time, rubbing her thumbs over the fabric, knowing what she was about to do but unable to stop herself from doing it. She raised them to her face, closed her eyes, and drew in a deep breath.

Did she only imagine she could smell something of Robert on the shirt, or that Joel's funky baby smell still clung to the rabbit? After four years could there really be anything but the smell of cardboard box and wardrobe? She wanted to believe there was.

In the lounge the phone waited. For perhaps three or four seconds she entertained the thought of slipping on the shirt, pushing the wedding band onto her finger and curling up in her bed with the rabbit crushed to her chest, but she didn't. She refolded the shirt and set it back in the bottom of the box, put the knitted rabbit and the ring box on top and fixed the lid back in place, surprised, as she always was, how much strength these simple actions demanded.

The box required respect, chiefly because the items it held were, under certain circumstances, hazardous. Like radioactive treasures, the trio of innocent looking items had the potential to wither the spirit and poison the soul, something a widow, a childless mother, would be foolish to forget.

Kate lifted the box back onto the wardrobe shelf, pushed it out of sight and tugged the old blankets over it. The bedside clock read six thirty-five am. She went to call the hospital.

The switchboard answered straight away. She gave the receptionist the pertinent details, and endured a short but agonising wait to be offered some in return. The news that came back was good. Her father had slept through the night without incident, and had not long ago eaten a little breakfast.

Kate expressed her thanks and set down the phone. It was the very best news she could have hoped for.

Why then did it merely feel like a reprieve?

Chapter 7

"You scared me."

"Darling, I scared myself," Kate's father replied, fidgeting some in an attempt to get comfortable on a quartet of hospital pillows. "It's not like I planned to have a heart attack, you know? I wasn't thinking to myself, 'Hmm, you know what James? Today seems like the perfect afternoon for a myocardial infarction."

"There's no need to get smart."

Kate was sitting beside his bed in the ward. He was still hooked up to an ECG machine, but the IV line and the oxygen mask were, to her relief, no longer considered necessary.

He looked a whole lot better too. True, he was unlikely to be entering any triathlons in the immediate future, but he did look a good deal closer to his old self. This, together with the gentle, ambient bustle of the ward, helped distance Kate from the awful dread of the previous night. She wasn't foolish enough to think he was completely out of the woods yet, but it at least felt like they could peek between the tree trunks and glimpse where their old world lay.

"So what happened?" she asked.

Her dad shrugged. "I ate my breakfast, went out to fetch my paper as usual, except when I got back and let myself in I heard a strange noise from upstairs, a thump? I don't know. Anyway, I went to the foot of the stairs and listened for a bit. Then, just as I was beginning to think I'd imagined it, someone appeared on the top of the landing and came thundering down at me. I didn't have time to do much of anything, least of all get out of the way, so he just barged me aside and shot out the front door. I started after him, and suddenly had this terrific pain shooting down my arm. Then my chest began to hurt. Next thing I knew I was in the back of a speeding ambulance with a paramedic beside me."

"It sounds like we owe this neighbour of yours a big thank you. If she hadn't seen the guy running away and decided to check things out, she wouldn't have found you lying in the hall… She performed first aid on you and called the ambulance."

"Which neighbour?"

Kate tried to recall. "Holloway? Ms Holloway? I think that's right."

"Janette? Janette did all that?"

"If by 'Janette' you mean 'Ms Holloway' then yeah."

"Goodness," he said, presumably marvelling at Ms Janette Holloway's estimable resourcefulness. "And the house is okay?"

"The police told me it was secure."

"You wouldn't mind checking the place over all the same would you, just to set my mind at ease? See if anything looks to have been taken or damaged?"

"Of course I will, but I don't want you worrying about any of that. You need to focus on getting well. That's all that's important right now."

She leaned over and took his hand, kissed him on the cheek.

He squeezed her hand. "Ah, where would I be without you, Katie?"

"Hey, where would I be without you?"

Her retort was meant to have been offhand, flippant, but as soon as the words left her mouth their weight settled on her. No, really, she thought, where *would* I be without you? I'd have no one, no one at all. Something in her face must have betrayed her, because her dad suddenly squeezed her hand again.

"It's okay." he said firmly. "*I'm* okay."

"You really did scare me, Dad. I thought…"

"I know, but you should know I'm not planning on going anywhere, okay?"

"Can I have your word on that?"

"I promise to do my best," he said. "Is that good enough?"

Not really, she thought, but what she did was nod.

—

Home.

Kate parked up in front of her mum and dad's house, a traditional three-bed semi in a quiet avenue in Croydon. This was where she had spent her childhood, her adolescence, those early years of young adulthood, and barring minor changes it was the same as it had always been, which was to say beloved, safe, a place of countless happy memories.

Where most of the street had surrendered to the toothpaste-white lure of PVC double-glazing, the house still had its original hardwood sash windows, maintained by her father's own carpentry skills, same as the wooden garage doors, equally rarefied in a street full of metal up-and-overs. If maintaining the house had been her dad's preserve, then care of the small front garden had been her mother's domain. As a child Kate had spent whole afternoons helping her tend the borders and pots, planting, pruning, weeding and feeding. Since she had gone her dad had done his best to keep things looking tidy, but the result lacked something. While perfectly neat, there was something undeniably workmanlike about the job, a case of preserving what had existed when her mother was alive rather than breathing new life into it. It was hard not to feel sad about something organic and alive appearing to remain so fixed. As a retired carpenter, the workshop was where her father's interest lay. The simple truth of it was he preferred his vegetation cut, seasoned, and ready to saw, shave and chisel. A garden consisting of shingle and hardy alpine shrubs would have suited him better, and been less work...

"Excuse me?"

The voice, friendly, yet unexpected, made Kate start. She turned to find a woman standing at the foot of the driveway. She looked to be in her late fifties, well turned out and attractive, in an understated way.

"Sorry, I didn't mean to startle you," she said. "I just wanted to a... Your father, how is he?"

For a couple of seconds Kate was lost, and then the penny dropped.

"Ms Holloway?" she asked, somehow knowing already this was who the woman was.

"Sorry." Ms Holloway shook her head, admonishing herself. "I should have introduced myself. Yes, but please call me Janette." Janette Holloway advanced, extending a hand. "And you're Kate, of course," she said as they shook.

There was a queer moment in which Kate couldn't shake the impression she was being studied, almost like when someone recognised her, but couldn't place it was from seeing her on TV. You could see a person trying to work it out, struggling to reconcile how one part of him felt sure he knew her when another part insisted he didn't. This was similar, but somehow different.

"He's doing well, all things considered," Kate said. "The doctors seem pleased with his progress. I saw him this morning and he looked worlds better than he did last night. They say there's every chance he'll make a full recovery. I imagine a good part of that could be down to you finding him so quickly and taking care of him. If you hadn't got to him when you did, well, I'd rather not think about what might have happened," Kate finished.

Janette Holloway looked slightly abashed. "Well, I'd like to think I only did what anyone else would have in the same situation. When I saw that man running off I knew something was wrong, you know? I'm just relieved to hear James is alright."

Kate smiled. This was the kind of comment you would expect someone to say, except Ms Holloway—sorry, *Janette*—did genuinely appear relieved. Actually, some might think almost too relieved for simply a neighbour from across the street. Kate got the feeling she was missing something. She took a closer look at the attractive Ms Holloway. Well-groomed. Attractive. No wedding ring.

James?

Janette?

"Well," said Janette Holloway, "I'm sure you've plenty to do without me holding you up. It was nice to meet you Kate, and please send my... best wishes, to your father."

"Yes, of course. It was... nice to meet you too, and really, thank you, for everything."

With a parting smile the handsome Ms Holloway retreated down the drive. Kate stood for a moment doing her best to look like she wasn't watching her as she crossed back over the road to her house.

Her dad had been a widower now for, what, approaching twenty years? He had been a single parent before the phrase had even been coined, and yet he always seemed happy, despite having never met anyone else. Kate had occasionally wondered if that was simply the way things had turned out, or if it had been a conscious decision on his part. He had still been relatively young when they lost mum. Had it been a case of him not looking for someone else, or not finding anyone? As the years passed she had assumed it was the former, but she had no real way of knowing save to ask, and while she and her dad were close, there were still topics she would feel too embarrassed to raise, and this was one of them. Her dad had always seemed happy with his lot. He had his carpentry business and his workshop, and once retired he had just been free to spend more of his time in the latter. Nevertheless, it was hard not to view her dad's life as somewhat static, and quite solitary, especially since she had flown the nest.

Was it so astonishing that this Janette Holloway might be interested in him? Objectively, her dad still had plenty to offer. He was smart, kind, and attractive enough for an older chap, she supposed. Was the attraction mutual? Was something already going on? The prospect felt... strange. Sixty-five wasn't exactly ancient, and yet the idea of him romancing some chick over the road proved difficult for Kate to picture. Rather than try, she resolved to shelve these unexpected questions of her dad's potential romantic adventures for another time, and get down to the business of checking his house over.

She wasn't sure what she had been expecting once she got inside, but was almost surprised to find the hallway looking perfectly normal. She wandered through the downstairs rooms, finding them likewise undisturbed. She scaled the stairs, checking each of the rooms in turn, at last encountering evidence of the burglar's work. This wasn't to say everything had been turned upside-down, though, far from it. While the two bedrooms and dad's study had clearly been disturbed, the way in which they had was downright weird.

All the drawers from her dad's wardrobes and cabinets had been removed from their runners and laid on the floor in neat rows. It was all so ordered, so tidy, almost as if her dad's intruder was the world's only chronically afflicted OCD burglar. Why else the careful organisation? Had the thief hoped to conceal the break-in by putting everything back just as he found it, all save for a few valuable, well-chosen, pickings? Maybe buy days or even weeks before his crime was even suspected? If so, then what had been taken? It was impossible to know until her dad was able to go through everything himself. She stared at the orderly row of drawers on the floor, and shook her head, eventually concluding the best thing would be to leave everything in situ for the time being.

She patrolled the house, retracing her steps, checking all the doors and windows from top to bottom until she was satisfied they were all secure, and then let herself out. By the time she emerged it was mid-afternoon.

Hospital visiting hours didn't begin for a few more hours, more than enough time to drop by the production offices. She owed Henry an update.

Chapter 8

Bennett White's modest production offices resided in an unassuming Guildford business park. Nothing special to look at from the outside, they were for the same reason, agreeably quiet and anonymous.

After stopping by briefly in the small hours of the morning to check everything was okay, primarily that the stuff they had captured the previous evening had been backed up, Henry had returned home and grabbed a few hours' sleep before returning around noon. Truth be told, he couldn't really concentrate.

His mind kept turning to Kate and how her father was doing. From what Kate said, her father was the only family she had, something personally Henry found it hard to get his head around. His own family was huge. There was his mum and dad, his brother, his three sisters, and a whole bunch of aunts and uncles, not to mention around two dozen cousins and a brace of nieces and nephews. They were a pretty tight clan too. At a White family occasion, pity the photographer who neglected to bring his wide angle lens. When your entire family was reduced to a single person, though, what must that feel like? Especially when they had just suffered a heart attack...

He was aimlessly poking through paperwork in his and Kate's shared office when Ray Darling rapped on the door. Henry invited him in.

Ray was *Where the Dead Walk'*s chief researcher and location scout. A solid-looking gent with cropped greying hair and a quiet but attentive air about him, Ray was, at fifty-five, the oldest member of the Bennett White production crew. A former police detective who had left the force to start his own private detective agency, he was five feet eleven and thirteen stone of pure investigating machine. His agency had operated for five years before he had grown weary of tracing bad debtors, shifty insurance claimants, spying on suspected adulterers and finally chosen to enter early retirement.

When Henry and Kate were setting up Bennett White and scouting for staff, Ray had been recommended to Henry by a former client of Ray's. The format of the show demanded the production crew also appear on camera, making personality as important as their practical skills. Henry's friend believed Ray would make a great fit. After meeting him, Henry had agreed. Ray Darling came across as honest, earthy, and real. What Henry and Kate hadn't anticipated was the strength of Ray's imagination and tenacity. He had a way of burrowing into a place's history and unearthing just the sort of juicy details required to give it the aura of foreboding a *Where the Dead Walk* location begged for.

Henry set aside his paperwork.

"Hi, Ray, what's up?"

"I've just been on the phone to a chap named Sebastian Dahl, about a place he has on the south coast. Could be good."

Henry's interest was immediately piqued. It was rare for Ray to get worked up about a location, but something about this one had clearly got his attention. It wasn't that Ray was a curmudgeon, just that the majority of the locations they were approached with tended to fall into three predictable categories. Henry had dubbed them historical, entrepreneurial and delusional.

Historical sites were usually pretty fair game. Often they were looking for little more than to enhance their visitor numbers and maybe encourage folk to take an interest in their local history. If nothing else, they almost always promised decent atmosphere. Old buildings are apt to creak and groan almost constantly, and at night when it was deathly quiet the results can be conveniently eerie. They tended to enjoy grisly histories too, if you were willing to look hard enough. There was also the benefit, call it a mental tick, that people simply seem more willing to believe old buildings might be haunted. Henry found this pretty wonky logic, along the lines of if Loch Ness were twice as large then it should also be twice as likely to contain a sea monster, but so far as the show went, though, it didn't hurt any.

The next category was places owned by businesses hoping to gain some level of notoriety, and the increased custom that came with it. Usually these were pubs, hotels, or bed and breakfasts. You'd be surprised what a pet ghost can do for the old bottom line.

The last category was places owned by fantasists, those people inclined to see paranormal forces at work everywhere they looked, the sort of nuts who contact national newspapers because they find a crisp that looks like The Virgin Mary—if you hold it to the light, and squint a bit. Henry was eager to hear what category this Sebastian Dahl's house fell into and what made Ray think it was different.

"Okay, Raymond. Tell me, what we got?"

Ray was about to do just that when Kate appeared in the doorway. He caught Henry's eye and each knew the other was thinking the same thing: was Kate carrying good news or bad? She must have read the trepidation on their faces, because she immediately said, "He's doing fine. The doctor said he might even be able to go home as soon as next week."

"That's great news," Henry said.

"Terrific," Ray added.

"You have no idea," Kate beamed. "I take it everything is fine here?"

"Peachy," said Henry. "Actually, Ray was just about to tell me about a prospective location he's got. I get the impression it might be something special."

Kate raised an eyebrow. "Really?" She drew the chair from behind her desk and sat down. She looked keen to take a break from what must have been a very tense twenty-four hours. Henry could sympathise. Work could be a marvellous distraction from the real business of life sometimes.

"A bit special, hm?" she mused.

Ray leant forward, very nearly smiled. "Okay. Here it is. We got a call this morning from a property developer, a Sebastian Dahl. Claire gave me the basics and I got back to him. This chap, Dahl, claims to have a house that's stood empty for a decade because it's haunted."

"What's his angle?" Henry asked.

"Not quite sure yet," said Ray. "He developed the property from scratch, bought the site, and oversaw the design and construction of the place. It's a big Victorian style affair, incredible location, on a cliff-top on the south coast with an unobstructed view out to sea. His vision, he told me, was to create the type of house that's always in demand, but in equally short supply." Ray arched an eyebrow. "According to Mr Dahl, things worked out somewhat differently... He claims he's let the place sit vacant for so long simply because he doesn't really know what to do with it. Says he doesn't feel right about selling it, given what he knows."

"Pretty decent of him wouldn't you say?" Henry commented, making no attempt to hide his scepticism.

Ray's mouth curled into an arid smile. "Hmm. I believe I made a comment to that effect myself. Our Mr Dahl responded by informing me money wasn't really an issue. Apparently, he's built something of a property empire. Felt the need to tell me he made his first million at twenty-two and never looked back."

"I see," said Henry.

"So where do we come in?" Kate asked.

"He said he's seen our show, and was curious to see what we might be able to achieve. He mentioned Charles's efforts assisting troubled spirits to move on to the other side, and wondered if whatever was haunting his place might be similarly engaged with, moved on, so to speak. If the house was 'cleansed', then he would have no qualms about putting it on the market. If he had an angle, then I guess that could be it, but only if you believe *he* believes the place truly is haunted."

"Do *you* think he believes the place truly is haunted?" Henry asked.

"He seemed serious enough. Claims to have tried renting the house out a few times early on, only to have each of the tenants move out in a matter of days. Eventually, through a mixture of frustration and curiosity he decided to try living there himself for a while."

"And?" asked Kate.

"Said he lasted three nights."

"What happened?" asked Henry.

Ray's arid smile was back. "Noises, turning his back to find objects had been moved around, abrupt drops in temperature, all sorts of weird stuff. Claims after a couple of days his nerves were shot..."

"Okay," said Henry, pursing his lips. "It's interesting, Ray. How about we do a bit of digging on the place, and on this Sebastian Dahl bloke too? See if his story stands up. If it does, have Claire get back in touch with him and arrange a meeting for us at the site."

Like a fisherman who spies a tremor in his line, Ray nodded and was on his feet. "Leave it with me," he said, and added, "Glad to hear your dad's on the mend, Kate. If there's anything I can do, don't hesitate to ask, okay?"

48

"Thanks Ray."

Once the investigator had closed the door behind him, Henry turned to Kate.

"So how are you?" he asked. "Really?"

"I'm fine," Kate answered. "*Really*. My dad seems to have been pretty lucky. He's going to have to take it easy for a while, and there'll be some rehabilitation, I'm sure, but, yeah, it actually seems like everything's going to be okay."

"That's great. I'll do what I can to take the pressure off you here. Whatever time you need, we'll work around it. Okay?"

"Thanks Henry. You're not—"

"So bad?" he smiled.

She smiled back.

Chapter 9

Nadine twisted, reached back, pushed aside her long dark hair and appraised herself in the mirror. A series of angry red welts laddered her pale back. The scarlet strap marks climbed from the top of her buttocks to below her shoulder blades. As always Sebastian had been considerate, kept the strap's kisses where they could be easily concealed.

Nadine stared at the Nadine in the mirror, regarded her with a tight uncharitable grin. She held the gaze for a spell, then wheeled, scooping her robe from Sebastian's bed and slipping it onto her naked body. A brief frisson ran through her as fabric brushed against tender skin. It hurt, but only a little. Not enough to bother. Nowhere near enough to please.

One note does not make a song. For a song you need melody and rhythm, a variety of instruments. Hurt was similar, when executed skilfully by the right conductor it was sweet poison, pure black bliss.

Sebastian knew. He understood part of her needed the hurt, that if deprived of it she simply suffered in a different way; she began to feel detached, her grip on the world uncertain, everything threatened to grow mute and monochrome. Without ever being told, Sebastian knew how the hurt served to make everything real, more *there*…

And yet, it hadn't always been this way. Nadine could still remember, dimly, a time when the hurt had been inflicted mindlessly, for the sole gratification of others. Once, the hurt had brought only fear and misery, her first tastes born of her father's explosive temper. The old man's beatings would strike without warning, like lightning from a blue, cloudless sky. And later, after she had tired of his oppressive rule and decided to take her chances on the streets, there had followed the dull and boringly predictable violence of her clients, and the realisation some men were prepared to pay far more to indulge their sadistic appetites than others were to sate their sexual ones.

Somewhere along the way there had been a shift, though, the line got blurred. Where once she had feared hurt, then, in time, had learnt to tolerate and profit from it, eventually she had grown to need it.

She had been on a dangerous path, and had Sebastian not found her she was in no doubt she would have followed it to its inevitable conclusion. Like a junkie who little by little loses sight of how much is too much, she had been pushing further and further. Then he had come, and had shown her a way to master her appetite.

Oh yes, Sebastian understood hurt, maybe understood it better even than she did. He knew it was complex, potent. He had shown her how it could be channelled, harnessed as an instrument of power to achieve things beyond most people's pitiful imaginations.

He had helped her to see she was special, something he had identified from their very first encounter. He had plans for her. Together they were going to do something incredible, and afterwards he would love her forever.

Chapter 10

Kate collected her dad Tuesday morning. He had been hoping to get out of the hospital before the weekend but they wanted to monitor him a little longer before releasing him back into the wild.

Most of Sunday had been spent over at his house, giving it a quick once over, although to be fair it hadn't taken much to set things straight. James Bennett was an orderly soul. Even his workshop in the garden was neat and tidy. Every tool had a home, not to mention all those segregated drawers brimming with screws, nails and panel pins, and different grades of sandpapers... Kate had made a sortie to the local supermarket and filled his fridge, freezer, and cupboards with enough food to see out a siege. Her dad wouldn't have to worry about shopping for at least two weeks, which was good because he needed rest and recuperation, and Kate was determined to ensure he got it. The week he had spent in hospital had forced him to take it easy. Now he was home he would need to be reminded not to get carried away. She had almost succumbed to the temptation to fix a padlock on his workshop's door, lest the lure of timber, dovetail joints and the smell of sawdust got the better of him, but ultimately she had given him the benefit of the doubt.

She parked in front of her dad's drive and walked around to open the passenger side door for him, but before she had chance to it popped open and he climbed out. He appeared perplexed to find her standing with her hand outstretched for the handle, and then after a second or two of confusion he joined the dots.

He looked at her and let out an exasperated sigh. "Good lord, Katie, I'm not an invalid."

"You've just had a heart attack."

"From which the doctors say I can likely enjoy a full recovery." He looked her in the eye, inviting her to disagree. Tempting though the invitation was she chose to decline it. He seemed satisfied. "Come on, let's get ourselves inside, I'm ready for a decent cup of tea. That heart attack may not have seen me off, but too much more hospital catering might have."

Kate shot him a disapproving glare, but the result was pretty half-hearted. She was simply too happy to see her old dad back. The pale doppelganger she had encountered lying in the Coronary Care Unit scarcely a week ago had scared her badly. She would be prepared to do almost anything to never see that fragile facsimile of her father again.

They were hardly inside the house before her dad was filling the kettle. He busied about choosing a pair of mugs and giving them a precautionary rinse under the tap while the water came to the boil. His hospital holdall could be sorted through later, he argued, and as for the burglary, if anything had been taken it wouldn't be any less taken by the time they finished their drinks. They carried the tea through to the lounge, Kate watching her dad savour the simple pleasure of being back beneath his own roof, the feeling of having things returning to normal. She shared the sentiment. Sipping tea in the cosy front room where she had watched what seemed like a billion episodes of *Blue Peter* and *Take Hart*, a cataclysmic event like her father's heart ceasing to beat seemed as unthinkable as England winning the Eurovision song contest or Rosemary Conley serving up bread and dripping.

Eventually, though, when the mugs were drained, and her dad's hospital holdall had been emptied, there was the business of the freaky lined-up drawers to attend to. Kate followed her dad upstairs and showed him how they had been taken out and laid carefully upon the floor in neat rows, the ones in his bedroom, and the ones in his study.

"Well," he said, after pondering them for a spell, "it's a bit odd, isn't it?"

"I wondered if perhaps the burglar was intending to steal a few high value items then conceal having broken in by leaving everything exactly as it was. Failing that, maybe he was just the methodical type and he was determined not to miss anything? The only other explanation I can think of is he was looking for personal information, you know, bank statements, birth certificates, insurance policies, that sort of thing, to use for identity theft? Secure a bunch of fraudulent loans, something like that?"

Her dad looked unconvinced.

"Is that what burglars do these days in lieu of stealing your things, break in and sift through your paperwork?"

Kate shrugged, not entirely convinced herself they did. Wasn't the identity theft thing all done on the net? Breaking and entering to do it didn't strike her as making much sense. Once you've gone to the trouble of getting into someone's house, why not just rob them the good old fashioned way?

Her dad was still considering the neatly arranged drawers.

"I suppose I had better go through it all in that case, then," he said, "see if anything has been taken."

So he did. For almost two hours, he carefully sifted through the drawers checking for missing paperwork or other items.

"Anything?" Kate asked, not for the first time, when the last drawer had been examined.

Her father seemed to waver momentarily, but then said, "No. Everything appears present and correct."

"Are you sure, there's nothing at all missing? Jewellery? Cash? Anything?"

"No. I don't have much jewellery, you have your mother's things, and I don't keep much cash in the house, and the small amount I do keep to hand is still here."

Before Kate could quiz her father further, her phone started to ring. The caller ID informed her it was Henry. She excused herself and went out onto the landing.

"Hi, Henry."

"Hi. I just wanted to confirm our plans for tomorrow afternoon."

They had arranged to travel down to Cornwall to meet with Sebastian Dahl and view his 'haunted house' for a prospective *Where the Dead Walk* location. Ray had done a bit of digging on the place and Dahl's story about the place being empty for a decade appeared to check out. Henry was going to drive.

"You'll pick me up around nine?" she asked.

"Yeah, that should give us more than enough time to get there by two."

"Great. See you in the morning then."

When she returned to the study and slipped her phone back into her pocket, Kate noticed rather than her dad's attention being on the paperwork in front of him, it was on her.

"What?" she asked.

"Nice chap that Henry White."

"He's alright."

"You know, the last time I saw you together I came away with the impression he's quite fond of you. Very attentive, as I recall."

"We're business partners Dad. That's all, and besides, Henry's quite fond of women in general, if you know what I mean."

"Oh." Her dad looked a little disappointed. "Oh. I just thought, maybe..."

"Dad, don't."

"Don't what?"

"You know."

"I just want you to be happy, Kate. Is that so wrong?"

"I'm okay, Dad, really I am."

"Are you, though? I can't help worrying. You're still young, Katie. You could meet someone else, have another—"

"*Dad*."

Silence reigned for a moment. What had meant to be a plea for clemency had emerged as a rebuke.

"I'm sorry," she said, more softly. "I know you mean well, but I'm not ready for that, not yet."

"I know, I was only..." He stopped, defeated. "I do understand you know. I lost my wife far too early too, and had I lost you at the same time..." He paused, contemplating a hurt of such magnitude perhaps, but his eyes never wandered from hers. "This business?" He tapped the spot on his chest beneath which his heart lay. "It's made me realise something more than ever, Katie. We don't have forever to take what we want from life."

"I have everything I want."

His response was a taciturn nod that wouldn't have fooled a stranger, let alone his only daughter.

—

James Bennett accompanied his daughter to the front door.

"I'll be over tomorrow evening," Kate said. "Call me if you need anything, otherwise I'll see you then, okay?"

"Katie, I'll be fine."

"You'll keep the mobile phone I got you close, at all times?"

He couldn't help rolling his eyes, and briefly wondered if it wasn't worth pointing out who was the parent here. "Yes, Kate," he said instead. "At all times."

She hugged him then, a proper hug—the kind you don't get nearly so often once your child is all grown up. He hugged her back, and then she was disappearing down the drive and climbing into her car. He waved as she backed onto the road and drove off.

Then he shut the door and walked straight back upstairs.

He went to the drawer and pulled the large manila envelope out. The envelope had clearly been torn open and the adoption papers containing the information about Kate's birth mother and what had happened to them both all those years ago removed and gone through. He knew this because the sheets were out of sequence and creased a little, as though they had been hastily stuffed back into the envelope. Why on earth would a burglar be interested in them? The documents had no value to anyone but Kate and himself. Kate had never even seen them, had never wanted to. He and her mum had always made it clear they were available should she want to, but she had been resolute. The past wasn't important. As far as she was concerned, she said, her childhood had started the day she had become their daughter. James had always respected her wishes, but also knew she may feel differently one day. Circumstances change, and with it often one's perspective follows suit.

Carefully, he sorted the papers back into the correct order and put them into a fresh envelope, sealed it and returned it to the bottom of the drawer.

It took him a long time to fall asleep that evening, and once he did he didn't sleep well.

He woke in the small hours from a disturbing dream in which Kate was a little girl again. They were both trapped in a strange house, a wall of fire separating them. In the dream Kate was screaming for help, except when he tried to reach for her through the spreading flames she shrank back, eyed him like a stranger, and only screamed louder.

Chapter 11

Henry obeyed the sat-nav's synthetic schoolmarm's instructions as she guided him southward to the coast. The traffic was light and Henry and Kate chatted easily. The journey flew by and they reached the coastal village upon the outskirts of which Sebastian Dahl's 'haunted house' lay in good time.

Following a series of narrow snaking lanes flanked by rolling fields and hedgerows, they eventually arrived at the neck of a decidedly unkempt private road where the sat-nav schoolmarm informed them they had arrived at their destination.

They rumbled down the overgrown, gravel-studded dirt track for about a hundred metres until they encountered a gate and were forced to stop. The track continued past the gate for a further two hundred metres or so up to the house. Henry got out, intending to open the gate so that they could drive on and park in front of the house, a plan that was scuppered by a mammoth tangle of weeds, grass and bramble that had grown up around it. He engaged in a short bout of tugging and shoving, but it was no good, the gate was stuck fast. It would swing wide enough for someone to walk through, but that was about it. If they were going to get any nearer to the house it was by foot.

—

Kate watched Henry wrestle with the gate. She was getting out to help when he gave up. Once closer she could see it was a lost cause. The gate opened a little, but appeared unlikely to budge further for anyone not wielding an industrial strimmer, flame thrower, or failing these a tractor doing, oh, say forty? Henry's Aston Martin was staying right where it was. She joined him and they stared up at the house on the hill.

"Well," Henry said after a moment, "it at least looks the part doesn't it?"

Kate knew what he meant. Sebastian Dahl's faux Victorian house looked grim indeed. Its once presumably white-washed rendered exterior had weathered to a grubby sullen grey and great swatches of it were choked in creeper from the surrounding garden, left to roam unchecked. The house had gone feral. It seemed to brood atop the hill, isolated and unloved, daring them to approach.

She was saved from further idle anthropomorphising by the throaty growl of a car engine. She and Henry turned to see a sleek black car approaching them up the track. It drew up, parking beside Henry's Aston Martin. The Ferrari had scarcely come to a stop before the door popped open and a lean dark-haired man hopped out. Kate took him in. He was handsome and well-groomed. Understated, yet expensive, shirt. Designer jeans paired with dress shoes. Tastefully subtle tan. Colgate smile. George Clooney gene-spliced with a youthful Richard Branson. He strode over to meet them, hand outstretched.

"Kate Bennett?" he asked.

Kate shook his hand. "Sebastian Dahl?"

He smiled back, studying at her for a beat longer than might be considered well-mannered. He seemed to realise it too, because when he broke off the handshake he said, "Forgive me, but television doesn't come close to doing you justice."

Kate accepted the compliment with grace. "Thank you."

Dahl turned to Henry now. The hand was out again, the winner's smile ready. "And Henry White? I'm a huge fan of your show."

Henry hesitated, and for moment Kate was weirdly certain he wasn't going to shake Dahl's hand. It hung in the air between them for a beat, and then Henry stuck out his own.

"We do our best," Henry responded.

"Well, with that in mind," said Dahl drawing an almost theatrical breath, "I imagine you'd both like to see my haunted house?"

—

"So the house was built around ten years ago?" Henry asked, as they climbed the rise, beating a path through the knee-high wild grass.

"Yes," Dahl replied. "Planning had already been secured for an eight-bedroom dwelling on the plot when I acquired it. It seemed like providence, ideal for the project I had in mind."

"A large period-style property?" said Henry.

"That's right. I think I'd just reached a point where, personally, property development had moved beyond simply making money. I had a different goal in mind. I wanted to create somewhere special. Buildings can survive for centuries. I suppose I wanted to make one I would be proud to have standing long after I was gone, and not some indulgent architectural avant-garde confection, but a *real* house, to be lived in by generations, loved. When a business acquaintance, another developer, brought this site to my attention, it seemed a perfect fit. My beautiful house would get an equally beautiful setting."

"I see."

"The project grew into something of a labour of love. I fear I got carried away; the original budget was revised, and then revised again. Not a single corner was cut. I sourced only materials authentic to the Victorian period, and the construction enjoyed the same exacting detail and care. I was determined to craft something that transcended brick and mortar. I wanted to craft a building that had..." Dahl stalled for a moment while he searched for the right word, "... a soul." He offered Henry an apologetic smile. "I know that may sound somewhat pretentious, but it's an honest summation of how I felt at the time."

"Not at all," said Henry, reflecting on all the plastic mock-Georgian mansions that passed for luxury dwellings these days. In comparison, Dahl's goal sounded quite admirable. Whatever the guy's faults might be (and Henry already suspected rampant narcissism and over-confidence were at least two) the desire to build a beautiful, painstakingly authentic, period-style property wasn't among them. Henry was a fan of the solid grandeur of Victorian and Edwardian buildings himself, all that lovely incidental detail wherever your eye fell.

They crested the rise and fell under the house's dour shadow. Freed from the silhouette the sun's aspect had imposed upon it from the bottom of the hill, the building looked, if anything, even bleaker. Up close, they could see just how eerie and decrepit it really was. Henry had visited his fair share of supposedly haunted buildings in the course of filming the show, but this grim stack of tile, masonry and timber fit the picture of what a haunted house should look like more than all the others combined. Hell, it gave the house from the opening credits of Scooby-Doo a run for its money.

They stopped on the front porch while Dahl sorted through a set of keys. The tumblers in the lock growled as the key turned and the hinges squealed in sympathy as Dahl pushed the front door wide to reveal a dusty, cobweb-draped, entrance hall.

—

Dahl held his arm wide, inviting them to step inside. Kate let Henry enter first. They paused in the gloomy hallway, letting their senses sample the atmosphere and collect conscious notes of their first impressions.

The conclusion Kate quickly arrived at was this: If the rest of the property packed even half the punch of this modest space, they'd been handed an absolute gift. Everywhere you looked there was cobweb coated Victoriana, manna from heaven for a show like theirs. If you set out to construct most people's mental picture of what a haunted house was supposed to look like you would have been hard pressed to get much closer. She turned to Dahl, still in the doorway.

"Mind if we take our first look around the place alone?"

"Not at all. Feel free to look wherever you like. I'll be waiting here if you have any questions."

Kate turned to Henry. "You want to take upstairs? I'll do down here?"

"Sure."

Henry approached the entrance hall's ornately carved mahogany staircase. An impressive sheet of cobweb spanned the wall and bottom post. He drew a finger through the top. The web sagged and then collapsed.

He cast a look back at Kate and arched an eyebrow. She knew what he was thinking. It was almost like being on the set of a Hammer Horror movie.

He began to climb the staircase, venturing bravely into the unknown. Once he was out of sight, Kate weighed her own options.

Four dark panelled wood doors beckoned, one to her left, two to her right, and one ahead. Where to begin?

She went for the first door on her right and grasped the dusty brass handle. She was unable to keep herself from smiling as it swung wide with a pleasingly clichéd screech of parched hinge. A large dining room lay behind. She stepped inside. The door swung shut behind her and immediately, even knowing Dahl was on the other side and with Henry's muffled footfalls upstairs, she felt queerly isolated. A moment later this thought too garnered a grin. It was yet another positive sign.

Splitting up on initial viewings had quickly become the cornerstone of their evaluation process. Given that places simply aren't as creepy in the cold light of day, going solo provided something of an antidote. If roaming a location alone in the day was enough to provoke 'the creeps', then you could be pretty sure it would deliver in spades in the dead of night with company. For a location to work it had to be capable of getting under the crew's skin, everyone's unease had to be, at some level, genuine. Faking it wasn't an option, because if your viewers began to suspect that was what was going on you were in big trouble. Credibility was paramount. Squandering it had sunk similar shows. Honest to goodness, authentic spookiness was vital.

Kate meandered through the dining room, allowing the right side of her brain to soak up the ambience while the left took note of details. The house had never been broken into, or at least there were no obvious evidence of it having been. There was no graffiti on the walls or other signs of vandalism. True, it was located in a pretty rural area, but nevertheless the city girl in Kate found the idea of the house being empty for a decade without attracting the interest of squatters or criminals surprising. Like the hallway, the dining room exuded the stale and musty scent of disuse. It also shared a similar dressing of dust, cobwebs and period-style decor. Kate could imagine it being eerie as hell at night, not just due to its creepy aesthetics, but also from the knowledge it had been sealed up for so long, tomb-like, as though it had been buried or left to slumber, to wait for...

Kate frowned.

To wait for...? For what? Now where the hell had that idea come from? After a beat she continued; this place really was getting to her. She pressed on, circling the huge table in the centre of the room, barely resisting the urge to drag a finger through the thick blanket of dust on its surface, to the door leading to the next room. Another wonderful creak afforded access to a huge kitchen. The house's Victorian decor had been adhered to here too, in a room where a good many property developers might have felt tempted to compromise with something more modern.

Kate cast her eyes about, found no fridge freezer, no microwave or dish washer, and yet at the same time she strongly suspected they were here, artfully tucked away somewhere. Putting her theory to the test, she opened a nearby cabinet door and immediately discovered a dishwasher. Behind the next cupboard door along she found a fridge freezer, and behind another two a tumble dryer and a washing machine. She left the doors open for a moment.

Finally, with these things in plain sight something of the house's spell broke, its true age was suddenly rudely exposed. While it begged you to believe it had stood for a perhaps century or more, in truth it was bereft of any genuine history at all, had scarcely even been lived in. Its only inhabitants were a few extremely short-lived tenants and Dahl, who hadn't even lasted a week himself.

Her building impression of the house being perfect for the show suddenly faltered. In one respect it was perfect, visually it was the quintessential haunted house, and yet... What if, during filming, as the night wore on it was this feeling that prevailed? What if the house came across as nothing more than a well-crafted prop, like a movie set that looks utterly convincing, until you pop your head around a corner and find nothing but struts and plywood and fresh air?

They had fast discovered that when it came to locations older buildings were the easiest sell. If a building had history then somehow the prospect of it being haunted seemed more credible, and the older the building the more pronounced the effect. History becomes ingrained in a building. People leave something of themselves in the places they inhabit, not in a supernatural sense, but in a tangible, physical way. They leave wear and tear in their wake. They alter the architecture, they extend, divide, update the decor to suit the age. They do things that make a place famous, or infamous... Incident, event and location are the warp and weft that form the canvas we call history.

But what had ever really happened here?

She closed the cupboards, hiding the white goods away, and moved on, through the kitchen and another door into a spacious lounge. Again the décor and furniture, a large leather sofa and two leather armchairs, a tall cabinet and a card table, were all in the Victorian style, but it was no good, she feared the mood was spoiled. Disappointment beckoned. She circled the room, reached out and ran a hand along the wall. It was cool, just a little damp and—

She listed as the room began to roll queasily, stumbled, lurched for the nearby sofa for support, but the spinning sensation only intensified and the room darkened. She drew in a few deep breaths and scrunched her eyes in an effort to shake it off, clear her head.

It didn't help.

Crimson fractals danced dangerously behind her eyelids. Shit, I'm going to collapse, she thought, clinging to the sofa like a shipwrecked mariner to a lump of driftwood. She tried to call out for help, but she wasn't sure anything came out...

The room dimmed and grew darker still, and then there was light, strobing like a train window speeding though tall buildings, dark, light, dark, light— And all at once she was no longer alone in the room, because—

A succession of dark shapes was filing into the room, shadowy figures, fluttering, shifting, moving toward her. She struggled to make out faces, discern details, but everything was muddeningly vague, smoky, smudged and indistinct. The figures were fanning out, arranging themselves into a circle, with her at the head...

Kate.

The circle was parting to allow two more figures to enter, but they...

Kate?

"Kate? Miss Bennett?"

The darkness lifted like a veil, light returned with the blunt immediacy of heavy drapes being thrown back. Kate was suddenly aware she was being held. A pair of arms was wrapped around her, supporting her. She groped for purchase...

"Miss Bennett?"

"What...?" Her voice seemed to reach her from somewhere far away. Small and low, it quickly grew louder, building Doppler-like... And then, just like that, everything snapped back. She was in the lounge—and Sebastian Dahl's face was very close to hers. He was staring down into her eyes.

"Kate?" he asked again. "Are you all right?"

"I... I think so..."

"I heard you cry out. When I got through the door you were white as a ghost and clinging to the sofa. I asked if you were okay, but you didn't seem to hear me.

Then you started to slide... Fortunately I managed to get to you before you fell."

"You... Pardon?" she shook her head, trying to shake off the feeling of fuzziness. Slowly the weirdness began to bleed away... What the hell had just happened?

Another voice called her name from across the room.

"Kate?"

She looked over. Henry was standing in the doorway. She saw his eyes move from her to Dahl, and then back again. A small *v* appeared between his eyebrows.

"Is everything okay?" His tone was almost accusatory. "What happened?"

"I..." Kate struggled. What had just happened? Had she just had a hallucination, a vision, what? Before she had opportunity to put a name to it she heard Dahl's smooth Oxbridge accent say, "I believe Miss Bennett suffered a dizzy spell."

Almost at once, Kate grew uncomfortably aware she was still clinched in the arms of a near stranger. She started to politely disentangle herself. Taking this as a cue she had no further need of his assistance, Dahl immediately released her and took a step back.

Henry strode over eyeballing Dahl with poorly concealed suspicion. He put a hand on her shoulder and asked, "Are you sure you're okay? I think it might be a good idea for you to sit down." He looked around, trying to find a surface not covered with dust.

Kate waved it off. "I'm fine. It was nothing. Just got a little light-headed for a moment, that's all." But even as the words left her mouth she knew they weren't true. What she experienced had most definitely been 'something'.

Chapter 12

They covered the remainder of the house collectively, although in truth most of Kate's mind was elsewhere, chewing over what had happened in the lounge. Like a dream after waking, the details already seemed eager to slip away. Henry was clearly distracted too. Kate caught him glancing at her intermittently, as if he expected her to flake out at any moment. Sebastian Dahl trailed a half a dozen paces behind, offering the odd, and usually redundant, comment such as, "This is the bathroom," or, "This is one of the larger bedrooms." Heaven knew what he was thinking.

As they progressed, though, Kate became aware she wasn't solely responsible for Henry's apparent distraction. The inattention he paid to the last handful of rooms they passed through revealed the greater reason. He thought the house was a dud. All the initial interest he had shown inside the entrance hall had long since evaporated. There was a perfunctory air to his questions now. Were he still keen, talk would have already turned to practical considerations, dates, site access and so forth. Although Henry's instincts were usually sound, Kate believed he may have passed judgement too quickly this time.

Tour complete, they returned to the front porch. Dahl locked up and they started to head back down the hill to where the cars were parked. They slipped one by one through the gap in the weed-choked gate. Dahl went last and wrenched it closed behind him.

"Is there anything else you'd like to see," he asked, brushing flakes of rusted metal from his hands, "any additional information you need?"

"I think we got everything we needed, thanks." Henry replied, to Kate's ear rather too curtly.

"Obviously we have other locations to review before deciding which ones will best suit the show. We'll be in touch as soon as we come to a decision."

"I see," Dahl answered slowly, looking between Henry and Kate. "Well, I look forward to hearing from you in due course then, Mr White." Dahl offered Henry his hand, and then Kate. When they shook, she again got the impression Dahl was studying her.

"And from you too, Miss Bennett," he said, a beat before releasing her hand.

"Thanks again for the catch," she said.

Dahl looked mystified momentarily, a tiny frown crossing his handsome features.

"In the lounge?" she explained.

"Oh," Dahl said belatedly catching her drift. He smiled. "Not at all, my pleasure."

When Kate turned, Henry was already on the way to his Aston Martin. She caught him casting a grumpy glance at Dahl's brand-new Ferrari before sliding into his own seven-year-old sports car. To her eyes, both were very impressive cars, but she knew what boys were like about such things. She thanked Dahl again and joined Henry, slipping into the passenger seat beside him.

"Hardly subtle was he?" Henry mumbled.

"What do you mean?" she asked.

"Dahl. You're not honestly saying you didn't notice he was coming on to you?"

For no better reason than idle mischief, Kate feigned ignorance. "Really? You think so?" She pretended to digest the prospect for a moment before shrugging. "I don't know. I'm not sure he's really my type."

"No?" Henry said, quickly adding, "Yeah, I mean, of course. A bit full of himself?" He fired up the car's engine, appearing, at a stroke, markedly more relaxed.

Kate turned to the window. Dahl was sitting in his Ferrari; busy on his phone. She looked him over afresh.

The expensively understated clothes, the well-judged tan, the impeccable dental work, and mischievously responded, "Hmm, a wealthy, articulate, handsome bachelor. What's to like, right?"

She had expected Henry to respond with some witty riposte, but to her surprise he just let out a short grunt and pulled away. They trundled down the uneven track to where it met the narrow country lane, leaving Dahl behind them in his Ferrari, still talking into his phone. Henry paused at the neck of the hedgerow-clogged driveway to check nothing was coming down the country lane curling away out of sight to their left, and then pulled out.

As soon as they met the road Kate saw the flash of colour speeding round the bend, and yelled, "Henry, watch out!"

Henry had seen the car too, and was hastily throwing the Aston Martin into reverse, but despite having to have seen them the vehicle showed no sign of slowing—

Kate experienced the singular sensation that often accompanies an accident, of things playing out in sickly slow motion. The car appeared to sail around the curve with preternatural unhurried clarity. She saw the driver finally become aware of them halfway out in the road, saw him screw up his eyes and wince as he belatedly pumped his brakes, and heard the squeal of rubber peeling onto road as momentum carried his vehicle onward regardless. It was at this point she screwed up her own eyes and awaited the impact. Henry must have known the car wouldn't stop in time too, because suddenly she felt him throw an arm across her, shielding her.

Then there was a colossal metallic bark, like someone dropping a giant mess of wrought iron and glass from a top story window. Kate felt the Aston Martin shunt violently sideways, at the same time she and Henry were snapped by inertia in the opposite direction. Her seatbelt bit sharply into her waist and neck.

And then it was over.

She blinked, opened her eyes, and heard Henry's voice over the ringing in her ears.

"Kate? Are you okay?" He stared into her face, and then her body, frantically scanning her for signs of injury. "Kate?"

"Wha—yes, yes. I'm fine, I think."

She looked down to reassure herself she was still all in one piece and saw that, yes, she was fine. The car's interior appeared largely unchanged, the outside, however, was another matter. Through the windscreen she could see the front passenger side wing of Henry's Aston Martin now had a small blue Fiat imbedded in it. She met the shocked expression of the other car's driver. He looked dazed, eyes saucer-wide with disbelief, complexion white as an Apple store interior.

She and Henry cracked open their doors and climbed shakily out onto the road. Perhaps prompted by this, the other driver emerged too. He was a parker-clad, bearded man of indeterminate age, sporting a corduroy flat cap and a pair of heavy framed glasses. Like Henry and Kate he appeared shaken up, but otherwise uninjured. He was first to break the silence.

"Oh my goodness. I'm so sorry. I just didn't see—and when I did I tried to stop, but..." he stammered wretchedly. "Are either of you hurt?"

Henry advanced on him, bristling. "*You didn't bloody see us?* What the hell were you doing?" he demanded. "Taking a nap?"

The man recoiled, flustered. "My attention must have wandered... As soon as I saw you I tried to stop..." he mumbled contritely. "You seemed to come out of nowhere. I know that's no excuse, but... I'm really very, very, sorry. Goodness, look at your car. My insurance will take care of everything, of course..."

Buried beneath an avalanche of apology, Henry's ire fizzled. Kate watched him sigh, shake his head in exasperation, and gaze at his Aston Martin in anguish, contemplating the damage wrought upon his beautiful machine, the buckled front passenger side wing and wheel arch, and the bonnet, one side now crooked into what looked like an ugly sneer. He was still staring at it despondently when Dahl's Ferrari drew up behind them.

–

Insurance details were exchanged. Recovery trucks were called, they arrived, and then departed. Sebastian Dahl, to his credit, did much to help move things along. He proved particularly invaluable when it came to the other car's driver, who seemed unable to help himself offering a relentless, effusive, and very quickly irritating, stream of apologies. By the time they finally got him in the passenger side of a recovery truck and on his way it was a blessed relief to be shot of him.

When Henry's Aston Martin was winched up onto the second recovery vehicle, the question of what they were going to do next arose. The prospect of sitting in a recovery truck in rush hour traffic while Henry's Aston Martin was towed to his preferred garage in London wasn't especially enticing, but then neither was messing around organising an insurance company loan car, taxis or train tickets. It was Dahl who again stepped forward to offer a helping hand.

"This is only an idea," he said, "but if there's no pressing reason for you to travel back this evening, I've an acquaintance who owns a small hotel not too far from here. If I call, I'm sure I can get you rooms. It's a charming little place, and to be honest I can't help but feel partly responsible for what happened. I should have warned you about that corner. There was a mirrored disk fixed to the wall once, but it went by the way years ago. Please, let me call my friend? It's the least I can do."

Henry looked to Kate.

Dahl waited.

Kate was sold. The day had been unexpectedly eventful to say the least. She felt wrung out; the option of drawing the day short at a charming little hotel sounded like a terrific idea. She looked to Henry, who just shrugged as if to say *whatever you want*.

"Alright," she said. "If you could arrange that, Mr Dahl, we'd be very grateful."

"Please, call me Sebastian," Dahl replied, taking out his phone.

Chapter 13

"No Dad," Kate insisted, "I'm fine. It was just a little bump, that's all." Henry smiled at her in sympathy and mimed raising a glass. Kate nodded and he took his leave for the hotel's diminutive bar. She was already regretting mentioning the accident. All she had really needed to do was call and tell her dad she would be back tomorrow afternoon instead of today. A simple omission, not even a white lie, would have done the trick. By mentioning the accident she had worried him, and now had to answer what felt like a thousand questions.

"No. Honestly, Dad, the only harm done was to Henry's car. I'll be catching the train back in the morning. Yes Dad. Honestly. See you tomorrow. I know. I love you too."

Henry was back. He set their drinks down on the table while Kate put her phone away.

The hotel was, as Dahl had promised, charming. Presently they were in its compact but comfortable lounge. Somehow an afternoon of location scouting had turned out to incorporate a weird dizzy spell and a minor car crash. Both she and Henry were in need of some winding down. A few drinks wouldn't hurt to smooth the day out, and perhaps even help Henry cope with the harrowing trauma of what had befallen his beloved Aston Martin.

A few pints of predictably bizarrely named real ale (two Smooth Hoperators and a Theakston's Old Peculiar) and sure enough the cataclysmic magnitude of the calamity appeared to diminish. Henry relaxed, became more talkative, and inevitably the conversation turned to Sebastian Dahl's house. Kate's impression that Henry had left unimpressed proved correct.

"You think it's a dud?" she asked, surprised he seemed so sure.

"It looked promising at first, but the more I saw of it the more... It just came across as... flat, you know? I'm not saying it didn't look the part, visually it's as close to the picture of a haunted house as you could want, but then you could say the same thing about the Haunted Mansion ride at Disney World, couldn't you? The real problem is there's no story, no history beyond, guy builds house—house is haunted. We've more than enough prospective locations for the series already, why bother with somewhere we're not sure will work out?"

"I want to do it."

"Why?"

"The place is short on history, true, but I still feel there's something there, something beyond the creepy old furnishings, the dust and the cobwebs. I think it will play well on the show."

Henry looked doubtful. "You think?"

"I do. My gut tells me we'd be stupid to pass the place by."

"I don't know, Kate."

"There's something there, I know it."

Henry looked unconvinced, then after a moment's thought a look crossed his face and he said, "Please tell me this hasn't got anything to do with that funny turn you had, because if it does, I'd be reluctant to put that down to Dahl's house. If you take into account everything you've gone through lately, worrying about your dad, before that the pressure of trying to get this second season together, and then the stuff with John Dickinson... You've been stressed out. A cocktail of fatigue, a little elevated blood pressure maybe, and a late-afternoon dip in blood sugar... Come on, tell me I'm wrong?"

Kate wanted to. She knew in her bones what happened in Dahl's house was something different. She'd experienced something she didn't understand. The problem was how exactly she was supposed to articulate that to Henry when she couldn't really explain it to herself.

"Look," she said, "everything you've just said is true, but even so something tells me Dahl's house is different." She stopped short of saying more, knowing how it would sound.

Henry knew her too well, saw she was holding something back.

"Alright," he insisted, "let's have it."

"What?" she said, knowing full well what.

"*Kate.*"

She sighed. "Okay. My 'funny turn'? Well, it didn't feel like any ordinary dizzy spell. There seemed more to it. It felt like..." She held back, didn't want to say it out loud.

"Go on," Henry prompted.

He waited patiently, expectantly. Did she really want to start down this road? She trusted Henry perhaps more than anyone she knew, save for her dad, but still... Oh screw it, she thought, and rolled the dice.

"It seemed like there were people in the room with me, or some room somewhere at least," she said, "but more than that it felt like someone was, I don't know, in my head. It wasn't like a hallucination, or a daydream... It felt more like some kind of vision..."

She stopped, attempted to read Henry's face.

"Okay, forget I said anything."

"What?" he said.

"What? I don't appreciate being patronised. There's no point you pretending to take what I'm saying seriously when you're not."

Henry started to say something, thought better of it, exhaled.

"Look," he said, "put yourself in my shoes. We've been to, supposedly, some of the most haunted buildings in the country, and yet never once have we experienced anything we couldn't put down to us simply getting the creeps or someone in the crew being responsible, but now you're telling me you've had some kind of... supernatural vision?"

"No," she said sharply, "what I'm saying is I experienced something unusual, that's all, something I haven't experienced in any of those other places or anywhere else. There's something about Dahl's house, I know it'll deliver, and we both know it will look fantastic on screen. Consider it women's intuition if it makes you feel better."

Henry screwed up his face. "I don't know Kate..."

"Henry, you know me. Would I go out on a limb if I wasn't sure?"

He seemed to think about it. "No," he said at last, "you wouldn't."

"Alright, how about this: what if we split one of our forthcoming locations into two shows, one of the larger buildings, say, that theatre in Liverpool? That would give us wriggle room to drop a location in the event Dahl's house turns out to be a dud."

Henry gave it some thought. "It's feasible, and I suppose it wouldn't add too much extra work, maybe a couple of hours longer at the site, some additional editing... We've had locations before that produced enough footage for two shows."

"So Dahl's house is in?"

Henry grimaced, but a smile was already putting a crimp in it. "Okay, you persuaded me. It's in, it's in..."

—

It was still fairly early when they left the bar to retire to their rooms, but it felt later. All in all it had been a strange day and Kate was ready to turn in. She and Henry had adjacent rooms. Kate bid him a good night in the hallway outside and closed the door behind her. She took a quick shower and slipped into bed. Almost the instant her head hit the pillow she was asleep.

The dream flourished like a flame struck in the dark, bright, vivid, cohesive in the way dreams rarely are.

The room is large, poorly lit. They enter silently and congregate to form a circle. Kate finds her place, walking hand in hand with another. Together, they fill the gap, close the circle.

Glancing sideways, she meets her companion's eyes and her lips curl into a smile. The man is in his late middle age. His grey hair shows signs of thinning and his face looks drawn.

She makes a gesture with her hands and the circle breaks apart. A woman leads a small figure into the centre and then melts back, retaking her place in the ring. A moment later a second woman echoes her actions, guiding a second small figure to stand beside the first. Unlike the first woman, she does not retreat immediately, but lingers, kneeling to whisper something into the small figure's ear, hushed words that do not carry.

Watching impassively from her place at the head of the circle, Kate feels restless, wants to urge the woman to hurry up. From inside the circle, the kneeling woman's eyes flash upwards and meet hers, and for an instant she fears everything is going to unravel. Except it doesn't, because the woman rises and falls back into her place in the circle. The ring of shadows joins hands. The circle closes.

Two small figures stand like totems, surrounded. Kate's eyes move over them and she experiences a flashing stab of jealousy, so sharp and sudden it grips her like empty-bellied hunger. She opens her mouth and begins to speak...

Kate woke with a start.

Her heart was hammering and she was slick with sweat. She tried to make herself breathe slowly, in an effort to calm down, but the pitch-black dark of the room wasn't helping. Images of the dream lingered against the black canvas of her eyelids. She swung her legs out of bed and groped on the bedside table for the lamp switch, pawing blindly until she finally located it. The wall lamp's glow immediately charted the room. She was not in the strange room from the dream, but a hotel room. It should have helped, but didn't. She still felt jittery, disoriented.

It had just been a dream, a stupid dream. It meant nothing. The images were just a meaningless jumble of flotsam and jetsam bobbing atop the sea of her unconscious. Random junk, meaningless, she reasoned. Problem was, in the dead of the night reason wasn't always the best form of argument. She felt weirded out, dislocated, and despite waking the images persisted, skulked in her head like a greasy meal in the gut, heavy, indigestible.

Her phone lay on the bedside table. She prodded it awake. The display informed her it was a little after two thirty in the morning. She got up, padded to the bathroom and turned on the faucet. She was about to bend and drink water from the tap when she glanced in the mirror, caught her face, and was almost surprised to see herself reflected back. She stood staring at herself.

Whom exactly had she been expecting to see? She watched her brow pinch, her eyes narrow, cognitive friction flutter across her features. She felt... odd. She forwent the drink and used the cold running water to douse her face instead. It didn't help.

The room, the ring of shadows flashed into her head again, as though her mind was on a rail it couldn't jump. She swallowed, refused to give in to the panicky feeling that wanted to take hold...

—

Henry was roused by a rapping on his hotel door. He fumbled the lamp on and got up, sleep was a heavy blanket; it took him a few seconds to shrug it off. He yawned and checked his watch. It was still the middle of the night. Something had to be wrong. He grabbed his jeans, climbed hastily into them and made for the door, anticipating a member of the hotel's staff on the other side. There had to be some kind of emergency to be waking guests at this time of night. Only when he opened the door, instead of a member of hotel staff, he found Kate standing before him, clothed only in a bed sheet.

"I had a bad dream," she said opaquely.

"Oh?" His mutinous eyes wandered. Kate's bed sheet had a tantalisingly low thread count. "Really?"

"Hm. Fancy helping me to take my mind off it?"

He was about to ask how when she stepped forward and kissed him. The next thing he knew she was gently driving him back into the room and palming the door closed behind them.

Chapter 14

Henry traced the path of the scar with an idle finger. Kate's head was on his shoulder, her arm slung across his chest. He had been drawn to her scar unconsciously, simply seen the pale track of tissue snaking up her neck and wondered how it felt. The answer was smooth, vaguely waxy, to the touch. Kate's own fingertips moved to the scar too; she ran them in the wake of his, making him aware suddenly of what he had done.

"Sorry," he apologised. "It doesn't hurt does it?"

Kate tilted her head back to look up at him. "No." Her voice was warm, almost dreamy, "Not much feeling there at all, actually. I feel the pressure, but that's about it. Does it bother you?"

He took in the scar. It seemed such a natural part of her. As long as he had known her she had never made any attempt to hide it or give any impression she was self-conscious about it, so it seemed strange somehow that anyone else should have an issue with it. He craned his neck to kiss her head. "No." He smiled. "I find every square inch of you nothing short of mouth-watering."

She drew back to look up into his face, adopted the demure drawl of a southern belle and said, "Why, Mr White, you are quite the silver-tongued devil..."

Henry replied in kind, his best stab at a Rhett Butler, "And you, my dear, are enough to tempt a saint to sin."

She smiled, tweaked his nipple, and settled her head back on his chest. He could feel the smile on her lips in the contours of her face. It felt good to have her lying there, like morning would never come, like they wouldn't go on as before and quickly pretend like it never happened.

The question popped out, almost as much of a surprise to him as it likely was to her.

"What are we doing here, Kate?"

"What do you mean?"

"You know," he swept a lazy arm at the bed and them in it, "this business. How's the saying go? 'Once is an accident, twice is just careless'?"

"So?"

"So... what does it mean?"

Kate paused to think about it. "Well," she said after a moment, "the way I see it, we're friends, right? Only now and again we're slightly friendlier friends than usual. You're not looking to get involved and neither am I, so where's the harm?"

Where indeed, thought Henry, and before he could think better of it said, "But what if I did want to get involved? What then?"

Kate drew back again and studied him. That was fine by him. He wanted her to see he was serious. He held firm, awaiting her response.

For what seemed like an age she just looked at him, and then abruptly she snorted. He wasn't sure what he had been expecting, but it wasn't laughter.

"Oh, that was good," she said, not quite wiping tears from her eyes from mirth, but uncomfortably close. She rabbit-punched him playfully. "Honestly, you almost had me for a moment there." She shook her head, still grinning.

He couldn't believe it. She thought he was fooling, pulling her leg... He had three, maybe four, seconds to decide upon his response. He could correct her, tell her he *had* been serious, or he could scaffold together a grin and laugh along, because all at once he understood. He got it, the reason why she felt so comfortable about inviting herself into his bed. It was because she felt safe there was no risk of any emotional complications. As far as she was concerned the last thing on earth he wanted was a monogamous relationship. Which, to be fair, was not the wildest conclusion to draw. His relationships with women had generally been of the somewhat... relaxed variety. How did the joke go? Monogamy, it leaves a lot to be desired?

The irony bit deep. She was able to do what she had done precisely because she didn't really want him, or at least not in the way he was growing to realise he wanted her.

He marshalled a smile, hoping it looked more convincing than it felt.

"Yeah... Heh... almost got you for a moment there..."

—

In the room two doors along, the other room adjoining Kate's, Nadine was clearing up.

She went about the task methodically, taking care of the messy items first, the crocodile-clips and pins, the blood-stained antiseptic wipes and band-aid wrappers. Her forearms sang, but not excessively. The hurt had shrunk to a dull throb she scarcely even acknowledged. Like labourers' hands, calloused through a lifetime of use, her body had grown accustomed to discomfort. This done, she turned to the band of salt that cut a half circle around the room. The arc began at the skirting that adjoined Kate Bennett's room and swept out, terminating back at the skirting board a few metres along. Nadine worked her foot back and forth through the salt, dispersing the grains into the carpet until they vanished into the pile.

Finally, she collected the items inside the salt circle's boundary, taking care to meticulously store each one away. Some had been tricky to obtain and were irreplaceable. Sebastian would be unhappy were they to get lost or damaged.

Sebastian would be unhappy…

Not for the first time, Nadine was forced to confront the realisation of just how much she had come to need him, and how dangerous she knew it was to succumb to that kind of need. Dangerous because dependency makes you vulnerable, truly vulnerable, inside, where it mattered.

Nadine was no stranger to the perverse mechanisms of attraction. She knew how cruel the levers and pulleys were that made victims and villains of people. She knew all about the gravitational pull damaged people exert on those who like to damage. There was nothing profound about the insight; it was a simple case of supply and demand. Was Sebastian a villain in waiting? She didn't think so. Not once had he laid a finger on her, or at least not without prior invitation. Many wouldn't understand the distinction, but she did, and believed Sebastian did too. It was just one of the things that made him different.

Nadine knew she was broken, knew her experiences had misshapen her, pushed her proclivities and tastes beyond the realms of what most considered 'normal'. What she had not known, not until Sebastian had shown her, was that she was special too, and how it was the particular way in which she was broken that made her so. Sebastian didn't want to discard her because she was broken, or, heaven forbid, try to fix her; no, he welcomed her for the broken thing she was, and had taught her how she could turn all her raw and splintered edges into something she could use.

Her attention hovered momentarily upon the coarsely cut band-aids stuck here and there over the pale scarred skin of her arms. She recalled the sensation of being connected, of tugging at invisible threads, sending, seeing… Her skills were growing. She was using them with more confidence, becoming attuned to the ebb and flow of the workings, and while she still had a huge amount to learn, Sebastian assured her there was time. A world of dark wonders awaited, she only needed to continue peeling back the edges of this one to reach them. Sebastian would show her how.

She lifted the bag from the bed and cast a final look around the room. Satisfied, she eased the door closed and sneaked out, moving through the dormant hotel's corridors, ghost-silent.

She found Renwick parked outside the hotel as arranged. Slipping into the passenger seat, she immediately noted the marked change in his appearance. His hair had been clipped short and his face was now clean-shaven. Shorn of his usual shoulder length hair and beard he looked starkly different, and Nadine knew at once the change was no accident. Renwick's transformation was in some way just one more element of Sebastian's plan.

Chapter 15

The crew gathered in the Bennett White production office's meeting room. Claire kicked off the proceedings, outlining the meeting's rough agenda. The mood was positive. They had lost a little time due to Kate's dad's heart attack but the schedule for the remaining locations was, with a modest amount of crunch, still perfectly achievable. All in all, season two of *Where the Dead Walk* was coming together nicely. The shoot a few days before in a derelict theatre in Liverpool had gone great. They had captured some wonderfully atmospheric material and Charles had been in prime form. In a séance conducted on the dilapidated main stage, he had produced some startlingly accurate details regarding several key figures associated with the theatre's heyday. True, the same information could be easily obtained from a book written about the theatre by a local historian, but surely only the most cynical of souls would be bold enough to suggest this was how Charles came by it...

Throw into to the mix some poorly maintained pre-war plumbing, and the crew were treated to more bumps and queer gurglings than an entire coach load of restless spectres could have mustered. They had easily got enough footage for two episodes, which meant the heat was off. With three locations still to film, if one turned out to be a horrible dud they had their spare to take its place.

Once Claire was done, Ray took the reins. A converted church in Worcester was the next shoot, in a fortnight. Dahl's cliff-side faux-Victorian house had been confirmed for the week following this, and the week after this was their final location, an empty three-wing building that once served as a mental institution.

Ray summarised his findings on the Worcester church first, and then moved on to the Dahl house.

"It's got to be said, the site isn't exactly brimming with history," Ray commented, consulting his binder. "I've had a fairly good look, and nothing seems to have been built on the site before, at least not in modern times. It's entirely possible, that something was, of course, predating the records I was able to find, but that doesn't really help us in terms of lending it some colour."

Kate leant forward. "What about the wider area?" she asked. "Any historical stuff locally that might prove interesting?"

"Well, everywhere has its stories," said Ray. "If I broaden things out then I'm sure one or two local legends will pop up…"

"Okay. Give it a try. See what you can find."

Ray was about to flip to the next tab in his binder when he frowned and let the pages fall back, ran his finger down the page."Before we move on, there was a small discrepancy I wanted to raise concerning the Dahl house. When I spoke with him he told me he had acquired the site with existing planning permission for an eight-bedroom dwelling?"

"Hm, I remember him saying something along those lines," said Henry.

"Well," Ray continued, "it's just that he didn't. From what I found it actually took his company a couple of years to obtain planning permission for the house. Judging from the paperwork I'd say it probably took quite a bit of effort too."

"Dahl's a property developer," Kate said. "He's probably submitted more planning applications than most people have had hot dinners. Maybe he got it confused with another project?"

Ray shrugged. "I suppose…" Then he seemed to remember something else. "Oh, while we're talking about getting details confused." He found the next tab down on his binder and flipped a bunch of sheets over until he found what he was looking for. "The converted church in Worcester? Well, remember the story about the monk who was alleged to have been pushed from the tower and fell to his death..."

The meeting rambled on. Kate recalled how things had been the year before when she and Henry had put season one together, how it had felt like they were flying along by the seat of their pants. It had all been so exhilarating, assembling the crew, getting the shape of the show down, every idea fizzing with potential, and no previous ratings to beat or be judged against... Looking back now there had been more to it than that, though. Founding Bennett White, creating the show, had inadvertently marked a threshold, separated her past from her future. Setting up the company and crafting the show had required her to draw that line, and gave her what she really needed, a life she could imagine inhabiting going forward, an existence defined by something other than the cavernous hole of what was gone.

They wrapped up the meeting around lunchtime. Kate attended to a few loose ends, and ducked out early. She had told her dad she would drop by around five. Just passing through reception, almost on her way out, Claire saw her and waved to catch her eye. Kate stopped, bemused, as Claire cast a distinctly furtive look around, before disappearing, only to reappear moments later with a huge bouquet of flowers.

She handed them to Kate.

"These were delivered earlier," she said. "I thought you might prefer I put them to one side."

Kate read the small card fastened to the bouquet.

Dear Kate,

Delighted you've decided to take a closer look at my haunted house. Very much look forward to seeing you again.

Sebastian

Kate plucked the card free and slipped it into her bag. Claire had been right; she did appreciate her putting the flowers to one side. The bouquet, together with its accompanying message, and the fact Dahl had scribbled his mobile number onto the reverse, might invite someone who saw them to get the wrong idea, especially after they met the man who sent them. Dahl was an attractive, successful guy, and modesty didn't appear to be part of his makeup. Understatement rarely comes in the shape of designer suits and black Ferraris...

Kate felt he had been mildly flirtatious when they met at the house, and evidently Henry had thought so too. Now he had sent her flowers and a note stating how much he looked forward to seeing her again... Kate wasn't quite sure what to make of it, not that it mattered either way. She most certainly wasn't in the market for a man, and the next time they met she would just have to find a tactful way to make that clear, and hope Sebastian Dahl wasn't afflicted with a fragile ego.

Claire lingered. "Lovely aren't they," she said, giving the flowers a nod.

"They are," Kate replied. "I don't suppose you could make use of them?" She offered the bouquet to Claire.

"You don't want them?"

Kate wrinkled her nose, and executed a small shake of her head.

"It would be a shame for them to go to waste."

"Well," Kate smiled, "that settles it doesn't it."

—

Kate stood at her father's door, leaning on his doorbell, again. Hold on now, she reasoned, there's no need to freak out. Yet.

After a further minute of the doorbell going unanswered she got her phone out and called the house. She heard the faint trill of her father's phone. She waited, but like the doorbell got no response. Okay, she told herself, no need to panic. He was likely just down the garden in his workshop. She tried the number for the mobile phone she had got him, and again she heard a distant phone begin to ring. For a second she thought it was from inside the house, and then realised it was coming from behind her. She turned to see her dad crossing the road, prodding awkwardly at his mobile's screen. Kate terminated the call; her dad's phone immediately fell silent.

"Have you been here long?" he asked.

"Only a couple of minutes, where have you..." Then she saw where he had come from. Across the street, Ms Janette Holloway's front door winked closed.

James Bennett followed his daughter's eye-line.

"I've just been over to see Janette," he mumbled. "Janette Holloway? The woman who—"

"I remember Ms Holloway, Dad."

He unlocked the front door. Kate followed him inside.

"Janette has the proper sash windows on her house, like ours, but one of them has got stuck shut," he explained. "She saw we still had ours and asked if I knew anyone who might be able to fix it. So I told her I was a joiner by trade and I saw to ours. Said I'd be more than happy to take a look at hers, see if I couldn't fix it."

Kate followed her dad into the hallway. "I see. That's very... neighbourly of you."

"Something funny?"

"What? No. Nothing funny. So were you able to help?"

"Damp's got into one of the corner joints and made it swell. Just needs to be stripped, planed down a touch, sealed, and it'll be good as new. Fancy a cup of tea?"

Chapter 16

The Andrew Mulligan Show was a weekday afternoon talk show broadcast live in front of a studio audience from a television studio in north London. Kate and Henry were appearing as guest panellists, and to indirectly publicise the launch of season two of *Where the Dead Walk*, the first episode of which was airing the coming Monday evening. They had already appeared on a Capital Radio spot earlier that morning, and had numerous other media spots scheduled for the rest of the week.

They had finished in makeup and were on their way to the green room. The floor assistant had just been called away to take care of something pressing, leaving Kate and Henry to make their own way down to the studio. Kate picked up telling Henry about dropping in at her dad's the previous day, and her subsequent suspicions regarding her father's romantic status, i.e. no longer single.

"So you think your dad might be getting friendly with this Ms Holloway then?" Henry asked, clearly amused. "Would that be so terrible?"

"No... It's just, well, kind of weird, the idea of him with someone other than my mum."

"He's been a widower for how long?"

"About twenty years."

"Does she seem okay, this Ms Holloway?"

"I guess so... Yeah, she seems nice."

"But you feel awkward about it?"

"I'm not sure how I feel about it. I suppose I assumed he was happy as he was."

"Maybe he was, until he met Ms Holloway. Things change, Kate, people change. You think you have your life just the way you like it, you're having fun, no one to worry about but yourself, and then all of a sudden something changes, something seems to be missing..."

"I suppose..." Kate said.

"I imagine, I mean," Henry added, "that can happen sometimes. And let's not forget this Ms Holloway practically saved his life. That's got to leave quite an impression on a bloke."

"Well just so long as she doesn't end up giving him another heart attack," Kate responded tartly.

Henry laughed. "You want my opinion?"

Kate looked at him sceptically. "I don't know. Do I?"

"The last time I saw him, your dad looked all grown up to me. He's capable of making his own decisions about what he wants, and let's face it, it's not like you could place him under curfew even if you wanted to."

Kate sighed in defeat. "Ah, who knows? Maybe I'm just imagining it all. Perhaps all she's interested in is getting her sash window fixed."

"Yeah," Henry agreed. "There's probably no more to it than that."

"Really, you think so?" Kate said optimistically.

Henry let her hang for a moment before answering. "Nah."

–

The Andrew Mulligan Show had a topical bent. The talking points were a pick-n-mix of stories pulled from the headlines and subjects germane to the day's guests, incorporating live phone calls offering blistering analysis and insights from the public at large. The afternoon's topics were, in order, the barring of a pensioner from a local shop for racist language, a story from one of the day's redtops, followed by discussion of the Royal family's place in contemporary Britain

(Mulligan's first guest was a former BBC royal correspondent, now retired, promoting his recently released autobiography) and finally the question 'Do ghosts really exist?', offering Kate and Henry ample opportunity to plug *Where the Dead Walk*'s season two debut.

At the top of the show Mulligan introduced the talking points and his guests/panellists. Kate and Henry smiled from behind a long curved lime green desk, against a backdrop designed to look like a series of arched windows offering a view out onto the city. Mulligan probably liked to think he provoked biting discussion across an eclectic range of subjects; in reality the discourse was usually tamer than a vegan in handcuffs.

Kicking off with the 'racist pensioner' story, Mulligan made clear his own maverick view on the acceptability of racial prejudice up front—he was dead against it—before canvassing opinions from the panel, the audience and a couple of callers. The segment concluded with the general consensus that the corner shop incident was most likely due to an octogenarian's outdated use of language than any real intent to cause offence.

After an ad break, the Royal family were up for discussion. Elderly ex-Beeb royal correspondent, Stewart Burlington, was given opportunity to recount a couple of mildly amusing anecdotes from his innumerable encounters with the Royals, and along the way deliver a tetchy riposte to a female caller who dared forward the opinion she shouldn't have to contribute to keeping some family who had 'nout whatsoever to do with her' living 'quite literally' like kings, while she worked sixty hours a week between two minimum wage jobs. Kate and Henry did their best to contribute without taking either side until Mulligan introduced his final topic, 'Do ghosts really exist?'

Kate and Henry talked a little about their experiences filming season one of *Where the Dead Walk* and their excitement about embarking upon a season two. Mulligan, a former newspaper editor who knew attracting interesting guests was largely achieved by plugging their wares, sought to mask it by asking the occasional 'tough question'. In truth, these 'hard-balls' were invariably nothing of the sort. They sounded vaguely challenging, but usually just offered the guest a further chance to push their agenda or plug their product. He served Kate and Henry one such question now.

"So," Mulligan asked, adopting a sober no-nonsense tone, "what do you think makes your show any different from all those other paranormal investigation shows that sprang up a few years ago?"

Kate smiled and shared a look with Henry. "You know, I don't think we really look at it that way. I think both of us found some of those shows very interesting, and as for why most of them went away, I don't think it was necessarily because they did anything wrong, more that the public's appetite got slightly worn out. A lot of similar shows tried similar things, and unfortunately too many of them leaned toward being 'entertainment' rather than serious attempts to gather evidence of the paranormal. I found that disappointing. I've always been fascinated by the subject, and always wanted to see it done in a particular way. In the end I decided to see if I couldn't do that myself."

Henry nodded, and chipped in, "I think before our show and others, one thing has always been true, and that's if you ask people, quite a lot of them will say they've had experiences they would categorise as being paranormal in nature."

"How about you Andrew?" asked Kate playfully. "Haven't you ever had a strange experience you couldn't explain away?"

Mulligan appeared to think for a few seconds. "Well, there was one hotel my wife and I stayed at where we were disturbed by unusual noises coming from the room above, although on further investigation it transpired we just happened to be located beneath the honeymoon suite." Mulligan chuckled at his own gag before turning to his other guest, the retired Royal correspondent Stewart Burlington, "How about you Stewart, any strange encounters with the paranormal?"

Burlington seemed not merely surprised to find himself drawn into the discussion, but practically offended. "I'm sorry," he offered tartly, "but I find it ridiculous people are willing to entertain this kind of superstitious mumbo jumbo, and without wishing to offend your guests here, to waste one's time investigating such nonsense the very definition of pointlessness."

Kate smiled agreeably and appeared to give Burlington's point of view some consideration before responding. "I think what is and isn't pointless tends to be informed by personal experience. I'm sure there are scores of people who would consider reporting upon the coming and goings of an all but powerless monarchy a waste of time too."

Burlington coloured. "My dear, I am a journalist. I report facts. What you propagate is fodder for fools. To my mind, encouraging people to believe such simple-minded rubbish is quite irresponsible, and potentially damaging."

"Damaging? How so?" Kate asked.

"You said you have a so-called medium on your show, I believe? Well in my experience such charlatans exist only to prey upon bereaved, quite often grief-stricken individuals. They peddle them nonsense and charge them for the privilege. I have a dear friend who was fleeced of almost two thousand pounds by a woman who claimed to be in communication with his deceased mother."

Kate nodded, waiting for Burlington to finish. "I don't entirely disagree," she said."I imagine there are unscrupulous individuals out there like you mention, but what we do is very different—"

"Yes, yes, I'm sure you think it is," said Burlington with undisguised scorn, warming to his theme, "but pretending that ghostly spirits exist only serves to feed the culture of mumbo jumbo that underpins these fraudsters' activities. To turn the exploitation of emotionally wounded people into entertainment is, to me, deeply distasteful, and quite honestly I would have thought someone who lost her husband and child as you did would be more sensitive to the issue."

Kate's composure vanished. A slap across the face couldn't have wrought as abrupt a change of expression. If Burlington realised just how colossally insensitive he had just been, he didn't show it. The majority of the daytime audience knew it though, as did Andrew Mulligan, as did without a shadow of a doubt the show's producer in the gallery. Henry could only imagine what was now being hastily barked into Mulligan's earpiece, although 'Shut that stupid old duffer up' was probably not far off the mark.

It took effort, but Henry remained in his seat. Had Burlington been closer he feared he might have surrendered to the urge to knock the pompous prick flat on his arse. Beside him, Kate was fighting to recover her game face.

Mulligan interjected suddenly, "Ah, okay, we have a caller on the line, let's see what they've got to say on the subject of ghosts... Are you there caller? I believe you had a restless spirit in your home?"

The caller's voice was piped into the studio. "Yes Andrew. As I told your researcher, my husband and I used to live in a beautiful old tenement flat in Edinburgh..."

Owing to the broadcast delay, and/or the request to turn down the sound on her television, the caller evidently hadn't been privy to the previous minute or two of the show, and rattled away blissfully unaware of what she had missed. Mulligan was delighted to let her fill time. He was no dummy. The show had only a short while left to run. By the time the caller had recounted her tale and Mulligan had asked a question or two, Kate had composed herself. Burlington must have finally twigged he had put his foot in it too, because he had fallen silent and had a chastened look about him.

They limped along for a further few minutes until the close of the show. Mulligan thanked his guests, briskly plugged their respective wares, in Burlington's case his book, 'available at all good book bookshops now' (and likely a good many charity shop shelves a couple of weeks later) and Kate and Henry's show *Where the Dead Walk*'s season two premieres 'exclusively on Viva TV this Monday evening', and finally they were done. The floor manager whisked Burlington away and deftly manoeuvred Henry and Kate in the opposite direction. Kate was quiet, and neither of them mentioned Burlington's remark until they were out of the studio.

"You okay?" Henry asked.

When Kate answered her voice sounded flat and weary. "I'm fine, Henry, honestly."

"That bloke Burlington's an idiot, but then if you spend your whole career brown-nosing aristocracy that's probably not so surprising is it?"

"It's okay."

"No, Kate, it's definitely fucking not. An arse like that shouldn't be let loose on live television."

"Look, someone's always going to bring up Robert and Joel. It's just one of those things people associate with me. It'll always be that way."

As depressing as it was, Henry knew she was right. Even he had attained his own degree of celebrity shorthand. Henry White, the guy who was nudged out of presenting children's TV because he was snapped by the paparazzi tumbling out of London nightclubs with a (delete as applicable) blonde/brunette/redhead a little too often to maintain a squeaky clean image, condemned at the dock of supermarket-stand journalism, *Heat* magazine and *Closer* acting as the prosecution. It was one of the reasons he had abandoned presenting and moved into producing. Nobody cares what the people behind the camera get up to, and when he eventually got back in front of the camera to co-present *Where the Dead Walk*, it wasn't because people had forgotten his indiscretions, more that it was old enough news they no longer cared. The difference was, he had stopped falling out of nightclubs with dolly birds, or at least learnt to be more discreet about it, but Kate's husband and son would always have died in a tragic accident. Kate was right, so long as she was in the public eye, someone would always bring them up.

She must have sensed his frustration, because she said, "Let it go Henry. I lost my husband and my little boy, but I can't crumble every time someone brings them up, even if it's a dickey-bow wearing dickhead while I happen to be on live TV. And you shouldn't feel bad about it either; I have a life I like now. I have my work, and I have my dad."

"And you have your friends."

"Yes," Kate agreed, "and I have my friends."

TV PRESENTER'S HUSBAND AND SON KILLED BY LORRY

Driver dies at wheel

By COLLEN PIKE

Husband and son of Kate Bennett, presenter of C4's E-world, were killed yesterday in a tragic road traffic accident.

Thirty-five-year-old Robert Harding and two-year-old Joel Harding suffered fatal injuries and died at the scene after a heavy goods vehicle lost control in Howarth High Street, Harrogate. The driver of the vehicle was also declared dead at the scene.

Kate Bennett's E-world co-presenter, Hailey Willet, offered the following comment this morning: "It's devastating, absolutely horrible. They're such a wonderful family. I haven't been able to talk to Kate yet, but I know I speak for everyone else on the show when I say she's in our thoughts and prayers."

WHEN RED LIGHT SHOWS WAIT HERE

WHERE THE DEAD WALK MONDAY 9.00 PM

VIVA TV. ☆ ☆

The spook hunting show is back. Season two kicks off with Kate Bennett and her intrepid crew spending yet another night fumbling around in the dark to reliably inconclusive results, this time at a sixteenth century coaching house in the West Midlands. While occasionally still fun, 'Medium' Charles McBride is as always wonderfully (if wholly unintentionally) amusing, the only fear you are likely to experience while watching is that the format may already have run out of juice.

Chapter 17

It was approaching noon when the car, transit van and motor home transporting the equipment and crew of *Where the Dead Walk* rumbled up the uneven track to the weed-choked gate barring access to Sebastian Dahl's cliff-side house. Their small convoy drew to a stop and almost at once the vehicles' doors swung open. The crew: Henry, Kate, and Ray the show's historian/researcher/investigator; Claire the investigator/production assistant technician/logistics tech; Mark the principal camera operator; Keith the second camera/sound/tech guy; and finally, of course, Charles, the resident medium/psychic climbed out, keen to stretch their legs.

It was a lean team, but this only benefited the show's aesthetic. The shaky handheld camera work, the murky, claustrophobic night vision and raw sound were all intrinsic to producing the anything-could-happen immediacy and spooky mood it demanded.

Henry stretched and gazed up the rise to the sullen faux-Victorian building perched there. It protruded from the hilltop like an ugly, plaque-encrusted tooth. He had already noted Dahl's black Ferrari parked on the other side of the track, confirming the man himself was somewhere nearby. As if summoned by the mere thought alone, Dahl emerged from the house's front door. He saw them and raised a hand in greeting, and started to descend the hill.

Henry watched his approach. Something about the man irritated him. He didn't like Dahl. But why? Was it the whiff of over-confidence, the suspicion he thought rather too much of himself, or was it simply that Dahl fit so comfortably into the mould of the privileged public-school-educated capitalist? Henry came from humble stock himself. He had grown up on a council estate, got his education in the local comprehensive. His father had been a union foreman, until Thatcher set about cutting the union's balls off and one by one his old man and his mates were made redundant, or found themselves working the same job for private outfits, for less pay and half the job security. Any one of these reasons may have been enough, but none seemed quite close enough. Henry wanted to put his finger on the definitive source of his dislike. Maybe it would come to him today. After all, they were likely to be rubbing shoulders for much of the next sixteen hours.

Dahl slipped through the gate and extended a hand. "Good journey?"

Henry reciprocated, but took Dahl's hand with the same kind of enthusiasm he would reserve for licking the lid of a swing-top bin. Dahl didn't appear to notice. For his part, Henry found Dahl's greeting reminiscent of a used car salesman's—a baked Alaska of a welcome: warm enough on the surface, but ice cold beneath.

After the obligatory introductions to the crew, Henry accompanied Dahl back up to the house. Henry outlined how an episode's filming usually went as they walked. Due to the nature of the show, the structure was fairly simple, in as much as most of the filming was done in chronological order, as it would appear on the show.

They would begin with a brief monologue from Kate, where she would introduce the location, touch upon its history and summarise some of the paranormal activity alleged to have occurred at the site, then next up was Ray. He would delve a little deeper, detailing the historical background of the location and highlighting people or events Charles might perhaps pick up on. Henry's piece came next. Taking the role of the show's resident sceptic he would suggest alternative possibilities for some of the described paranormal activity, legends and phenomena surrounding the site. He might highlight things like uncommonly strong electromagnetic fields, or local hallucinogenic plant life and fungi and suggest ways they might explore or measure them. After Henry's bit they often included a brief interview with the location's owner or caretaker, in which they were encouraged to recount personal anecdotes of paranormal experiences at the site, unless, as in this case, the owner/caretaker didn't want to contribute. From the very outset Dahl had declined all invitations to appear on camera.

The first major segment of the show followed: the daytime walkthrough with Kate and Charles, the medium. This served to set the scene, build atmosphere and acquaint the viewer with the general layout of the site before the night-time vigil, which was useful considering most of what followed would take place in muddy monochromatic green night vision. Charles would perform his shtick, try to discern the presence of any 'dominant spirits' or 'forces' haunting the site and propose which areas or rooms might prove most worthy of attention later. Next came the core of the show, the night-time vigil. This was where the crew split up into small groups and explored various locations to see if any paranormal activity could be captured on camera, thermal imaging, or audio.

The last two segments, Henry explained, were filmed the following morning. The first being where the crew discussed any interesting events and reviewed notable video or audio material, and then finally Kate's concluding monologue.

Dahl listened, nodding studiously. As they neared the house, Henry asked Dahl one last time if he wanted to appear on the show. Most people who approached them were usually keen to appear on camera, enjoy their five minutes of fame. Others simply welcomed the opportunity to voice their experiences in a context that took them seriously, or at least purported to. Henry had been surprised to find Dahl so resolutely uninterested in taking part.

"You're quite sure?" he asked, as they fell under the shadow of the gloomy building.

Dahl seemed distracted; his gaze kept wandering down the hill. "No. Honestly, I would prefer to just… observe." He suddenly flashed an impossibly wide and white smile and said, "Miss Bennett."

Belatedly, Henry understood. Kate had been climbing the rise to join them. He turned to find her standing behind him.

"Mr Dahl," she replied. She was smiling, and yet Henry detected a definite coolness to the greeting. Evidently Dahl did too because his ultraviolet smile momentarily deserted him.

"Mark's scouting a good spot to shoot the opening from," Kate said, almost as if Dahl wasn't there. "I should go and prepare. Are you okay sorting out everything up here?"

"Yeah, although if you could tell Keith to come see me that would be great. We need to discuss where we're going to place the ambient sound recorders and fixed point thermal cameras."

Kate nodded and started back down the rise to where the rest of the crew were busy unloading and sorting equipment.

—

Things kicked off smoothly. Kate delivered her monologue, Ray and Henry did their pieces and they were ready to move on to the daytime walkthrough.

Keith was sorting out Kate's radio-mic. He had already done Charles's. Right now, the medium was over by the gate with Mark and Claire, regaling them with an anecdote, possibly ribald judging from his face and a suspect hand gesture. Regardless, Mark and Claire were laughing. Kate smiled. It would be fair to say she liked Charles from the first.

When she and Henry began developing the show they had decided after much discussion that the crew should include a medium. Previous shows in the genre had demonstrated they were popular, and so long as they made it abundantly clear the medium simply offered one more perspective, and was in no sense a voice of authority, they still felt confident of adhering to the objective stance they were shooting for. Their search for a medium had brought them into contact with many prominent names on the spiritual circuit, and no shortage of oddballs.

The criteria were simple enough. They needed someone who was comfortable in front of a camera, likeable, entertaining, sufficiently convincing for those inclined to believe there really were people who could speak to the dead, and yet sufficiently tolerable to those who didn't.

It seemed to make sense to start with mediums who performed live stage gigs, reasoning anyone accustomed to performing in front of an audience should be at least part way convincing in front of a camera. What they hadn't anticipated was how huge the spiritual/medium circuit was. There were dozens upon dozens of potential candidates, many of whom had succeeded in turning their 'special gifts' into lucrative careers. Every night, it seemed, venues large and small up and down the country were packed with punters eager to receive a message from beyond the grave. The reality was rather less astonishing. To Kate's ear the overwhelming bulk of the 'messages' passed on were either hopelessly vague or generalised to the point where they likely applied to a good portion of any audience, laser precision communications like, "I have an elderly lady here who crossed over a while ago... She's got *lovely* white hair, just lovely... I'm getting... Rose? Ruth...? Definitely an 'R' name...", or, "I'm seeing a photograph... of a beach? There's sea in the background and a girl in a swim suit...?", or, "Your brother says he loves you and to take care of Mum, and, oh! He says get ready, someone in the family is going to be blessed with a baby soon..."

At first Kate had been stunned to discover what a thirst there was for such fuzzy guff, and (as much as it chafed to find herself in agreement with a twit like Stewart Burlington) there was often the strong whiff of vulnerable people being taken advantage of. The audiences seemed to feature too many bereaved individuals desperate to hear a word or two from the loved ones they had lost, all of them willing to pay good money for the slim chance they may be one of the couple of dozen lucky enough to be singled out from the, often, several hundred gathered before the medium on stage.

Kate was never sure what to think. If these people in some way gained comfort or peace of mind through the messages delivered by one of these mediums, might there not be some good done? It was, she supposed, a question of degrees. Forking out ten or twenty quid for a show was one thing, but then there was the whole business of private sittings to consider. Many stage mediums also engaged in one-on-one private sittings, for 'donations' ranging from twenty or thirty pounds to several hundred. A bargain, one might argue, if they really were communicating with dead spirits, practically a daylight mugging otherwise.

Eventually she and Henry had narrowed their search to a dozen or so mediums they thought could be a good fit for the show, then invited each of them to discuss the possibility of taking part. A few Kate was able to rule out after the first meeting, others took a little longer for her to grow uneasy about. Charles McBride had been different. Kate liked him straight away, and only warmed to him the longer they talked. True, he came across as being a trifle prim, but there was a geniality, humour and intelligence there too. Some discreet digging revealed that while he had a respectable enough reputation, Charles kept his venues small and his ticket prices modest, and although he did occasionally offer to do private sittings, he didn't charge for them. Furthermore, in addition to the usual woolly messages, he occasionally appeared to produce some genuinely surprising information, really quite specific details. There were, of course, lots of ways this could be achieved, plants in the audience or prior research can make any 'medium' look amazing, but ultimately even if this was the secret to Charles McBride's success it didn't really matter. She and Henry were chiefly looking for someone charismatic and convincing, and whatever his methods Charles fit the bill perfectly. In the context of the show, there would never be any suggestion the rest of the crew believed he was actually communicating with the dead, anymore than they would argue anomalies on the thermal cameras, fluctuations in the electrical magnetic field detector or changes in temperature necessarily meant anything concrete either. They would simply present the material and let the viewer decide. Charles had been offered the gig and become one of the Bennett White family.

Kate joined Mark, Claire and Charles by the gate.

"Ready to do your thing?" she asked.

Charles checked his tie and straightened his suit. "As ever, my dear."

"Great. Mark?"

"Ready when you are, Kate."

–

They scaled the overgrown path leading to the house's front porch. Unlike the rest of the crew Charles had not been inside the building yet. He preferred to enter places with a 'clean palate'. It was the way he liked to work and Kate had no objections. Charles was an important element of the show's chemistry. The viewers liked him, so Kate and Henry afforded him latitude, and to his credit he hadn't turned prima donna on them yet.

They met Henry and Ray at the front of the house. Mark was ready at his camera. Charles tugged at the cuffs of his suit jacket, smoothed his hair and took a deep breath that was pure theatre. Together, they approached the house's front door—only when Charles set foot on the front porch he stopped dead.

Kate was about to ask what was wrong when she saw his face and the question died on her lips. Charles looked stricken. All the colour had drained from his face. He looked ashen, sweaty. Kate mind immediately leapt to her father and heart attacks. Charles was trying to say something, his mouth was working, but no words were coming out. He stared at the front door, then back to Kate, and then, consciously or not, he started to back away from the house. It was only then that Kate realised Charles wasn't having a heart attack. He was just scared, absolutely scared stiff. She went after him.

"Charles? What on earth's the matter? What's wrong?"

"I, I think…" he stammered, the words finally coming, staring back at Henry, Ray and Mark who was still filming, regarding them with a look of bewilderment, "I think we should leave."

"What? You mean take a break?" Henry asked, his eyes flicking to the others to see if they were as lost as he was.

"No," Charles replied, still backing away, distancing himself from the house. "I think we should seriously reconsider filming here."

"Not film here?" asked Kate. "Why?"

Charles was a good way from the porch now, but he continued to eye the house the warily. "Because this house is haunted."

Kate was struggling to work out what the hell was actually going on.

"Erm, I don't want to point out the obvious, Charles," she said, "but isn't that the idea? Isn't that what we do?"

"No, Kate. It's not." He looked at her, deadly serious. "'What we do' is go to places that are *supposed* to be haunted. We creep around making a meal over the slightest creak, and pretend not to notice the difference between poltergeist activity and Claire knocking things over... That, Kate, is 'what we do'. This is altogether different. This house isn't *supposed* to be haunted. This house most definitely *is* haunted. And I don't think what's inside is good."

Chapter 18

Kate, Henry, and Charles sat in privacy at the rest of the motor home.

"Alright, Charles," said Henry, "what's this all about?"

"Is that door shut?" Charles asked, leaning to look down the vehicle.

Henry took the key fob from his pocket and pressed the button. The muffled click of the motor home's central locking followed. "It is now." They waited for Charles to speak. Kate caught Henry's eye.

"Charles?" she prompted. "Are you going to talk to us or what?"

"What do you want me to say? I've already given you my opinion. I think it would be a bad idea to encourage anyone to enter that house, let alone spend the night in it."

"Because it's haunted?" Henry said soberly.

"Yes, because it's haunted," said Charles. "There's something ugly in that house. I felt it."

"And it doesn't want us to intrude?" said Henry.

"I've absolutely no idea what it wants, but I can't imagine it's anything good, and I don't think I'd be much of a medium, or a very good friend, if I didn't strongly urge you to let this place go."

Henry looked to Kate, trying to judge what she made of it all. She seemed as perplexed as he was.

"Charles, we have to do this place," Henry replied. "I understand you feel like you tuned into some weird vibes, but—"

"*Do you?* I don't think so," Charles replied with flinty exasperation. He glanced along the length of the motor home again, checking they were definitely alone. He vacillated, exhaled, and all but blurted, "Look, I

114

know you both think I make it up, alright? And that's fine because... well, most of the time that's precisely what I do."

Henry shot Kate a glance. This was quite an admission. Had Charles really just confessed to inventing stuff purely for the camera?

The medium shrugged. "Look, the truth is very simple," he said, "and it's that very few places are actually *haunted*—spirits are rarely tied to specific locations, and even when they are? Mostly all I'm able to catch are faint impressions from them, images, if I'm very lucky something audible. There *are* people more sensitive than I, who might see more, or hear more, but for the overwhelming majority of mediums it's nothing more than weak echoes, fragments... When I stepped up onto the porch of that house, though... Only once or twice have I experienced anything like that in all my years." He looked at Henry and Kate intensely. "Presences as strong as that are extremely rare. Do you understand?"

Kate said nothing. After a beat, she looked Charles in the eye and asked, "Have you been talking to some other production house, Charles?"

"What?" the medium asked, appearing genuinely thrown.

"Has someone offered you your own show? Is that what this is really about?"

"No," Charles protested. He turned to Henry. "You think I'm trying to sabotage the show?"

"No," said Henry quickly.

"I'm not sure what to think," said Kate.

Charles looked wounded. "I'm your friend, Kate, and for your information I would never *ever* do anything to harm the show, or either of you, come to that. That's why I'm imploring you not to stay here."

"What exactly are you afraid will happen?" Henry asked.

"I don't know," Charles said, "and I'd rather not find out. All I know is there's something in that house, and its bad news."

Henry looked to Kate.

"Charles, would you give us a moment, please?"

Charles looked between them, offered a curt nod and got to his feet. "Not at all." He strode down the length of the motor home and let himself out.

Once he was gone, Kate said, "So? You think he's on the level?"

Henry dragged a hand across his chin, let out a big sigh and stared down the motor home. After a few seconds he said, "I think he believes what he's telling us, but where does that get us? If we're going to film here, we need him. It's not like we can rustle up a replacement medium at this kind of notice, and besides, the viewers expect to see Charles. We've discussed this already."

So they had. From very early on they had acknowledged a big part of the show's appeal could be attributed to Charles. The viewers liked him, found him entertaining, some because they believed he had a gift, others because they found his flamboyant personality amusing. It was a win-win thing. Together with Kate he was emblematic of the show, and had become a modest celebrity as a result.

They had briefly debated having guest mediums for season two, but ultimately decided against it. The only real reason for doing so would be to insure them against the prospect of Charles becoming bigger than the show itself, and if his replacements didn't deliver the show would only be weaker as a result. They had stuck with him.

They had since heard through the grapevine that midway through season one Charles had been offered a show of his own by another production house, but that he had politely declined. Even so, just because he had

116

said no thanks once, didn't mean he wouldn't fold some point further down the line. He might still go, Kate felt, if a juicy enough offer came along.

"Do you think we can persuade him?" Kate asked.

"To go inside that house?" said Henry. "I don't know. Maybe? Want me to talk to him?"

"No. We should do it together, strength in numbers."

Henry got to his feet. "Fair enough, I'll go get him."

—

The effort was concerted and uncompromising, and after nearly half an hour of cajoling and coercing Charles started to wobble. To begin with, he had resolutely refused to be involved if they insisted upon going ahead. Henry told him they *were* going ahead. It was as simple as that, with or without him, and had been quick to point out how much damage it would do to the episode not to have him involved. Kate agreed, and while she never actually said *outright* they would be forced to reconsider his position as resident medium on the show if he chose to bail on them, she did remind him how much the show had done for his profile and reputation. Nor did Henry say, *out-and-out*, how tarnished that reputation might become within television production circles if it became common knowledge he had dropped out of a show with such short notice…

They knew they were being hard on Charles, preying upon his loyalty and pride, but their backs were against the wall. There wasn't time to be nice. If they didn't start filming again soon the whole thing would be a bust anyway. Ignoring their grumbling consciences they drove a wedge into the thin crack they had created.

"I hear what you're saying, Charles, and that's why I promise, absolutely promise you," Kate implored, "if anything too freaky happens, we'll pull the plug and be out of that house at once."

Charles lips were pressed into a thin seam. He eyed them both wretchedly.

At last he said, "I have your word?"

There it is, Henry thought, he's going to do it.

"Cross my heart," Kate assured him, "hope to die."

Charles's jaw tightened. "Let's hope it doesn't come to that."

Bless you Charlie, thought Kate, never one to let an opportunity for melodrama slip by.

–

Mark tracked Kate and Charles through the entrance hallway. He adhered to a pure vanilla shooting style for the daytime walkthrough, framing steady, movement measured, simple and conventional, consequently invisible. The aim was to make the viewer feel comfortable, safe, so that when the lights went off for the night-time vigil and he took up a looser, shaky, traditionally handheld style the contrast would amplify everything, lend it more immediacy, make it feel intimate and spooky.

Kate and Charles were walking the entrance hall, making observations. Kate had her work cut out. They had been filming for around ten minutes and so far Charles's performance was, not to put too fine point on it, as wooden as a pirate's leg. Mark had been baffled when Charles had freaked out earlier. He had wondered if maybe the whole thing had been staged, Charles's seeking to kick things off with a good dollop of foreboding, but it soon became clear there was more to it than that. For one thing, Charles's fear was a tad too convincing, and secondly Kate seemed genuinely pissed to have to halt filming. The resulting delay meant the schedule on the daytime walkthrough was now uncomfortably tight, enough that if Charles didn't start loosening up soon they might not get anything worth using at all.

And on that count, Mark had his doubts. Charles still appeared tense and distracted, a million miles from his usual confident persona. When Kate, Henry and Charles had emerged from the motor home and said they were ready to begin filming again, Mark assumed everything had been sorted, but evidently it wasn't. Whatever had got Charles into a spin was still rattling him and interfering with his performance, and while Kate was doing her best to prod him into life, Mark could see it was tough going.

They progressed through the creepy-looking hallway into the house's lounge. Kate remarked on how if someone wasn't aware of the true age of the property they could easily be forgiven for taking it for an authentic Victorian property. Charles mumbled a few words in agreement, his mind still plainly elsewhere. Kate stuck at it, though.

"Can you sense any activity in here?" she asked, in an increasingly blunt effort to get something useful.

"Oh, erm, yes," Charles belatedly answered, at last seeming to pick up on Kate's growing exasperation, "there are definitely presences... present."

Mark bit down on his lip and fought to keep the camera steady. *'Presences present'*? Oh man... He wondered for a moment if Charles was deliberately winding Kate up, then caught the look on the medium's face when he realised what he had just said. Charles *was* trying, but it just wasn't happening. He must have known it too, because he appeared to make a renewed effort to get his act together. He straightened up and started to breathe deeply as if tasting the room's flavour, letting his eyelids droop shut.

When they opened again a moment later he said, "I can feel a number of different energies, although none appear linked specifically to this room…"

Mark could almost feel Kate's relief. Finally, Charles had shown a glimmer he was finding his groove.

"Can you tell if they're male or female, adults or children?" she asked.

"A man, I think…" Charles said, cocking his head slightly. "Hmmmm..." His eyes stared dreamily into the middle distance. "Yes, a man," he said with more certainty. "Not a bad man exactly, but firm. 'Rules must be observed,'" he said with a slight West Country lilt. "Yes. 'Rules must be observed.'" Then Charles seemed to surface from his daze. Kate placed a hand on his arm.

Good old Charles, Mark thought, you might be a ham, but by golly it's quality bloody ham.

They explored more of the house, and with every room Charles became more his usual self. By the time they finished the daytime walkthrough his earlier dire warnings were a fading memory.

–

"That was great Charles," Kate beamed, as they emerged from the house and set off for the vehicles parked down the rise. Claire was setting out a trio of cool boxes. "I don't know about you, but I'm ready for lunch." After a few steps she stopped; Charles was still standing at the foot of the porch, staring back up at the house.

She glanced back. "Everything okay?"

Charles frowned. "Yes. It's strange, but whatever I felt earlier, well, I think it's gone."

"Hey, maybe you just got a bad reception," Kate ventured.

"A bad reception?" he repeated aridly.

"Henry and I, we appreciate you not bailing on us, Charles. Really, we do."

"Does that mean you no longer suspect I'm off to get my own show?"

Kate winced. "Yeah… Sorry. I've been a bit stressed out of late. I guess I got kind of paranoid for a moment there. Think you can forgive me?"

"Already have. I still have your word, though? If anything I don't like happens while we're in that house, then we quit and get the hell out of there, right away?"

"If you say we should get out, then that's what we'll do," Kate agreed, walking back and hooking an arm inside his. She gave him a gentle tug. "Come on; let's get down there before they eat all the best sandwiches."

Chapter 19

On the cliff-top where Dahl's house stood isolated and alone a dank breeze rolled in off the ocean, spawning a mist that blanketed the coastline. Aided and abetted by a low ceiling of bruised cloud it brought the day to an early close; darkness fell quickly. Dahl had already informed them the house's diesel generator was out of action, so they had brought their own portable generator, which was just as well, because without it the hilltop would have been darker than Batman's armpit.

The *Where the Dead Walk* team followed the usual routine. Everyone knew his jobs. They broke into small units, each choosing a location within the house to investigate. Henry and Ray wound up lurking in the attic. Kate and Charles the kitchen and the small lounge at the rear of the house, and Mark, Keith and Claire chose a stint in the master bedroom.

The results were the same for everyone: disappointing. Despite game attempts at making something out of nothing—the old 'What was that?', 'Did you hear that?' sort of stuff, nothing of note actually happened. They changed things up, swapped partners, and relocated to different areas, to similarly fruitless results. Scarcely halfway through their customary six hours Henry was seriously beginning to question what kind of show the Dahl house was going to make, if they were able to make a show out of it at all. The extra material they had shot at the theatre in Liverpool was starting to look like a pretty shrewd investment, because if things continued as they were, a two-part show featuring the theatre would trump watching forty-five minutes of Dahl's dreary dump hands down.

Around two thirds of the way in, they changed things up again, swapped partners, swapped areas. They needn't have bothered, because still nothing happened. Eventually, Henry imagined he could almost hear the uneventful seconds ticking by. He was irritated with himself. He should have trusted his own judgement, his impression of the place, the feeling of flatness and sterility the house had. Instead he had caved in to Kate's desire to include it, when really he should have concentrated harder on talking her out of it. Truth be told, though, even he hadn't believed it would turn out to be this comprehensive a dud. You would imagine any decrepit and deserted property in the dead of night would produce some interesting material. The creak of settling floorboards was usually enough to secure one or two reasonable scenes. Hell, were he on his usual form, Charles would have done most of the house's work for it, but whatever had spooked him earlier had left him distracted and delivering what could at best be described a workman-like job. The Dahl house was by far the dullest location they had yet visited. In comparison the rest were wall-bleeding, 'get out'-breathing, demonic-flies-swarming Amityville fucking horrors.

By the time he checked his watch and found they had less than an hour and a half to go before packing up the vans and setting off all he could do was shake his head and look forward to some sleep.

—

Kate found Henry moping in the hallway. The crew was taking a short break before starting what would be the final part of the night-time filming: a séance conducted by Charles in the lounge. Henry was at the foot of the stairs, drinking from a thermos. Kate sat down beside him.

"You can say 'I told you so' if it helps."

He looked at her and smiled, but a long night of futility soaked up much of its punch.

"Hey. You win some, you lose some, right?"

Kate shrugged. "Nah. Looks like you had it pegged right. You know, I was so sure this place would have something, and then when Charles freaked out... Well, you'd have thought that would have primed the crew to be jumping at the slightest bump, but everyone seems more bored than spooked."

"You never know how somewhere will play until you try it, so don't be so hard on yourself. Some will pop and some are bound to fizzle." He rocked sideways, gave her a playful bump. "And who knows, the night's not over yet," he said, "perhaps the séance will get the doors banging and the windows rattling?"

"Will you be offended if I don't hold my breath?"

The door across the hallway swung open and Dahl appeared from the lounge. Kate wondered if he had overheard their exchange. Dahl had spent the night observing the filming of the show quietly and from a distance, diligently staying out of the way. He tipped them a nod in greeting, and returned to the lounge where Mark and Keith were setting up for the séance.

"Think he heard us?" Kate asked.

Henry shrugged, suggesting he didn't much care one way or the other.

"Come on," Kate said, "let's get this done and go home."

—

When Henry joined the rest of the crew in the lounge, Dahl sought him out to ask if he could sit in and observe the séance. Henry said he didn't see why not; he would check with Mark to see if it would cause him any problems filming. Mark said no problem, just so long as Dahl stayed behind the camera and kept quiet so as to not get picked up on the boom mic. With Dahl watching, Mark filming, and Keith holding the boom, the séance was comprised of five people: Henry, Kate, Ray, Claire, and Charles. They arranged themselves around the card table in the lounge, hands splayed flat on the table-top, pinkie fingers touching to form an unbroken ring.

A quartet of candles burned in the centre. They were an intrinsic element of Charles's method of performing a séance, but had the effect of rendering the scene too bright to be filmed in night vision. There was some compensation, though. The candlelight offered some terrifically atmospheric lighting of its own. Mark had once remarked how it lent an almost Rembrandtesque quality to the way the light caught the crew's faces, made them 'melt from the darkness'. Henry reckoned the effect was more 'torch under the chin' B-movie horror, but kept the observation to himself.

Once they were all comfortable, Charles begged them for silence and let his head drop forward, causing his eyes to vanish into deep wells of shadow. His chest rose and fell as he drew in a series of deep breaths. When he at last spoke it was with a dead of night voice, an empty church voice, a low sepulchral murmur.

"Spirits? I call upon you. Come forward, do not be afraid, cleave to the flame's light and warmth. Find us at this table. Enter into our company... Make your presence known to us. Make a noise if you are able, move the table if you are able..."

Henry caught Kate's eye, and saw the same thing on her face as must have been reflected in his: weary disappointment at what was shaping up to be a complete waste of twelve hours filming. Their mutual gloom was a tacit acknowledgement that they were now simply going through the motions until they could pack up and head home. Charles, to his credit, seemed to be soldiering on in a last ditch effort to salvage something from the night even at this late stage. Henry appreciated the effort, but almost felt like telling him not to bother.

"There's nothing to fear," Charles cooed, "we seek only to communicate, to understand why you cannot leave this place. If you are lost, we can help you to cross over..."

Henry's gaze wandered from Charles to the others sitting around the table; Ray, whose eyes seemed irresistibly drawn to his wrist watch, Claire, who was staring into the candle's flame, valiantly trying not to fidget and failing, her index finger absently worrying a small scar in the table's surface, repeatedly tracing the shallow groove as though trying to smooth it away, Kate, who was trying to look like she was paying attention when Henry was sure her mind was probably miles away.

"Come to the light," Charles urged softly, "come—"

Henry stifled a yawn; Ray must have seen it, because almost immediately he too was fighting one back. He succeeded long enough for Mark, who was moving steadily clockwise around the table, to get round to filming the back of his head before succumbing. Ray's resulting exhalation disturbed the candle flames, causing them to flicker. Charles elected not to notice this, choosing to attribute the disturbance to some paranormal entity instead.

"That's right, spirit, come into the circle," he coaxed in a dramatic whisper, although comfortably loud enough for the boom mic to pick up, naturally. Then he was off. The stern male presence he had 'sensed' earlier

126

made a dramatic reappearance. Charles convened with the spirit. The 'dialogue' went on for around five minutes, during which everyone, although mainly Kate, dutifully asked the spirit questions before Charles finally guided him via the candlelight to the 'light in the darkness'. With a final flourish the medium closed his eyes and let his head fall forward, announcing breathlessly, "He's crossed over, finally he's at peace." And then they were done.

Henry couldn't remember being more ready to call a night quits. An hour of packing up, a short drive, and he could slip his weary body between the crisp bed sheets of a motorway access sited hotel.

Then, just as everyone at the table was about to break contact, push back their chairs and get to their feet, just as Mark was about to power down his camera and Keith his boom mic, something happened that stopped them all dead in their tracks.

Kate let out a cry, a low keening howl of pure anguish that made the hairs on the neck of every living soul in the room stand on end. It was the moan of something unimaginably lost and wounded, and it sliced through the room like a slow-drawn razor, freezing everyone in place.

The moan decayed to an eerie silence.

All eyes fell upon Kate, to find her stock still, head bowed, face veiled in deep shadow. No one seemed to dare move; all were reduced to bewildered inaction. Henry recovered first and reached across the table for her hand, her name on his lips. His fingers were on the verge of making contact when she suddenly threw up her head. What he saw caused him snatch back his hand quick sharp. The woman in Kate's seat wasn't Kate at all; someone else had taken her place.

Or at least that was Henry's first thought, but then he saw he was wrong. It *was* Kate—and yet it wasn't. From behind Kate's eyes stared a stranger.

A few months previously a sketch show had poked fun at *Where the Dead Walk*. In the skit, a female comedian had done an impression of Kate, and although the physical resemblance had been superficial at best, the way she had captured her voice and mannerisms was uncanny. What Henry saw now was oddly reminiscent of that, only hideously inverted. Instead of an unfamiliar face mimicking the mannerisms of someone he knew and loved, he was confronted with a face he knew and loved bent into the shape of a stranger, and it scared the living fuck out of him.

"Kate? Quit it," he demanded. "This isn't funny." He reached out again, tentatively, determined to make contact. Before he could she whipped her head in his direction, only to stare straight through him. Her gaze appeared frantic and yet blind, as though she were gazing into darkness, or something worse.

"Lawrence?" she asked, almost in desperation, but like the mannerisms, the voice was not really Kate's.

Henry looked to Charles, but the medium appeared nearly as lost as the rest of them, and yet he had it together enough to ask the very question Henry was about to.

"Who's Lawrence?" Charles asked.

If Kate heard, she showed no sign of it.

"My child, I can't—where is—I can't..." She shot clumsily to her feet, pushed back from the table. "Lawrence?"

Her chair over balanced, toppled over, and she began to back away, but as she did so she started to list. Henry could see she was going to fall. He was up, trying to round the table to catch her, but Charles was up too, and he was closer.

A scream suddenly filled the room.

To begin with Henry thought it belonged to Kate, only a moment later did he realise it had come from

Charles. The medium's reaction couldn't have been more violent had Kate suddenly bared fangs. He took his hands off her at once and reeled back, eyes wide in terror, his gaze whipping madly around the room. While Kate crumpled to the floor, he back peddled frantically, collided with the wall and then ricocheted like a pinball off a bumper, rocketing toward the doorway, still shrieking and now beating at his chest and head with his hands.

Henry heard Mark's shocked voice sputter, "What the fuck..." Whether through instinct or sheer habit his camera was still up, filming the whole crazy episode.

Henry suddenly broke from his own shock-induced paralysis and went after Charles, yelling back at the dumbstruck crew, "Help her, for god's sake, someone get her out!"

He crashed into the hall in time to see Charles flailing crazily towards the front door. He caught up with him at the threshold. They all but tumbled onto the front porch together. Charles hit the deck hard, but didn't stop; he seemed to be torn between the urge to thrash at himself and get away from the house. He scrambled off the porch onto the dewy grass, where Henry caught up to him. Seizing his jacket, Henry wrestled Charles over, ready to slap him out of his hysteria if necessary, but then, as suddenly as if someone had flipped a switch, the medium fell still.

Henry bent over him. "Charles? Talk to me, what is it? What happened?"

Charles was red-faced and breathing hard. He looked up at Henry, who had him by the lapels, and blinked as though waking from a nightmare.

"The fire..."

"What?"

"The house, the fire," Charles babbled, "all those people—didn't you see...?" He trailed off, staring over

Henry's shoulder at the house looming over them. "For heaven's sake, get them out Henry. All of them. Now!"

One look at Charles's face was all the convincing Henry needed. He scrambled up and ran for the front door, but before he reached it the crew was already spilling out. The last to emerge was Ray, and with him, her arm slung over his shoulder, looking thoroughly dazed, was Kate.

Before Henry could put voice to the question on everyone's lips, Kate asked it for them.

She stared at the pale, shaken faces of the crew to Charles sitting in the mud and wild grass fringing the porch, his once neat suit now damp, dirty and crumpled.

"What the hell just happened?"

Chapter 20

"Are you sure you want to do this?" Henry asked.

The crew was gathered in the rear end of the motor home, solemn faces trained upon the TV screen Mark's DV camera was hooked up to. It was cramped to say the least, but no one complained.

Kate turned to Charles. "I need to see it."

Charles held her gaze for a moment, before turning to Henry and giving a tiny assenting twitch of his head.

Henry sighed. Instinct counselled him not to play back what Mark had captured, and yet despite this he stabbed the play button. Later he would recall that even as he did he knew it was a mistake, that what he should have done was delete the damn video file and weather the furore that followed. It would have been a small price to pay to avert what followed. So what stopped him? Simple. It was that black kernel of curiosity that lies within all men, the voice that whispers from some dark corner and urges us to turn and glimpse the grisly road accident as we pass by. Part of him wanted to watch the video too.

The screen came to life; it showed the candlelit lounge, the card table and the crew seated around it. Henry skimmed forward to where they settled down and touched hands, and then let it run at normal speed. The séance commenced.

They watched Charles begin his performance, his conversation with the house's 'unhappy spirit', to what should have been the close of filming, where he assisted it to 'cross over'. About thirty seconds after this, when the whole thing looked done and Mark must have been an instant away from hitting stop, came Kate's chilling moan...

In the back of the motor home they watched the next part out until finally the video snapped to black.

Kate broke the silence. "I don't remember saying any of that stuff," she said, looking adrift, although Henry thought he saw something else in her face too... "I remember us sitting down around the table, forming a circle, and I remember Charles doing his thing, helping the spirit cross over, but then... nothing. The next thing Ray was carrying me and we were all piling out of the house. Charles?"

Charles looked haggard. His signature neatness and serenity had deserted him. His suit was dirty and crumpled and so was his face. "When you got up from the table?" he said. "You looked like you were about to faint, so I jumped up and reached out to steady you, but when I touched you..."

"What?"

"The whole room was ablaze. There were flames, everywhere. It was so vivid... I could feel the heat scorching my skin, the smoke filling my lungs and... I lost it. All I could think about was getting out, getting out before I was roasted alive."

"What does it mean?" Kate asked. "Who's this Lawrence, and what do you think I meant when I said 'My child?'"

Charles shook his head. "I honestly don't know, Kate. I'm sorry."

"You asked where they were, I think," Claire said. "You really don't remember saying any of it?"

"Not a word," said Kate. She stared at the blank screen the video had just played on, as though the answers where there somehow, hidden behind the glossy black panel. "Does anyone feel ready to go back inside yet?"

"What?" Henry asked her, astonished.

"Absolutely not," said Charles getting to his feet. "No one is going back inside that house. *No one*."

Henry put a hand on Charles's shoulder. "Charles, relax. You're right, no one's going back, not tonight, if ever."

"You're not serious?" Kate snorted, on her feet too now. "None of you want to go back?" She looked around the cramped rear of the motor home. No one responded. To Henry they all looked shell-shocked, their silence spoke for them. Just to be sure, before anyone for whatever misguided reason could decide returning to the house was actually a good idea, he moved to put an end to it.

"Kate, we need time to think about what happened." He grabbed the remote and turned the flat-screen off. "Everyone start packing up, we're leaving in an hour, earlier if that's possible, but not a second later. I've no idea what happened tonight, and for the time being I don't particularly care. I just know it scared the living fucking daylights out of me."

"No," said Kate. "We finally have something happen that might actually be genuinely paranormal, and you just want to up and out? I appreciate some of you might feel a bit shaken up, but honestly, let's stop and think about this. What we have on that camera is dynamite, *dynamite*, and if we leave here now it could be all we ever get." She looked at them all, incredulous. "You're really ready to simply walk away?"

"Kate, you didn't have to watch yourself in there, or Charles," Henry shot back. "Yeah, right now walking away sounds like a bloody excellent idea."

"And you all agree with that? None of you are willing to go back in?" Kate asked, looking around.

Again no one answered. Henry saw their discomfort, a blind man could have. Kate wasn't being fair on them. It was wrong for her to test the crew's loyalty like this. He was on the verge of telling her so when a voice issued from the back of the motor home. It belonged to someone Henry had all but forgotten was around, someone standing alone in the gloom at the foot of the motor home.

"I'll go back in," Sebastian Dahl said. There was an accusatory tone in his voice. "I told you the house was haunted. I can only assume you thought I was lying."

Apparently Henry wasn't alone in having momentarily forgotten Dahl. The house's owner had everyone's attention now though. He stepped forward and stared at the doubters assembled before him, trying to appear indignant, the slighted witness whose honest word had been doubted. Henry didn't buy it.

"Excuse me for being blunt," he said, "but we've been doing this show for a while now, and we've been to dozens of the country's allegedly most haunted buildings, *dozens*, and do you know how many honestly inexplicable paranormal events we've experienced in that time?" He wasn't interested in Dahl's response, so didn't wait for it. "Precisely none. So at the risk of offending you or denting your ego, Mr Dahl, let me confess that, yeah, I kind of assumed you were spinning us a whopper."

"I see," Dahl replied, but his eyes were on Kate as he said it.

Henry turned back to the crew. "Come on, we're packing up and then we're leaving. Kate?"

Kate glanced from the blank television screen to Henry, to Dahl, and finally back to Henry. She looked less than thrilled.

"For what it's worth," she said, glaring at him, "I think this is a huge mistake, but I can see I'm in the minority. My apologies Mr Dahl, but it looks like we'll be leaving."

—

It took half an hour to scrape together the gear. Henry retrieved the stuff installed in the house, insisting the crew stayed outside. They ferried the equipment back down the hill and bundled everything into the vehicles. In just short of forty-five minutes they were done and on the road. Henry was keen to get some distance between Kate and Dahl's house, leaving Dahl behind was just an added bonus.

There was a strange mood among the crew as the coast disappeared behind them; they were subdued and maybe a touch deflated too. Now they were actually leaving he suspected one or two of them might be wondering if Kate was right. Were they letting a once-in-a-lifetime chance slip by them? Maybe they were even considering the possibility Kate and Charles had duped them, that the whole incident had been staged for the camera. As much as he and Kate had tried to distance them from John Dickinson's posturing, they could have got the vibe Viva TV wasn't as keen on the show as it once was. They might be asking themselves whether what they had seen was real, or just a scheme Henry, Kate and Charles had cooked up to juice the show. If so, Henry almost envied them. He had to deal with the knowledge that what happened was real. Kate and Charles hadn't been faking. Kate's resentment over him calling time on the shoot was one hundred percent real too. He had tried to talk to her while they were packing up and got a serving of cold shoulder for his trouble. Only once they had checked into the hotel had she deigned to speak to him, and then all he got was a terse, "Get Charles, we need to talk."

They met in the hotel bar downstairs. Due to the hour it was closed, and for the same reason conveniently deserted and private. Charles was last to arrive. He had changed back into the suit he had travelled in earlier, and was again neatness personified.

They took a table in the corner. Kate seemed calmer, but no less determined.

"Back there, at Dahl's house," she asked simply, "what happened, Charles?"

Charles studied them for a while. "Why don't you tell me?" he said. "Seriously, I think it might be valuable for you both to say what *you* think happened, out loud."

Henry thought Kate would make him say it first, but she didn't.

"Okay," she said, "I think... I think a dead person spoke through me."

Charles nodded. "Henry?"

Henry sighed, shrugged and said, "Yeah, I'd say that about sums it up."

Charles seemed satisfied. There was nothing smug about it; he just seemed content they were all in agreement on this fundamental point. Although, in light of the way he and Kate had practically bullied him into taking part after him warning not to go ahead, Henry wouldn't have blamed him if he'd felt tempted to serve them each a big ol' dollop of 'told you so'.

"I've seen channelling before," Charles said, "although not often, and never through someone without the gift."

"Channelling?" Henry said. "You're saying Kate was acting as medium to some spirit in that place?"

Again, Charles nodded. "Channelling is a form of mediumship, but one that's rarely practiced. Even for an experienced medium it can be a difficult process. To channel a spirit takes uncommon sensitivity, and even then it isn't something to enter into lightly."

"Why?" Kate asked.

"Because," Charles said, "it requires submission. To allow a spirit to use your body as a vessel of communication is to allow it control over you. An extremely gifted medium, adept at channelling, would be one confident of submitting just enough to facilitate direct communication, but no further. This is crucial, because without firm boundaries there's no knowing what a spirit might seek to do. It could attempt to use the medium's body as a weapon to attack the living, or even try to make the medium harm herself. You need to understand that a great many spirits are angry and confused. This can be the very reason they were unable to cross over in the first place."

"You say you've never seen anyone without the gift channel a spirit before," said Kate. "What if I do have the gift?"

"If you had the gift, you would know," Charles said simply, as though stating the obvious.

"How?" said Kate.

"Mediums are usually quite young when they realise they can see and hear things others, generally, do not."

"What age were you?" Kate asked.

"Three, perhaps, four years of age? One of my earliest memories is sitting on my grandmother's lap talking with my grandfather. Not so unusual, you may think, were it not for the fact my grandfather died in France during the war, over twenty years before I was born.

"My grandmother had the gift, as had her mother before her. She recognised that I had inherited it too. She helped make sense of it for me, explained to me how we were different. She told me that people like us were gifted. It was nothing to be afraid of—so long as you were careful." Charles smiled. "I was very fortunate to have someone who understood. Children are not good at keeping secrets, keeping the things they see and hear to themselves. Commonly such stories will be attributed to an overactive imagination, a propensity for imaginary friends... but as the child grows older...

"My grandmother explained it all to me in a way I could understand; she told me how while most people's spirits cross straight over when they die, go to a place distant from this world, a few linger. Some stubborn souls like my grandfather stay because they're not yet ready to leave the ones they love in the realm of the living. Others, she said, become lost, or stuck, and some of these can be helped to cross over. My grandmother would help such souls when she was able to.

"I have encountered many a gifted medium who struggled or suffered for years until they made sense of what they were going through. I know one who spent over a decade in psychiatric care, trusting the doctors when they assured her she was suffering from schizophrenia. Our society has ways of dealing with people who hear voices others cannot." Charles smiled sadly. "To be sensitive to the spirit world can be... difficult sometimes. Occasionally, I still wonder how I may have coped with my own modest gift had I been left to make sense of it alone. Thankfully, I wasn't. I had my grandmother, and her gift was very keen indeed.

"She was able to channel spirits, but rarely chose to. As I said before, channelling is not something to be entered into lightly. My grandmother believed a spirit who will only communicate in such a way was generally best avoided. She regarded them as arrogant bullies, too proud to have their words interpreted, at best obnoxious, at worst dangerous."

Charles regarded them. Perhaps he doubted they were taking what he was saying seriously because a few moments later he said, "I'm not a fool—I knew from the outset you considered my contribution to the show as harmless theatre, enjoyable nonsense to add a dash of colour and heighten the mood, and I won't deny it, that's most often been the case. So you're probably asking yourselves, if I do indeed have the gift, why don't I just earn my keep and converse with real spirits?

Well, I'm afraid the truth is rather dull. As I said previously, most buildings just aren't haunted, and even when they are making contact with the spirit therein may be beyond all but the most sensitive medium. I have a gift, but not to the extent my grandmother had. It was keener when I was young, and quite intense for a spell during puberty, but in the main it tends only to be strong enough for me to see, hear, or feel spirits who are determined to make their presence known to me. Sometimes I'm able to pick up images and feelings from people who have a close connection to a lingering spirit. A spirit can show me things only these people could know. By passing this information on I can occasionally bring them comfort and reassurance, let them know that while their loved ones are no longer with them, they are not entirely gone.

"And yet, often it does not require any special gift to bring such comfort. If one asks the right questions, and listens carefully, people will usually tell you what they need to hear to set their minds at ease."

Henry said nothing, neither did Kate. They had both heard Charles admit to engaging in what psychic debunkers called 'cold reading'. *If one asks the right questions, and listens carefully, people will usually tell you what they need to hear to put their minds at ease.* It was a confession that, were it to get out, could kill Charles's career stone dead. Given all three of them knew this, the admission was in effect an expression of how much he trusted them.

"I do this with a clear conscience because I know spirits *do* exist," he continued. "I'm content to offer these people the comfort they require, because I sympathise with their need to feel that while their loved ones are no longer part of their lives they still continue to exist somewhere, that one day they may be reunited. I understand that need, Kate," Charles said kindly, fixing his gaze on Kate. "So why don't you tell me why you're really so eager to go back inside Sebastian Dahl's house?"

"I don't know what you mean," Kate said, although to Henry's ear it sounded like maybe she did.

—

Kate knew when she'd been busted. She considered playing dumb for a moment before giving it up.

"My mother died when I was fifteen," she sighed. "She wasn't ready to go, and I wasn't ready to let her go. Isn't that how the restless spirit thing works?"

"Not always..." said Charles.

"You heard what I said," Kate continued, "or rather whatever the spirit speaking through me said. 'My child'. What if it was my mother? What if she was trying to contact me? You said you've never seen anyone without the gift channel a spirit. What if the reason I was able to was because it was my mum?"

Charles did a poor job of concealing his scepticism. Worse still, Kate saw a similar look on Henry's face too.

"I'm sorry, Kate," Charles said, "but I think that's very unlikely."

"But possible?" she retorted. She wished she could describe how she had felt watching herself on the video of the séance. She had felt... hope?

"A good many things are possible," Charles conceded diplomatically, "but what you're suggesting... I don't think so."

"What about this Lawrence?" Henry interjected. "Does the name mean anything to you? Did your mother know anyone called Lawrence?"

Kate gave it some thought. Admittedly the name didn't ring any bells. Her mum and dad didn't really

140

have any extended family, and she couldn't recall hearing her father mention anyone called Lawrence, but that didn't mean there couldn't have been someone connected to her mother with the name. An old friend, perhaps, or a distant relative…

"No, but—"

"Kate," Charles said, "the presence I felt in that house was not one I would characterise as warm and welcoming. I can't say why the spirit chose you as its conduit, and in some respects that's what worries me most. There's something very wrong with that house, and I for one would be happy to live in ignorance as to what it is rather than see you put yourself in danger to find out."

"But don't we have a responsibility to find out?" Kate said, "If we run away from this, doesn't that prove we really are just a bunch of charlatans? I know we've 'creatively edited' the show for dramatic effect on the odd occasion, but I never viewed that as an alternative to capturing something authentically extraordinary on camera; I honestly believed we were looking to document something truly supernatural. I never once guessed that if we finally did encounter something our response would be to just go 'oh shit' and split."

"And I felt the same way, Kate, until tonight," said Henry. "You didn't have to watch yourself during that séance. And before you say it, it's not the same thing seeing it played back on a TV screen. No, I'm afraid I'm with Charles on this one. I find it hard to believe whatever got into you had anything to do with your mother. I think we need to get some distance from this. You've gone from being open-minded and on the fence to being a true believer all in one night. Hell, *I've* gone from being a sceptic to true believer in one night, but surely that's all the more reason to step back, take stock?"

Kate looked at them both; their concern was heartfelt, of that there was no doubt. They were possibly even right. It didn't matter.

"Take stock?" she said at last. "Okay, I'm all for stepping back and taking stock. It's ruling the place out completely I have a problem with. Which is it we're really talking about?"

Henry and Charles exchanged looks. Then Henry said, "I'm not ruling it out, not yet. Let's just take time to consider it with cooler heads, okay?"

"Just so long as you know I'm not about to let it go without a damn good reason."

—

Henry pulled a detour before retiring to his room. He wanted to have a word with Ray. When he knocked the door to Ray's room he found him still up.

"Henry?"

"Hi Ray. Good, I was hoping you hadn't turned in yet."

"Let's just say dropping off hasn't been easy. Strange old night, eh?"

"To say the least. Listen, I need a favour. It looks like Kate isn't about to let Sebastian Dahl's house go without some convincing. I'd like you to see what you can find out about the guy. There's something about him I don't like. I can't quite put my finger on it, but..."

"Say no more. I'll do some digging."

"Oh, and I'd rather you didn't mention any of this to Kate."

"Mention what, mate?"

"Thanks Ray. You're a star."

142

Chapter 21

Seeing is believing.

Was any idiom truer? Not in Kate's book. During the past week she had lost count of how many times she had watched the recording of the séance, partly out of simple fascination, partly because she was gripped by the tantalising conviction that if she only watched it carefully enough some previously overlooked detail would reveal itself. If that was the case, though, she had yet to spot it.

In the days following the incident at the Dahl house, work had become a peculiar blend of familiar routine set within a strange new context. The crew couldn't help but be affected by what had happened. While they made the usual arrangements, continued with the established shooting schedule, they all knew something had changed. The question as to whether entities like restless spirits really existed was not nearly as open as it had once been. They had been robbed of the small kernel of doubt that immunized them against creeping around dark, empty, sometimes decrepit, buildings. Everything was the same. Everything was different. As they prepared to shoot the final location the crew's collective tension built to a pitch.

The real surprise turned out to be how temporary the effect was.

The final location for season two was a deserted three-wing building that once served as a mental institution. The daytime walkthrough went smoothly enough, and the crew quickly began to loosen up. By the time they reached the night-time vigil everyone seemed to have settled back into their comfortable old grooves. The building was a bit creepy, a bit dank, prone to lots of echoes and creaks, but nothing they hadn't experienced before. Charles recovered his usual flamboyant form and the rest of the crew threw themselves into things in the usual way, which is to say, they were soon acting like a bunch of big kids tooling around in a spooky abandoned building. It appeared the adage of climbing back onto the horse that threw you held water. By daybreak it was as though the thing at Dahl's house had never happened, or for the rest of the crew at least.

For Kate, Dahl's house remained an itch she couldn't scratch. For her, it felt like they were just spinning their wheels. When Dahl's house existed, every second they spent in the retired mental institution seemed a waste of time. She did her job, she was a professional, but something fundamental had changed, and she doubted there was any going back.

She almost felt sorry for Henry. She wasn't trying to be difficult, but she refused to pretend she had left what happened at the Dahl house behind her. She wasn't stupid; she knew he had been hoping that if he could just kick it into the long grass, she would let it go, move on, while she knew all the 'taking stock' and 'getting perspective' in the world wasn't going to change a damn thing. She found it infuriating no one else seemed willing to acknowledge what had happened and meet it head on.

Perhaps if Henry had been more receptive she mightn't have been so quick to accept Sebastian Dahl's invitation to meet up.

He had called Bennett White a couple of days after the debacle at the house. Henry had fielded the call, and summarised the conversation for her later, conveying Dahl's 'disappointment' over the way they had abandoned the site so abruptly. Kate was pretty sure Henry was grossly understating Dahl's perspective on the matter. She recalled the way Dahl had spoken out following the séance. He'd been pissed. He had told them the house was haunted, and hadn't appreciated the assumption he had been lying.

Regardless of how Henry and Dahl's conversation had actually gone it had clearly failed to placate Dahl because he called back again the following day, this time specifically asking to talk to Kate. When told she was unavailable, he had left a fairly blunt message. It was simple enough: 'Could he request *Kate Bennett* call him back'.

Had Henry got wind of the message, Kate suspected there was a good chance it may have somehow got mysteriously lost. In the event, though, Claire had taken the call, and dutifully passed it along.

Kate had returned his call.

Chapter 22

Summer was performing as British summers so frequently do: fitfully. Like the mercurial engine of a vintage sports car, still capable of surprising performance when everything behaves itself, the past week's weather had sputtered out a couple of sunny days, followed by one or two that were nearly duffle-coat chilly, before launching into a truly sweltering weekend potent enough to have the most prepared ice cream van proprietor running short on his 99s.

As Kate joined the sludge of cars making an exodus to the coast, intent upon beaches, sun-tans and donkey rides, she had ample time to question why she had agreed to meet with Sebastian Dahl. In the end it came down to this: when she had asked who was willing to go back into the house following the séance, Dahl had been the only one to speak up, the only one there seemingly as keen as she was to find out what the hell had actually happened.

She called him a couple of days after getting his message. Conveniently, the card bearing his personal number that accompanied the bouquet was still knocking around the bottom of her bag. Despite everything, Dahl was nothing but courteous. He had thanked Kate for returning his call and asked if she would meet with him. He wanted to discuss what had happened, he said, share some ideas with her about whom he thought the spirit she had channelled might be. Kate had attempted to quiz him on this latter point, but he had said it was something he would prefer to talk about face to face. He was hosting a small celebration this coming Saturday, to mark the anniversary of a charity he was involved with called *Doorways* that endeavoured to help young homeless people back into mainstream life and work. He wondered if she might like to come along as his guest. Maybe he had judged she would feel more comfortable meeting him somewhere there would be other company around. If so, he had judged right.

Kate continued to progress southwards. The motorway gave way to a series of A-roads, to B, and finally to a string of spindly country lanes, until she at last arrived at the address Dahl had furnished her with, what turned out to be a large and beautiful Edwardian country house, *Doorways*'s headquarters.

Kate viewed it through a set of tall wrought iron gates. A high red-brick wall surrounded the property, beyond which lay pristine gardens, lawns, flowerbeds, meticulously clipped topiaries, and an immaculate gravel drive that swept in a grand arc up to the house's impressive front entrance. One might be forgiven for assuming minor aristocracy dwelt inside; the reality was quite different. The house was, for the most part, occupied by youths whose previous residences had been shop doorways and cardboard boxes.

A deeply engraved brass plaque on the wall beside the gates simply read, 'The Retreat'. Kate waited as the gates opened with a motorised whine, allowing her access. A young man posted on the other side directed her to the parking area beside the house. She wasn't the only new arrival. A group of young men and women were just ahead of her. She followed them into the house and spotted Dahl across the way; he was standing beside an intense-looking younger man with close-cropped hair who appeared to be intently focused on what Dahl was saying.

Dahl's gaze wandered across the room. He saw her and immediately shot her a smile. He said something to the man, who responded and promptly disappeared. Dahl took a brief detour and appeared in front of her moments later holding out a flute of bubbling liquid.

"Champagne?" she said. "Before noon?"

"Ah, no. Carbonated grape juice, actually. Many of the young men and women staying here have alcohol issues, so we don't permit alcohol within the grounds. Sometimes the best option is to simply remove temptation." He flashed her another smile.

He really was quite handsome, she thought, in a clean, clipped and groomed kind of way. Not that she was remotely interested, of course.

"Thank you," Dahl added, "for coming. I wasn't sure you would."

"Me neither. How long has your charity...?" Kate tried to recall the name.

"*Doorways,*" said Dahl.

"How long has *Doorways* existed?"

"A decade now. One day I woke up and was no longer able to ignore I had the resources and skills to offer young people who'd suffered experiences akin to my own a chance to escape their circumstances, that I had the means to help them try to change their lives."

"Experiences akin to your own?"

"Sleeping rough, on the streets."

"You slept rough on the streets?" Kate said, surprised.

"For nearly five years. I was taken into care at the age of ten. Let's just say it wasn't for me. I was placed with a foster family, but that didn't suit me either. So I ran away, lived on the streets, in squats, learnt to fend for myself."

"That's dreadful."

"Maybe, but in the end I was lucky. Through good fortune, a few tough life lessons and hard work I succeeded in making something of myself. And yet I'm only too aware things could have turned out differently. In similar circumstances many young people become dependent on drink, on drugs; some get drawn into prostitution..." Dahl looked genuinely despondent. "At

148

the same time they're often already dealing with deep emotional problems. Many will come from violent or abusive backgrounds. We aim to offer young people like this, youths who have no one and nothing, youths who could vanish off the face of the earth tomorrow and scarcely be missed, a second chance. They're given a room here, three meals a day and, crucially, a mentoring scheme to give them direction, with the ultimate goal of guiding them into education or work. It's proved to be an effective model. Many of our former beneficiaries have returned to volunteer as mentors themselves. Unfortunately, our capacity is painfully limited, but we do what we can…"

"I suppose it's easy to forget not all families are happy ones."

"It is, but there's more than one definition of family. I would argue people can forge bonds far stronger than blood. Shared beliefs, shared experiences, loyalty, obligation, duty and love… These things bind people powerfully too." Dahl caught himself and smiled. "Am I sermonising? Please, forgive me."

"No need." Actually Kate agreed. Her mum and dad weren't her birth parents, her blood, but she couldn't imagine loving them any more had they been.

"After things wind down this afternoon," Dahl said, "you'll perhaps stay for a while? We can share a bite to eat, discuss what happened back at my house? I've a few ideas I'd like to share with you about what happened and why, things that, on reflection, I think might be relevant…"

—

Dahl guided Kate through to the gardens at the back of the house. There was a large marquee set up, offering non-alcoholic beverages and what her dad would have called a good spread and some welcome shade from the glare of an over-enthusiastic English afternoon sun.

Dahl mingled as they wove a path through the guests, stopping to shake hands and chat. Kate was always introduced and often recognised. Being Julia Roberts might be a pain in the bum, but in truth the life of a C-list celebrity wasn't so bad. Kate was occasionally stopped and asked for an autograph when out and about, but never often enough for it to have become a chore.

As Dahl socialised, Kate reflected upon what he had said earlier about having no one, about being taken into care and then fostered. While he hadn't said it had been a bad experience, not explicitly, Kate suspected it must have been for the prospect of running away and living on the streets to seem more appealing. Had it been better, she wondered? His desire to help other youths who found themselves alone or abandoned with nowhere to call home suggested it couldn't really have been.

She found herself obliged to reappraise her view of him. Sebastian Dahl was a man it was clearly unwise to make assumptions about. Take his vaguely upper class accent; this was something she had taken as a sure indication of a privileged public school education. In reality, it seemed the core of his education had been conducted in the rather less exclusive school of hard knocks. Where then had the posh accent come from? If she were to speculate she was inclined to guess he had cultivated it to appear more credible in his business dealings. It's unfortunate, but people are frequently reassured by a posh accent, the clear ring of public school enunciation tends to open more doors than the blunt glottal stop of an inner city comprehensive.

And then there was the Teflon-slick self-assured exterior. This was something else Kate assumed was a result of a privileged, silver-spoon background. Knowing what she knew now, it seemed far more likely a front, a survival mechanism. Considering the sort of sketchy individuals a youth might encounter sleeping rough on the streets, she imagined a confident shell was essential to deterring predators on the lookout for a soft touch.

And what of the smart suits and expensive Italian sports car? Rather than being the trinkets of someone accustomed to finery, they now looked like the spoils of a man who knew what it was to have nothing at all. The thing that most called for a reappraisal of Sebastian Dahl, though, was his charity. It appeared he had dedicated a decade of his life to helping the sort of kids some might cross the street to avoid. Dahl, it appeared, truly was a riddle, wrapped in a mystery, inside an enigma, inside... well, some pretty expensive Savile Row tailoring. To her surprise, Kate found herself warming to this new Sebastian Dahl. It caused her to think on something else too. How differently might she have turned out had she languished in care or been bumped through a series of foster homes, and not been adopted by two loving parents? Without the unconditional love of her mum and dad, would she still be the same person? Would she still have found success without their love and support?

Maybe.

Maybe not.

She thought about the young people populating the party, former and present guests of The Retreat. How many of them had enjoyed the unconditional love of a parent, of anyone at all? How many received any kind of help, until Dahl's charity found them? She was pulled from her thoughts when she noticed a young man striding over. He appeared to be making a beeline for her. A few more paces resolved it was actually Sebastian he was heading for. Kate had seen him earlier. He was the intense-looking man talking with Dahl when she had first arrived.

The man reached them and said, "Sebastian?"

Dahl turned, saw him and smiled, "Afternoon, Simon. Is something wrong?"

"I'm sorry to have to bother you, but the site foreman at the Juniper Grange development wants to discuss something with you, something unexpected has come up, something to do with the drainage."

Dahl grimaced good-naturedly and shrugged at Kate. "How does the saying go? No rest for the wicked? Mind if I take a moment?"

"Of course not."

"I shouldn't be too long. In the meantime I'll leave you in Simon's capable hands. Simon? Perhaps you'd like to give Kate a quick tour of The Retreat? You'll almost certainly do a better job of explaining what goes on here than I could."

The young man smiled. "I'd be delighted."

They watched Dahl head back into the house. When Kate looked back the man was holding out his hand.

"Simon Renwick," he said.

Kate shook his hand. "Kate Bennett."

"I know, I'm a huge fan of your show, but I imagine you get that all the time."

"Not so often it isn't still welcome. You work for Sebastian?"

"Actually I work for the charity technically, but seeing as *Doorways* wouldn't exist without Sebastian I do tend to think of myself as working for him. Like many people you'll meet today, I owe him a huge debt. I used to live here," Renwick added, as though this explained everything.

"I see."

"If it wasn't for Sebastian, I'm pretty sure I'd either be in prison or dead by now. There really aren't many people like him around."

"You sound very fond of him."

"I'd do almost anything he asked."

Kate felt herself smile uncertainly. She couldn't say why, but there was something about what Simon Renwick had just said, or perhaps the way he said it, she found unnerving. He was looking at her, and she realised that something of what had passed through her mind must have shown in her face.

"Sorry, I suppose that sounds a bit, well, melodramatic," said Renwick, "but it's true. When Sebastian found me I'd been living rough for a while and things weren't going well. I'd been in the armed forces; my home situation hadn't been great, so I joined up as soon as I was old enough. It was alright for a while, and then... well, it wasn't. I did three years, gave my year's notice, and got out. I thought normal life would be easier. It wasn't. I struggled to find regular work, ended up getting myself evicted from the place I'd been renting, wound up on the street. From there things only got worse. I fell into doing shady stuff to get by, thieving mostly. I was probably not far from being nicked for something and doing a stretch when Sebastian found me. At a point in my life when I had nothing and no one—and to be brutally honest really didn't care about anything or anyone, other than where my next hit was coming from—he offered me a way out."

"You had a drug problem?"

"Was I a junkie? Yeah." He said it as though there were few things worse. "And like most junkies, I was a stealing, cheating, lying, poisonous, wretched waste of space. Sebastian offered me a deal. He said he helped people like me. He said if I came with him he would give me a place to stay, three square meals a day and the chance to build a future for myself. I pegged him for some liberal do-gooder, reckoned I'd string him along, take what he was offering until I got fed up, or more likely he got fed up and kicked me out. It's not like I had anything to lose... He brought me here, and he kept his word. I got a room, three square meals a day, but more important than both, I was suddenly surrounded by people who *used* to be just like me, people who were now fighting to build themselves new lives, and actually seemed to be succeeding. In each other, they had people who cared about them, and people they'd grown to care about... I won't say I changed overnight, but..."

"You saw what your life could be like?" Kate suggested.

"Yes," Renwick agreed simply. "I saw what my life could be like."

Kate couldn't help but be moved by Renwick's honesty and slightly ashamed again at her original assessment of Sebastian Dahl. How many people change another individual's life the way he had changed Simon Renwick's?

"Sounds like the world could do with a few more Sebastian Dahls."

A look crossed Renwick's face; Kate thought she detected genuine affection in it, but there was something else too, a sliver of... what? Before she was able pin it down it was gone. All she was left with was Simon Renwick's affable smile.

"Come on then," Renwick prompted, "I'll give you the grand tour. Here, let me get that."

He reached for her glass, once filled with fizzy grape juice, but now empty. As he relieved her of it she felt a strange sensation across her forefinger and almost dropped it. Fortunately, Renwick had it. She looked down to find her finger dripping blood. Renwick saw too. In a flash he produced a handkerchief from his pocket and offered it to her. "Here, it's clean. I promise."

She was about to protest about it only being a nick when she saw how much blood there suddenly was. It had started to drip in fat ruby droplets from her finger tip. She accepted Renwick's handkerchief and pressed it to her finger. When she lifted it to examine the cut she found a neat slice across her fingertip, not terribly deep, but enough for blood to already be oozing up to obscure the cut again.

"Like this," said Renwick said."You should keep pressure on it." He took back the handkerchief and wound it carefully around her finger. She held the makeshift bandage in place as Renwick tilted the glass to the light.

"Ah," he muttered, "it's chipped. We'd better get rid of this." Before Kate had chance to look he had caught the attention of a young girl standing nearby, handed her the glass and instructed her to dispose of it.

"Come inside," Renwick said. "We'll get that cut washed out and dressed."

Chapter 23

The Retreat's kitchen managed to somehow be both huge and homely at the same time. A long dining table dominated the room, long enough to seat perhaps twenty or more people. Kate guessed it was where The Retreat's residents gathered to eat their meals. The image that came to mind was a cosy one.

Simon Renwick was picking through one of the kitchen cupboards. He emerged with a first aid box, which he set down on the work surface before calling Kate to the sink. He peeled off the handkerchief and got her to hold her finger under the cold tap. Slowly, the thin stream of water ran from red, to pink, to almost clear. Renwick dipped into the first aid kit and removed a bright blue plaster. He tore off a couple of sheets of paper towel, dried her hand off and deftly applied the plaster.

"There, done," he said, stuffing the blood-stained handkerchief back into his pocket. "Sorry about the plaster. I knew there'd be some in here, but I forgot they would be the blue catering type."

"No apology necessary. Blue or otherwise, at least I'm not sploshing blood all over the place."

"Still interested in getting the grand tour?" Simon Renwick extended an arm toward the door leading to the hall.

Kate smiled. "Lead the way."

–

Simon showed her around The Retreat, starting with what he called the common spaces. These comprised two large lounges, a well-equipped gym, an I.T. suite, and even a swimming pool. Renwick told her there were thirty guest rooms, usually all occupied. The length of stay depended on the individual. Some just needed a chance to get back on their feet before once again grasping the reins of their lives, he said, while others needed a longer stay before they were ready.

When the tour was done, Kate and Simon rejoined the garden party. Dahl must have dealt with his business matter because he was back too. He caught Kate's eye and beckoned her over. A few of the charity's ex-beneficiaries had asked for the opportunity to say a few words. Simon appealed for quiet, and a handful of young men and women stepped forward to offer praise for *Doorways* and thank Sebastian personally for his help and support. When they were done, Sebastian thanked them for their kind words and begged everyone present to join him in a toast to *Doorways* and its continued success. A collection of grape juice-filled glasses were enthusiastically raised aloft.

Eventually, evening rolled around and the event began to wind down. A series of goodbyes left the garden empty of all but The Retreat's current residents, at which point they all pitched in to tidy up. Kate watched them as they worked, talking, laughing, teasing each other good naturedly while they cleared everything away. They looked like a family, like brothers and sisters. Not *The Waltons*, perhaps, there were a few too many tattoos and piercings for that, but a family all the same.

Dahl suggested they take advantage of the fair weather to eat alfresco on one of the rear gardens' patios. The unexpectedly hot afternoon had tapered off to a pleasurably warm evening. A table was set out for them. Dahl drew out a chair and invited Kate to take a seat. Dahl's 'bite to eat' turned out to be a three course gourmet meal: insalata Caprese, followed by some incredible smoked salmon ravioli, capped off by pecan-maple ice cream. It was delicious. Dahl explained how Carl, the young man who had prepared and served it, was one of The Retreat's current residents. Once a commis chef in a smart London restaurant, he had developed a taste for cocaine, which he had eventually traded for a crack habit. Unemployment and destitution followed. After eighteen months at The Retreat he was again cultivating dreams of opening his own restaurant one day. When he returned to collect their empty dessert bowls and replace them with two midnight-black espressos, Kate made a point of telling him how amazing the meal had been.

When he left, she turned back to Dahl. "You must feel immensely proud. Even from what little I've seen today it's clear you've achieved something remarkable here."

Sebastian considered her. "Thank you. We work at it, but that said, you should take care not to be misled by appearances. Our efforts don't always bear fruit. Not everyone who comes here finds their way back onto their feet. For every Carl, there are others who vanish without even a goodbye. We find their rooms empty, their belongings, and occasionally some of ours, gone. I imagine most wind up back on the street. It takes courage to start again from scratch, to commit to reinventing one's self. Not everyone can do it."

"But you offer them a chance to. Isn't that all anyone *can* do, and more than most in their situation usually get? Who knows where I'd be now if my mum and dad hadn't adopted me? If they hadn't given me a home, a life, a chance to be part of a family... Would I even be the same person?"

"I think you would have survived," Dahl said. "You seem like a survivor to me."

Kate immediately thought of Robert, of Joel. Reluctant to wade in to those particular waters, she instead deflected.

"What about you?"

"What about me?" Dahl echoed innocently.

"Were you always a survivor?"

"I survived my childhood. I survived the streets. I survived having no parents. I survived the fire that took my mother."

Kate's jaw literally dropped. She recalled Charles back at the house, telling Henry and her about what he had seen. The fire, the bodies... She became aware she was staring, her mouth all but hanging open like a lobotomy patient's.

"Your mother died in a fire?"

"Yes, a house fire, along with several others. I escaped, mostly unscathed." Dahl unbuttoned the left hand cuff of his shirtsleeve, pulled it back to expose the skin on his forearm. There was scar tissue running to the elbow, scarring caused by burns. The damaged skin was puckered pink and waxy, like her own. Almost involuntarily, she reached up, touched her neck.

Dahl rolled the shirt sleeve back down. "I need to know what happened at the house that night, Kate. Someone there chose to speak through you, and I can't help but feel they're connected to me."

"Why would you think that?"

"To begin with, there's the obvious, that house is *my* house. It was my passion. I designed it. I sourced the materials, orchestrated its construction... I put my heart and soul into it, so much of myself... and finally there's what your friend Charles experienced, his vision of a fire, the plea you made, or rather the spirit made through you, searching for their child? It all fits, doesn't it?"

"How old were you?"

"When I lost my mother I was approaching eleven years of age."

Ten years old, thought Kate. A year spent in care and with foster parents, meant Dahl must have been on the streets, alone, at barely eleven or twelve.

"I'm sorry."

Dahl stared down into his espresso. "It's okay. If I'm honest, I don't really remember a great deal about her, or the fire which took her life." He sighed. "Is that better, do you think? Sometimes I think it is, sometimes I'm not so sure. It can make it feel like somebody else's past." He lifted his gaze. "I invited you here today because I wanted to know if you'd be willing to help me, if you were still interested in finding out what happened. If you might return to the house with me, either as part of your show or outside of it. I'd be more than happy to cover any expenses you incurred." Dahl looked at her, his eyes imploring. "I need to know if she's there…"

"I understand," Kate heard herself reply, and she did. She knew perfectly well how Dahl felt, because somewhere deep inside her the notion that the spirit was her own mother still clung. Like Dahl's own belief it was nebulous, irrational, hard to articulate, but surprisingly tenacious. Even now after what he had told her, it wouldn't shake free.

"Will you help me?" he asked.

Kate tried to look like she was considering it; in truth she already knew the answer. She'd known it before setting out this morning. If Dahl wanted to go back then she wanted in.

"I'll try."

"What about your partner, Henry? I get the feeling he isn't particularly fond of me, and perhaps even less keen to return to my house."

It was true, Henry would need some convincing. He had made no secret of it. He would be perfectly happy

160

if they never saw Dahl's house ever again. He thought they should let sleeping dogs lie, but she needed to prod the dogs, hear them bark, check their eyes and teeth and ears, and most of all find out whom they belonged to. Despite Dahl's argument, she couldn't shake the feeling that the spirit in his house was connected to her somehow. Why else would it choose to speak through her when there was a medium sitting at the very same table?

"I think Henry might be swayed," she said.

Dahl appeared unconvinced. "And if not?"

"I'll talk to him. He thinks it's safer to let it go, that he's protecting me, but I need to know who spoke through me that night, and why. If I can make that clear, make him understand how important it is to me, hopefully, he'll respect that."

"I hope you're right."

"Um, and while we're on the subject of making things clear..." Kate felt herself begin to squirm slightly at the prospect of broaching the topic on her mind, but if they were going to be spending further time together it was best to set things straight from the get go. "Oh, god, this is probably going to make me sound like a raving narcissist, so forgive me, because it's perfectly possible I'm way off the mark here... but I got the impression that, well, you might be interested in me, and I just thought I should make it clear that while you seem like a great guy... I'm not looking to get involved, with anyone. The flowers you sent were very nice, but..."

"But you would prefer I don't send any more?" Dahl said amiably with a resigned smile. "I appreciate your honesty."

"No hard feelings?"

"None at all."

—

As Kate departed The Retreat's red-brick walls, the gates whining shut behind her, it was with plenty of food for thought. Her mind was already working furiously, digesting what she had learnt, and calculating how to convince Henry to return to Dahl's house.

She had come away feeling different toward Sebastian, warmer and more sympathetic. He was a considerably more complex individual than she had initially taken him for. She wondered, had his achievements, the wealth he had accumulated or the youths he had helped been an effective salve to what he'd lost so very early on? No stranger to loss herself, she knew better than most how deep some scars run. She had been robbed of two mothers, her birth mother and then her adoptive mum. Nearly two decades had passed since the cancer had taken her, and yet all too often it felt a fraction of that. When she lost Robert and Joel the grief she suffered as a teenager had reverberated with such ferocity that for a time, during the worst of it, the two events had become disturbingly intertwined. The year or so following Robert and Joel's deaths had been bad. Even now she tried not to think too long or hard about that time, when she had almost been broken on the wheel of what she had lost. Throughout those bleak interminable months, something cold and dark had stolen into her soul, a spiritual malady whose chief symptoms fluctuated between numbness and despair, the conviction everything was meaningless. At perhaps her lowest ebb, she had arrived at the belief, sober and chillingly logical, that she would prefer to feel nothing at all than endure the relentless gut-chewing exhaustion of grief any longer. She had come dangerously close to taking her own life. Only the thought of what it would do to her father had kept her from the precipice.

Instead she carried on. She ate. She dressed. She slept... and the darkness lifted, not all at once, but slowly, little by little, the way winter bows to spring. It was like rising from the depths of a cold dark riverbed toward the surface. She would occasionally catch glimpses of sunlight, shafts piercing the gloom. The current of life began to tug at her, draw her back into the world and the light, where people and purpose existed. It was almost as if something began switching on long dormant functions within her. Feelings ceased being abstract concepts and returned to being something she actually experienced, murky myopic corridors began to widen back into vistas.

Looking back, she realised how close it had all come to destroying her, and while things were better now, she knew she could never really be the person she was before. Once you know how cold and dark it is down there in the depths, there's no unknowing it. Part of you is always feeling for the undertow waiting to suck you back down. So you do what you can. You turn your face to the light. You keep kicking. What you certainly don't do is idly tread water, dwell on your bad times, count and re-count all you've lost. A husband, a child, a parent...

Sebastian believed the spirit she had channelled was connected to his mother somehow. He seemed to think there were answers to his past hidden in his house, to the life he had lost.

Kate thought about those cold dark depths and wondered how strong a swimmer he was.

—

Sebastian, Renwick and Nadine looked out of the window from the study on the second floor. Nadine had something in her right hand. Renwick had given it to her only moments before. It was a neatly folded handkerchief, stained with dried blood.

The trio were silent as Kate Bennett drove away, disappeared from view.

Renwick had been apprehensive about meeting Kate Bennett again. Sebastian had been confident she wouldn't identify him as the driver from the car accident she had been involved in leaving the house. Renwick hadn't been so sure. In the event, Sebastian had been right. The hat, glasses, and beard had proved an effective disguise. When Renwick introduced himself to Kate she hadn't shown as much as a flicker of recognition.

"Well," said Sebastian, "I'd say that went rather well, wouldn't you?"

Chapter 24

When Henry had asked him to take a deeper delve into Sebastian Dahl's past, Ray had started with the obvious stuff first, the electoral roll and other low-hanging fruit in the form of the most common online social network sites. From there he had moved to business and property searches, criminal records and such, and worked steadily backwards. Most of what emerged tallied broadly with the picture Dahl had given them, until Ray hit the period around Dahl's sixteenth birthday when the trail screeched to an abrupt halt.

This was after around a day and a half's digging, and while Ray could have called it quits and left it until the following morning to try and pick up the trail, he found he didn't want to. The sudden brick wall had fired his curiosity. He refilled his coffee machine and rolled up his sleeves. He started by reaching for his contacts book emailing a couple of colleagues from his private investigation days, people he knew had some valuable, if slightly unorthodox contacts. He gave them what he had on Dahl so far, and said he would make it worth their while if they could add something.

Despite much effort, and no small amount of midnight oil being burnt, the trail remained cold for two more days, until one of these colleagues got back to him with something that suddenly got it toasty again. The piece of information in question was plucked from the private database of one of the country's larger deed poll issuers. It was a name, or rather a pair of names, one old, one new.

Things opened up again and pretty soon Ray had stuff on Dahl right back to the day he had been born. This was when he went to Henry to share what he had found.

"There, I knew there was something shifty about that guy," mumbled Henry. "I bloody knew it."

He sat bent over his desk in his and Kate's shared office at Bennett White, poring over the notes Ray had handed him following the investigator's brief potted history of Sebastian Dahl's life story. "I knew it the second I met him."

It was hard to know precisely what to take from what Ray had unearthed. It only made an already strange business stranger still. Dahl was up to something alright, there was little doubt about that, but what exactly wasn't so easy to say.

"We need to talk to Kate," said Henry.

"And say what?" Ray asked.

"That Sebastian Dahl can't be trusted, for starters, that he's been lying to us."

Kate found Henry in their office. He was with Ray poring over some paperwork. She rapped lightly on the door before walking in. Henry and Ray both looked up, and upon seeing her appeared almost… guilty?

"Henry. Ray."

Ray smiled back uncertainly. "Hi Kate."

Henry returned her smile too, but for some reason Kate thought he looked slightly shifty too.

"Kate."

The entire morning she had been trying to think of a good way to broach the topic of returning to Dahl's house with Henry. Based on what Dahl had revealed to her about his past there was no question of not going back, but it was awkward. She had deliberately chosen not to tell Henry she was going to see Dahl, precisely because she knew he would try to persuade her against it. By going ahead without him she had expressly broken their agreement to put some distance between themselves and the incident at Dahl's house. She had to find a way to get Henry to see past this and focus on the important part: what Sebastian had told her, information that cast what had happened in an entirely new light. She toyed with a multitude of approaches from pushy to charming. Ultimately, she went with simple honesty.

"Henry, there's something I need to discuss with you."

"I was about to say the same thing."

"Oh?"

"Hm. I asked Ray to look into something for me, and he's made some very interesting discoveries about—"

"Henry, I went to see Sebastian Dahl yesterday."

Henry frowned, traded a look with Ray. "You did?"

"Yes. I attended an anniversary bash for a charity he's involved with, *Doorways*. They help young homeless people? Anyway, I talked with him, and told him we're still interested in going back to investigate his house again."

"Look, Kate—"

"I know what you're going to say, but just let me finish, okay? He told me some things that might make you see things differently. Just hear me out. Please?"

Henry traded another look with Ray, and again she thought she saw something pass between them, but Henry simply said, "Okay, what did he say?"

Kate almost asked Ray to leave them alone, but then thought, where's the point? If they were returning to Dahl's house the crew would need persuading too.

167

Some a little, some, like Charles for example, quite a lot.

"Dahl grew up in care. The reason he grew up in care was because his mother lost her life in a house fire. He believes she was the woman who spoke through me during the séance, or someone connected to her."

Henry appeared to think about this. After a long pause he said, "I see."

"Do you? It makes sense, kind of, doesn't it? When I—or rather the spirit—made a plea for a child, and then Charles's vision of a fire?"

Henry looked oddly unmoved. She felt a flash of irritation. Didn't he get it?

"What else did he tell you?" asked Henry.

Kate wondered if she hadn't made herself clear enough. What else did Henry need?

"Isn't that enough?"

Again Henry looked to Ray.

"There was nothing more?"

"What are you getting at?"

"After we got back from the house that night," Henry said hesitantly, "I asked Ray to see what he could dig up on our Sebastian Dahl. I was sure there was something iffy about him."

"And?"

"And what he told you is true, I can't argue with that…"

"But…?"

"It's not the whole story, not by a long chalk. You might want to sit down."

Kate opened her mouth to speak, only to discover she didn't have anything to say after all. They had a corner sofa in the office, she sat down in it. Henry nodded to Ray.

"The man we know as Sebastian Dahl hasn't always gone by that name. His name used to be Timothy

Lamb. He changed his name by deed poll at the age of sixteen."

Kate nodded. "Go on."

"What I've got is pieced together from dates and names from records," Ray said. "It's sketchy in places, but close enough I reckon. It goes something like this.

"According to a Birmingham Evening Mail news story dated September 23rd 1989, Sebastian Dahl's mother was one of six people who perished in a house fire in the Edgbaston area of Birmingham. Timothy Lamb, as Dahl was called then, was one of the lucky three to escape the blaze. He was just ten years old.

"If Timothy had any other close family they chose not to take him in. He was taken into local authority care, where he remained until around the age of twelve—when he ran away. Four years after this he changed his name by deed poll to Sebastian Dahl, the name that subsequently appears in all the records attached to Dahl Developments, a property development company that in a few short years became very successful. Dahl, as he's now called, made a lot of money very quickly. A few years later he established a charity, called *Doorways*, a kind of refuge for the damaged and dispossessed, homeless youths, ex-teen-prostitutes, ex-cons and the like."

Kate took a moment to consider what Ray had said, but struggled to find anything especially damning in it. To summarise, as a child, Sebastian Dahl had lost his mother, been taken into care, and from these tragic and disadvantaged beginnings had managed to fight his way to success, even going so far as to dedicate himself to helping others who had suffered similar misfortunes.

"Okay... Am I missing something?" Kate said, at last.

Henry turned to Ray, and said simply, "Show her the story."

Ray nodded and held out a sheet of paper. Kate took it from him. It was a digitally scanned printout of a newspaper story. The date and the subject identified it as being the 1989 Birmingham Evening Mail story Ray had referred to previously. She read it.

Three survive house fire which claims six lives.

A 52-year-old man, a 10-year-old boy and girl of seven years escaped a fire that started late Thursday evening in a three-story house on Oakbourne Road, in the Edgbaston area of Birmingham. Six people are believed to have perished in the blaze.

Although several of the house's occupants were recovered by the emergency services, all were pronounced dead at the scene.

Describing the scene, Mr Albert Hope, a neighbour, said, "I've never seen anything like it. The heat was incredible, like standing in front of an open furnace.

"The firemen did their best, but you could see no one else was getting out of there alive by the time they arrived."

Police Superintendent Stuart Rose commented, "It appears the fire started somewhere in

*the ground floor of the house.
Fire-fighters attended the
scene until midnight and
investigators are due to
return this morning in an
attempt to establish the
cause."*

*The identities of the surviving
man and two children are
currently being withheld,
pending investigations.*

Kate re-read the story from the top, and then turned to Henry.

"Doesn't this just support Dahl's story?"

"It does, but..." Henry trailed off. "Kate, take a look at the date."

She did, the article was dated September 23rd 1989. She frowned.

"You attended junior school in Birmingham. I remember you telling me that was where your mum and dad lived before you moved to London...? Your birth mother died in an accident, isn't that what you once told me? The date and your age at the time, they match. You would have been seven years old then." Henry tapped the printed sheet of paper gently. "Dahl was the boy who escaped that fire. I think you might be the girl."

She heard the words leave her mouth slowly. "But that's..." She was about to say crazy, but it wasn't. The situation might be crazy, but Henry's conclusion made an awful kind of sense.

"Dahl must have known." Henry added, "When he contacted us, Kate, he must have known it."

Kate felt queasy.

She swallowed. "I think I need to speak to my dad."

171

Chapter 25

Kate turned into her father's avenue, drew near his house and parked up across the road. She was about to get out of her car when she realised her father was outside in his front garden, and that he wasn't alone.

He and his companion were kneeling side by side on a pair of foam gardening pads next to a soil border, her dad had a trowel and his companion was handing him bulbs out of a brown bag. He was planting them in a row, carefully pressing them into the soil and dumping a scoop of compost on top.

It was then Kate noticed how the borders had been artfully reshaped. They'd been cut deeper into the lawn in a pleasing sweep. A collection of council garden refuse bags full of culled turf sat beside the drive. Her eye picked out other changes too. A run of wooden trellis had been screwed to the wall between the porch and front window, and below it a big terracotta planter. The tendrils of a flowering climber with crimson-red buds had been teased into the trellis's criss-crossed nooks and crannies. Her dad and Ms Janette Holloway looked to be chatting easily while they worked. They appeared comfortable together, relaxed and happy.

The garden looked different, and when the new plants and bulbs bloomed next year it would look even more so—for the first time since her mother had died. Kate thought about this for a moment and found, almost to her surprise, that she approved.

She made herself get out of the car, before either her dad or Janette Holloway could spot her watching them.

She called out, "Hi," as she approached them.

Her dad turned, first looking delighted, and then, unless she only imagined it, just a pinch uncomfortable.

"Katie."

He climbed up from the foam kneeling pad and gave her a hug.

Ms Holloway got to her feet too. "Hello Kate."

"Hello Ms— Hello, Janette."

"I was just lending your father a hand. He claims gardening's not his forte."

"From the looks of it all he needed was a little help."

Perhaps detecting something beneath Kate's veneer of cheeriness, her dad said, "Is everything alright?"

"I need to talk to you about something." She paused. "It's a kind of private thing, though…"

"Oh? Oh, right." James turned to Janette. "Janette is it possible Kate and I could—"

Janette was already collecting her gardening gloves and kneeling pad. "Of course." She gave them both a smile, warm and genuine. "Bye, Kate. It was lovely to meet you again."

"You too, really—and sorry for crashing the party; the garden really does look terrific."

"Thank you."

Kate and her father watched Janette cross the avenue to her own house, then began to gather up the remaining gardening tools. "So what exactly did you want to talk about?

"I wanted to ask you about my biological parents."

"Oh. Right." His expression changed, betraying apprehension and resignation. "Maybe I should put the kettle on."

—

Kate watched her dad read the Birmingham Evening Mail news story. He went through it slowly, handing it back to her when he was done.

She took it from him. "Dad, did my birth mother die in this fire?"

He nodded unhappily. "Yes, I think she may have. The date and the location fit the small amount of information I and your mother were given."

"My biological father, he wasn't there, though?"

"Kate... Please, after reading this I appreciate you must have a thousand questions you'd like answered, but as much as I'd like to, I'm not going to be able to satisfy many of them. The truth is I don't have a whole lot more to tell you than you already seem to have discovered for yourself."

"When you adopted me didn't they tell you anything about my family background? Didn't you see birth certificates, stuff like that?"

"I'm afraid not. I'm sorry to say I can't even tell you for certain what your birth mother's full name was, much less your father's. The information your mother and I were given was rather sparse, simply because not much was known for certain. The sum total amounted to this: We were told your birth mother died in a house fire, which you escaped, but for your burns. We were told your mother went by the name of Valerie Jones, but there was some doubt as to whether this was actually her real surname. No documents were found to confirm her identity, which of course made tracing any extended family you may have had all but impossible. The coroner estimated your birth mother to be in her early twenties when she died, and with you being around seven it seemed likely she had got pregnant in her early teens. Perhaps she had been thrown out by her parents, or maybe she had run away. With no way of finding relatives to take you in, you were placed under local authority care. Apparently during this time you were severely withdrawn, you wouldn't speak. Slowly, though, over the following twelve months or so you started to open up. Efforts were made to try to get you to talk about what had happened. I believe you were under a child psychologist for a time.

"You seemed to have no memory of your life before the fire and entering care, and yet apart from being unwilling or unable to talk about the past you were beginning to socialise with others around you. As things went on you were assessed and deemed to be developing normally. The burns on your chest and your neck healed, leaving only moderate scarring, and there was good reason to believe you were healing psychologically too. After just over a year in care it was decided adoption would be in your best interests. Your mum and I were the couple lucky enough to benefit from that decision.

"We were advised that someday you may be ready to confront what had happened to you. If you were blocking traumatic memories then eventually they could surface, perhaps even many years later, when your unconscious felt better equipped to deal with them, or when some other event or experience triggered you to recall them. We accepted that one day you might want to talk about your mother's death and the fire. We were prepared for it, but the day never came. Over the years we built our own family and our own history and it seemed less and less of an issue somehow, almost like you never had a life before you came to us.

"Mum and I never pretended you weren't adopted and we were always in agreement; if you wanted to know about your past we'd offer you what little information we had, but as the years passed it became evident you simply weren't interested. You seemed to accept your birth mother was gone, and we were your parents. You were happy and healthy, and when it came to those years before you were our daughter, those years you couldn't remember, you were always adamant: you insisted they didn't matter."

Kate nodded without even meaning to. It was true. Even now, if she tried to turn her mind back to the years before she entered her parent's lives she found she didn't really want to. Why? Was it due to a sense of loyalty, plain disinterest, or something deeper rooted? She tried to dredge up a memory from before she was adopted. She couldn't. Her mind met resistance; a hard knot wanted to form in her gut, and a feeling of ill-defined unease...

She found herself suddenly reluctant to even try, which in itself suddenly struck her as strange. She had always told herself those years didn't matter, that she wasn't interested, but what if there was more to it than that?

"But you want to know now?" her dad asked, and then after a moments silence, "Is it because of my heart attack?"

"No," Kate protested, shocked. "Why would you think that?"

He didn't answer, but she fancied she knew what he was thinking. If the heart attack had proved fatal, if things had turned out differently, she wouldn't have a single soul left she could call family. For a second she considered telling him everything, all about Dahl's house, the séance, the spirit, but only for a second. What good would it do? It was just too weird. He would only fret about it.

So in the end she said, "I suppose finally I just got curious." The explanation sounded lame as she uttered it, but from what her dad asked next he seemed to buy it.

"So you really don't remember any of it? The fire, your birth mother? I didn't think you did, but I suppose I was always wary to ask for fear of triggering anything. If you blocked it all out, maybe there's a good reason why. I did some reading on the subject a while back, retrograde amnesia they call it. It can sometimes be a response to emotional trauma. It's thought to be a defence mechanism. The mind attempting to bury a frightening or traumatic experience… Perhaps some things are best left forgotten. It hasn't always been easy, though. A few times you asked me how you got your burn scars, do you remember? Maybe you don't; it was when you were little. I never knew what to answer for the best. I suppose that's why I told you I didn't know."

"Don't feel bad. I'd have done the same thing in your shoes, I think."

"So how did you come across that newspaper story?"

Kate froze. Shit. She could have kicked herself. She'd been so caught up with questions she hadn't stopped to think about how she was supposed to have come by the news story.

"I… hired an investigator to look into it, and when he came back to me with this… well, that's when I realised I should have just spoken to you instead."

"You should have. Are you okay?"

"I'm fine. I was curious, and now I know as much as I needed to I guess."

He looked at her. She saw love, concern, tenderness, and felt her heart strings draw tight. She felt sorry for him. Like any parent, he just wanted to make everything right. Who wouldn't fold the world up like origami to better fit around their child if such a thing were possible?

In lieu, he simply said, "I love you, Katie."

It was almost enough.

—

Kate left feeling unsettled and strangely guilty. She hoped she hadn't left her father suffering too much disquiet. Her own disquiet she buried until she was a road or two from his house, far enough to be safely out of sight to pull over and call Henry. He answered almost at once, like he'd been awaiting her call.

"Henry, it's me."

"Have you spoken to your dad yet?"

"Yeah. And it looks like you were right. The girl in the newspaper story? It was me."

She heard him exhale on the other end of the line. "So what do you want to do now?"

The answer was simple.

"I want to talk to Sebastian Dahl."

Chapter 26

Kate wanted to speak to Dahl alone, but Henry had kicked up such a fuss she had relented and agreed to confront him together. On reflection she accepted it was probably a wiser move. If Dahl, not unreasonably, assumed she had been successful in convincing Henry to return to his house, he was apt to be less prepared, perhaps more likely to let slip his true agenda.

Claire made the arrangements. She contacted Dahl and asked if he would like to meet with Kate and Henry to discuss returning to the house. Would he perhaps be able to drop in at their production offices for a chat? As Kate anticipated, Dahl hadn't needed much encouragement; as chance would have it, he said, he would be in London the following week. Remarkably convenient.

Kate and Henry had smiled and welcomed him cordially on his arrival, led him through into their shared office space and closed the door.

When Kate produced a printout of the Birmingham Mail story and handed it to him, Dahl had looked puzzled, until he scanned the story and confirmed beyond a shadow of a doubt he knew. There was maybe half a second during which Kate saw him deliberate between feigning ignorance and coming clean.

"Ah," he said uncomfortably, looking between them.

Kate could practically feel Henry holding himself in check beside her. She put a hand on his arm. She wanted Dahl to speak and reckoned silence would achieve that sooner than heated accusations.

Dahl exhaled, resigned, it appeared, to coming clean.

"It was your burn scar," he said, "on your neck. That was where it began, what made me think it was you. I can still remember it livid and fresh, you know, sitting in the dark outside the burning house where it happened..."

"You remember the fire?"

"I was ten years old. I nearly died. My mother and five other people I knew did. Yes, I remember. Evidently, though, you don't?"

"No."

"I saw you on television, around eight months ago. Your scar captured my attention, and coupled with your name... 'So what?' I told myself. We live in a nation of sixty million people; there must be several women around your age named Kate with burn scars... Once the possibility surfaced, though, I found it impossible to ignore. Could you really be *the* girl I knew named Kate, the same one I climbed out of that burning house with? And that you presented a paranormal investigation television show... I don't know if I believe in things like fate and such, but it seemed to mean something. I was in possession of a haunted house and there you were presenting a paranormal investigation show? Given what had happened, I couldn't help but wonder. If I got you there, would you experience something similar to what I had, would you see anything, feel anything too?"

"What do you mean?" Kate asked.

"Do you remember your first visit to the house, your dizzy spell? You saw something, didn't you? I could tell. Soon after the house was completed the same thing happened to me. I blacked out momentarily, experienced something like a vision, a series of flashes, images, of fire, of people... I came to lying on the floor, staring at the ceiling. The only difference was I made the connection at once. I thought immediately of the fire that took my mother's life but spared mine. I had built a life, moved on, so I had believed, until that moment. At a stroke, I felt my past dragged cruelly into my present. I fear I became somewhat obsessed with

180

the house then, found myself drawn to it. Instead of selling it as I had intended, I kept it, and started spending more and more time there, hoping to see something else, make sense of it all. The fact that we're sitting here right now should tell you I failed. After those first few flashes the images stopped, and while other strange things happened, noises, things moving, sudden changes in temperature, they told me nothing. It became infuriating. I knew something was in that house, something connected to my past, but beyond that—" Dahl's confession petered out. "So, in an effort to see if it was just me, to reassure myself I wasn't losing my mind, I rented the property out. A few tenants were enough to settle my mind on that score. None of them stayed long.

"When I quizzed them about what they had experienced," Dahl continued, "why they chose to leave, they all said the same thing, unapologetically, point blank, the house was haunted. They described phenomena similar to that I had experienced, noises, strange sensations, abrupt changes in temperature, the feeling of something being in a room with them, but none mentioned experiencing visions. That seemed unique to me. Was that because I had put so much of myself into the building, or because, as I'm now even more convinced, the spirit or spirits that haunt the house are connected to me? Somehow knowing further tenants would tell me little more than I already knew, I was at a loss. I couldn't bring myself to sell the house, and yet I didn't know how to get the answers I craved, so I mothballed it. Sealed the place up, tried to forget it, and that was how things remained until—"

"You saw me," Kate finished.

"Yes," Dahl admitted. "Until I saw you."

"You lied to me, if not outright, then by omission."

Dahl was quiet for a spell. "Yes, I suppose that's fair."

"You should have told us there was more to it," Henry said, stony-faced.

"Try to see it from my point of view," Dahl countered. "For all I knew nothing at all would happen when Kate walked inside the house. What I knew, about my own past, and Kate's, was a considerable bag of worms to open if there was no cause to. If Kate walked around the house and left unaffected, if she experienced nothing akin to what I had, then I had every intention of calling you a few days later to tell you I'd changed my mind and no longer wanted my property to be considered for your show." Dahl looked at Kate. "And you would have continued with your life none the wiser. Except you *did* see something, you did experience something. That's when I became convinced it was linked to the fire we escaped, perhaps to someone who hadn't escaped? For what it's worth, I am sorry, but Kate, you more than anyone must understand... I needed to know what it all meant."

Kate should have felt angry; she had been misled, manipulated, used even, but anger wasn't among the things she felt. What she chiefly felt was ignorant, in the strictest definition of the word. She knew practically nothing about those early years of her life, recalled nothing about the woman who had given birth to her, the fire that took her life and spared Kate's own. To save her distress, her mind appeared to simply have erased it all, which made sitting in front of Dahl, who did remember and yet had clawed his way to success without the love and support she had enjoyed, slightly uncomfortable. She didn't feel angry, she felt like a coward.

"What did happen in that house fire, Sebastian, when we were children? Why don't we start there? What do you remember?"

"Fragments. It was a long time ago, and I was only ten years old myself, and I had ample reason to want to forget. It wasn't something I made a habit of thinking back on, until that house made it impossible for me not to.

"The house where we lived, the one that caught fire, was a kind of commune. I think there was around a dozen or so people living there at the time, mostly young people. A couple of them had children, your mother and mine. From what I can recall it was a good place; I remember it feeling friendly, like we were part of a big family. I think my mother and I had been there for around a year prior to the fire, and I'm almost certain you and your mother were already there when we arrived. An older couple owned the house. I'd guess they were hippies in the sixties, 'free thinkers', 'counter culture', what by the late eighties people might have called 'new-agers'." Dahl smiled, but it quickly faded. "I'm not sure how the fire started. The inquiry said it was an accident, and I've no doubt that was true. If I had to guess, I would hazard an unattended cigarette or joint was responsible. Either way, it must have spread quickly. When I try to think back to the fire, all I remember is heat and smoke, and the terror, being dragged through the house, eyes stinging. The man who owned the house got us out. We were terrified, crying, everything seemed to be on fire. At some point through the house part of the ceiling gave way. We were knocked to the ground. It was like being doused in hot coals. I remember trying to scream, but I couldn't, and then just when I was sure I was going to die, I was hauled from beneath it all. It was the man, pulling me to my feet. We found a window and managed to climb outside. There were sirens, and I remember looking at you. You were mute, blank-eyed, and your neck was burnt..."

Dahl stopped, shook his head as though this was where his memory ran dry.

"Afterwards, I was put into a local authority care home, and I assume you were too. I never saw you again, or not until you appeared on my television, that is. I understand the man who saved us suffered a mental breakdown. They put him in a psychiatric hospital. He died around a year after. I never got the chance to thank him for saving my life."

Kate heard herself mumble, "Good lord."

"So there you have it." Dahl opened his hands. "My cards are on the table, so to speak. I'm convinced there's something in that house that's trying to communicate. With me, but with you as well; that has to mean something, doesn't it?"

It was Henry who asked, "Why?"

"Isn't it obvious?" Dahl swept a hand around him. "Mr White, I'm a property developer. It's Miss Bennett here who's the paranormal investigator. You think that's simply a coincidence?"

Kate felt Dahl's eyes on her. "Why was it you chose the paranormal in particular to make a television show about?"

Kate wasn't sure how to answer, so she plumped for honesty. "I don't know. I've always been interested in that kind of stuff I guess…"

"In light of recent events, doesn't that seem, I don't know, *significant?* The incident at the séance, you've never experienced anything like that before?" Dahl leaned forward, there was suddenly a light in his eyes. "Please, try to remember. Anything similar? Maybe—"

Henry cut across him."Okay, that's enough. In fact I think that's more than enough for now. Kate and I are going to have to talk about this. We've got your number."

Dahl began to protest, "Hold on, you can't—"

"Yes, I can." Henry was on his feet, staring down at Dahl. "I'll have Claire show you out." Henry walked to the office door and held it open.

Dahl didn't budge. Instead, he looked to Kate, asked her, "Do *you* want me to leave?"

Kate was confused. Henry was right. What she needed right now was some time to think, time to process what Dahl had told them.

"I think it might be best, but we *will* call you. And thank you."

Dahl gave her a curt nod, and left without sparing Henry so much as a glance.

Henry waited until he had gone and sat down beside her.

"Are you okay?"

She wished she knew.

"It's one thing to read a newspaper story, another to hear about it from someone who was there... Why don't I remember any of it? You'd think I would, something at least."

"I'm not sure that's true, Kate. You were a little girl, seven years old. In all honesty I can't say I remember too much about my life at that age, and even less the further I go back."

"But if you almost died in a fire? Don't you think that might be something that stuck in your memory?"

"Have you considered you might be better off not remembering?"

"I don't think it's about being better off or worse off at this point. I *need* to know. Was there something more to that fire, like maybe it wasn't an accident? Something in Dahl's house tried to communicate with me, show me something, why?"

Henry looked troubled. "I don't know, Kate, but I know I don't trust him, Dahl, and I don't think you should either. It's nothing personal—"

Kate couldn't hide her scepticism at that one.

"Okay," Henry conceded, "it might be a bit personal. I don't like the bloke, but even if I did, hasn't he already proved he can't be trusted? He put you inside

185

that house hoping, *hoping*, that something would happen to you, and he only came clean about it when we cornered him. Tell me I'm wrong."

"I can't. But he was right about one thing: I do understand why he did it, why he led me into that house. He experienced something, and he needs to know what it means. I understand because now I need to know too. I have to go back there—and soon. Preferably as part of the show..."

Henry didn't respond. He wasn't dumb. She had just made the alternative, unspoken, clear enough. If he refused to get involved she and Dahl would go it alone.

"Okay," he breathed unhappily, "we'll look at the schedule. See if we can fit it in."

"In the next week?"

"Kate…"

"It has to be soon."

She held his gaze; she needed him to accept she was resolute.

"Okay... If Dahl's willing, we'll go back next week."

"Good enough."

"But I still think it's a bad idea."

Chapter 27

Henry wove his way back over to Ray and the table they had bagged beside The Red Lion's almost medievally huge fireplace. Henry had caught up with Ray after the meeting with Dahl and asked if he would be open to grabbing a pint or two. He had something he wanted to discuss, preferably outside of the office.

The business with Dahl had left him with a nasty aftertaste. Paradoxically, Dahl coming clean had only made Henry trust him less than ever. To begin with, Dahl had done little more than confirm what they suspected or already knew. By confessing to concealing he had known who Kate was he appeared, perversely, to have regained her trust in a single stroke. He was still manipulating her, insinuating their shared experience meant no one but Kate could really be expected to understand what had motivated him to lie. What made it more frustrating was Kate actually seemed to be buying into it. Despite having exploited her, and then misled her, Dahl had somehow won rather than lost her sympathy and trust. It was maddening.

By the time Henry had filled Ray in they were into their second round of drinks. Ray's considered response was a heavy exhalation and a "So we're going back?"

"I don't see what choice I have. If I refuse, I think Kate will just go back alone, and there's no way I'm about to let that happen. Dahl knows way more than he's telling. I'd stake my life on it. I want to see if I can find out more about that fire, and about Dahl."

"And you could do with some help?"

Henry nodded.

Ray rubbed a hand over the fine grey stubble covering his jaw. "Paper trails are all well and good, but they're only so useful. If I were you I'd want to talk to someone who remembered the incident first-hand."

Henry thought about it. "Like the neighbour from the newspaper story? What was his name..? Albert Hope?"

Ray nodded. "If he's still around he'd be a good start, but also, what about the journalist who wrote up the story? Most stories have more than makes it into print, mostly just for brevity's sake, sometimes because the information leans too close to rumour and innuendo. Who knows, the reporter who wrote that Birmingham Mail story might have heard something like that? A house full of hippies that burns to the ground, killing the majority of them? I'll bet the neighbours had plenty to say."

"It's been twenty odd years, though. Would a journo be likely to remember a story after that long?"

"True, it's a fair way back," Ray admitted, "but from my experience, most journalists have pretty tenacious memories. Why don't you let me see if I can track him down and we'll find out? If you're lucky the neighbour might still live at the same address he did back then."

"Maybe."

"Henry?"

"Hm?"

"What are you worried Dahl's up to? Don't get me wrong, I'm not calling your judgement into question, I've always believed in trusting your instincts, worked well enough for me when I was in the force, but this bloke's clearly got under your skin..."

"That's what's driving me crazy about all this. He's dragging Kate into the unknown and we can't know if it's dangerous or not. He has an agenda, for sure, but I'm dammed if I know what it is. If the spirit in that house is connected with the fire he and Kate escaped, then the only way I can hope to find out what he's up to is by discovering as much about that event and the people involved in it as I can."

"Can't you just persuade Kate to let it go? I'm no chicken but I'll admit to not being eager to spend a night in that house again. There's part of me still wants to believe it didn't happen the way it did, that Kate and Charles freaked out and acted weird for some other reason... exhaustion, auto-hypnotic suggestion, something like that..."

"But we both know that's not how it was, don't we? And as for Kate letting it go..." Henry shook his head. "If we don't go back, she'll go alone."

Ray didn't disagree; he obviously knew Kate well enough by now to feel Henry was right. "Okay," he said, "let me see if I can find that journalist. I'll see what more I can find out about the house too while I'm at it."

Chapter 28

The boy checked the street one more time. It was deserted. As he hoped, the early hour ensured most were still in their beds. Only the distant whine of an electric milk float shattered the illusion of him being the only waking soul for miles around. He crossed the street for the house and the driveway's padlocked gate.

He looked again to make absolutely sure he was still alone and no one was watching from one of the neighbouring houses before jumping up, grabbing the top of the gate and quickly clambering over it. The entire movement took less than ten seconds to execute, but to the boy's ears the shaking clank of the gate, padlock and chain rang out with wince-provoking volume against the early morning quiet. He dropped down on the other side and sprinted for the cover of some bushes, sure curtains had to be twitching, curious eyes trying to identify what had been responsible for the noise.

When he peeked through the foliage, however, everything was just as still and silent as before, which was good. The last thing he needed now was a run-in with the police. If he were caught they might find out he had run away from his foster home, and then things would get messy. Content he had traversed the gate unseen, he made his way around to the back of the house, pushing through the overgrown bushes and weeds trying to reclaim the garden and paths around the property.

The rear garden was conveniently obscured on all sides by fences and tree foliage. While the boards covering the back door and windows had seen some graffiti, the property had remained secure. The boy pulled a heavy-duty screwdriver from his pocket and set to work on the board covering the kitchen window. It was hard work, but eventually he prised a corner free and levered the board off, tossing it into the long grass. The window behind was broken, blown out in the fire. He used the screwdriver to dislodge the shards of glass still left in the frame and climbed through into the house.

Save for the light spilling through the window the interior was all but black. He took out a small pocket torch and thumbed the switch. A disc of light appeared and skittered about, revealing snatches of degraded and lumpy kitchen wall. He advanced, directing the torchlight down ahead of his feet so he could see where it was safe to tread. The house smelt damp, and as he left the tiled floor of the kitchen for the hallway the floorboards creaked ominously. The torchlight illuminated ragged carpet and scorched wood. The fire had reduced the patterned wallpapered walls to mottled black canvasses, furniture and fixtures to misshapen lumps of debris. A pervasive black tar seemed to coat everything, sticking fast to his fingertips wherever he touched.

He pressed on, through the hallway to the threshold of the lounge. The door was missing. He spotted it a moment later in the centre of the room where the floorboards were mostly gone, incinerated to charcoal, leaving a cavity where joists poked out like the ribs of an eviscerated beast. The door was half-submerged in the under floor cavity, as black and ravaged as everything else.

The boy placed a foot upon the nearest joist and took a testing step. Despite its blackened appearance the timber seemed solid enough. He ventured a second step forward, spreading his arms wide like a tightrope walker. Four more steps brought him to the centre of the room, where he lowered himself to sit on the beam, letting his legs swing idly beneath him.

He moved the torchlight slowly around the room, trying to reconcile the ruined planes of scorched plaster and wood with the room he remembered. In one corner he identified the remains of a chair, in another a charred black box that might have once been a sideboard. Finally he switched the torch off, allowing the darkness to swallow everything. The room appeared in his mind's eye, as it used to be.

"I haven't forgotten you," he whispered. "You know that don't you?"

In the silence that followed came his answer.

Chapter 29

The ringing tone repeated, unanswered. Henry knew it was something of a long shot to expect the neighbour from the newspaper story, Albert Hope, to still be living at the same address twenty years later, but not completely unreasonable. He was just about to give up and try again later when someone picked up. An old man's voice came down the line, thin and tremulous.

"Hello?"

"Mr Hope? Albert Hope?"

"Yes? Who's this speaking?"

"Hello Mr Hope. My name's Henry White. I'm trying to find out about a house fire that occurred in 1989, on the road where you live, Oakbourne Road, Edgbaston, in Birmingham?"

"Yes..."

"You were quoted in a news story reporting on the tragedy at the time. I'm trying to gather some information about the event. I wondered if I might ask you a few questions. Do you remember the incident?"

There was long silence on the other end of the line. Henry was about to repeat the question when Hope answered.

"I don't suppose I'll ever forget it. You don't, not something like that."

"Can you tell me what happened, maybe something about the people who lived in the house?"

"Well... I can't really say I knew them all that well."

"Really, anything would be appreciated."

"There were a bunch of them living there. Young people, mostly. Eight, nine? The house belonged to an older couple; although you'd have been forgiven for thinking it was a squat or something if you didn't know that. I'm not sure any of them actually worked. My wife, god rest her soul, she had them all pegged as a bunch of layabouts."

"Did they cause trouble?"

"No, nothing like that, just the place could look a bit untidy. They weren't much for mowing the lawns or that kind of thing, but they didn't cause any real bother. They were sort of like hippies, I suppose. They kept chickens in the back garden, grew their own veg. There were a couple of children; they were among the few who got out when it caught fire. A boy and a girl. Awful tragedy, terrible... and the older chap from the couple who owned the house, he was the only other one to get out..."

"That's what it said in the newspaper story. You didn't know him at all, the homeowner?"

"Not really. We exchanged the odd greeting now and then, but that was about as far as it went. They kept themselves to themselves. Whatever they got up to in private was their own business..."

Something about this comment or the way Hope said it made Henry prick up his ears.

"And what were they getting up to?"

At once Henry knew he had asked too quickly, sounded too keen. At a stroke he had abruptly derailed the casual path the conversation had been taking. He had sounded too interested, and made Hope suddenly uneasy. The continued silence on the other end of the line confirmed as much.

When Hope did finally respond his tone was suddenly guarded. "Who did you say you were again?"

"Henry White."

"And why is it you wanted to know about this business?"

Henry grimaced. Tell the truth, or fib a little? He decided on somewhere in between.

"I think I have a family connection to someone who perished in the fire."

194

"Oh..." Hope still sounded unsure. "Well, Mr White, it was a long time ago, and I doubt there's much I could tell you beyond what's in that newspaper story you mentioned."

"What about the night of the fire? Could you tell me what you remember about it?"

There was another pause.

"Mr Hope?"

"As I said, it was a long time ago."

"If you could just—"

"I'm sorry, I'd like to help, but I have to go now. Goodbye, Mr White."

Henry heard the click as Hope set his phone down. He stared at the phone in his hand for a while, convinced Hope's memory was sharper than he claimed, but equally sure he wasn't going to get anything more out of him over the phone.

Chapter 30

Eight days. Eight interminable days. The wait had been excruciating. After getting Henry to agree to return to Dahl's house Kate had wanted to get in touch with Dahl immediately to request another visit, but Henry had pulled her up short. He said he wanted to do it. This, she figured, was his way to try and keep things on a professional footing, or perhaps reassure himself it was still to some extent about the show.

Henry and Dahl's conversation had been conducted over speaker phone in the office, with Kate listening in. Henry had been direct, but courteous, and for his part Dahl met their request with grace, offering to make the property available to them at their convenience. The date was set for eight days' time, Wednesday of the following week. Henry thanked Dahl (although to Kate's ear a little like someone thanking a dentist for a filling) and ended the call. The next step was to call the crew together for a meeting and inform them of their intentions.

They had already agreed no one should be pressured into returning to the house if they didn't want to. While it was true they all worked on a paranormal investigation show, and should probably have anticipated paranormal encounters could well be part of the gig, Kate accepted the present situation was different. Their goal was no longer simply trying to capture interesting footage for a TV show.

They explained how they intended to return to the Dahl house in just over a week, but that each and every one of them was free to opt out if they wanted to. They could operate with either a skeleton crew or hired help if necessary. They shared what they had learnt about Dahl's past, and how it was connected to Kate's. They told them about the house fire on Oakbourne Road in '89, the deaths of Kate's and Dahl's mothers and the others living there. To Ray, of course, it was old news, but for the rest of the crew it cast things in a whole different light, and was an admission the reason they were returning to the Dahl house was really not for the show, but for Kate.

Claire responded first. Without a fuss, she simply raised a hand and said, "I'll go."

Kate could have hugged her.

"Count me in too," said Keith, close on Claire's heels. "If there's ever any chance of us getting something paranormal on camera it's in that house. I might have to double up on underpants, but I'll be there."

This earned a chuckle or two, before Mark chipped in, "Fair enough. I'm in too."

Ray executed a quiet nod. It was enough.

That only left Charles.

His face was inscrutable, but Kate feared she already knew what lay behind his silence. In a moment he would speak, tell them they were fools, declare them out of their depth, implore them to remember what happened last time, and then he would get up and leave.

It was Kate he looked at when he finally sighed and breathed, "You're determined to go back?"

"I am."

"And there's nothing I can do to persuade you otherwise?"

Kate shrugged. "Charles, I have to."

"No," he said sadly, "you don't, but if you're absolutely intent upon it, I think it's only best that I go with you."

She was astonished. "You'll come?" She was so sure he would steadfastly refuse.

"At least if I'm there," he added with a wan smile, "I might be able to stop you from getting into too much trouble."

And so, eight long days later, they were finally back at Dahl's house.

Kate leant against the motor home and stared up the hill to the bleak looking building perched atop. If anything, it looked even less inviting than she remembered. The weather had turned. The day was damp, overcast with clouds the ugly grey of day old bruises stretching out to the horizon, fusing the sky and ocean beyond the coast into an unbroken band of white noise.

They parked the vehicles in the same spot as before and everyone threw themselves into their preparations, unloading gear and the like, and yet their industry seemed to Kate more an effort to distract themselves than an indication of enthusiasm. Certainly no one seemed in any hurry to go near the house itself. Kate wondered if one or two of them were regretting their decision not to bow out.

Dahl had arrived a little after they did, but more or less kept out of their way. Seeing him again, Kate was uncertain how she felt. After her visit to The Retreat she had warmed to him, then she had been forced to reassess him yet again. While she sympathised with his need to know what was in the house, she would never have done what he had, but then her teens hadn't been spent in shop doorways or filthy squats. She had never grown up feeling robbed and alone.

Sebastian Dahl, once a boy called Timothy Lamb, who sat outside a burning house beside a suddenly mute girl who buried the memory of that night so deep it still lay beyond her reach.

Looking up at the house now she experienced a flicker of doubt. Was it possible she had been so intent upon convincing everyone to return that she hadn't given sufficient thought to whether they really should? The house held a secret, a secret it seemed to want to share, but like the memory of that night, was it one she would be better for knowing? Could there be a line here, behind which lay her life as it existed now, untainted by events of the past, and beyond this another life... a different life?

When Henry rounded the motor home, appearing right in front of her, she almost jumped.

"Ready?" he asked.

For a second, maybe two, she almost said no.

"Kate?"

Instead, she marshalled a smile. If Henry got the slightest whiff what had just passed through her mind, he would begin herding everyone back in the vehicles to head home.

"Yes?"

"Charles would like a word." Henry gave her an arch look. "I think he wants to extract a few pinkie swears out of us before we get started."

—

Despite Henry being right beside her, Kate knew full well what Charles was saying was directed squarely at her.

"And even if, as last time, nothing occurs during our daytime walkthrough or during the course of the night-time vigil, and we do decide to conduct another séance, you promise you'll follow my guidance?"

Kate nodded dutifully.

Charles continued, "If you feel anything strange, anything similar to what you experienced last time, you *must* attempt to resist it. Focus your attention on the physical as we discussed. Direct your senses toward your immediate surroundings. Wall yourself off mentally. Try to avoid directing your thoughts toward how people around you may be thinking or feeling. The goal is to force the spirit to speak through me, indirectly if possible, although I'm prepared to channel it should that become necessary."

Kate frowned. "Didn't you say channelling spirits was something a medium shouldn't enter into lightly? You said it could be dangerous, that the spirit could try to harm the medium or someone else?"

"All of which I still stand by, but if it becomes a matter of me channelling the spirit in place of you that would be my preference. My only stipulation is as before: If I judge things to be getting out of control," Charles said, "then we get out of that house straight away, no hesitation, no arguments."

Kate could almost feel the weight of Henry's eyes on her as she replied, "You have my word."

—

They marched up the hill together.

Kate was mentally going over the opening monologue she was about to deliver in front of the house. She and Henry had written the script together. It would recap the explosive outcome of their previous visit and acknowledge the crew's anxieties over coming back, how they were prepared to face their fears and venture back into the unknown. It was all good stuff, a bit melodramatic, but that was no bad thing. Personal motives aside, they were still here to film a television show.

Kate beat a path through the long grass.

Claire walked beside her, a clipboard in hand. "You sure about this?" she asked.

"It's entirely possible nothing will even happen."

"If you really believed that we wouldn't be here."

Kate was surprised. Claire wasn't usually so direct.

"No," she admitted, "I guess not."

They walked the rest of the way in silence, like a clan marching into battle. Who knew? Maybe they were. Charles still seemed convinced whatever was in the house wasn't friendly. They crested the hill and gathered near the porch, although Kate noted no one actually chose to set foot on the porch itself.

"Okay," Henry said, "let's approach this the same way we would anywhere else. We'll do our jobs and see what, if anything happens. Mark you ready to roll?"

"Just give me the nod."

"Keith?"

"I'm good."

"Kate?"

She nodded and stepped forward, setting a foot onto the first step of the porch. Part of her half expected... what, the porch to rattle beneath her feet? She suppressed a nervous laugh and took a second step up. When she got to the door, she turned to face down the hill, the rest of the crew, and Dahl standing away at the back. She mentally rehearsed the opening lines of her monologue in her head, and positioned her body in front of the doorway, slotting her hands into her coat pockets, only to find her phone still there. She fetched it out and quickly set it to vibration only. Claire usually took care of it for her when they were filming. She had forgotten to hand it over. Claire saw and moved forward to collect it. She was about to place it into her outstretched hand when it began to vibrate. She was ready to let the call go to voice mail when she saw who it was from.

She looked to Henry. "It's my dad."

"It's okay, take it. We can wait a minute or two."

She turned her back, wandered off a few steps and answered the call.

"Dad?"

The voice that came back threw her. It wasn't her dad's voice, it was a woman's, and she was clearly distressed. Kate knew who the voice belonged to, and suddenly felt the slosh of oily dread in her gut.

"Kate? Is that you?"

"Janette?"

"I'm calling from your father's mobile phone... I knew your number would be in it. I saw him slip it into his pocket before we went outside..." Janette Holloway was babbling. "We were in my garden, having lunch and... Oh, Kate, your father... He had another heart attack."

Kate felt blood begin to roar in her ears. She fought to gather her wits, focus. She had to get going, her dad was sick. She needed to be with him.

"Janette? Where have they taken him? Which hospital?"

There was a pause. Kate was on the verge of repeating the question when the reply came.

"Kate I'm so sorry..."

Janette Holloway's voice crumbled into a choked sob that told Kate all she needed to know.

Chapter 31

There are cultures where dropping to your knees, wailing and rending your clothes is considered a perfectly proper way to conduct yourself at a loved one's funeral, expected even. Standing at the foot of her father's grave, Kate wondered how the modest gathering here would react were she to take this approach. With mixture of shock, she imagined, embarrassment, pity?

Why? It seemed to her an honest way to mourn the loss of someone you love, more genuine than dabbing your red-rimmed eyes with a hanky while attempting to stoically 'keep it all in'. Which begged the question then, why *was* she keeping it all in? Certainly not because she wasn't hurting. Maybe it was because she feared if she started wailing she wouldn't be able to stop, she would just wail and wail until someone called the men in the white coats to take her away?

The vicar reached a break in his prescribed duties and fell silent. The rite, however, continued. Kate watched as the funeral directors started to lower her dad's coffin into the refrigerator-sized hole that had been cut into the ground to receive it, a hole beside which lay the plots of her mother, her husband and her son. The void inside her felt monstrous and raw, a malignant oscillating black hole that threatened to tear pieces of her away until there was nothing left.

She wondered if she shouldn't be inured to grief by now, or at least accustomed to it, an old hand whose heart had grown callused, hard as leather. How could this loss hurt every bit as much as the others? How was that possible?

The funeral directors were done and again melted in the background. Now her dad's coffin rested at the bottom of its hole the vicar's droning monotone resumed, "Forasmuch as it hath pleased almighty God of his great mercy to take unto himself the soul of our dear brother here departed, we therefore commit the body of James Scott Bennett to the ground; earth to earth, ashes to ashes, dust to dust; in the sure and certain hope of the resurrection to eternal life, through our Lord Jesus Christ; who shall change our vile body, that it may be like unto his glorious body, according to the mighty working, whereby he is able to subdue all things to himself."

Kate bent to scoop up a handful of dirt from the graveside. She stared at the wooden box holding her dad's body and, with more effort than the simple act should have demanded, she scattered the dirt over it. Henry stepped forward and threw another handful down, as did several others in turn, but Kate was already somewhere else. She was in her dad's strong hands, being hurled into the air, only to be caught a moment later when gravity triumphed. She was at her university graduation, spying her dad's beaming face in the crowd. She was handing Joel, small and crinkly, newborn, into his awkwardly cradled arms...

The vicar's voice called her back. He was dispensing the final blessing. Prayer, Kate reflected, part conversation, part poem, part wish, part spell, magic words for the faithful. Amen.

It was done.

—

The service was lovely; it must have been because in the last ten minutes six different people told her so. Kate had politely nodded to each of them and agreed, yes, it had been a lovely service, although in truth she remembered only fragments. Her dad hadn't been an especially religious man; like her and a good many others he was Christian by default: Church of England, C of E, to Kate's mind. The magnolia paint of religions: the church you could worship between meals without ruining your appetite. The vicar hadn't known her dad personally, so while she was sure his words had been very nice, moving even, in an abstract way, for her they were tinny and hollow. Death is sad, but to those closest to the deceased it is greater than that, it is a catastrophe, an off-the-Richter-scale, ground-shaking earthquake, a gale force fuck hurricane, a three-story-high rolling tsunami that knocks you flat, sweeps you away and strips you bare. While she surveyed the devastation, the vicar would return home and get on with his life unaffected, get on with doing whatever it was vicars did, eat scones, leaf through their Bibles, raise funds to fix the leaky church roof, with scarcely a thought for her dad and the colossal hole his passing had left in her life.

The wake was made up of around two dozen people, which if Kate discounted herself and the crew who had turned up for moral support, left just over a dozen who were present because her dad actually meant something to them. The absence of family relatives, because there were none, left a handful of old work colleagues and a few neighbours, including Janette Holloway, to make up the numbers.

It was a sparse gathering, not that Kate cared. She was familiar with the adage 'to know the worth of man you need only count the mourners at his funeral' but believed it was horse shit. Whatever the turn out, she knew her father was worth ten of most people. He had just been a quiet, private man who had given the best of himself to Kate and her mum. Had he instead chosen to slice his time, friendship and affection into tiny slivers and serve it up to a cast of hundreds then perhaps a larger room would have been required for his wake, but her share would have been all the smaller and right now she felt like she had been robbed enough already.

She tried her best to be a good host, she truly did, but the whole celebrating a life lived thing was for people who perhaps hadn't lost quite as much as she had, and after a while, in ones and twos, people began to offer their polite excuses and drift away.

Henry stayed at her side the whole time. An onlooker may have been forgiven for thinking a contract had been taken out on her life and he was her bodyguard, ready to hurl himself in front of the assassin's bullet at a second's notice. She appreciated his concern. It was nice to know he cared, but her feelings were too volatile, the emotional equivalent of a magic 8 ball. At turns she found herself wanting to lean on him, and then yell at him to fuck off, him and everyone else in the small function room. How dare they pretend to feel even a fraction of the pain she did? Instead, she accepted their condolences, engaged in small talk, and waited patiently until they said their goodbyes and left. The crew were among the last to go.

Eventually only she and Henry remained, or at least she had thought so. As they were preparing to leave, Janette Holloway appeared from the corridor leading to the rest rooms. She spied Kate, took in the empty room and walked over. Her face was friendly, but she looked wrung out. Her makeup had the same tested appearance Kate's own had exhibited when she last caught herself in the mirror. As she neared, Henry, ever tactful, suddenly remembered something he needed to attend to and excused himself.

Kate had last spoken to Janette at the hospital, the afternoon her father's heart had stopped for a second and final time. She and her dad had been taking advantage of a sun-kissed afternoon to enjoy lunch in Janette's back garden. Janette was inside fetching dessert when she heard a plate smash. She had rushed outside to find Kate's dad slumped on the patio, had checked his pulse, found nothing, and immediately began performing CPR and yelling for help, praying a neighbour would hear her and come see what the problem was. When a couple of minutes passed and no one came she ran into the house and called an ambulance. She was still performing CPR when it arrived.

"I wanted to thank you," Janette said, "for inviting me."

"I thought you would want to come."

"It was very thoughtful. How are you?"

Kate shrugged. For some reason the facade she had maintained for everyone else suddenly seemed unnecessary.

"It's hard to accept that he's gone, isn't it?" said Janette.

"Very."

"I don't know how much your father said, whether he told you about how much time we'd been spending... We were becoming quite close..." Janette struggled, and then stalled. "I'm sorry."

"Don't be. Janette, are you trying to tell me that my dad and you were a couple?"

"No, well, sort of..." Janette sighed in frustration. "We were taking things slowly, but I think we both believed things were heading in that direction. We were enjoying getting to know each other. He told me about how he lost your mother, how his life had changed. I know how hard that is. I lost my husband too, four years ago. He talked about you all the time, he was immensely proud of you, of how clever you are, how creative, how brave."

Kate felt her throat tighten. She tried to smile. "I suppose most dads have a blind spot when it comes to their daughters, eh?"

"And sometimes I imagine they're simply right," Janette said firmly.

"I don't feel very brave right now."

"Well, I think bravery is sometimes more a matter of what we do than how we feel. You, your father, and I, we carried on when life dealt us the worst of blows, didn't we?" Janette's eyes wandered from Kate to Henry, hovering near the bar. "If nothing else it taught me I should be wise enough to seize happiness whenever it dares stray within my reach."

Kate suddenly wondered exactly what else her dad may have discussed about her with Janette Holloway.

Janette smiled, and Kate smiled back. She realised she liked this woman, and wished she and her father had been given time to reach where their relationship was heading.

Janette's eyes shifted to Henry. "I think I'm going to be off now. I believe your friend is waiting for you."

"I believe so. Goodbye, Janette. And take care."

"Goodbye, Kate. You take care of yourself too."

As Janette Holloway disappeared through the door leading outside, Henry returned to her side, again ready to take the assassin's bullet. How was he supposed to understand it was already too late, that she had nothing left to lose?

Chapter 32

Henry was making coffee in Kate's kitchen. He had insisted she sit down in the lounge. She looked spent. The service and the wake had required her to put a public face on, but now it was over she was withdrawing again. She seemed distant, lost. Her father's death had hit her hard. He worried about her. Her flat, usually smart, clean and tidy, betrayed evidence of her mental state. The sink was stacked with dirty cups, plates and pans and what appeared to be the last week's post was strewn unopened across the breakfast bar.

He carried the drinks back into the lounge and found her staring toward the window, expressionless. She seemed oblivious to his return. He set the coffee mugs on the coffee table in front of her.

"Kate? You okay?"

When she turned sluggishly to look at him he saw, unvarnished in the pale light spilling through the window the dead, crushing weight of her sadness bearing down on her. When she responded it was in a tone so flat and bare he thought for a moment she was talking to herself.

"Do you think it's possible," she said, "for a person to be cursed?"

Uh, oh. He could almost feel the ground shifting beneath his feet.

"I think," he said very carefully, "that some people can have way more than their fair share of bad luck."

"Bad luck, eh?" Kate seemed to consider this for a moment. "I wonder, though. How would one know the difference?"

He sat down beside her, looked into her face. "I don't know, Kate, but the way I see it, if someone starts believing they're cursed, that means they can only expect bad things to come their way, whereas if they choose to accept they've just suffered more than their share of bad luck, at least the future still holds some promise. Bad luck, good luck, in the end isn't it just things happen that are beyond our control? Some will be good, some bad, some so bad a person might just begin to lose faith. It may feel cruel and unfair, but those things are still random. I don't believe in curses."

"Random?" Kate echoed the word in the same awful monotone. "I've lost two mothers, a husband, a son, and now my dad. I'm alone, Henry, I've lost them all, and I have to say, from where I'm sitting, it doesn't feel random. It feels like someone's got it in for me."

"But you're not alone. You have friends, people who care about you. *I* care about you."

"I know." She tried to smile but the result was closer to a grimace. "You should watch yourself, caring about me appears to be terminal."

"Don't talk like that. You'll get through this. I know you will. *You* know you will. Whatever you need, whatever I can do to help, you just have to ask. I'm here. You can count on me."

"There is something you can do to help me."

"Consider it done."

"You might not be so eager when I tell you what it is."

"What do you need?"

"I want to go back to Dahl's house. No, I *need* to go back to Dahl's house."

She was right. Whatever he had expected her to say it hadn't been this. Why the hell would she want to go back to that grim pile of masonry, especially now?

"I really don't think that's what you need right now, Kate."

"I think it's exactly what I need. It's where my first mum died. That's where it started. I think that if maybe

I can make sense of how I lost her then I might be able to make sense of the rest. You say you don't believe in curses? Help me prove to myself that I'm not cursed. Maybe then I can get on with grieving for all the people I've lost and see a way forward."

He wanted to say no, every instinct told him to say no, but he knew with or without his help she would do it anyway. If he refused, she would go to Sebastian Dahl and they would mess around in that god-forsaken house and with whatever was festering inside it. As fragile as she now was, that scared him. At least if he was involved he could protect her, try to prevent her from getting in too deep, watch out for trouble...

"If you think that's what you need to do, if you really, honestly, believe it will help, then alright, I'll go back there with you."

"Thank you." She leant in and lightly kissed his cheek. As she pulled away she paused and took in his face, then she was back. This time it was to kiss his lips. He responded. When she began unbuttoning his shirt, though, he broke away.

"Kate..."

"What?"

"You're sure this is what you want? Your head's got to be all over the place... Don't get me wrong, I do want to be with you, but..."

She smiled at him, a beautiful smile laced with sorrow.

"Then be with me."

Chapter 33

The last time they had called Sebastian Dahl, Henry had insisted on doing the talking, this time they both knew it was Kate's call, in both senses of the word. Henry resigned himself to listening in over speaker phone.

To Henry's ear, Dahl did not seem especially surprised to hear from Kate. In fact, it was almost as if he had been expecting her call. As ever, slick as a greased seal on a water slide, Dahl's first words were of condolence, voicing how very sorry he was for Kate's loss. Kate thanked him but briskly moved on to what they all knew was the real business at hand.

"We still want to return to the house," she said, straight and to the point. "Is your invitation still open?"

"It is."

"And if I said we wanted to return," Kate said, "not to film for the purpose of the show, but on a private basis? Would that be a problem?"

There was a pause, before Dahl said, "I think we both know it wouldn't. I should tell you, however, that things have progressed since we last spoke. I've been exploring ways I might move things forward on my own, and... I think I've found someone who might be able to help. She's agreed to meet with me, tomorrow afternoon as it happens."

"I see."

"After the séance, and your abrupt departure," Dahl continued, "I was forced to review my options. The obvious conclusion was that I might want to investigate enlisting the aid of a medium of my own. To this end, I began exploring potential candidates from the spiritualist circuit. As you may be aware from your involvement with your own Mr McBride, there's quite a large pool to choose from, although it seems the most prominent names are not always the most well-regarded. There was one name, however, that kept coming up, a medium called Nadine Smith. Despite not being involved in 'the circuit' itself, many on it seem to be aware of her talents, if grudgingly. From what I understand she holds a dim view of mediums who reduce their gift to a side show. If she's aware of your show, it's likely she may view your involvement with some suspicion."

"I'll complicate things?"

"Perhaps, perhaps not. If you're willing to join me tomorrow we may be able to convince her otherwise."

"And Henry will be welcome too?"

There was a slightly lengthier pause than previously before Dahl answered, with only a hint of detectable resignation, "If that's what you want."

"It is. So where will we be meeting this Nadine Smith?"

Chapter 34

The following afternoon, when Henry and Kate arrived at the address Dahl had furnished them with, they found him already there waiting; a black Ferrari is hard to miss. They went through the motions of exchanging pleasantries and approached Nadine Smith's apartment block. Dahl scanned the intercom panel, located Nadine Smith's buzzer, pressed it and waited. A moment later a woman's voice crackled over the intercom.

"Hello?"

"Miss Smith. It's Sebastian Dahl, and the other interested parties I mentioned?"

There was a buzz, a click, and the entrance door's catch released. Nadine Smith lived on the third floor. They climbed the stairwell and Dahl executed a smart rap on her front door.

A striking woman who could only be Nadine Smith opened it. The medium was darkly attractive. Pale as porcelain with ink-black hair, a tail of which snaked over her right shoulder, the first four buttons of her equally black shirt were unbuttoned, revealing a swell of cleavage Henry gamely fought the urge to check out, with questionable success. He judged her to be somewhere in her early twenties or thereabouts.

Dahl introduced himself. Kate started to do the same for herself and Henry. "Hello Miss Smith, my name is—"

"I know who you are," Nadine Smith said bluntly, unimpressed. She turned on her heel. "Come through."

The interior of the apartment wasn't at all what Henry had expected. The decor was sober, tasteful, wheat-coloured walls married with Scandinavian furniture. He had thought the medium's home would be... different. How? Beaded curtained doorways, a gloomy gypsy-esque cave of a dwelling? Woven wall coverings and crystal balls? He realised, ruefully, this wasn't so far off the mark.

"So," asked Nadine Smith, inviting them to sit in the lounge, "what might I do for you?"

Dahl, with occasional contributions from Kate, summarised the situation remarkably succinctly. He had built a house. The house was haunted. The entity haunting it seemed to be connected to him and Kate somehow, and a fire they had both escaped in their childhood, a fire in which six people, including both their mothers, had lost their lives.

Finally Dahl said, "I was hoping you might be willing to visit the house with us, help us discover what's going on there, and why."

Nadine Smith appeared to consider this, and then turned to Kate.

"Miss Bennett, before we go any further, you should know I've no intention of taking part in any kind of televised paranormal investigation."

"I understand. Sebastian made your views on the subject clear, and I can assure you, despite how this all started, at this point it's a strictly private matter. We've no interest in broadcasting anything that might occur inside that house. I just need to know what it's all about... what the spirit who spoke through me there wants."

Nadine nodded. "How much do you know about the spirit world, Miss Bennett?"

"Honestly? Not a great deal," Kate confessed, "a few perspectives picked up throughout our investigations with the show, and of course things Charles has told me. Charles McBride, our show's medium?"

Nadine's mouth curled into a dry smile. "Hmm. I'd recommend not placing too much stock in Charles

McBride's views. While I'm sure for the purposes of a ghost hunting show he's very entertaining—" Nadine Smith stopped, appeared to reconsider what she had been about to say. "Forgive me. Please, go on."

Henry who had promised himself he would take a watch and listen approach to the meeting found he couldn't help himself. "Would you like to tell us how the spirit world works? As *you* see it?"

Nadine regarded him coolly, but the dry smile never completely disappeared. "I can tell you it isn't a science. By its very nature the spirit world is a mystery, a realm we, the living, can never truly comprehend. A sensitive, or medium, is afforded a view, but only through a small and hazy window. What lies beyond is often distorted and indistinct. Imagine a deaf person facing an orchestra. They will feel the vibration of the music, discern rhythm and patterns, but the music's true essence will always be beyond their grasp. I suspect few of the ways we negotiate the physical world, through sight, sound, touch, smell and the passage of time have much meaning in the spirit realm. When communicating with spirits these aspects always feel ill-formed to me, almost as if the spirit is forced to resort to a near-forgotten language, rusty and half-remembered. Thoughts and feelings are what carry most clearly."

"When we die, though, we do continue to exist, somewhere? Communication is possible?" Dahl asked.

"Yes, although the majority of spirits are not easily reached, even by the most gifted sensitive. Some spirits seem closer, those perhaps torn between our world and the one beyond. Frequently these spirits are drawn to people and places where the source of their unrest lies. Of course, it's equally possible the gulf between the living and the dead is not as great as we imagine, but most spirits simply don't feel compelled to acknowledge us."

"You can communicate directly with those spirits who do wish to make contact?" asked Dahl.

"Yes and no. When I talk about communicating, I don't really mean communication in the common sense, verbally. While I may speak out loud when conversing with a spirit, perhaps appear to be talking directly to it, ultimately my words are largely unimportant. They're merely an aid, something to help lend shape to my thoughts. The real conversation is unspoken, conducted in images, memories, and feelings. Emotion is the common language." Nadine smiled thinly. "An infinitely more direct and honest way than we, the living, choose to communicate, wouldn't you agree?"

"What do you think the spirit in the house may be trying to tell us?" Kate asked.

"It's hard to say, but that it's trying to communicate at all, and especially in such a direct way, to channel through you, makes me inclined to believe it's something important, either to it, or to you."

"Charles told us we should be wary," Henry interjected. "He said a spirit who wants to communicate that way is best left alone."

"And as much as it pains me to agree with the illustrious Mr McBride, on this matter he has a point. I certainly wouldn't advise you attempting to make contact with this spirit again alone. I was speaking from the perspective of me guiding you."

"So you'll help us then?" said Dahl.

"If you're sincere about it being a private matter, then yes, however if in due course I find my name connected with your television show it will mean an immediate end to my involvement. I value my privacy and have no interest in celebrity, none at all."

"We assure you, at this point it is a strictly private matter," Dahl said. "Kate?"

"I agree."

"In that case I'm willing to offer you whatever help I can."

—

"So?" asked Henry. They were back outside, in Kate's car. Dahl had just driven away.

"What?" Kate asked.

"We're going back to Dahl's house, with her?"

"We both know Charles isn't keen on going back. He might agree to if I asked, maybe, but I'm not going to. Look, I'm not rubbishing him here, but even by his own admission he isn't the most gifted medium out there. Perhaps this Nadine woman is better equipped to help us."

As much as Henry would have liked to argue otherwise, he couldn't. There was something about Nadine Smith, an innate confidence, and a comforting lack of flamboyance that set her in stark contrast to every other self-proclaimed medium Henry had met. But still...

"I don't know. I think we should try to find out a bit about her before we commit to anything."

"Alright, that seems sensible, but let's not take too long doing it. I want to go back soon."

"I know. Just give me a few days, okay?"

—

Henry wasted no time. The moment they got back to the office he hit the phone, contacting some of the same people he had back when they had been searching for Charles.

The word on Nadine Smith appeared to support Dahl's own findings. She was, according to a collection of anecdotes Henry was given, the real deal. While none of the people he spoke to claimed to have actually met her in person, more than a few were able to share second- or third-hand tales of her successes dealing with troubled spirits. The most common account (Henry heard three independent versions) centred upon the haunting of a young boy. Some of the finer details differed, in one version the city was simply 'somewhere up north', in another it was Newcastle, in yet another Leeds, but the broad details matched up.

The story concerned a boy, who was the victim of poltergeist activity practically from the day he had been born. The episodes frequently left the child with bruises or abrasions. The family moved house, several times, but after a brief lull the attacks always resumed. In his first year at infant school a staff member informed child services about his injuries, prompting his parents, at their wits' end, desperate their son could be taken away from them, to look for help. After a number of false starts they found it in the shape of Nadine Smith. According to all versions of the story after a mere handful of visits Nadine dealt with the spirit and the attacks ceased, this time for good.

And yet, while it appeared Nadine Smith's name, deeds, and reputation were known, it still troubled Henry that no one claimed to have seen her work first-hand. Kate, though, was more forgiving. Given Nadine Smith's dim view of her peers, she argued, was it so surprising no one in the spiritual circuit knew her personally or had seen her work first-hand? If she valued her privacy, and exercised discretion regarding her clients, weren't accounts of her work almost inevitably destined to be second- or third-hand? Ultimately, Kate seemed to feel what Henry had discovered was sufficient.

A date was set. They would return to the house the following week.

Chapter 35

It wasn't like Renwick was an especially picky eater. Three years in the armed forces had left him with a pretty forgiving palate, and living on the streets had only served to further lower this already low bar. There was a time, not so long ago, where a square meal could mean two litres of White Lightning and a Snickers bar. A man adjusts to comfort quickly, though, and Simon was surprised to find couple of days snacking on hastily purchased garage snacks and warm soft drinks was testing his constitution. Movie stake-outs might look cool, but in real life they just made your arse ache and your shoulders stiff. Pissing into pop bottles to reduce the chance of missing something important wasn't super cool either.

Simon arched his spine in a vain attempt to stretch, but the van had somehow shrunk over time. He ached for a chance to stretch his legs, for a tall drink of ice-cold water, to eat something that hadn't come out of a cellophane wrapper clad in cold puff-pastry. Nevertheless, he stayed right where he was, kept his eyes pointed across the street on Kate Bennett's flat.

From his vantage point, inside a van with tinted windows and decals for a landscape gardening business, he had watched the previous evening as Kate Bennett and Henry White had entered the flat. Twelve hours later and White was yet to leave. This alone all but confirmed Sebastian's suspicions, but 'all but confirmed' wasn't the same as knowing for sure.

Simon was halfway through a jaw-creaking yawn when Kate Bennett's front door at last opened. Bennett was in a bathrobe. White was dressed, and leaving. They shared a few words and kissed, and not in the way you'd kiss your granny either.

Once White had got into his car and left, Simon made the call. It was still early morning, but Sebastian would want to know at the first opportunity his suspicion was well-founded. There was no doubt about it, Kate Bennett and Henry White were romantically involved, and Simon knew without asking that something was going to have to be done about that.

Chapter 36

They had arranged to meet at the house.

Sebastian Dahl and Nadine Smith were already there waiting when Kate and Henry arrived. Henry parked his recently repaired Aston Martin beside Nadine Smith's Volkswagen Polo and Dahl's black Ferrari.

Nadine soon took the reins. They would walk the house's interior, she said, and then she would decide where to go from there. Once inside, they were to do exactly as she instructed. If she told them to do something, they should do it at once and without question. She would be perfectly willing to explain herself later, but while in the house she was in command. If they felt unable to agree to this they should say so here and now, save her the bother of progressing any further. Encountering no dissent, she gave a nod of approval and led them up the hill toward the house.

She called them to heel at the foot of the front porch, instructed them to wait, and scaled the porch steps to the front door. There was a brief pause where she seemed to study the door, and then she reached out, pressing a hand to it, palm flat, fingers splayed. They waited.

After perhaps half a minute she turned. "Okay, I want each of you to join me now," she instructed, "one at a time. We'll start with you Mr White."

Henry joined her on the porch. Hand still pressed to the door's weathered surface, she called forth Dahl next, who followed suit. A moment later she beckoned Kate forward too, only unlike Henry or Dahl, the instant Kate's foot touched the porch step Nadine stiffened slightly, her back arching ever so as though a mild electric current were passing through her. Uncertain, Kate froze.

But Nadine had already relaxed. She lifted her hand from the door. "Hm. Interesting… Mr Dahl? I'd likc to take us inside now."

Dahl unlocked the door and Nadine led the way. She entered the hallway, hesitated, and then made for the door to the dining room, the same one Kate had chosen on her initial visit. She took the same route too, passing through the dining room, the kitchen, and into the lounge where Kate had experienced her funny turn. as Henry had put it. Nadine, though, didn't seem inclined to linger. Before long they had completed an entire circuit of the ground floor and were back in the entrance hall, where she turned and immediately began to scale the staircase to the first floor.

The remaining tour of the house was conducted in the same manner, brisk and largely silent. Kate wasn't sure what to make of Nadine Smith's no-nonsense approach, and judging from Henry's body language he didn't either. It was hard to tell if Dahl too had been expecting something different. They covered the topmost floors of the house as fast as the first and soon enough were back in the entrance hall, where Nadine headed directly to the front door, her only comment being, "We'll talk outside."

Once they were clear of the front porch the medium was immediately more talkative.

"Okay," she said, "given your past experiences, I don't imagine this will come as a surprise, but that house is host to a powerful presence. We were surrounded by it the instant we crossed the threshold."

"But out here, now?" Henry asked.

"Nothing," Nadine answered. "I'm almost certain the spirit is confined to the house itself, almost as though it forms a focal point for its energies. There could be a number of potential reasons why this is… Mr Dahl, you mentioned the house was initially something of a labour of love, a passion project? That could be significant, and Ms Bennett, your connection to Mr Dahl, what happened to you both, that could be important too. The spirit responded to both of you, but Ms Bennett most powerfully. If you still want to make contact with it I doubt it'll require much effort."

Kate looked at Henry, and also at Dahl.

"I haven't changed my mind," said Dahl. "I need to know what's going on here, and why."

Kate looked at Henry, and said, "Same here." She found Henry's eye and held his gaze, extracted a reluctant nod in return. He would stick by her, despite his misgivings.

Nadine studied them, maybe gauging their resolve.

"Okay," she said, "let's get this done."

—

Nadine wanted to conduct the séance in the dining room, as this was where the spirit's energy appeared most concentrated.

Nadine eschewed the use of a table and instead had them stand in the centre of the room, Dahl facing Nadine, Henry facing Kate. Kate asked Nadine if she wanted them to join hands, but she only shook her head and said, "Something tells me that won't be necessary."

The medium, or sensitive as she preferred to be called, closed her eyes, tilted back her head and took a series of deep, languid breaths. When she spoke it was in a relaxed, almost conversational tone of voice.

"Spirit? My name is Nadine. Come forward, introduce yourself. You've nothing to fear. I'm here to help; if that's something I can..." Nadine broke off, looked about her.

"Is it here?" Kate asked, following Nadine's gaze.

Nadine's mouth opened to answer, but Kate never got to hear her response, because suddenly the room shifted. Kate was still staring at Nadine's face as the walls began to contract. The colour and light began to leach away. A tiny crease formed between Nadine's eyes and her lips were moving, but Kate couldn't hear her words. The room collapsed, folded into darkness. Then, just as quickly the darkness was gone, exchanged for dazzling sunlight, and—

The hand in hers is soft, and larger than her own. Kate looks up to find a woman with a curiously familiar face looking down at her. The woman is her mum and she is talking to her. Everything will be okay, she says, there is nothing to be nervous about. They're going to be happy here.

The house that stands before them is huge and old. Her mum tells her it will be better here than the flat, and mostly because of the tired look on her face Kate nods and smiles, but she hadn't thought the flat was so bad, not all of it. The stairs were tiring, because the lift always seemed to be broken, the walls and floors smelt funny and she definitely didn't like the bugs that lived under the kitchen cupboards, but you could see for miles from the windows, miles and miles. She used to cup her hands around her eyes, press her face to the window and pretend she was flying they were so high up.

Her mum gives her hand a squeeze, then a gentle tug. They cross the road to the house, pass through its gate and walk to the front door. Her mum presses the doorbell. They wait. She shuffles closer to her mum's side.

The door opens. A man and a woman stand in the—

Darkness, and then something surfaced from the void— Henry's face, etched with concern, staring at her. Kate could see his mouth moving soundlessly, and then like a distant radio station being tuned in—

"—you okay? Kate?" he was asking. Henry looked ready to say something else when Nadine Smith's voice stopped him dead. Except it wasn't really Nadine Smith's voice, it belonged to someone else, someone she, Henry and Dahl had all heard before at the first séance at the house, although that time the voice had come from Kate.

"Lawrence? Please, I can't— My child, I can't— Where is— I can't... Where is my child!" Like the voice, Nadine Smith's features had been hijacked by a now unnervingly familiar stranger who stared wildly about the room. "I can't—"

She broke off and snapped rigid suddenly, convulsed once and then again, in the grip of an internal struggle. She bared her teeth.

"No." The voice was again Nadine's own. "If you want to communicate we can—" She convulsed again, her spine flexing hard and straight, shuddered, and the stranger was back, eyes darting about the room, wild with panic. Another spasm and Nadine reasserted control. "Enough!" she barked firmly, taking a decisive step back. "Everyone outside. Quick as you can, please."

Nobody argued. In a few moments they were back outside on the hill.

For Kate, the shock of what had happened was already ebbing away, was being swept aside by a mounting excitement. The spirit had shown her another vision. She could scarcely believe it. She had actually seen her birth mother's face, heard her voice, and held her hand... She could still see her features, a good many of which she shared. Elated and heady, she stifled an almost manic giggle. The séance may have got a bit bumpy, but ultimately Nadine *had* kept things under control, mostly.

227

But these were small concerns. What mattered was her mother was trying to communicate with her, show her things, about her past...

"Okay I got the beginning," she blurted, "and I got the end. What happened in between? What did I miss?"

Before Nadine could answer, Henry beat her to the punch, and from the very first Kate knew he wasn't happy. He looked fit to start pacing and was eyeing Dahl and Nadine darkly. "Same thing as last time," he spat, "except this time she managed to snap you out of it, which might have been more comforting if she hadn't started freaking out instead... but I think you caught that part."

Where she felt excited, Henry was just wired and shaken up. Kate had to remind herself, he hadn't seen what she had. From his point of view what had just gone down wasn't a whole lot different from the last séance. For her, what she had seen changed everything, dwarfed the stuff that was bothering him, rendered it trivial in comparison. Without the benefit of the vision, all Henry was left with was watching her become someone else momentarily, someone clearly distressed, crying out in panic. She tried to sympathise with him, see how that might be... uncomfortable. She had a little taster of it herself watching Nadine Smith suddenly being worked by a will that wasn't her own, had heard her plead and shout—

That's when it hit her; Nadine had channelled the spirit too. Had she shared the same vision Kate had? She had to know.

"Nadine? Did you see anything? When you were channelling her, did you see anything?"

"See anything?" Nadine said vaguely.

"Yes, a sort of vision, something like that?"

"You saw something?" Nadine asked.

"Yes, my mother—my birth mother. I was a little girl. She was holding my hand. She had dark hair and her eyes looked like mine, the shape of her face too... We were in front of an old house, it was big. We were going to live there, I think."

"Do you think it was *the* house," asked Dahl, "the house that we escaped from?"

Kate couldn't keep from grinning. "It has to be, doesn't it? My mum was taking us there... It was on a street full of similar houses, lovely big houses with tall oak trees lining the road."

Dahl turned to Nadine. "Did you see anything like that?"

Nadine shook her head. "No... But given how focused I was upon keeping the spirit in check that's not surprising. The spirit we're dealing with is, in the walls of that house at least, very strong, powerfully driven. It wants to communicate, there's no doubt about that, but as we already suspected it wants to do so directly. As you saw, I had to offer myself as a channel to prevent it from using Ms Bennett. I was able to assert control, but it required some effort."

"She's trying to show me something," Kate said, "something to do with the house where Sebastian and I used to live, I think."

"How do you feel about trying again?" Dahl asked. "Going back inside?"

Kate was ready. She wanted to go again, as soon as possible. Nadine had proved she could keep control of things, and Kate knew her mother had more to show her. Where was the point in waiting? She recalled the comforting feeling of her birth mother's hand in hers, and she wanted to see her face again, with features so much like her own. She was ready alright.

"Nadine?" Kate asked.

Nadine pursed her lips and then said, "I've no objection—so long as you feel comfortable."

"What?" Henry said, incredulous. "You have to be joking, right?"

"We're here to find out what's going on," Kate said, "and that's not going to happen standing around out here, is it?"

Henry stared at her, apparently lost for words, then said, "Can I have a moment?" His eyes flashed to Dahl and Nadine. "In private?"

"Of course," said Kate.

Kate followed Henry down the hill, until they reached a distance he presumably judged out of earshot. When he turned to speak, resistance was writ large on his face. She wanted to go back into the house. Clearly Henry did not.

"You can't honestly be serious about going back in there. Don't you think we should be treading a bit more carefully?"

Kate could almost feel him winding up, getting ready to argue, or guilt trip her into letting it go. She felt bullied suddenly, disliked his tone. "Carefully?" she retorted, "or slowly?"

"Whichever is safer, you pick. Look, this is all moving too quickly for my liking. You can't even be sure what you just experienced *was*."

"But I do, Henry. It was a vision, a message from my birth mother."

"How can you know that? Couldn't it have been, I don't know, say, a memory?"

"A memory?"

"It's possible isn't it? Or at least as likely as it being a vision, right? A buried memory, triggered by the situation? You say you can't remember anything from your early childhood, but those memories still have to be there, buried away in your subconscious. What if you just unearthed one of them?"

"But it was so vivid..." Kate heard herself say, hating the way her voice suddenly sounded hesitant and uncertain.

"Memories can be vivid too." Henry reached for her hands, made her look him in the eye. "I think we're dealing with too many unknowns to act impulsively."

"And what if Nadine isn't up for running down here time and time again?"

Henry cast a glance up the hill to where Dahl and Nadine were waiting. "Oh, I wouldn't worry," he said dryly, "I'm pretty sure Dahl will make it worth her while."

"And what if Sebastian doesn't want to wait? What if he just chooses to carry on without me?"

"I'd fret even less about that. Whatever's in that house seems far more interested in you than him, and you can bet that hasn't escaped his notice. If you say you need to go slowly, he'll go slowly."

"What if *I* don't want to go slowly? I thought you were with me on this."

"I am, but I'm asking you to trust me." His voice softened. "Kate, you're too close to this, and with everything that's happened... I'm worried about the effect all this could have on you. All I'm asking is—"

"I'm not a child, Henry. You don't understand. There are answers waiting for me in that house, and I want to know what they are."

"You can't know that, you can't! For all you know what you experienced was a memory, one you've suppressed for a very long time."

"It wasn't. You're trying to confuse me."

"*I'm* trying to confuse you?" Henry protested, again his eyes flicked up the hill to where Dahl stood waiting.

"Is this really about the house," she asked, "or is it about him? What are you, jealous or something? Is that it?"

"Oh please, do me a favour," Henry retorted sharply, his voice dripping with scorn.

"I'm going back in there."

"Not if I can help it."

They glared at each other. The stalemate lasted perhaps half a minute, until Sebastian Dahl approached them, hands held up apologetically.

"Forgive me, but it seems sound carries rather too well on this hill. I couldn't help but overhear. Kate, on reflection I think Henry has a point. Like you, I'm afraid I may have got slightly carried away. Maybe it would be best if we slowed things down a little. I've spoken to Nadine; she's perfectly happy to return with us in a few days' time."

Kate looked at Dahl, to Henry, and then to the house where her birth mother's spirit waited for her. The truth was she didn't want to wait. She wanted to strike while the iron was hot, but it appeared Henry's qualms had given Sebastian Dahl cold feet, either that or Dahl didn't want to feel responsible for causing friction between them.

Kate suddenly found herself outnumbered. Not that she liked it, not one bit. In fact she was seething.

"A few days?"

Dahl nodded. A moment later, with some reluctance, so did Henry.

Chapter 37

Kate's demeanour was distinctly frosty on the car journey home. Henry was content to weather it. He was just relieved to be putting some distance between Kate, Dahl's house, Dahl himself, and, for good measure, Nadine Smith. In short, all the screwy shit he was increasingly certain was unhealthy for her. She was brooding right now, but she would calm down soon enough, and then they would be able to talk about what had happened a little more soberly. He was in no doubt, preventing her heading back inside the house with Dahl and Nadine Smith had been a smart move, even if, irritatingly, it had been Dahl who had ultimately swung things…

He almost admired the swine's deviousness. By stepping in to lend Henry his support, Dahl had not only come out of the situation looking as concerned about Kate's welfare as Henry, but had also managed to set the date they were to return to the house, in a matter of mere days, uncomfortably soon in Henry's book. It left him under a tight deadline to persuade Kate whatever lay inside the house was best left alone, especially with Dahl hovering in the background providing his counterpoint: a willing, seemingly reasonable and cautious collaborator. To say he was growing to really dislike the man was a bit like saying slugs weren't big fans of salt.

They arrived back at Kate's flat just shy of five p.m. Henry planned to wait until they were inside, and then he would apologise, turn on the charm and talk Kate into allowing him to take her out for the evening. A little wine and dine to begin smoothing things over and he could work on getting back into her good books, which was where he had to be to stand any chance of talking her out of returning to Dahl's house. He was about to get out of the car when Kate stopped him in his tracks.

"I don't want you to stay tonight."

"What?" He was taken aback. "Why?"

"I think I need some time to myself."

For a moment he was speechless. Here he was worried stupid about her, trying to support her, watch out for her, and this was his reward, a childish and blatantly spiteful measure designed to punish him for not letting her get her way?

"Why?" he demanded. "So you can obsess over what happened in that miserable fucking house? Kate, honey, trust me, that's the last thing you need."

"And you're an expert are you, on the topic of what I do and don't need?"

"I know you're still coping with losing your dad. I know that kind of loss takes time to adjust to. This business with Dahl and that house, it's not healthy— even if the spirit there *is* your birth mother, and you can make contact with her in a way that doesn't involve you blacking out and gibbering like a crazy woman, it's not going to fill the void. It's not going to help you make sense of *anything*. Can't you see that?"

Kate stared at him, her face almost white with fury, and at once he knew he'd scored a direct hit. He knew nearly as quickly that he'd scored an own goal. Even the worst student of body language could have seen her defences slam down.

Close to shaking with anger, she glared at him, disdain thinly covering the hurt beneath. "Spare me the amateur psychology," she said witheringly, "and stop trying to pretend you know what I'm going through. It's insulting. I've lost *everyone* I ever loved and you've spent your whole adult life worrying about no one but yourself. Really? What the fuck would you know about loving and losing anyone?"

As she was already getting out of the car, he guessed the question was rhetorical.

"Kate—"

Her parting words drifted through the car door before it slammed closed, scalding, "Get fucked, Henry!"

Get fucked? Get *fucked*? The problem was he did care! How could she say he didn't? His temper got the better of him. He inched down the window and the words were out before he could call them back.

"Maybe I fucking will!"

She didn't even turn around. Within seconds she was inside her flat, door slammed in her wake and in his face.

–

The door crashed shut, shuddered in its frame. Kate stormed into her flat and paced in the centre of the lounge, hands balled into tight fists, fizzing with anger. Who the hell did Henry-fucking-White think he was, and how dare he—how *dare* he—agghh! She felt like screaming!

Why couldn't he just help her, help her do what she *needed* to do rather than chip away at her resolve, muddle her mind and make her question what she knew. The spirit in Dahl's house was her birth mother, and there was something she wanted to tell her. How could Henry think that was ever going to be something she could simply forget about?

She turned and saw through the blinds he was still outside; his Aston Martin idling at the kerb. Why the hell couldn't he just help her? Why couldn't he... just...

Because he cared about her, not Dahl's house and not the spirit inside it. Her anger fizzled. The simmering resentment she'd nursed throughout the journey back, culminating in that one vengeful act, the thing she knew would sting him, that she didn't want him in her flat or her bed tonight, evaporated; she saw it for exactly what it was, what Henry must have: petulant, spite-fuelled and brattish.

She made for the door. He hadn't driven away yet. She could still call him back inside, make peace. Try again to make him understand why she was never going to be able to just let Dahl's house go. She would be as honest as she could, *make* him understand, but as her hand reached for the door she heard his car's engine fire up. Then, before she could stop him, he was gone.

She stared at the empty kerb, strangely shaken. He had gone, just like that.

Well, a cold inner voice spat, *you got what you asked for, didn't you? You get to sleep all alone tonight, for the first time since you put your dad in the ground.* She had told Henry she didn't want him around to hurt him, and had only succeeded in spiting herself. She had said she needed some time to herself, but in one awful sense she was never alone.

Dahl's house wasn't the only haunted building she had inhabited today; the flat she stood in had its fair share of ghosts too. They vied for her attention at every turn. On the bookshelf her mum smiled from a sun-bleached photograph. From the picture frame next to this beamed the three of them: Mum, Dad and a primary school version of herself, all enjoying a summer break in Brighton, Kate in the middle holding a dripping ice cream, drizzled in strawberry syrup, Cadbury flake listing in the heat...

Not all her ghosts were so bold, though. Robert and Joel's lurked in a box in her wardrobe in the form of a shirt and a knitted rabbit, each smelling less of husband and child and more and more of musty cardboard box as the days, weeks, months and years passed.

236

Photographs of them were still too much to deal with on a daily basis.

Selling the big family house they had shared and moving to this flat was supposed to have helped her to escape their ghosts, but she had discovered almost at once that ghosts are quite amenable to travel, and don't require nearly as much space as you might imagine, more than a few can squeeze into a modest two bed flat.

Kate stared out the window to the vacant kerb, surrounded and alone all at the same time.

–

Henry swerved and pulled in, screeching to a stop at the side of the road. He was wound up, bristling, and it was making his foot heavy. He felt hurt and angry, but more than this he felt exasperated beyond belief. He was annoyed with himself for losing his cool and biting back. Kate had lashed out at him precisely because part of her knew damn well he had a point. Deep down she had to realise the whole thing was no good for her, but like the sore you can't stop scratching even though you know you're only making it worse, she couldn't help herself. If she didn't call him tonight, then he would call her, try to make peace. There was no point right now, not until she had calmed down and was ready to talk properly.

And when she was calmer, what then? Henry wondered. Did he think he could persuade her to let the whole thing go, just walk away from Dahl and his crazy house? If she was truly convinced her dead birth mother's spirit there was trapped in the house for some reason, the answer was probably no.

Unless…

Dahl was the key. Dahl had dragged her into all this, and the one driving her forward. Oh, he was subtle about it, Henry gave him that, but Dahl *was* pulling Kate's strings and he had to find some way of cutting her free. If he could expose Dahl as fundamentally deceitful, discredit him in Kate's eyes, maybe then he could get her to view the situation objectively. The good news was he knew Dahl was dodgy as all hell, knew it in his bones. The tough part was finding an ironclad way of proving it to Kate. He needed to find out what Dahl's real agenda was... He and Kate were connected by the house—the original house—the one they escaped, the house back in Birmingham...

Henry thought back to his phone conversation with Hope, the neighbour from the newspaper story, and how he had been left with the feeling the old guy knew more than he was willing to share with a stranger over the phone.

Henry got out his phone and found Hope's number. After a few rings someone picked up. Henry waited a moment, until he heard a voice.

"Hello?"

The voice was Hope's.

Henry adopted the blandest bright and breezy persona he could muster, and then added a slight northern twang for good measure. "Hi there, my name's David, and I'm calling from Wonderful Windows. We're canvassing in your area this coming week and I was wondering if you would welcome the opportunity to meet with one of our representatives for a free no obligation quote on our triple A quality range of double glazed doors and windows?"

"I'm sorry, but no thank you."

"There's no reason to make a decision right away. Should you change your mind, don't hesitate to call us back and arrange an appointment. You can speak to someone at our sales office on—" Henry reeled of a string if digits he felt confident Hope wouldn't even jot down, let alone call, and added, "Thank you for your time."

Henry quit the call, having confirmed Hope was at home. He punched the old guy's address into the satnav, fired up his Aston Martin and pulled back onto the road. Birmingham was less than two hours' drive away.

–

Approximately one hundred metres further down the road Simon Renwick watched Henry White's Aston Martin speed past him. After what had looked an awful lot like an argument outside Kate Bennett's flat, White had torn off and Simon had very nearly lost him. He had caught up with him just in time for White to suddenly stop a couple of miles down the road. Simon had sailed past and pulled in himself a little further on. Now White was on the move again, and moving with a purpose it seemed. Simon waited a few seconds, indicated and took to the road again to resume trailing him.

Chapter 38

Henry turned into Oakbourne Road. A string of large detached properties screened by towering oaks ran down each side. He progressed until he reached Albert Hope's address and pulled up.

Oakbourne Road lay in a suburban area of Birmingham called Edgbaston. The neighbourhood appeared affluent and sleepy. Behind a red-brick wall topped with dense privet and screened by tree foliage, Henry made out the upper half of Hope's beautiful Victorian house.

Before he arrived at Hope's doorstep, though, he had a prior port of call. He crossed the road and walked down a short stretch until he reached house number 65, the spot where a young Kate Bennett had once escaped a house fire. He looked down the drive, and saw immediately the original house was gone. Where the old building had stood there was a more modern example. The original had evidently been demolished some time after the fire, perhaps because it was damaged beyond repair, perhaps because it would forever be the house where six people lost their lives. It was the sort of detail that, while never in an estate agent's particulars, tended to find its way to prospective buyers. Either way, the place had been torn down. He loitered for a moment, although in truth there was really nothing left to see. The new number 65 Oakbourne Road could impart little about what had happened to Kate all those years ago, but there was someone nearby who might. He crossed back over the street to Albert Hope's house.

In contrast to the house he had just been looking at, Hope's home was an archetypal example of Victorian arts and crafts. It sported expansive bay windows,

Flemish bond brickwork, decorative bargeboards at the roofline and porch, and a stained glass windowed front door with an ornate brass knocker, which Henry approached and made use of. About half a minute later he spied movement through the stained glass diamond patterned glazing. Then the door opened, on a security chain. An elderly gentleman with white hair and thick glasses squinted at him through the gap.

He eyed Henry with the caution elderly people are advised to show toward strangers who present themselves at their door uninvited.

"Hello?"

"Mr Hope? My name's Henry White. We spoke on the phone a while ago? I wanted to ask you a few questions about a house fire that occurred over the road there, in 1989?"

"Yes... I remember, although, as I recall, I told you there wasn't much else I could tell you."

"If you'd just be willing to let me ask you a little about the incident perhaps something might surface? My friend is one of the two children who survived the fire. She lost her mother in it, and recently she's grown... curious about her past. Anything you could tell me about the house, about the people who lived there, would be much appreciated."

"What precisely are you hoping to find out?"

"Whatever you can tell me."

Hope appeared to think for a moment.

"This friend of yours...?" Hope trailed off, presenting a void that begged to be filled with a name.

"Kate," Henry answered promptly. "Her name is Kate." And in the same instant, Henry knew, just knew, it was the name Hope had been waiting for, even after all these years he remembered the name of the little girl who had made it out alive.

"This Kate," Hope asked, "she's a close friend of yours?"

"Yes. Someone I care a great deal about."

Hope nodded. "And she knows you're here?"

"No. She doesn't."

Hope took a further moment, presumably to chew this last piece of information over, and then without a word he unhooked the chain and opened the door.

—

"So who exactly lived in the house?" Henry asked.

Hope regarded him. "You mean apart from the older couple who owned the place? Around half a dozen young people. The couple began to take them in as lodgers," Hope said, "or we assumed they were lodgers. Most of them scarcely looked out of their teens, some of the older ones, maybe their early twenties? None of them appeared to work. You didn't see much coming or going. We assumed the couple had taken it upon themselves to put a roof over their heads. To be honest most of them looked a bit lost, the sort who don't have anyone to look out for them."

"Was it always the same half dozen youths?"

"No, there was a bit of a turnover, I think, especially early on. We'd see some new face, and then a few weeks later they'd move on. Things seemed to settle down after a while, though. I think most of those who died in the fire had lived there for a year or so. I think by then they'd become quite a tight group, like a family almost."

"The ones who had children, the boy and my friend, Kate, do you remember them?"

"Not really. As I said, they tended to keep themselves to themselves."

"You remember the fire, though?"

242

A look passed over Hope's face. "I doubt I'll ever forget it. My wife spotted something was up when she was calling the cat in, saw flames and smoke coming from the windows in the front room. She ran in and said I should call the emergency services, get a fire engine out. By the time I'd finished doing that you could see it was serious. We went outside and found a few neighbours on their way over too. Jim, our next door neighbour at the time was already across the street and running up the drive, so I went after him. It didn't take a genius to work out that anyone inside could be in big trouble.

"I can remember the heat to this day. It was like standing at the edge of a bonfire, which I suppose we were. We began hammering on the front door, then we tried to force it open, but it wouldn't give. We were trying to find another way in when a couple of the downstairs windows blew out. We tried kicking the door in again, but it was no good. It was like being cooked alive, and the smoke pouring out of the broken windows was thick and black. It made my eyes and chest burn. Even so, we were still trying to get the front door open when we heard another window shatter, this time upstairs, above the porch. We got ourselves clear, in case there was falling glass, that's when we saw the window hadn't blown out because of the fire; someone had smashed it out on purpose. There was a boy climbing out of it, down onto the porch roof. Before we knew it he'd jumped off. He hit the ground pretty hard, but seemed okay.

"Then someone else appeared at the window, a little girl, couldn't have been more than six or seven. She started to climb out too, and there was someone with her. It was the fella who owned the house, Lawrence? Lawrence Hawley? He was helping her. I yelled to him, told him if he got her to jump from the porch I'd catch her. Poor child looked more dazed than scared, but she had to have heard me because she did jump. I caught her okay, and then the fella, Lawrence, started to climb down. I remember the look on his face, like he was in some kind of daze too. He looked... bewildered, like he couldn't understand how he came to be there, clambering out of his blazing house, smoke and flames belching from the windows..." Hope shook his head. "Jim helped him down, and then we just stood for a bit just staring up, hoping someone else would appear at the window I suppose. No one else did though. No one else got out."

"What happened next?"

"We heard sirens. By then we'd got the kids and Lawrence away from the house and nearer to the street. A fire engine rolled up and they got to work on the fire. Even by then though, I think we all knew nobody else was coming out that house, not alive at least. I was in shock, I think. I still had the little girl with me, and she looked in shock too. Her little body was shaking and she had an awful blank look about her. She never made a sound, though, not a word. My wife took her from me, and set about trying to comfort her. That's when I noticed what was happening with Jim. He was busy with the old fella, Lawrence. He was getting all worked up. I wondered if he mightn't be drunk or something, because he couldn't seem to co-ordinate himself properly, and on top of that he'd started yelling. I could see Jim trying to calm him down, but he was having none of it. Then I heard what he was shouting and realised what he was after. He wanted to get hold of the lad who'd escaped. He was across the drive, and one look was enough to tell you he didn't want to be anywhere near that Lawrence fella. I went to give Jim a hand, try to settle the chap down, but he wasn't having any of it. Soon, me and Jim were practically wrestling with him. He was thrashing like a wild thing, trying to throw us off so he could get at the boy. As you can imagine, what with the fire and everything going on too, it was like bedlam. No one seemed to notice us struggling with him. He was raving, but even though his speech was slurred I was still able to make out what he was saying. He was roaring the same thing over and over. He must have thought the lad was responsible for the fire, because he kept shouting, 'What did you do? What did you do?'"

"And then?"

"The ambulance and the police arrived, and they took charge, thank heavens. The ambulance men saw to the children, they'd both suffered burns that needed attention, and the police took Lawrence off our hands. He was still acting up, though. The police had to practically drag him away. His eyes never left the lad, not once. He was still raving as the children were put into the ambulance, only now he was screaming, 'Where are you taking me? Where are you taking me to?'" Hope shook his head. "To be honest, I think he'd lost it."

"And after?"

"Once the fire was dealt with and the police had asked their questions? We all went back to our own homes."

"No, I mean, later, did you hear what happened to the children, and to that Lawrence guy?"

"Oh, the odd snatch, here and there. The children, Kate and Timothy, a neighbour told me their names, they were taken into care I believe, and Lawrence, well, if what I heard was true, he had something of a breakdown. Judging from the way he behaved that night, it was easy enough to believe. The whole thing, all those young people burning to death in his house, his own partner too, I imagine it was too much for him."

"Did you ever find out how the fire started?"

"Not really, but I don't remember there being any talk of foul play."

"So the boy wasn't responsible then?"

"Nothing I heard suggested he was. The general thinking around here was one of the kids had probably been smoking some wacky-baccy and dozed off, or perhaps popped some pills and left an electric fire on in the wrong spot.... something like that. Although to be fair, we never knew for sure."

"The girl, my friend, Kate, do you remember anything about her mother?"

"Sorry, but I don't," Hope said apologetically. "As I said they didn't mix much. A very tight group, they kept themselves very much to themselves."

Henry tried to imagine a tight knit group of youths and a pair of aging hippies living quietly across the street in the place where a different house now stood. The thought prompted another question.

"Was the house demolished soon after the fire? I saw there's a different one there now."

"Soon? No, not really. It just stood there, boarded up and empty for the longest time, years actually. Then about, oh about...?" Hope's already wrinkled brow crinkled further as he troubled his memory. "About, ten or so years ago, I'd say, it was knocked down, or took apart or whatever it was they did, and shortly after they built that new house there."

"Sorry? What did you say?"

"They built that new house there."

"No before that, the part about it being knocked down, or *taken apart?*"

"Well, yes, I suppose dismantled would be more accurate, almost brick by brick, it seemed like. They didn't just demolish it, pile it into skips, as you'd expect, more took it apart and kept everything they thought was salvageable I suppose, loaded it onto lorries and took it away. I imagine they sold it all or

246

something, like on those property renovation shows you see on the telly? Those shows are always going on about the value of 'period features' and 'authentic materials' aren't they? Although at the time, watching them drive off with those half burnt windows and timbers, and scorched bricks and tiles neatly stacked up, I remember thinking how strange it was."

—

Back in his Aston Martin outside Hope's house, Henry immediately called Ray.

"Ray? Hello mate, I've got something I need you to get your teeth into; I need to find out something about that house in Birmingham, the one on Oakbourne Road—"

"The one in the fire?"

"Yeah, the very same. I need to know who owned it and who ended up inheriting it."

"And judging by your voice, 'yesterday' would be the optimum timeframe we're talking about here?"

"Ray, mate, yesterday would be awesome."

"I'll do my best."

"How did the thing go this morning, at Dahl's house?"

"Kate might tell you it went great. I'd beg to differ."

"And this thing with the Oakbourne house, it's connected?"

"What I'm thinking is crazy, but I think so. I'm going to check something out. I'm hoping between the two of us we'll know a lot more soon."

Henry put his phone away and reached for the sat-nav. He navigated the menu to 'recently visited' and selected the address of Dahl's cliff-side house.

Chapter 39

By the time Henry pulled onto the track leading to Sebastian Dahl's cliff-top house the light was fading. He needed to get a move on. He drew to a stop and jumped out, his new toy in hand: a brand new, oily blue-black crowbar, purchased from a hardware store on the outskirts of Birmingham. The bar was larger, heavier and cruder than a set of keys, but he reckoned it would get him past the front door just as surely.

The house Henry had quickly grown to despise lay ahead. Was it normal, he wondered, to feel this level of antagonism towards something inanimate? Probably not, but somehow this collection of brick, slate and timber had set its rotten roots in his life. Insidious and malignant, they had spread, worming their way into the psyche of the woman he loved. If there was a way to cut them out he was going to find it.

He began to scale the hill.

Beyond the cliff's edge, the sea whispered in tongues of white noise. Henry tried to discern murmurs of encouragement rather than the hiss of dire warnings. He came to the porch, and kept going, jamming the business end of the crowbar into the seam by the door's lock. He took a firm hold and levered the bar back; the door popped open with a satisfying crack. He stepped back, surveyed his handy work.

A good-sized chunk of wood around the lock had completely splintered free, leaving the remains of the lock hanging loose like a rotten tooth. There'd be no concealing someone had broken in. Henry didn't really care.

He pushed the door wide and stood at the threshold, was about to toss the crowbar aside and thought better of it. The light was fading fast and suddenly he didn't fancy stalking around empty-handed.

He stepped through into the entrance hall, eyed the tiled floor for a moment, and went to the bottommost step of the carpeted staircase. He slipped the pronged end of the crowbar beneath the carpet's edge and tugged free the stretch covering the bottom-most steps, exposing the wood beneath. The timber beneath showed clear evidence of having been scorched. He stripped more of the carpet back. Several other sections were similarly scorched, some quite badly. He got his phone out and took pictures. This done, he left the hallway and entered the lounge. He picked a corner of the room and repeated the process, peeling back several feet of carpet. Again, the exposed timber was a hodgepodge of virgin wood mixed with aged and scorched boards. He took some more pictures, and then stood, thinking for a while.

There was a dresser against the far wall. He walked over, grabbed a side and swung it away from the wall. He drew the crowbar back and took a swing. The impact shot up his arms as the crowbar connected with the wall, leaving a deep dent where the wallpaper split and old plaster peeked through. He took another swing at the same spot. The plaster started to crumble. Doing damage to the house felt satisfying, cathartic even.

He swung again. This time a big section of plaster broke away and the area around it crumbled, only the wallpaper held it in place. He reached out, tore the paper off and the rest of the plaster fell away, exposing an area about a foot square bare to the brick.

Henry stepped forward, hunkered down on one knee and set the crowbar down. He ran his hand over the masonry, brushing away plaster dust to better examine the bricks beneath. They were dark, much darker than normal brick, and oddly mottled. He reached for the crowbar again and used the end to chip away at one of the bricks. Beneath the surface layer it was paler, normal brick colour. Like the timbers, the bricks showed evidence of having been scorched. He took half a dozen more pictures for good measure and decided he'd seen enough. There was no doubt in his mind now; the house he was in was built from the remains of the house that had once stood on Oakbourne Road. Ray was sure to be able to find something to connect Dahl to the purchase of Oakbourne, damn him as the lying shit he was. If that wasn't enough to convince Kate that Dahl couldn't be trusted nothing would.

He used his foot to sweep the loose plaster against the wall and then pushed the dresser back into place, neatly covering both the mess and the damage. Someone would have to look pretty close to detect anything. After this, he went to the corner where he had exposed the floorboards and carefully rolled the carpet back into place, treading it flat.

Back in the hallway he tidied up in similar fashion before retreating out onto the front porch. The lock was ruined, and there was nothing he could do to disguise it. When he returned, Dahl would know someone had broken in, but he wouldn't know why and who, not for sure, although Henry suspected he might come to Dahl's mind, sooner rather than later. He pulled the door shut and wedged a splinter of wood into the frame to stop it from blowing open.

It was darker on the rise now. Evening was becoming night. Over the cliff's edge, the sun was already three quarters dunked in the sea. In less than an hour it would be pitch black.

Armed with what he prayed was enough evidence to force Kate to see Sebastian Dahl not only couldn't be trusted, but was actively plotting something, he started back down the rise to his car.

The arm looped around his neck, catching him completely unawares. Before he could even process what had happened, a boot smashed down behind his knee, driving him to the ground. He grappled at the arm around his throat, fighting to break its grip, but whoever had him was strong and practiced. A fist or maybe a knee slammed into his kidneys and he buckled, crumpling onto the grass. He tried to get up but his head was slammed violently back into the coarse grass, an instant after this one of his arms was wrenched up behind his back, pinning him to the ground.

Black spots dimpled his vision, and a small thread of his consciousness calmly informed him he could well be in some considerably deep shit. He struggled, turned his head, glimpsed the house. It seemed to tower over him like a sheer rock face, a grim monolith, impossibly huge...

The last thing he would remember before oblivion swallowed him whole was the sharp sting of needle being jabbed into his arse.

—

Renwick rolled Henry White over and went through his pockets, taking his phone and his car and house keys, before dragging him down the hill and bundling him into the passenger side of the Aston Martin. It was heavy work and he was still breathing hard when he slipped into the driver's side to call Sebastian.

"Got him," Simon said simply.

Sebastian quizzed him.

"A few hours at least," Simon replied. "I'll give him a second dose if he stirs. Susie will meet me at his flat?"

Sebastian answered in the affirmative.

251

Simon put his phone away and started the car. There was much to do before morning.

Chapter 40

Kate switched off the television. In all honesty, she hadn't really been watching it anyway. She had come to a decision. She was going to call Henry, tonight, before it got too late.

She had lived with the feeling all day, the feeling you have following an argument in which it increasingly dawns on you that you were the one in the wrong. The further from the row she got, the more disproportionate and unjustified her reaction seemed. She had wanted to go back inside Dahl's house, strike while the iron was hot, and Henry had thrown a stick in her spokes. She had been frustrated by this, but even so, she struggled now to see what had made her respond with such petulance and spite.

She didn't want the day to end with Henry thinking she was still mad at him. She didn't want it to end with him thinking she didn't care. What she really wanted was to go to sleep with him lying next to her. If eating a little crow was what it took to set things right, maybe even get Henry to climb in his car and come over, then hand her the knife and fork, she was ready to chow down.

She tried his mobile first. It came back with a number unavailable message. Henry must have switched his phone off. She tried his home line. It rang out for a while and eventually went to his answer-phone. This suggested two possibilities. Either Henry wasn't in, or he was and had seen her number on the caller ID screen and chosen not to pick up. She listened to the invitation to leave a message, very nearly did, and then at the last moment decided against it. She was wary of saying something in case it somehow came out wrong and ended up stuck there recorded, for him to

253

listen and re-listen to, only making things worse. Mostly, though, she felt stupid. She should have called him earlier. She hadn't, and that was nobody's fault but her own. If only—

The phone rang, causing her to jump, swiftly followed by a rush of relief. It had to be Henry. He had been home after all, seen her call, thought about it, and decided to call back.

"Hello?"

"Kate?"

She was thrown for a second or two. The voice on the other end of the line wasn't Henry's, but Sebastian Dahl's.

"Sebastian?"

"Sorry, I know it's late, but I've been in two minds all day as to whether I should call you... I wanted to explain you see."

"Explain?"

"My actions, why I felt it necessary to intervene this morning? I could see you weren't exactly thrilled when I sided with Henry about slowing things down. It wasn't my intention to gang up on you, but it was impossible not to see the direction your conversation was going in... And, of course, I knew the reason. I'm not an idiot, Kate. I know Henry would prefer you have nothing to do with the house, and I can even understand why, I suppose. He doesn't share our perspective, so it's hard for him to understand why we're so keen to push things forward."

"He thinks he's looking out for me, that it would be better for me to let it go."

"But you can't can you? No more than I can."

"No."

"That's why when I saw an argument brewing between you this morning I decided to step in. I was just trying to avoid unnecessary friction..."

"I see, although I'm afraid we wound up having words anyway."

"Ah…"

"Hm. Actually I was just trying to call him to make peace, but he's not answering."

"*Ah*," Dahl said.

"Why do we say things we don't mean when we're angry?"

"Because we're only human?" ventured Dahl. "Look, I'm sure Henry will see you were simply frustrated. Give him some time. After a night's sleep things often have a way of looking different, a way of falling back into their proper perspective. Would you like my advice?"

"Go on."

"Go and see him in the morning, in person, things can so easily get misconstrued over the phone and an apology carries a great deal more weight delivered face to face. Say sorry, but be honest. Tell him how important it is to you to see this through, give him a chance to understand how important it is to you. If he truly cares about you then he'll support you, I'm certain of it."

Kate reflected for a moment. Dahl's advice seemed well considered. Perhaps giving things a night to cool down was best. She would go see Henry first thing tomorrow, set things straight.

"Maybe you're right. Actually, I already feel better."

"Good. So I'll see you in a few days?"

"Yes. Whatever it takes, I'll make Henry understand, somehow."

"Good night, Kate."

"Good night, Sebastian, and thank you."

"Not at all."

When Kate put the phone down, she realised she really did feel better. She would fix everything tomorrow. Dahl was right, a night's sleep and things were sure to look different in the morning, hopefully to Henry too. It felt like a plan, one that served to ease her mind enough for exhaustion to check it over and stamp its approval, because less than half an hour later she was asleep.

Chapter 41

Dahl's assurance that things would look different in the morning held water. Kate woke up feeling a lot more positive. The previous day's events and her subsequent argument with Henry didn't feel nearly so cataclysmic. She would go see him, say sorry, take him out for breakfast and try again to explain why she had to get to the bottom of what was going on in Dahl's house.

Sebastian's late night call had helped pull her jumbled thoughts into focus, enabled her to cut through the gloom, spy a shaft of sunlight and acknowledge something she had been resisting—that she wanted to be with Henry. She wanted him to be part of what she dared hope for, a chance to start anew. Wasn't that what her dad had wanted for her, a future that included love, and one day perhaps even to be part of a family again?

In her heart, though, before she could truly believe that dream was possible she had to find out what her mother was trying to tell her and why. She had to prove to herself there was nothing else at work, that there was no curse, otherwise the people she had loved and lost would continue to cast a shadow over her life. Perhaps then she might finally be free to look forward again without fear or the constant pang to look back. If the answers she craved lay inside Dahl's house, she had to find them, and she wanted Henry beside her to do it.

These were the thoughts that swirled around her head as she approached his flat and pressed his doorbell. She was just beginning to think he wasn't home when she heard the door's catch turn. A moment later it swung open, only the person who opened it wasn't Henry.

The woman couldn't have been more than twenty-five. She had tussled candy-red hair and mascara-ringed panda eyes. She blinked at Kate from Henry's shadowed hallway and squinted into the morning light. She was wearing a man's shirt, clutched loosely around herself. It came down just below her knickers and there was clearly nothing else beneath. She looked Kate up and down, and gave the shirt a casual downward tug, as though it might magically stretch a further foot and cover her black lace g-string and fake-tanned legs. The shirt was Henry's. It was the one he had been wearing the day before.

For a moment or two Kate actually tried to give Henry the benefit of the doubt and think of an innocent scenario which explained what she was being presented with. She failed.

Something dawned on the girl's face. "Shit!" she suddenly blurted excitedly, "you're Kate Bennett... Oh, wow. This is so cool. I'm a massive fan of *Where the Dead Walk*. Are you here to see Henry? He's in the—hey!"

But Kate had stopped listening. She pushed past the girl into Henry's flat and thundered down the hall directly to his bedroom. The curtains were drawn, but even in the gloom Kate had no trouble digesting the scene.

Henry lay sprawled naked on his bed, face forward, snoring loudly. His mouth was smeared with traces of red lipstick, and there were actually scratch marks on his back. The quilt was half-on half-off the bed. Before she even knew she had done it Kate had taken a swing and slapped him so hard across the face it made her hand sting.

—

Consciousness arrived rudely, with a sharp explosion of pain that left a hot stinging sensation across his face. Henry cracked open a set of impossibly leaden eyelids and groped for something that would tell him where he was and what the fuck had just happened.

In the dull gloom he made out a shape looming over him. It resolved into the blurry form of a woman, and then sharpened further into the form of Kate. He fought to keep his eyes open. It proved no small feat. He tried to get up, and found it not merely difficult, but impossible. It felt like someone had pumped wet concrete into his veins. He abandoned trying to get up and redirected what little vim was at his disposal into thinking. His mind worked sluggishly, like a clockwork mechanism dipped in treacle, but eventually it divined the following insight.

Kate was clearly still not happy with him.

He tried to speak, ask her what had happened, but his lips, tongue and throat were just as impaired as his body and mind. The sound that escaped his throat was redolent of a hernia-afflicted wookiee trying to move something heavy.

Kate stared down at him, and her face underwent a terrible transformation. Her jaw began to tremble and the taut anger in her expression suddenly evaporated, leaving her looking simply wounded, terribly, terribly wounded. Then, with an absent shake of her head, she turned her back on him. He tried to call her back, tell her to wait, beg her to explain to him what the hell was going on, but all he could manage was a feeble "Kaaa..."

In the half darkness, her silhouette was briefly framed in the doorway. He tried to keep his eyes open...

Sometime later, what could have been minutes or hours, someone lifted one of his eyelids. A young redhead swam into focus. She brought her face close to his and peered into his eye, cocking her head to one side.

"You still with the living, pal?"

He tried to respond.

"Whuurg..."

"S'okay, don't bother yourself. All this? I just wanted to say it was nothing personal, okay?"

She released her thumb from his eyelid, and to his surprise he mustered enough strength to keep it open. Not only this, but he succeeded in prising his other one open too. He even managed the colossal triumph of swivelling his head to watch the redhead vanish through the same door Kate had. This was when he realised he was in his own bedroom.

The curtains were drawn, but a laser-like blade of sunlight, bright enough to fry a vampire, streamed through the gap where the drapes met. He fought to remember what the fuck had happened, why his limbs felt like lead and his head hurt like hell. It drifted back in fragments. He had been at Dahl's house. He had broken in, the floor boards had been scorched... and then... Oh fuck.

He had to talk to Kate, tell her what he'd found out!

He pushed a leg towards the edge of the bed and felt it flop over. Buoyed by this victory he tried an arm, and eventually this flopped over the edge too. He clawed at the side of the mattress and eventually slid off onto the floor in an ungainly heap, breathing hard, staring up at the ceiling. The exertion had got his head pounding and he felt shaky and nauseous.

After a while the pounding and nausea subsided enough to attempt moving again. He crawled on his hands and knees and discovered his trousers lying in a heap on the floor. He went through the pockets. His mobile phone was there, but it was powered off. He held the button down and waited for it to come to life. His reward was a bubble of sick dread in the pit of his stomach. There was one missed call, from Kate late the previous evening. She had tried to call him. Where had he been at the time? He groped for his buttock and located a spot that still felt tender. This was where the needle had stuck him, but a needle full of what? Something strong enough to put him out of action for a while that was for sure.

He pulled up his contact list, thumbed down and tried Kate's number. It attempted to call out but then informed him the number was unavailable.

He swore, before thumbing down to Ray's number, he tried that.

"Ray?" Henry heard his own voice, still groggy and thick.

"Henry, that you? You sound terrible."

"I'm at my flat. Could you come over, kind of straight away?"

"Yeah... Is everything alright?"

"No, Ray, I've a nasty suspicion everything's a bit fucked."

Chapter 42

Kate sat in the park, near the duck pond, watching the light play on the oily green surface, an unhappy stew of emotions swilling inside her. She had transitioned from feeling foolish, to feeling stupid and naive, to feeling wounded and angry, although even the anger was bleeding away now. In its place was a queer numbness she wasn't sure was better or worse.

She knew she didn't want to go back to her flat. Sooner or later Henry would turn up there, and right now she just didn't have the energy to deal with his apologies/excuses/bullshit. As far as she was concerned there was no excuse for what he had done, and no way she could ever forgive him for it, not after she had finally found the strength to trust him, so why go through the exhausting motions?

And even if she could be assured Henry wouldn't turn up at the flat she didn't really want to go back there. She wasn't ready yet to face the smiling photos of her dead parents and the lure of the box, Robert's musty shirt and Joel's knitted rabbit. What she craved most was to escape, to run away, but she kept being pulled back. She wanted a new life, or perhaps just the one she had lost. How different might things have been if not for that one tragic night, the fire that had claimed her mother's life and altered the trajectory of her future? It was so easy to believe that first tragedy had transmitted something, a disease destined to infect anyone she grew to love, a virus intent upon blighting her entire life. Henry refused to believe she was cursed, but that was a luxury she didn't have. She needed to prove to herself she wasn't.

Dahl's house was the key. She had to go back, find out what her mother was trying to tell her. In that respect, as much as it hurt, Henry's betrayal had simplified everything. Him, the show, her career, they all seemed trivial in comparison. They could all wait. Her past and her mother couldn't.

She took out her phone and turned it back on.

Dahl took a few seconds to answer.

"Sebastian?"

"Kate? You sound— Is everything alright?"

Her lip threatened to wobble, she bit down on it. "Not really."

"You spoke to Henry?"

"Henry's… not important anymore. If you were to call Nadine Smith, do you think she could be persuaded to perform another séance sooner than we'd planned?"

"What happened?"

"Let's just say I was wrong to think all Henry was worried about was looking out for me. The long and short of it is he's not in the frame anymore and I've decided to take a break from work." She heard herself issue a weird shaky laugh. "I think I need to get some distance from my complicated corner of the world for a while, go somewhere it can't bother me. I want to focus on the house, communicate with my mother's spirit and find out what it is she's trying to show me, why she's stuck there… I'm going to look for somewhere to stay, somewhere closer to the house."

"I see." Dahl was silent for a moment, and then said, "Kate… You don't have to take me up on this, but if you're looking for somewhere to stay where the world can't bother you, I do happen to have just the place. How would you like to stay at The Retreat for a while?"

"Are you serious?"

"Of course. I can call Simon now and ask him to have a room made up for you."

It didn't take long to think over. She recollected the relaxed, tranquil atmosphere at The Retreat, the way it seemed like an oasis from the world outside. It was perfect.

"I'd really appreciate that. Thank you."

"It's nothing, honestly. I'll tell Simon to expect you."

"Then I'll throw a few things into a bag and be there by this evening."

Chapter 43

When Henry opened the door the expression on Ray's face confirmed he looked every bit as rough as he felt.

"Did you try Kate's place?" Henry asked.

"I did." Ray shook his head. "She's not there. I've tried her mobile about half a dozen times in the past hour, she's not answering. I called Claire, asked her to try too. No joy there either. You want to tell me what the hell happened?"

"Someone jumped me, drugged me, and set me up, I think."

"Come again?"

"There's a longer version. Come on in."

Henry told Ray about the séance at Dahl's house with Nadine Smith, the argument with Kate afterwards and going to see Albert Hope, and what Hope had said about the house in Birmingham being more dismantled than demolished after the fire. Then he told him how he had gone to Dahl's house and broken in, about the scorched floorboards and bricks... about being jumped on the way out and the last thing he remembered being having a needle jabbed in his arse. Finally he told Ray about regaining consciousness in his own bedroom earlier, Kate's slap, and the redhead.

"Dahl's behind this. I was getting in the way, or getting too close."

"To what?"

"Whatever it is he's up to."

"Which is what exactly?"

"I don't know; something to do with Kate and him, the house in Birmingham and the house with the spirit inside it, and—" Henry heard himself. "Shit... I know how this all sounds, but something's going on here and I need to get to the bottom of it, for Kate's sake."

"Okay. Let's assume for a moment this *was* all Sebastian Dahl's doing. What would that take? It would take him having been keeping an eye on you, to have seen your argument with Kate, to have followed you to Hope's house in Birmingham, to have followed you from there to his house on the coast, to have been ready to jump you, dose you, and then have the means to organise a red-haired young lady to be ready to answer the door to Kate the next morning and be complicit in the scheme." Ray dragged a thumb over his stubbly jaw. "All to drive a wedge between you and Kate?"

"When you lay it out like that it does sound pretty crazy, but I know I was jumped, and I know I didn't pick up that redhead, and she knew it too. 'Nothing personal' was what she said to me before she left. She knew she'd helped stitch me up. And it worked didn't it? Kate is lord knows where and right now the last person she's likely to listen to is me, even if I could get hold of her."

"So what do you think Dahl is trying to hide, what is it he's scared you might discover?"

"Well, there's no doubt in my mind that Dahl's house is built out of materials recovered from the house he and Kate escaped when they were kids—a house that now appears to have Kate's birth mother's spirit stuck inside it. I bet when we find out who owned that house and had it taken down it turns out to be Dahl. He must have been planning this for years."

"Planning what, though? If you're right about all that stuff, what exactly is he hoping to achieve?"

"Maybe the ghost isn't Kate's mum, maybe the ghost is Dahl's mum, or maybe he was hoping it would be his mum and it turned out to be Kate's..." Henry stopped talking. He was rambling and he knew it. It was infuriating. There was so much that seemed crazy, trying to employ logic to deduce Dahl's intentions was nigh impossible.

"Alright, here's what I think," Ray said. "First things first. We need to talk to Kate and tell her what you found out. We need to find out who that house in Birmingham was left to after the previous owners died, and finally we need to get you looked over. I know someone who can take a blood sample from you and get it checked out, see what you were dosed with, and make sure there was nothing nasty in the needle. Then we'll see where we are. How does that sound?"

"Sounds an awful lot like a plan, Raymond."

Chapter 44

The huge metal gate set into The Retreat's high red-brick walls opened with a whine of electric motors, permitting Kate to drive through. She found Simon Renwick waiting for her by the front door. He insisted on carrying her holdall, led her inside and showed her to her room.

He set the bag down just beyond the doorway and stepped back onto the landing. "A few of us are having a light supper in half an hour or so," he said. "You're welcome to join us if you'd like, or I can have something brought up?"

"Thanks, but I'm fine. I grabbed something to eat on the motorway."

"Well, perhaps I'll see you tomorrow then." He smiled sympathetically. "If there's anything you need, please don't hesitate to ask."

"Thank you, Simon."

He gave her a shy nod. "Not at all. Glad to help."

He left, leaving Kate to survey the room. It was nice, like a hotel room but somehow not as sterile. She approached the window. Beyond the red-brick wall a view of rolling countryside stretched out under a darkening sky. She already felt calmer. The Retreat was exactly the hiding place she needed, somewhere far removed from all the stuff she didn't want to deal with or think about. Here, she would be free to concentrate on the one thing that mattered now. Answers lay in Dahl's house, and she wanted them.

Fortunately she wasn't alone in this, she had an ally. Dahl wanted answers too. The fire that claimed their mothers' lives had left its mark on him as well, figuratively and literally.

She took out her mobile phone. It was still powered off. The last conversation she had had on it was with Sebastian by the duck pond. She tossed it into the depths of the holdall. Right now there was no one who might call her she wanted to hear from.

Chapter 45

"Anyone managed to get in touch with her?"

Henry eyed the wall clock in his front room, it was close to midnight, and he could almost see Ray shake his head on the other end of the line.

"No, but I just got a call from my doctor friend. He gave me the tests results, well most of them, the HIV test will have to be confirmed with another one in three months."

"And?"

"You were shot with a cocktail of benzodiazepines, including flunitrazepam. You'd probably know it better by its trade name Rohypnol?"

"So I was stitched up."

"Looks that way. So what do we do now? I still have friends in the force, if you—"

"Hell no. Let's not forget that prior to getting jumped I'd just finished breaking, entering, and not to mention vandalising Dahl's property. In hindsight I wasn't as circumspect as I should have been. Dahl proving I was there up to no good could turn out to be a damn sight easier than me proving he had anything to do with me waking up dope addled with a strange redhead in my flat."

"So what are you going to do then?"

"I'm going to find out what he's up to and then find a way to prove it to Kate, once I find her and get her to talk to me... We begin by finding proof it was Dahl who got hold of the house in Oakbourne Road, had it dismantled and built that house on the coast out of it."

"Do you think—" The line fell silent as Ray hesitated. "Do you think he knew that something, a spirit, would haunt that place if he built it out of stuff from the other house?"

It was the very question Henry had been asking himself.

"Sounds insane, but I think so. I have a bad feeling too much of what's happened is no accident. Kate thinks Dahl is searching for the same answers she is, but I'm not so sure. I wonder what used to go on behind the doors of that house on Oakbourne Road all those years ago. I wonder if that fire really was an accident. From what Hope told me, the old guy who escaped with Kate and Dahl didn't sound like he thought it was. In fact it looked like he thought Dahl, or Timothy Lamb as he was called then, had something to do with it."

"You think Dahl could have killed his own mother, Kate's mother and those other people?"

"I don't know, Ray, but I'm going to do my damnedest to find out."

Chapter 46

Whether through simple mental exhaustion, or her tranquil new surroundings, Kate slept ten hours straight through. She climbed out of bed and padded to the window, took in the rolling landscape, a patchwork of vibrant green and yellow under an impossibly clear blue sky.

Turning back to the bed she spotted a small folded sheet of paper near the door. She went to fetch it. It was a handwritten note.

Dear Kate,
I arrived early this morning, but didn't want to disturb you. I hope you slept well. When you're up and about, come and find me. I have good news.
Sebastian

She was showered and dressed less than half an hour later. She ventured downstairs and found Dahl talking to Simon Renwick in The Retreat's huge kitchen. They were in the company of around a dozen other people, all chatting and eating breakfast.

Dahl spied her hovering by the doorway.

"Kate. Please come in. Are you hungry?"

"A little."

She approached the table. Simon Renwick bid her a good morning and excused himself, offering up his own seat next to a petite mousy-haired girl. Dahl took care of the introductions. Most of the faces around the table were quite young. Kate would have guessed late teens to early twenties. She recognised many from her previous visit to The Retreat. Before they had come here these kids had lived on the street, and from what Dahl had said most were working through issues, drink, drugs, some may have prostituted themselves to get by, some thieved... not that you would know it now, they all appeared relaxed and friendly, healthy and cared for. Apart from the odd piercing and tattoo they looked remarkably wholesome.

"So, what would you like?" Dahl asked. "You remember Carl, our self-appointed cook? There's not much he can't fix up."

The petite mousy-haired girl sitting next to Kate jabbed a fork at the plate in front of her, where a few crumbs and traces of syrup lingered on an otherwise empty plate. "You should ask for waffles. Carl's waffles are fuckin' orgasmic."

Dahl shot the girl a look of mild disapproval. "Please, Helen, language, no?"

Chastened, Helen apologised, "Sorry, Sebastian. Sorry Kate."

Carl, however, just looked amused. He grinned. "No, it's true. I could make slaves of women with my waffles if I wanted to."

"Well then," said Kate, smiling at Helen, "I guess I'd be silly not to give them a try."

"Waffles incoming," Carl sang cheerily, brandishing his spatula with a flourish. "Anyone else care for some waffles orgasm?"

Helen shyly raised a hand.

"If it's no trouble, Carl?" A ginger-haired youth with a scrubby chin chipped in.

"No trouble at all mate. Anyone else? Going once, going twice..." Carl began cracking eggs into a bowl. "Last chance people..."

Several more hands went up.

During the following twenty minutes the table filled up as The Retreat's residents came down to share breakfast. Carl took more requests, deftly serving up bacon and eggs, omelettes, pancakes, a bowl or two of porridge. The room hummed with conversation, jokes, jibes and good-natured argument.

Then, at around nine thirty a buzzer sounded. To Kate's surprise the table instantly began to clear, after a brief babble of arrangements to meet up later, and a few nice-to-meet-you's cast in Kate's direction, only she, Dahl and Helen remained. The sudden hush was striking. Dahl caught her baffled expression and said simply, as though it explained everything, "Chores."

"Chores?"

"Yes, The Retreat's residents all have strictly mandated chores. It's the house rules. There's a lot of work required to keep a house with so many inhabitants running smoothly. We don't have hired help. Everyone has to pitch in."

"And today they're my responsibility," explained Helen, wafting a hand to indicate a tower of dirty dishes, cutlery, and cups, pots and pans.

"Well seeing as I'm a guest here too, why don't I give you a hand?" Kate started to get up.

Helen looked almost stricken. "No. You can't."

Had Kate imagined the girl's eyes flicking to Dahl?

"I mean, it's my responsibility," Helen said quickly. "That's all I meant…"

"Sorry, I didn't mean to…" What, thought Kate, what hadn't she meant to do? Helen had looked, well, not quite terrified, but her reaction had certainly seemed excessive.

Dahl got to his feet. "Come on Kate. Let's leave Helen to her chores."

Once they were down the hall, beyond earshot, Kate asked, "What was that all about?"

Dahl looked puzzled. "What?"

"That girl, Helen. Is she okay?"

"Helen? Yes, she's fine. Well, that's not strictly true. She has her problems, there aren't many here who don't, but if you're referring to the way she reacted to your offer of help with the dishes, I think I can explain."

"You can?"

"The young people who come here tend to have chaotic backgrounds. Many have grown used to living a hand-to-mouth existence, to treating others with suspicion. Often their ideas of what's right and wrong have grown quite murky. We try to offer them guidance, structure, discipline, encourage them to consider and care about others, and grow used to having other people care for them. Our goal is to install a sense of belonging, but we need them to understand that's something they must earn. Responsibilities are taken very seriously here. If they are given an instruction they must carry it out, without question. They must prove they're ready to contribute, to be part of something bigger than themselves. The way we teach that is by allocating responsibilities, establishing routine, structure, daily rituals... and we do this because when life's road gets rocky those are the things which often keep one afloat."

"I guess..." Kate wondered though. "So what happens if they don't play ball?"

"They're out. We're very clear about that up front. We can help, and we're committed, but we have very limited capacity. We can only help someone who truly wants to be helped. That may sound harsh, but that's the way it has to be."

"Hmm, so what chores can I look forward to?"

Dahl laughed. "I think you and I have enough on our hands with my house, don't you? Which brings me to my good news: I called Nadine Smith after speaking to you yesterday. I explained things had changed and we were interested in moving forward at a slightly quicker pace than we previously discussed. The result being I succeeded in persuading her to visit to the house with us later today."

"Today?"

"Yes, this afternoon." Dahl frowned. "I'm sorry I— That is still what you want, isn't it?"

"Yes, yes it is."

"Good. Well, then we'll need to leave in around an hour. Nadine will meet us—" Dahl broke off as the phone in his jacket began to ring. He took it out and checked the display, then said, "Sorry, Kate, do you mind?"

"No, go ahead."

He answered. "Hello?"

Dahl listened for a moment, said, "I see. If you'll excuse me for a momen..." Dahl put the phone to his chest and turned to Kate. "Sorry, I'm afraid I really should deal with this. Why don't you have a wander? I'll come and find you."

Kate left Dahl to his call.

–

Henry heard the call connect, and after a moment Dahl's buttery smooth voice answered, "Hello?"

"Sebastian. It's Henry White. I need to ask you something."

"I see. If you'll excuse me for a moment..."

Henry heard the phone being muffled, but was still able to make out the words, "Sorry, I'm afraid I really should deal with this. Why don't you have a wander? I'll come and find you."

Eventually Dahl's voice returned.

"Yes, Mr White. Sorry, you were saying?"

"That I need to ask you something. Have you heard from Kate since we left your house the other day?"

Henry had woken early following a restless night. With no idea where Kate was, or *how* she was, he had been too wired to sleep for more than fits and starts, nevertheless those meagre couple of hours had achieved something. The quiet machinery of his subconscious had put two and two together, and while he still didn't know where Kate had disappeared to, he had a fair idea who might.

"Sebastian?" Henry prompted.

"Actually," Dahl said, breaking the silence, "I have heard from Kate. Although from what she told me, I gather she doesn't want to see or speak to you at present."

Henry bristled. Did he imagine he heard pleasure in Dahl's voice, or was his dislike of him just causing him to think he did?

"Where is she?"

"Look, Henry, don't you think it would be best to let her contact you when she's ready? She has your number?"

Now Henry was in no doubt, Dahl was enjoying himself. Nobody could be that condescending by accident.

"If you speak to her again tell her to contact me."

"And why would I do that?"

"Because I'm her friend."

"A friend she doesn't seem to want to talk to right now."

Henry couldn't help himself. "I know you're up to something you shifty bastard. I don't know what it is yet, but I'm going to find out."

"I really have no idea what you're talking about Mr White."

"Just tell Kate—"

The line went dead. Dahl had cut him off. Henry didn't care, because he had a pretty good idea now where Kate might be.

Chapter 47

Dahl's Ferrari flew along the motorway, its motion succinctly encapsulating Kate's mood. She was moving ahead, free to begin unravelling the house's secrets unburdened by the creation of a television show or the weight of Henry's disapproval.

The journey was far swifter from The Retreat, in less than an hour they arrived at the house's gravel track road. Nadine's car was already parked up. Above, on the rise, Nadine herself waited on the house's steps.

–

"We'll proceed in the same fashion as before," Nadine said, once they were again in the house's gloomy lounge. "I'll seek to establish contact with the spirit and communicate with it. Kate, if you feel it trying to channel through you, you *must* try to resist. Focus on where we are right now, on the present, on the flesh? Do you understand?"

"I think so."

"The harder you make the spirit's attempts to channel through you, the more likely it is to choose to engage with me instead. Yes?"

Kate and Dahl both nodded.

"Good. Then let's get started."

They were arranged in a similar fashion as before, only with no Henry present to provide a fourth point they formed a triangle this time in place of a square.

Nadine fell still, tilted her head back and let her eyes fall closed. She began to breathe deeply, the silence growing fat and swollen until her voice, serene and even, broke the still. "Spirit, are you here? We have returned, to communicate, to help you if we are able to. Come forth. Speak to us, speak, speak..." Nadine's voice bled away, but her lips continued to form soundless words. Kate tried to lip read, but the words were too rapid, and then Nadine began to drift... Like before the room shifted and the walls began to contract, the light and colour leaching away before the room closed around Kate like a fist, folding into darkness. All at once she was somewhere else. She was—

—in the cosy living room of an unfamiliar house. A television glows in the corner of the room. Ronnie Barker is asking Ronnie Corbett for some 'fork handles', or 'four candles', the confusion is underscored with canned laughter. A girl sits watching the television, her legs curled up beneath her on the settee. She is smiling at the hardware store owner's increasingly comic exasperation. The room is dimly lit by a standing lamp in the corner. The girl's face is indistinct, daubed in shadow.

The doorbell rings and the girl springs to her feet. The light catches her face and Kate recognises her birth mother, Valerie. She looks much younger than before, though, in her early teens at best. She opens the door and a tall handsome man and an equally attractive woman step into the living room, a short exchange follows, Kate struggles to listen but it is difficult, like she is hearing the conversation from underwater. She makes out fragments: 'Have the children behaved themselves?', 'No, really, you've earned it. Five pounds is money well spent for a night out without the kids,' and 'Colin will drop you back'... Then Valerie and the tall handsome man are leaving. They are in a car, driving along a dark road. They are in a lay-by. They are making love, cramped and hurried. Valerie is getting out of the car, walking up a *path to another house where she lets herself in with a key...*

The scene collapses to black. And then—

The same house, but it looks different in the daylight. The door is thrown wide and several black bin bags fly through onto the path. Valerie scurries after them, tears streaking her face. She screams back into the open doorway, where a man appears, red-faced, angry. He begins shouting too. They are still screaming at each other when Kate notes the bump. Valerie's tummy betrays a small but unmistakable swell. Kate marvels, because she's almost sure she and the bump are one and the same.

Valerie scoops up the black plastic bags containing what Kate suspects are the sum total of her worldly belongings, and turns her back on the house and the angry man inside...

The images are moving more rapidly now, tumbling like the pages of a flip book; Valerie stands on another doorstep. The tall handsome man blocks the doorway. He glances furtively into the hallway behind him, shouts something about having to 'nip out for a moment', and all but drags Valerie and her black bags away from the doorstep. Then they are sitting together in a park, there is a lot of head shaking, from the man at least. Again Kate catches only snatches of conversation, talk of mistakes and clinics. Money crushed into Valerie's hand. The handsome man makes an ill-disguised threat and turns his back, impervious to a teenage girl's tears.

Kate already knows there will be no clinic. What she sees next is a train station, and a journey. Valerie sits, a hand resting protectively on her bump, gazing out of a window scarred with clumsily etched graffiti, watching the world glide past.

The darkness shifts, swirls, falls away—

Kate blinked, took in the faces in front of her, Dahl's furrowed brow and Nadine Smith's mask of intense concentration. Dahl's lips were moving but the world was still mute. Then, like someone twisted the cosmic volume knob up, Kate heard his voice.

"Kate, are you alright? It happened again. Nadine tried to... but—"

"It doesn't matter," Kate heard herself say. She felt giddy and still a little dazed. She wanted to cling onto what she had seen. Her mind fizzed with images and sounds... Her mother, still just a girl...

Dahl steadied her and asked, "What did you see?"

Kate was about to try and put some of it into words when something prompted her to hold back. She hesitated, found she didn't want to share, not quite yet. She had a powerful sense the things her mother had shown her were meant only for her. They had nothing to do with Dahl or Nadine Smith. She needed time to think. "It was all jumbled," she offered weakly.

"Was it like last time?" Dahl enquired. "Did you see the house again?"

She felt the weight of his scrutiny. For some reason she couldn't explain, she said, "Yes. And my mother, I think."

She saw Dahl's eyes flick to find Nadine Smith's. Kate thought she saw something pass between them, but couldn't say exactly what. Did they know she was holding back, was it that obvious?

"Anything else?" Dahl prompted.

"It was hard to make sense of... Sorry, maybe once I've had some time..."

"Of course," Dahl replied. "I'm sure you'll tell me everything once you're ready."

—

They were again outside the house. Nadine said she believed it would be wise to call it quits for the day. They should discuss their options before moving forward, she said, but was unwilling to elaborate. She agreed to accompany them back to The Retreat, where they retired to one of the gardens' large patios.

"I'm not sure I'm going to be able to do much more for you," Nadine said.

"What do you mean?" asked Kate.

"I don't believe the spirit in that house is prepared to communicate through me. Both times I've tried to engage with it, it's leapt directly to you, and when I've managed to wrestle it back, to channel it myself, it has ultimately rejected me, retreated away."

"Did you see anything?" Kate asked. "When you channelled it this time?"

Nadine shook her head.

"So what do we do now?" said Dahl.

Nadine looked pained, reluctant to deliver bad news. "I'm afraid the options I can offer you are limited. Perhaps someone else may be able to—"

"No," Dahl interrupted. "You were the one. I searched, and the people I spoke to said you were the best."

"You said our options were limited," said Kate. "So what are they—if we stick with you?"

"We, that is to say Mr Dahl and I, attempt to communicate with the spirit without you present."

"Or?"

"We give way and let the spirit communicate with us through you, try to engage with it, discover what it wants or needs that way. It's certainly not the route I'd prefer to take, but if you're determined to get answers, if you're committed…"

"We are," Kate said.

Dahl nodded slowly. "We are." He looked to Kate. "But only if you're completely sure."

"I am."

Nadine appeared to think it over, perhaps assessing just how serious they were. Then she sighed and said, "Okay. When would you prefer to return?"

"Tomorrow?" said Kate, looking to Dahl, who after a moment nodded in agreement.

Nadine studied them both, and then said, "Very well, tomorrow it is."

A polite cough came from the doorway, Kate looked over. An agitated looking young ginger-haired man was fidgeting at the threshold.

"Sorry to bother you, but someone's out at the gate, Sebastian. A Henry White? He wants to see Ms Bennett. Simon's dealing with him at the moment."

"How the hell did he know I was here?" said Kate.

Dahl winced. "I think that may be my fault. He called me this morning, asked if I had spoken to you. I said I had, but that I thought the best thing he could do was to give you some space, let you call him when you're ready to talk. I'm sorry. I thought he deserved to know that you were safe at least. I should have anticipated it might occur to him you could be staying here."

Kate felt weary suddenly. She didn't want to deal with Henry. She didn't have the energy, but she should have known he wouldn't leave her be. He had no right coming here, demanding to see her, not after what he'd done. She had every right to be left alone.

"You don't have to see him," Dahl said gently. "You really don't. I can talk to him, tell him to go away."

As tempting as this offer was, Kate knew it wasn't an option. Henry wasn't going to listen to Dahl, certainly not about this, about her.

"No. I'll talk to him, but at the gate. I don't want him in here."

"I'll come with you."

Chapter 48

Henry was finding it a truly Herculean effort to keep his cool. The man responsible for presenting the Olympian test to his patience stood on the other side of The Retreat's substantial gate.

As soon as his call with Dahl had ended, Henry had jumped into his car and hit the road. The journey had been lengthy enough for his anxieties for Kate and his darker feelings toward Dahl to simmer into a potent stew, the metaphorical lid of which was now rattling under the pressure.

"Look, I *know* she's here. All I'm asking *you* to do is tell her *I'm* here. I have to speak to her."

"*Look*, Mr…?"

"White. Henry White."

"*Look*, Mr White, you need to understand how things work around here. This is private property, home to a registered charity, a registered charity whose aim is to help troubled young people build new lives. If you read the brass plate on the wall just there you'd see this place is called The Retreat. It's called that because it's supposed to be somewhere the rest of the world can't easily invade, that's the point. As such, we're not in the habit of discussing individuals who may or may not be staying here to anyone who just turns up and leans on our bell. I'm sure you can appreciate that. However if you'd like to contact us by post or email I'm sure—"

"Kate's got nothing to do with your charity work, she's my close friend and business partner, and I really need to talk to her."

"A close friend and business partner who's staying here but hasn't left you any way to contact her directly?"

One of Henry's mum's favourite sayings was how one could catch more flies with honey than with vinegar; unfortunately right now Henry was all out of honey. He spoke slowly through gritted teeth. "There was a misunderstanding, we argued. She's upset with me. That's why I need to speak to her."

"And you think she's here?"

"I *know* she's here. I want to speak to her."

Slowly, as though he were talking to someone with a mental deficiency, the man reiterated, "Yes—and as I said—we simply can't divulge the identities of people staying here to just anyone who turns up at our door."

Henry, who feared he was on the verge of sliding deeper into seriously anti-Zen territory, drew a deep breath and thanked the gods there was a gate to save him from throttling the man in front of him. He knew, *just knew*, Kate was somewhere beyond the gate, probably within shouting distance, but this pedantic—

Hold on.

Within shouting distance. Henry side-stepped the man, cupped his hands around his mouth and began to yell at the top of his voice toward the house.

"*KATE! IT'S HENRY. I'M OUTSIDE, AT THE GATE. I NEED TO TALK TO YOU.*"

"Please sir, I'm going to have to insist you—"

"*KATE!*"

"Look—"

"*KATE, IT'S ME, HENRY—*"

Henry stopped. Dahl had emerged from the house, and Kate was with him. They were on their way over. Kate was saying something to Dahl, but they were beyond earshot. Dahl said something in return, equally inaudible. There was a glance in Henry's direction, more discussion. Kate put a hand on Dahl's arm, said something else, which earned a reluctant nod. Dahl stopped and waited in the shadow of the house as Kate approached the gate alone.

She addressed the man at the gate as she neared, "You can go, Simon. I'll take care of this."

The man shot Henry a distrustful glance and asked, "Are you sure?"

Kate nodded, the man exhaled and backed away, turning for the house. Kate stood behind the gate's wrought iron bars, her face an emotionless mask.

It hurt. Henry had to keep in mind how everything appeared from her skewed perspective. He needed to remember that she believed she was the one who'd been wronged, and after Dahl had done such an effective job of stitching him up who could blame her?

She stared at him coldly. "Why are you here?"

Her voice sounded flat, almost bored.

"To tell you that what you saw yesterday morning wasn't what it looked like."

"No?"

"No, I was set up. Dahl set me up. He's up to something and—"

"Dahl set you up?" she repeated, in the same flat matter of fact, perfectly reasonable, voice.

"Yes, I went to Birmingham, to speak to a neighbour who lives across the road from the house where—"

"*Dahl*, set you up?" In a flash Kate's detached monotone was gone, and her poker face along with it. She scorched him with angry, undisguised contempt. "Let me get this right, just so there's no confusion: Somehow Sebastian tricked you into picking up, taking home and screwing that little red-haired skank who greeted me at your front door yesterday morning? The same one who was wearing your shirt, a face full of slap and not much else? Really, that's the story you're going with?"

"You don't understand. I know it must sound—"

"Like bullshit?" Kate spat, but already she was teetering; her anger was changing into something else.

She looked on the verge of tears. It hurt him to see her suffer like this, wounded by Dahl's deception. If she would only listen...

"Kate. Just hear me out—"

"No, I'm done listening to you. I fucking *trusted* you, Henry, idiot I am. I thought you cared about me, really cared..." She stalled, shook her head ever so slightly, her lips a thin line.

"Kate, I do care about you, I—"

"Then leave me alone. Do whatever the hell you want with the company; hire some hot young chickie to present the show if you like. Right now I've other things on my mind."

"Kate—"

She turned her back on him, strode off, back towards the house. Dahl intercepted her half way. They shared some words in passing. Then she disappeared into The Retreat. Dahl made his way over to the gate.

"Henry—"

"*Go get her back.*"

Dahl raised his eyebrows, utterly unfazed.

"I don't think so."

They stared at each other between the bars.

Dahl shrugged. "Look, Henry, I think it would be best if you left now. You should give Kate some time—"

"I'm on to you. I don't know what it is you're up to yet, but you can be sure I'm going to find out."

Dahl smiled patronisingly. "Is that so?"

"You can fucking count on it."

"I see. Well, best of luck with that, but in the meantime be a good sport and hop in that car of yours and get lost, eh? You're becoming a nuisance, and should I involve the police I think you'd find them quite supportive of our desire to maintain a calm environment here. 'Young people struggling with real problems', and so forth..." Dahl stepped closer to the gate, so close that his nose almost touched the bars. He regarded Henry with sardonic amusement. "She won't listen to you, not now, and even if she did she wouldn't believe you. I saw to that." Then, to Henry's utter disbelief, Dahl winked at him.

What followed was a blur. Henry saw red. The next thing he knew, he had his hands through the bars of the gate, gripping the front of Dahl's shirt. Dahl's face was close, mashed against the bars, but instead of protesting he simply twitched his head, directed his eyes up and to the right.

"You see that security camera atop the wall there, the one that just recorded your attack on my person? Well, if you're not a least half a mile away from this property in within the next ten minutes, what it just captured will not only form the basis for the charge of assault I'll seek against you, but the restraining order I'll pursue to keep you away from this property and myself. Oh, and of course, Kate." Dahl's voice was low but serious. "Let go of me. *Now.*"

With a great deal of effort Henry unclenched his fingers and released Dahl's shirt. Dahl took a step back and made a show of straightening his clothing.

Henry glared at him. "I meant what I said. I will find out what you're up to."

Dahl looked unmoved. Like someone who's grown tired of the game he's playing, he turned on his heel and began to walk casually back toward the house. Without even looking back he said, "I doubt you're even capable of imagining what 'I'm up to'."

Henry let him get half a dozen steps further before he responded.

"I know about the house. I know it's the house that caught fire, the house you and Kate escaped."

Dahl's step hitched. He set his foot down slowly. Now he did look back. Henry continued to glare at him.

Dahl didn't look unmoved, not anymore, Henry thought. He looked just the tiniest bit ruffled.

Dahl looked him up and down, cool as a cucumber once more. He turned on his heel continued back to the house, but not without a parting shot.

"Bully for you."

Chapter 49

It was late afternoon. The Bennett White crew was assembled in the production office's meeting room at Henry's request, all save for one, whose absence was the very reason the rest were there.

"I thought it was time I brought you up to date on a few things," Henry opened, "like why we're running around three weeks behind schedule, and why Kate's not here. She's staying at a property that belongs to Sebastian Dahl, and in my opinion she's in real trouble."

"What kind of trouble?" asked Claire.

Henry told them everything.

"So what do we do?" asked Mark.

"We try to find out what Dahl's up to, what he wants with Kate, and I think we do that by finding out what actually happened all those years ago in that house in Birmingham. Maybe then we can convince Kate that Dahl is bad news and that she shouldn't trust him. The sooner the better, too. I don't like the thought of her being isolated at that place and under his influence one bit."

"I've no wish to worry you further," Charles interjected, "but after what you've told us, I fear the situation could be worse than you imagine. Everything you've said, the fact Sebastian Dahl knew who Kate was from the very beginning, that she appears to be the only one the spirit is interested in, that Dahl would go to such lengths to separate her from us all... It's all deeply worrying, but if you're correct about him deliberately dismantling and rebuilding the house where his mother, Kate's mother and others died, only for a spirit to inhabit it as a result... that concerns me even more, because it's indicative of two things:

symbolism and ritual, two elements that go beyond the world of spiritualism and mediumship to somewhere far darker."

"What?"

"Something as old as humanity, the sort of thing people used to get burnt at the stake for. I'm talking about the occult, Henry, witchcraft, black magic."

Henry wanted to believe Charles was joking, only the medium's face made it impossible. He looked as grim and serious as Henry had ever seen him.

"There's someone I know," Charles said, "someone we should talk to. He knows considerably more about that sort of business than I do. I only hope I'm wrong."

Chapter 50

Henry waited in the car while Charles hovered outside the tower block, talking animatedly into the building's intercom. The 'someone' he had brought them to see didn't appear to be thrilled to have visitors. Charles had described the man, Eamonn Lister, as his friend, but in Henry's experience friends weren't generally so reluctant to let you in when you dropped by.

He peered up through the windscreen at the tower block, pointing like an accusatory finger into the pewter grey sky. The tower lay in a gentrified neighbourhood in Hackney, and had the impressive moniker of Vista Heights. It had clearly started life as a council high-rise, which rather than being levelled like so many of its giant ugly concrete brethren had instead been sold to a private developer who had deftly knocked a few walls through and transformed its collection of pokey shoebox flats into a series of spacious upscale luxury apartments, replete with landscaped communal gardens and gated walls. Despite the developer's best efforts, it was still largely a huge concrete eyesore.

Charles returned and slipped back into the passenger seat. "It took a little persuasion, but he's agreed to see us."

"Right," Henry said. "Good."

The motorised gate retracted and they drove through into a private parking area. Henry slotted into a space in the non-residents bay and they got out.

He stared up. "So what floor's this Eamonn live on?"

Charles cocked his head back too. "The top."

—

As they entered the building and made their way to the lift, Charles explained Eamonn owned not just the penthouse apartment that encompassed the top floor, but the apartment below as well, although this was left empty. It was, Charles said, a buffer. Henry couldn't quite bring himself to raise the question of, a buffer against what?

"The top two floors eh? The medium business's been pretty good to your friend, Eamonn, then?"

"In some respects, I suppose, although Eamonn has never actively sought to exploit his gifts, quite the opposite. He's always tried to avoid drawing attention to them, but when your talents are as remarkable as his... Well, let's just say it's hard not to come to some people's notice. Over the years he's accumulated a small number of benefactors who seek his counsel occasionally, and are happy to compensate him for his trouble."

"Are we going to be expected to 'compensate' him?"

Charles shook his head. "Eamonn and I are friends—as much as he still has them these days. His gifts have always made it difficult for him to be around others, and over time he's increasingly ceased to make the effort. I'm afraid he's become something of a recluse. You're likely to find him somewhat... eccentric."

Henry cast Charles a look. "Eccentric, eh? What makes it difficult for him to be around other people?"

"Where there are people there will inevitably be spiritual activity. For someone as sensitive as Eamonn this can be very distracting, disturbing even, imagine a kind of persistent babble in your head. That's why he chooses to live way up here—there's considerably less activity than near ground level."

The lift slowed and came to a stop. Henry and Charles disembarked into a small square reception room with two doors, a front door and a fire door leading to the building's stairwell. Charles stepped forward and pressed the intercom button beside the front door and waited.

A moment later the door opened a crack. A pale blue eye appeared and examined them through the seam.

"Eamonn," said Charles cordially.

A quiet voice with an inescapable stammer responded, "Hur-hello Charles. This is your fur-friend, the wuh-wuh-one with the pur-problem?"

"Yes. Henry White. Henry this is an old friend of mine, Eamonn Lister."

Henry tried to smile reassuringly while Eamonn's skittery eye studied him.

"H-h-how exactly do you think I can hur-help you Charles?" Eamonn enquired.

"I'd appreciate your advice concerning something we appear to have stumbled into, an area I believe you know more about than I do."

There was a long pause, and then a reluctant, "I suppose you had buh-buh-better come in then." The door swung open; behind it the enigmatic Eamonn Lister stood in the hallway. After Charles's unintended build up, Henry's first thought was that he looked shockingly ordinary.

Below average height, afflicted with a bad posture and short sandy hair, this season the medium Eamonn Lister was sporting an ensemble comprising a worn zip-up cardigan, washed-out corduroy trousers and checked brown slippers. Henry had anticipated the individual whom Charles held in such lofty regard would be an imposing Svengali-type figure, practically oozing wisdom and razor sharp perspicacity. In truth, Eamonn looked like a middle-aged train spotter. He looked skittish and nervy, an impression not helped by his stammer and a nervous tick which caused his head to twitch sporadically as he looked them over.

Henry instinctively offered Eamonn his hand, and was slightly taken aback when the medium practically recoiled. Eamonn cast a flustered glance toward Charles, who before things could get any more awkward explained, somewhat redundantly, that Eamonn had issues with physical contact.

They were led into a sparsely furnished, dimly-lit lounge. Eamonn hovered in front of a big brown armchair, apparently the only seating the room enjoyed.

"There are sss-some chairs in the cupboard o-o-over there. Would you Ch-Charles?"

Charles nodded, crossed to the cupboard and came back with two deck chairs. He unfolded them, set them out and he and Henry sat down. With the situation becoming increasingly surreal by the second, Henry did his best to ignore the fact he was seated on garden furniture and reminded himself they were here because Charles insisted they needed this man Eamonn's advice.

Eamonn perched himself on the edge of his armchair. "Wuh-what's this 'something' you've sss-stur-stumbled into then, Charles?"

"You're aware of our show, *Where the Dead Walk*?"

"Yes, your shuhh-show… I think I saw an episode wuh-once."

Henry got the impression Eamonn was being diplomatic; Charles either didn't notice or didn't seem to care.

"Well, a few months ago we were approached by someone, a man called Sebastian Dahl who offered us the opportunity to investigate a property of his…"

"G-gurh-go on," Eamonn prompted.

So Charles did. He began with Sebastian Dahl's call to the offices of Bennett White and concluded with Henry's altercation with Dahl at the gates of The

Retreat the previous day. Henry chipped in occasionally, adding details he thought could be significant. By the time they were done an uneasy frown had ensconced itself upon Eamonn's brow.

"I think you've every rur-reason to be c-c-concerned," he said. "Without wur-wishing to alarm you, there are sss-strong indications of a 'wuh-*working*' in what you've just t-told me." Eamonn's pinched face was grave. "To build a house out of mmmm-materials recovered from a pur-place where a tragedy such as you've described occurred... s-six deaths, and then to just happen to have a pur-powerful spirit appear there... I don't like the s-s-sound of it Charles, nor the fact this Sebastian Dahl ss-seems so intent upon encouraging your furgh-friend to fool about with a s-spirit who refuses to communicate any other wuh-way but through her... I don't like the surghh-sound of it at all."

"You mentioned a *working*," Henry asked. "What do you mean by that?"

"A working is another name for wuh-what some would call a spell, or a hex, a charm, vurgh-voodoo, or black magic: the occult. The kurgh-kind of practices only the desperate or the corrupt are usually furgh-fool enough to meddle in…"

Perhaps only a couple of months ago Henry may have been required to stifle a smile at what Eamonn had just said, but an awful lot had happened since. That he had never felt less like smirking in his life was perhaps indicative of how far down the rabbit hole he had tumbled.

"The occult?" he repeated.

"Dur-don't get sidetracked by ter-terminology,"Eamonn replied, "We're talking about practices as old as mmm-man. It may go by different names, but at heart it all comes down to the surgh-same thing. In essence, a wuh-wuh-working is the process of encouraging, persuading, or duping spirits into carrying out acts of the purgh-practitioner's design."

"And how exactly does someone go about performing one of these workings?"

"It dur-differs from culture to culture, belief system to belief system, but ultimately two elements rugh-remain common, s-symbolism and ruh-ritual. These are the tools a practitioner employs to concentrate his wuh-will and mmm-make clear his desires.

"Charles may already have explained this to you, but surgh-spirits rarely communicate in the verbal sense. Wuh-when they converse it is almost always through ih-images and feelings. Divorced from the fur-physical form they carried in life, spirits become the distilled essence of the purgh-person they once wuh-were, more authentic, perhaps, but also more pur-pur-primal. They view our physical wurh-world dimly, as though through a s-scarred and pitted glass. When they become aware of the lur-living it is through our emotions, our feelings, the engines of our wuh-wuh-will.

"Intense emotions—love, hate, joy, and purgh-pain burn m-most brightly, but unfortunately they are usually as unfocused as they are brilliant. When they belong to one attuned to the spirits, but inexperienced, they can act like a lantern in the nur-nur-night, sure to draw moths, only for the creatures to buh-beat vainly against its glass. Poltergeist activity around gifted but emotionally volatile chur-chur-children is a common example. The ch-child attracts a spirit's attention, but wuh-without direction, without focus, the result is chaos. At one end of the scale this can mean objects being mmmuh-moved, broken, hidden or taken, at the extreme it can mmm-mean physical attacks on the chur-child or those around them.

"When you consider it, this is not so s-surprising. The living behave in much the same wuh-way. A mob gathers because s-s-something draws their attention, anticipation buh-b-builds. The mob gets wuh-whipped up, a great deal of excitement is generated... and then nothing hurgh-happens. Among the crowd there will always be some who'll act out to let off s-s-s-steam.

"The occult practitioner's gurgh-goal is to achieve this intensity of s-spiritual energy and attention, but to harness it to produce a specific action or surgh-series of actions. A working is how the practitioner overcomes the conscious mind's fundamental whuh-weakness: that it is a poor conduit for cuh-channelling emotion.

"Intense emotions are by their nur-nature anti-intellectual. While we are, of course, all *conscious* of our furgh-feelings, our unconscious is the crucible in whur-which they are formed. Our keenest emotions often fur-feel ih-irrational, precisely because they are. We don't decide to furgh-fall in love, and sometimes hate can be every bit as instinctive. These emotions tend to be the pur-pur-product of unconscious thought. Which bur-begs the question: how exactly duh-does someone go about s-shaping their unconscious thoughts, thoughts that by definition they are uh-uh-unconscious of?

"The answer is through s-symbolism and ruh-ritual. Through the repetition of ritual and the symbolism inherent in the objects a practitioner ch-ch-chooses to utilise, he can build within his unconscious mmmm-mind a s-s-specific composition. In this way his emotions can be amplified and chur-channelled into instructions the spirit can not only clearly discern, but furgh-feels compelled to act out."

Henry gathered he must have looked at least half as lost as he felt, because Eamonn immediately elaborated.

"Ter-take a voodoo doll as an example. Here, the occult practitioner construct an effigy, or d-doll, symbolising the person upon whom they wuh-wish to

298

focus a spirit's attention, and then, through ritualistic actions, s-stabbing the doll with a needle for instance, suggest a specific action he wishes the spirit to cur-carry out.

"It's not enough for the doll to simply ruh-resemble the victim, as this alone would create only a superficial connection in the practitioner's mmmm-mind. For the necessary impact on his sss-subconscious, a really pur-powerful connection, the doll needs to incorporate mmmm-materials of powerful symbolic value. These may include fur-fabric from the intended vurgh-victims clothes, hair from their huh-head, personal items that once belonged to them or bodily fluids, the mmm-most potent of which would be blood or s-semen.

"This process, cuh-cuh-collecting these items and constructing the doll is in itself ruh-ritualistic, each step serving to bind the d-doll and the victim as one in the practitioner's uh-unconscious. If properly done, acts then inflicted upon the effigy will enter his unconscious with the s-same gravity as if he had performed them on the victim himself, and are thus presented to the s-spirits with equal clarity."

"And the spirits will carry the act out?"

"If the practitioner is ss-skilled enough, if he is gifted enough, and his wuh-will strong, all manner of feats are possible. Spirits have the potential to interact with our world in ammmm-multitude of ways, and the prurgh-practitioner can utilise these to achieve his aims. Spirits can move objects, cuh-cause fluctuations in temperature, make things cold as ice or hot enough to buh-buh-blister, make things combust, act as observers for a practitioner, shhh-show him things occurring behind drawn curtains or locked doors hundreds or even thousands of mmm-miles away, they can strike or pinch, sometimes enough to buh-bruise or draw blood, they can influence animals, and particularly p-powerful spirits are capable of far wuh-worse."

"Like what?"

"Things like invading a living person's buh-body, gaining control of them. Cases of possession are rare, but not unheard of, and while the puh-possession will inevitably be fleeting—a living soul's connection to its body wuh-will always prove stronger than the invader—if real mmm-malice is intended even muh-momentary control can open the door to catastrophe. Huh-how long does it tur-take someone to k-k-kill himself, or someone else?"

"Was Kate possessed?" Henry asked.

"No, I don't think so, not from wuh-what you described. Superficially, possession mmm-may appear similar to channelling, but channelling demands compliance from the hurgh-host, at least at some level. Possession is an act of pure domination. The kinds of s-spirits who are drawn to such b-b-behaviour are invariably wretched souls, lost, full of anger, bitterness and confusion... Spirits of this ilk are dur-dangerous—to the practitioner almost as much as the intended target of the wuh-working. For a working, remember, the practitioner s-seeks control."

"And you think Sebastian Dahl could be trying to perform a working, that's why he rebuilt the house where his mother and Kate's mother died? But for what purpose, what's he trying to do?"

"I wuh-wish I could tell you. Workings are, at their most ehh-effective, intensely personal, apt to be as rurgh-reflective of the individual c-conducting them as the act they wuh-want to achieve. To discover the purpose of a working I'd ruh-recommend gathering as mmm-much information about the practitioner and their target as you can fur-find, and then to study every p-piece thoroughly. You should assume nothing you discover is wuh-without significance, duh-duh-dates, places, people and o-o-objects may all provide vital clues... Look closely for ritualistic elements, pur-patterns and instances of repetition."

"And then?"

Eamonn paused, let his gaze move from Charles to Henry and back again.

"Then you should a-ask yourself if you are truly ruh-ready to put yourself buh-between a person who would go to such lengths and the o-o-object of their desire."

—

As Eamonn's towerblock disappeared behind them it was Charles who voiced the question on both their minds.

"Do you think it's possible, that Dahl's trying to perform a working?"

Henry shook his head. "Charles, I'm not sure I know what to think anymore, but I'll tell you this: I intend to find out what happened in that house Kate escaped all those years ago, why out of nine people only she, Dahl and a guy who wound up in the nut house survived."

Chapter 51

The name of the reporter responsible for the Birmingham Mail piece on the fire at Oakbourne road hadn't exactly been difficult to find, it was right there in the byline to his story, Mathew Mears. Tracking the man himself down, though, took slightly more work.

Henry tried his old newspaper first. The person he spoke to seemed willing to help, but hamstrung. Staff records for the previous decade were kept on computer, he explained, but the late eighties was still a largely paper-based era; even if they still had records he wouldn't know where to begin looking for them. Henry had asked if there was anyone still around who worked at the paper back in the late eighties. The man took a moment to think and said there might be someone, a freelance photographer the paper still occasionally used. Henry asked if he might have his number.

A call was enough to confirm the photographer had indeed known Mathew Mears. Mears had been a staff journalist when the photographer had started doing work for the paper, and the two had become friendly enough to remain in touch after Mears retired. Better yet, he was still in touch with him, although he insisted upon knowing why Henry wanted to speak to him before he bothered his old colleague. Henry mentioned Mears's story covering the fire at Oakbourne Road and said, even though the incident occurred a long time ago, he was hoping he might remember it. It was a research thing. The photographer said he was willing to contact Mears, explain the situation, but it would be Mears's decision after that. Henry offered his thanks and crossed his fingers.

He shouldn't have worried. Mathew Mears called around an hour later. As it happened, he said, he did still remember the Oakbourne Road fire, and that possibly even a few details that hadn't made it into print. He would prefer not to talk over the phone, though. Henry asked how soon they could get together. Mears gave Henry his address and said he was welcome to drop by around noon the following day.

For the second time that week Henry found himself journeying up to Birmingham. Mears lived to the south of the city in a neat little cottage on a pleasantly green fringe of the suburbs. Mears's wife answered the door; Henry explained her husband was expecting him. Mears must have told her, because she immediately beckoned him in and through the house. She pointed a finger through the kitchen patio doors to the garden.

"You'll find Matt down there somewhere, near the greenhouse would be my best guess."

Henry found Mathew Mears two-thirds of the way down the immaculately tended garden, near a large greenhouse as predicted, turning the soil in a vegetable patch. Mears looked engrossed, and didn't appear to have seen him coming.

"Mr Mears?"

Mears quit working and straightened up, resting an elbow on his fork. He had green wellington boots on and matching green work-wear trousers. Beneath a faded brown-coloured bucket hat tufted some thick snow-white, wiry, unkempt hair, framing a ruddy face, healthy-looking in a weathered outdoorsy way. All in all, if jolly farmer were a 'look', then Mears had it down pat. He studied Henry for a beat, before wiping a strong looking right hand across his cable knit sweater.

"Henry White?"

"Mathew Mears."

"So you're the chap who's curious about that house fire on Oakbourne Road way back?" Mears said.

"I dug up your news piece, the one you wrote at the time. I know it's a while ago now, but I hoped you might still recall a few things about the incident."

Mears pulled what looked like a thinking face and leant on his fork again. His eyes even did that thing they do when someone's trying to recall something, sort of drift up and to the left, but while Henry wouldn't have been able to say why exactly, there was something in the way Mears did it that struck him as phoney. He was suddenly certain Mathew Mears had already done a fair bit of thinking prior to his arrival. When he had mentioned 65 Oakbourne Road on the phone, the impression he got was that Mears hadn't needed to scour his memory for one second to place the address. No, if Mears was thinking about anything, Henry reckoned, it was whether he was going to give up what he had or not.

"What do I recall about the fire on Oakbourne Road?" Mears mused, his eyes finding Henry's. "Mmmm. Quite a bit as it happens." He reached behind him and massaged his back. "Bits of me might be getting creaky, but thankfully my memory isn't one of them, at least not yet. If you don't mind my asking, though, what exactly's your interest?"

"I'm something of an amateur genealogist. I'm researching a client's family tree; one of the people who died in the fire at that house in Oakbourne Road was a close relative of hers."

Mears was silent for a spell.

"Really, that's your story?" he said finally. His smile was still pleasant, but behind the veneer of the amiable gardener Henry detected the restless ghost of a former newspaper journalist.

"Excuse me?"

Mears tilted his head. The smile grew wry. "Mr White. I'd have found out who you were back in the day soon enough, I was a good newsman, and we had pretty good resources at the Mail, a library, archives, records. *Words on paper,* you understand. The world's changed some on that front since, so I'll set my cards on the table. It took me all of... ooh, eight seconds to find out who you were on Google yesterday evening."

"Oh, I see."

"I *know* who you are, and the television show you make, *Where the Dead Walk*? I've even caught snatches of an episode or two, flicking through the channels as one does... More pertinently, perhaps, I know a few things about the..." Mears paused, "*things* that may have been going on at 65 Oakbourne Road before those people burned to death there that night. You're no more a genealogist than I am. So, to borrow a charming American expression, let's cut the crap, eh? What's your real interest in 65 Oakbourne Road? Just hoping to film a show there, use all that grisly history for flavour, or is there more to it?"

Henry was hesitant. Wellies and garden fork or not, Mears had spent the best part of his working life as a journalist, and it seemed the guy's radar for a story hadn't been decommissioned yet.

"Off the record?"

Mears snorted. "Good god, Mr White, I've been retired nearly fourteen years."

Henry merely repeated himself. "Off the record?"

Mears rolled his eyes, as though Henry was being ridiculous, but behind the amiable facade Henry identified an unmistakable edge of grudging consent in Mears's response. "Okay, Mr White. Off the record. You have my word."

"Part of what I said is true. I do have a friend whose mother was one of the people who died in the Oakbourne house fire," Henry began, "but I'm not looking to trace her family tree. I'm scared she's in trouble, and I think it might have something to do what went on in that house all those years ago. I think that if

305

I can find out who her mother was, and what happened there, then I might be able to help her."

"How can you be sure your friend's mother was in that house? Most of the people who died weren't even identified; most of them had likely been living rough before they wound up there was what I heard."

"I know because she was one of the three people who got out of that fire alive."

"One of the..." Understanding dawned on Mears's face. "She was the girl?" Mears took a while to mull this over, and then tugged his fork from the vegetable patch. "Let's go have a proper talk, shall we?"

—

Henry followed Mears to the foot of the garden, where a huge shed nestled under the droopy foliage of a willow tree. Mears unlocked a solid-looking padlock and ushered Henry in. The space inside looked more like a study than a garden shed. A desk, shelving crammed with books and binders and a pair of green metal filing cabinets took up one wall, with just enough space remaining to accommodate a pair of aging but comfortable-looking leather office recliners. Mears took the one nearest the desk and invited Henry to take the other.

As Mears eased into his seat, he said, "I thought there might be a book in 65 Oakbourne Road one time, or failing that a decent article. In the end, though, I let it go."

"Why?"

"We'll come to that, but let's start at the beginning, eh, with the piece I wrote about the fire—the one you dug up all these years later."

"I arrived at 65 Oakbourne Road the night of the fire around the time the blaze was finally being brought under control. The house was a big old Victorian job and looked just about gutted. Half the windows were blown out, black scorch marks topping the charred frames.

"I approached one of the coppers at the scene and then a couple of the fire service guys and nailed the basics down. The cause of fire was yet to be determined, but there were three survivors, the man Lawrence Hawley, and two kids, a boy and a girl. The remaining occupants were believed dead, around six they feared. Besides the emergency services, some of the neighbours were still milling around, so I went and had a word with them too, grabbed a quote or two."

"And one of them was Albert Hope?"

"One of the chaps who had helped get the kids out? Yeah, him, and a few others, but it was a teenager I got talking to who really piqued my interest. He lived across the street, was about seventeen I think. He said he wouldn't be surprised if the fire had been started on purpose, said everyone who lived nearby reckoned the house was full of weirdoes. I asked him what he meant, and he told me he had a friend who'd lived there for a bit, Sarah. Even she had said they were weird, said they were getting like a cult, that's why she'd done a runner. Free food and board or not, she said, that kind of stuff they were doing wasn't right.

"I asked where his friend Sarah was now. He said she'd moved 'up north'. I asked whereabouts 'up north', but he didn't seem keen to share. I kept nudging and eventually he said she didn't really want anyone to know. But he knew, I asked? And he nodded. She'd sent him a postcard a month or so after she'd left. To cut a long story short, I managed to convince him to give me the address. I don't know what I thought I was going to do with it, not then, but you learn to listen to your instincts about these things."

"And you found her?"

"A week or so later. I'd been on to a source I had in the local force, told him I'd heard murmurings the fire may have been started deliberately, maybe even as some kind of suicide pact—I was just fishing really, but he didn't know that. He told me from what he'd heard it was possible. One thing had been established, all the bodies were found downstairs, in the lounge, and this looked to be where the fire had started too. It had spread fast, fast enough that they were looking for traces of propellant, some kind of flammable liquid, although nothing had been found yet. Group suicide couldn't be ruled out, the possibility that the whole lot of them may have gathered in the lounge and set fire to themselves. Unfortunately, the only three souls alive who may be in a position to say for sure what might have happened weren't talking. The two kids who got out either wouldn't or couldn't speak about what had happened, and the guy who got out seemed to have lost it, gone mad as a bag of badgers."

"Group suicide… Jesus."

"Hmm." Mears looked grave. "Well, as you might imagine, I was suddenly a whole lot more interested in speaking to this girl, Sarah. As it happened it wasn't so hard to track her down. She was still at the address the kid had given me, a YWCA in Manchester. She was wary to begin with, of who I was and why I wanted to know about what made her leave Oakbourne Road—a decision that almost certainly saved her life. So I told her the truth: I was curious, and I thought there might be a story to be had. I wanted to see if I could get to the bottom of what happened, and assured her if she did talk to me I'd treat her strictly as an anonymous source.

She seemed uncertain, asked me about the fire. I told her what I knew and that got her to open up some. She said she'd tell me a bit about the house on Oakbourne Road if I was curious, but only so long as nothing she told me made into print. I haggled a bit, tried to talk her around, but she wouldn't budge. So eventually I agreed, telling myself that I could maybe talk her around later.

"First off, she said she didn't buy any group suicide theory. Without doubt there was some odd stuff going on in the house while she was there, but no one seemed unhappy, much less suicidal. In that case, I asked her, why had she decided to leave? Things were getting too weird, she said.

"She'd come over from Ireland, leaving trouble behind her. I asked what kind of trouble. The law? No, she said, family trouble. She headed for Birmingham because she didn't fancy London; Brum was big enough to get suitably lost in and find work. She'd been just sixteen at the time. The getting lost bit turned out to be no problem, the finding work bit proved harder. Pretty soon she ended up sleeping either in hostels or on the streets. Then a girl she'd grown friends with got a room at a house belonging to a pair of do-gooders, or that was the way her mate described them. After a few weeks she'd asked the couple if Sarah could share her room. They said maybe. Sarah went to meet them, so they could look her over I guess, decide if she was trouble. The couple seemed nice enough, and agreed Sarah could share her friend's room until she got herself on her feet. It seemed too good to be true, free board, no more hostels or doorways... Unfortunately, turned out it was too good to be true, because as time went on she started to feel uneasy about what was going on in the house.

"Apparently the couple who owned the place liked to muck around with Ouija boards and that kind of stuff, but it always seemed to be going further. Sarah hadn't been too bothered at first, but then they started fooling around with experimental rituals. It was all very New Agey, 'tapping into the universe's multitude of energies', that sort of nonsense, but Sarah wasn't so sure. There had been some casual drug use in the house when she had first got there, nothing heavy, mostly weed, but as part of their experiments they'd started messing around with hallucinogenic gear, brewing peyote tea, and dabbling with increasingly weird stuff... She grew scared some of the stuff she'd seen wasn't down to the drugs... I asked her what she meant by this, but she wouldn't say. She said she just wanted to put that time behind her.

"I tried to get her to tell me more, but she seemed to have decided she'd told me enough already, more I think than she'd intended to share. I got the feeling she was still scared, despite most of the people she'd lived with now being dead. So I took what I had, thanked her, and let her be.

"I kept at it for a while, though, found out what else I could. I discovered the kids had been taken into care, no relatives had been found, not so surprising when you consider most of the people in the house were still yet to be identified. Apart from the couple who owned the place, only one of the dead youths' identities was known for sure. The kids living there seemed to be there either because they didn't want to be found or because they didn't have anyone else who gave a fig about them anyway. If what Sarah told me was true, my bet would be that most of them had been sleeping rough like her and her mate before the couple took them in."

"So what became of the old guy, Lawrence Hawley, the one who owned the house?"

"Spent the rest of his days in a psychiatric hospital, although 'the rest of his days' turned out to be not all that many. After about a year or so in the hospital he slipped into a coma and died shortly thereafter. He had a brain tumour apparently. Nobody knew, or they hadn't taken his complaints or symptoms seriously."

"Jesus. Then what?"

Mears shrugged. "Then nothing, I had a family to feed, bills to pay, and other stories to write that would pay them. Eventually I just let the Oakbourne house story go. The police couldn't prove an act of arson, or the intention to conduct a group suicide, and as there wasn't a queue of curious relatives lining up demanding answers the case probably got filed away under 'if any new evidence comes up we'll look into it'. I doubt most of those who died have been identified to this day."

"Do you remember which psychiatric hospital it was Lawrence Hawley spent time in?"

Mears said nothing, but his eyes flicked to a dog-eared manila folder lying on the desk. It had been on the desk when they entered the shed. Henry wondered how long for, sometime after Matt Mears's photographer friend called him the day before would have been his bet.

"I doubt very much that the quack who treated him will talk," Mears said, reading Henry's mind. "The impression I got was a good deal of the fallout from the failure to diagnose Lawrence Hawley's tumour came down on him. Just how had the good doctor failed to notice his patient had a lump big enough to kill him growing in his head? He kept his job, as I recall, but that kind of black mark can follow you around. I think it's unlikely he'd discuss any of it with you, even after all this time," Mears said.

"Perhaps not."

Mears chewed his lip, studying Henry for a moment, and then without a word he picked up the folder, thumbed through it and scribbled something onto a post-it pad. He peeled the note off and handed it to Henry. There were two things written on it, a name and a place: Dr William Lockley. Thistlemoor Psychiatric Hospital.

"Thank you," Henry said. "I suppose I shouldn't ask how you came by this information?"

"What information?" Mears asked, lifting an eyebrow.

Henry nodded to show he understood. At the same time, though, he couldn't help pushing his luck.

"You don't happen to still have Sarah's address, and perhaps her full name?"

"Ah," Mears said, "I'm afraid that's a bit different."

"I'm not looking to harass anyone. I just need to know what happened in that house."

"What exactly are you hoping to discover, and why's it so important?"

"I have to find out my friend's mother's identity, and how she came to die in that fire, as to the question of why I need to know that—trust me, you wouldn't believe me if I told you."

"Try me."

Henry needed what Mears had. He knew to stand any chance of getting in touch with the girl, Sarah, perhaps the only person who could tell him about the people who lived at Oakbourne Road and what might have led to their deaths, he had to convince Mears to help him.

"This is still off the record right?"

Mears nodded, not even bothering to protest now.

Henry laid it out, every crazy detail, about Sebastian Dahl and his supposed haunted house, about the first séance where his friend, one of the crew, had appeared to channel the spirit of a dead person, his growing suspicions regarding Sebastian Dahl, his discovery that Dahl was once Timothy Lamb—the boy who escaped the fire, how the Dahl house was in good part actually the Oakbourne house, how it had been dismantled and resurrected, and finally he described how Dahl had stitched him up.

Mears was silent. After a long pause he said, "My friend, that, I have to confess, is quite a story."

"You're not kidding," Henry agreed.

"You honestly believe there's something, a spirit, trying to communicate with your friend?"

Henry shrugged. "It's irrelevant what I think really, isn't it? What matters is she believes it—the person I'm trying to help," Henry concluded. "She's become obsessed with it all—the house and the spirit she's convinced is stuck there. I think the key to breaking that obsession lies in the truth, in the past, in what happened in that house on Oakbourne Road. If I can find out that, then maybe I can help her, and this Sarah sounds like the one person alive who might have the answers I'm looking for."

Mears chewed his lip again, ruminating.

"How's this?" he said finally. "Give me the opportunity to see if I can find Sarah. Assuming I can, I'll tell her what you just told me and see if I can convince her to contact you?"

Henry suppressed the urge to wrangle. He'd already got way more out of Mears than he had dared hope for.

"I'd appreciate that very much."

Mears nodded.

Chapter 52

While Henry had a restless night of fractured sleep fuelled by the creeping anxiety time was running out, to the extent he finally admitted defeat and abandoned his bed in the wee hours to return to the internet to search for any information relating to a Doctor William Lockley, Kate couldn't have slept more soundly had she been shot with a Pygmy's dart.

She dreamt of her mother, young Valerie, who refused to get rid of her child, the girl who ran away from the people who had turned their back on her. She awoke from these dreams feeling strangely tranquil.

By midday she was with Nadine and Dahl in the lounge of Dahl's slowly decaying house on the rise. Soon she would make contact with her mother again. She was sure of it.

Nadine turned to her. "You understand that permitting the spirit full rein over you will further limit my influence over it. Wrestling control back from a willing host is markedly more challenging than from an unwilling one. It may take longer, and that could introduce a greater degree of risk."

"You said this was the only way forward. Do you still believe that's true?"

Nadine nodded. "Yes. Unfortunately."

"There's still the option of Sebastian and me trying to contact the spirit alone..."

Kate shook her head. "No. I'm sure it's my mother's spirit here, and I can't believe she wants to hurt me."

Nadine nodded again, and then went to her bag lying in the corner. She removed a tub of table salt and what appeared to be a small hessian bag. Brandishing them, she said, "Fortunately there are ways I can bolster my influence."

Nadine thumbed the pouring spout open on the tub of salt and started to circle Dahl and Kate, pouring a ring of salt around the spot where they intended to perform the séance. Once the tub was spent she tossed it to one side and stepped inside the perimeter. Next she handed Kate the small hessian bag.

"I've crafted you a charm. It's made up of things that will lend you protection, herbs mostly, together with few items that belong to me. View it as a kind of talisman, and hold on to it for as long as we remain in this house. Its purpose is to symbolise me, and afford me a focal point I can use to wrestle away the spirit's control over you. Do you understand?"

"I think so."

"Then I think we're as ready as we're likely to be."

Nadine commenced the séance the same way she had last time, and just like last time, she had scarcely started before Kate felt something happen. Almost at once the room shifted, grew dark and started to close in around her. The difference was this time she welcomed it. It felt like falling into somewhere comforting and warm, somewhere womb-like. The darkness swirled in the void like ink dropped into a glass, resolved into a room and—

She's under the dining table, playing, drawing pictures on butcher's paper with pencil crayons. A dark-haired boy is beside her. Most of his pictures are of superheroes. A voice comes from the other room, calling them in to help set the table for dinner...

The darkness shifts, shudders, folds—

The table is bustling with bodies. They are all eating, talking, and laughing. They're like a big family, over there her brother, there is granddad, granny and a bunch of aunts and uncles...

The darkness shifts—

It feels late. She must have fallen asleep on the mattress, still in her daytime clothes. Mum's kneeling

*beside her, gently shaking her awake by the shoulder.
She complains, she wants to go back to sleep, she's
tired, but mum says they're doing something special
downstairs—* 'Like a party?' she asks. 'Yeah, kind of,'
her mum replies, 'kind of like a party.'

'Is Tim awake?'

'Yes,' her mum says, 'he's coming too...'

The darkness shifts, expands, and then closes in fast,
deeper, darker and somehow denser than before. It
sweeps her up in its motion like a roller coaster in full
pelt; Kate's stomach lurches—

*The morning is cold. There's birdsong and a dank
breeze that clings. In a field, a rustic collection of
vehicles, wooden caravans and tepee-style tents enclose
a burnt out bonfire.*

*She is trying to rub some warmth into her knotty
wrinkled hands without waking her arthritis when a
child pokes his face out from one of the tents, spies her
and smiles shyly. He is missing a clutch of milk teeth,
but the middle few remain, rabbit-like. He rubs an eye
with a pudgy fist.*

*Her smile wilts; she feels impossibly old suddenly,
ancient—*

The darkness collapses in as though the scene were
a vacuum, swallowing everything; it feels close,
cloying, then—

*She is descending the staircase into the hall. Her
mum leads her by the hand into the dining room. The
grownups are standing in a circle, like it's a game. She
imagines them starting to skip, turning... Ring a ring a
roses, a pocket full of—*

The darkness is back, obliterating everything once
more, except this time it closes tighter still, contracts
around her, smothering, suffocating. She wants the
light back. She has the idea something is alive in the
darkness... She begins to panic—

316

The bolt slides back and the caravan door opens. The girl enters, insultingly fresh-faced and vital, carrying a meal. She smiles prettily. The woman forces herself to return the smile, works hard to make it reach her eyes. The girl is coming to believe they are friends. That's good, because only if...

The darkness binds around her. It's thick and heavy, like being smothered in tar. Kate wants to scream, but she is afraid the darkness will get inside her... Gush down her throat and fill her up. It feels like being buried, she wants out. This isn't like the other times—

She is in the dining room again, inside the ring. Each of the adults holds a cup. Someone is moving from one to the next, pouring something from a brass kettle—

Kate blinked, disoriented. It took a few moments to reassure herself she was truly back in the present. She felt fuzzy-headed, a dreamer waking from a long sleep. She looked down and saw her fingers were still clamped around the small hessian bag, the charm, crushing it in a white knuckle grip. Across from her, Nadine was straight as a rod, rigid, save for her lips which were forming rapid soundless words. Kate had time to wonder if there was something she should do, and then the medium's eyes snapped open and found her.

"Did something happen? Did you see something?"

Kate grasped for the words to explain. "It was... different. Something was different this time."

"Different how?"

"I saw some things, but they were more jumbled than before, they felt different too, like they didn't fit together. I..." She gave up. Suddenly the room dimmed, listed. Kate staggered, and reached out for something to steady herself. In her urgency she dropped the hessian bag. Then as fast as it had descended the

317

sensation lifted. Dahl took her arm. "I think we need to get you outside. Get some fresh air."

Dahl helped her from the room, through the hallway and into the light of day. She sat on the porch's bottom step and took a few deep breaths.

Dahl hovered, concern knitting his brow. "Are you okay?"

"Yes, much better, thanks."

"So you saw something?"

"It was all jumbled up. I saw my mum again, she was waking me up. There was a party, I think…"

Dahl's eyes shifted to Nadine.

"Please, go on…" the medium prodded.

Kate tried, but this time it was hard. Everything had been so disjointed. The things she had seen previously had formed a narrative of sorts, but this time… it felt different. Did that mean something? She wished she could summarise the experience neatly, if not to Dahl and Nadine then at least to herself. She wanted to understand, to put the fractured pieces together, but it was still difficult to think clearly.

She started to get up, instinctively wanting to get some distance from the house. As she raised herself off the porch step the world took a drunken lurch again. She stumbled and Dahl reached out to steady her.

"Kate? I think you should sit back down for a mo—"

"No." The world settled back on its axis. She regained her balance. "I want to go."

Again Dahl looked to Nadine, and then said, "Yes, of course. Here let me help you."

With Dahl at her elbow, Kate made her way down the rise toward where the cars were parked. As the house receded she began to feel more herself.

They were leaving, but she couldn't shake the feeling something important had just taken place, that something fundamental had changed. The shift was hard to articulate and strangely contradictory. If pushed, she would have said she felt like she was taking something away with her, or leaving something behind.

Chapter 53

Henry and Ray gained Dr William Lockley's address through a combination of deft investigation and bald-faced lies. In a series of telephone calls, Henry had posed as at least a half a dozen people in positions of officialdom, a move liable to land him in hot water if he was ever caught out. He didn't care. He had a horrible feeling time was running out, that Sebastian Dahl's maddeningly opaque plan, a plan that in some key way involved Kate, was speeding toward its conclusion. He needed to throw a spanner into the works before that happened.

Dr William Lockley had been in charge of Thistlemoor Psychiatric Hospital during the eighties, but had left the post somewhere during the early nineties. A Thistlemoor staff reunion page on a social network site proved very interesting. A few oblique comments alluding to the good doctor suggested he had perhaps grown a little too fond of the bottle. Further digging unearthed accusations of misconduct at the subsequent institution where he practiced. The doctor had taken early retirement soon after this, in ninety-five.

Henry was curious about Lawrence Hawley. Dr William Lockley might be in a position to shed some light. If only Henry could get him to talk.

Whatever the estate agent's inverse of 'up and coming' is, the area where Lockley's flat lay would surely have fallen into it. The run-down council estate probably hadn't been built more than thirty years ago, but already begged to be nuked out its misery.

Henry parked in a cul-de-sac surrounded by a trio of graffiti-tattooed flats. Lockley's flat was number 72, about halfway up the middle block. Retrieving what he hoped would prove to be his secret weapon from the passenger side foot-well, Henry offered a short prayer to the patron saint of television producers that his car would not be gutted and propped on bricks when he returned and got out.

Scaling the dank, piss-marinated stairwell to Lockley's door, Henry couldn't help but consider the question, how far can a man fall? Presumably, as the head of a hospital, there had been a time not too many years past when Lockley had lived a reasonably respectable, affluent existence. Henry's secret weapon seemed more and more certain to be Lockley's kryptonite.

He arrived at the doctor's door and was about to press the doorbell when he found it had been smashed off. A wire still protruded from the wall, but the button was long gone. Only a lozenge-shaped patch of mismatched paint remained. Henry gave the letterbox a couple of snaps instead.

The figure who opened the door around a minute later looked every bit as dismal and neglected as his surroundings. Thin and haggard, Lockley had greasy nicotine-stained hair, a scrubby beard, bad teeth, hollow eyes and a shirt featuring enough stains to keep a forensics lab busy for a week. He smelt pretty potent too, a high-proof liquid breakfast combined with poor personal hygiene created an olfactory cocktail on par with 'broken drain' or even the legendary classic 'wet dog'. It wafted through the open doorway while the man responsible for it regarded Henry with naked suspicion.

"Dr William Lockley?" Henry enquired.

The man cocked his head, wobbling slightly. "Yes. Who are you?" The accent was educated and sounded disconcerting coming from the shabby husk in the doorway. "My name is John Morris," Henry lied, handing him a fake business card, briskly mocked up and then printed out on the Bennett White office printer only hours earlier. "I'm a genealogist. I'm trying to piece together a family tree. I believe you treated a relative of my client's during the late eighties, while you worked at Thistlemoor hospital? I wondered if I might ask you a few questions about him, nothing confidential, naturally. The relative's name was Lawrence Hawley."

Lockley actually flinched, Henry was sure of it.

The doctor straightened up and put his hand to the door. "I don't believe it would be appropriate for me to discuss any cases I dealt with professionally. As you seem to be aware, there are questions of confidentiality."

Henry had anticipated this, and prepared to deploy his secret weapon. It was a low blow, maybe, but his conscience would have to wrestle with that later. He reached into the bag he was holding and produced a large and very decent bottle of single malt whisky. He arranged his face to appear disappointed. "Oh, that's a shame," he said convivially, "I was hoping we might discuss the matter informally, over a civilised drink or two? I wouldn't be looking for you to share anything of a sensitive nature. In fact, it's clarification I'm seeking more than anything..."

Lockley wasn't a fool. At some level Henry knew he saw the bottle for what it was, a bribe, and if that was all there was to the matter the conversation would likely have stopped right there, but it wasn't. Like all addicts Lockley was a man with a master. Good sense and clear judgement weren't in the driving seat. He eyed the single malt, doctor's ethics warring with the chronic alcoholic's desire for a stiff drink.

Lockley pulled his eyes from the single malt to Henry's face. "Nothing confidential?"

"As I said, I'm largely just looking to confirm a few things."

Lockley let the single malt inside. Henry joined it.

–

Henry refilled Lockley's glass, again. The former psychiatric doctor had been reluctant to talk much in the way of specifics to begin with, but half a bottle of good scotch was beginning to pay dividends.

In order to ingratiate himself, Henry had thrown back a couple of shallow glasses alongside the good doctor's more generous servings. At which point he had carefully nursed his third. He asked Lockley a bit about Thistlemoor to begin with, innocuous questions, but by the time Lockley had emptied his fifth glass, Henry began to circle the questions he really wanted answered.

"Tell me about Lawrence Hawley. What was he like?"

Lockley lifted his glass, drank deep, licked his lips and said, "As a man? Lost. As a patient? Fascinating. Lawrence Hawley suffered as complete a psychotic delusion as I've ever encountered. From the day I first met him to the day he..." Lockley paused, "to the day he passed away, he never wavered. Not once."

"What was the nature of his delusion?"

"He believed he was someone else." Lockley absently tipped his glass towards Henry, causing a little to slop out. "Such psychoses are not unheard of. The infamous trope of the mental patient who believes he's Napoleon or some other famous figure does have some basis in reality. While this might make for good drama or comedy, however, in reality such monothematic schizophrenic delusions are rare. Commonly such individuals will possess other delusionary traits. They may suffer from paranoia, hear voices, experience feelings of persecution and the like.

"One school of thought regarding identity delusions is that they are a coping mechanism. The theory asserts that an individual experiences some manner of emotionally traumatic event he is unable to accept. In order to avoid confronting the trauma he retreats into a secondary persona, a persona who is not himself and therefore absolved of facing or even acknowledging it. The persona will typically be a personality type, or sometimes an actual person, the individual admires, identifies with or feels he understands."

"Was this the case with Lawrence Hawley?"

"No. Hawley's delusion was far more unusual."

"How so?"

"Lawrence Hawley didn't simply believe he was someone else, he believed someone had stolen his body. He fully acknowledged that in a physical sense he was still Lawrence Hawley, but insisted that *inside* he was someone else. The distinction is critical, and is what made his case so unusual."

"So who exactly did he think he was, on the inside?"

"That's the truly fascinating part. He was adamant his true identity was Timothy Lamb—the ten-year-old boy who had apparently escaped the same fire Hawley had." Lockley knocked back the remains of his glass and poured a refill. He moved to top up Henry's glass too, but discovering it almost full, set the bottle down instead.

"Did he say why he thought that?" enquired Henry.

"He claimed Lawrence Hawley had stolen his body. This was the first thing he told me when I came to assess him after he had been sectioned and brought to Thistlemoor. At that time he was in a highly emotional state, confused and suffering from mental exhaustion. I don't believe he had slept for several days. He was extremely agitated, but at that juncture still

324

communicative. He seemed desperate to make someone listen, desperate to find out where he—or his body—was... It was distressing, for him and for the staff at Thistlemoor. For his own safety we sedated him."

"And later?"

"He was treated with antipsychotic drugs. He settled some, enough for me to begin to work with him. His delusion was undiminished, but his behaviour was certainly more rational. I was optimistic that through a combination of drug therapy and careful exploration of his delusion I might enable him to see flaws in his construct and help him to confront the trauma at the core of his psychosis. Of course I was unaware of his condition then... Unaware that neurological damage may be causing or at least contributing to his psychosis."

"You mean his brain tumour?" When Lockley looked surprised, Henry added, "It was on his death certificate."

"Oh, yes, naturally..."

"Please, go on. You were treating him?"

"Yes. I took things slowly, gained his trust, and began to gently challenge his construct. I was hopeful, but as time went on his complete refusal to confront his delusion eventually led us to a therapeutic impasse." Lockley sighed. "Hawley became progressively disengaged with the process, became by turns withdrawn and then prone to violent outbursts. Eventually his violent episodes diminished but his depression and internal retreat became more entrenched. I reduced the sedative element of his treatment, hoping to reengage with him, but he only continued to grow more docile, sleep for longer and longer periods. I persisted in my attempts to treat him, but by then he was refusing to even acknowledge my presence, let alone speak to me."

"When did you find out about the tumour?"

"After he slipped into a coma. One night he went to bed and never woke up." Lockley seemed reflective. "How was I to have known? He complained of headaches, but they were an occasional side effect of his medication. It's impossible to say whether his delusion was caused or exacerbated by the presence of the growth; the brain is incredibly complex, but a tumour can certainly occasion all kinds of curious neurological effects." Lockley ran out of steam, deflated. "It was a difficult time for me. I was accused of negligence. A lot of mud was thrown... assertions that I should somehow have identified the existence of the tumour. I'm a psychiatric doctor, for heaven's sake... And that Hawley's psychotic break coincided with the tragedy of losing his partner and several lodgers in a house fire... What doctor would have assumed a neurological cause?" Lockley stared into his glass. "I came under a great deal of pressure. That I was going through a divorce during the same period didn't help. Nevertheless, I believe to this day that my work never suffered. I admit, subsequently I made a few minor professional errors, errors I believe, because I was already under the microscope, were blown somewhat out of proportion... The pressure of it all took quite a toll on me, on my health and my own mental wellbeing."

And so you were advised to step into early retirement before you were pushed, thought Henry.

"I maintain to this day that I did everything I could to help Lawrence Hawley." Lockley's yellowed bloodshot eyes suddenly flashed with bitterness. "His death was *not* my fault. Even if his condition had been diagnosed his chances of recovery would have been slim. Despite all that, Hawley was my patient and it's hard not to feel some responsibility, however unwarranted."

"Of course," Henry agreed. "People often mistake doctors for miracle workers."

"Precisely," Lockley agreed, momentarily animated, his scotch sloshing in his glass.

"Is there anything else you can tell me?" Henry asked. "Anything you feel might be important?"

"Like what? Really, Mr Morris, I can't imagine any of this will do much for your client. Lawrence Hawley's is a depressing tale to pin to one's family tree. Not exactly one to regale the grandchildren with is it?"

"My client may feel differently."

"You think?" Lockley said, with an edge of alcohol-tinged belligerence.

Henry shrugged. "I'm just doing what I was hired to do."

"Hmm, well, it's a pity one of Lawrence Hawley's relatives didn't take more interest in him while he was in Thistlemoor. I was under the impression he didn't really have any kin. To my recollection during the entire time he spent at the hospital he received a solitary visitor, and that was his ex-wife." Lockley said the last word with something close to loathing. Clearly ex-wives were not well regarded in the world of William Lockley. It didn't matter. Henry's ears were suddenly pricked.

"Oh yes?"

"Transpired she wasn't greatly bothered either," Lockley said, in a way that suggested this was only to be expected of ex-wives. "Spoke to him for all of ten minutes, and then disappeared, never visited again. I tried to talk to her as she was leaving, but she looked more angry than upset. She was his ex-wife so she probably felt justified in telling herself he wasn't her problem anymore."

"Did she speak to you?"

"Briefly, but considering the nature of Hawley's psychosis I found her attitude somewhat ironic. To paraphrase, she said something to the effect that he 'wasn't the man she'd married'." Lockley snorted. "I refrained from pointing out that was somewhat the crux of the problem, and instead enquired if he had suffered any kind of mental health issues in the past. I shouldn't have bothered. The woman just looked at me as though I were clueless. I saw little point in pursuing the topic further, and as I said, she never returned."

–

Henry stopped off at a small greasy spoon before hitting the motorway. He needed to think. His visit to Lockley had provided plenty of food for thought. He demolished a bacon sandwich and a mug of milky tea and called Ray at the Bennett White offices. His request? To obtain Lawrence Hawley's marriage certificate or any other documents Ray thought might assist them in tracking down the former Mrs Lawrence Hawley.

Chapter 54

Kate woke from the nightmare with a jolt, heart thumping, slick with sweat.

Joel had been in the dream. He had been curled up in a small pool of light, surrounded by darkness and shadows, and somehow Kate had known the shadows were threatening. She made to rush forward, snatch him up and protect him, only to discover she wasn't really there. She could see her son, but nothing more... Frantic, she tried to yell, scream a warning, but she wasn't just without body but voiceless too... The shadows meant to take her baby, do him harm, and she was powerless to help. She was still screaming silently when they closed in, swallowed him whole. That was when she had awoken.

She should have felt relieved; it was only a bad dream after all, not real, not real, and for a moment relief had come, until she remembered reality was worse than any nightmare could match. In her dream, Joel was merely in danger; in real life he was already dead.

They had arrived back at The Retreat around two in the afternoon, and despite leaving Dahl's house behind her, the odd feeling Kate had departed with persisted. Dahl seemed concerned, and tried to encourage her to eat something, suggesting her blood sugar was low, perhaps, but Kate didn't feel like eating. Her head was churning with images, all she wanted to do was go upstairs and sleep, not because she was tired, more because she craved the temporary escape from her chaotic mind sleep promised. The dream had denied her even that.

She slumped back, stared at the ceiling. She felt wrung out, saturated with a hollow exhaustion that seemed to have nothing to do with physical or mental fatigue, but something deeper down, a weariness of the soul. It was a brand of exhaustion that caused her to feel numb, dislocated her from her emotions, both good and bad. It was a feeling she didn't like one bit. She was afraid of it, and with good reason. It was reminiscent of the way she had felt in the aftermath of losing Robert and Joel...

Fuck.

She needed to distract herself.

She mustered the effort to swing her legs out of the bed and get up. Upon opening the drapes she was surprised to find it dark outside. She must have slept for the better part of the day. She tied her hair back, climbed into yesterday's clothes and headed downstairs.

Descending the staircase she heard voices. Further down the hallway she located the source of them. They were coming from one of the lounges. Curious, she stopped to eavesdrop. Something like a monologue was being delivered, full of affirmations about positive energies. She leaned closer to the door to get a better listen and a floorboard creaked beneath her step. She froze, suddenly feeling vaguely guilty. Had somebody heard? Perhaps she should—

The door cracked open. Simon Renwick peered through, looking, Kate thought, somewhat twitchy. The room behind him appeared host to most if not all of The Retreat's wards.

Simon recovered himself quickly, smiled, "Kate? Is everything okay?"

"Yes, although I think I slept most of the day away."

"I did wonder where you were, but Sebastian told me not to disturb you. Are you hungry?"

She wasn't. "A little. I was on my way to the kitchen to find a snack."

"Look, we're just in the middle of one of our house meetings, but we shouldn't be too much longer. If you can wait I'm sure Carl would be happy to prepare something for you, or you're free to help yourself of course."

"Oh, I don't want to trouble anyone. I can take care of it."

"I'll catch up with you later then?"

Kate nodded.

Simon Renwick waited at the lounge door until she moved off, it wasn't until she stepped into the kitchen that she finally heard the soft bump of it closing.

Chapter 55

Henry had never been through Manchester's infamous Moss Side before, but like most he had heard stories about how infamously grim and sketchy an area it was. He supposed as with most places it had its fair and its rough parts. Unfortunately it looked like his destination belonged to the latter. When they arrived, the taxi driver even asked him, "You sure this is the place you want, mate?"

Henry had been pouring milk into his cereal when the call came. A woman asked if she was speaking to Henry White; she had a musical accent, three heaped spoons of Irish with a pinch of Mancunian thrown in. When Henry confirmed she indeed was, she identified herself as being Sarah O'Brien. The one time lodger of 65 Oakbourne Road was on the other end of the line. Henry restrained himself. Slowly, slowly, catchy monkey... They spoke briefly and arranged a meeting to meet in person.

The day centre where Sarah O'Brien volunteered had clearly once been a row of houses, since knocked together to form one large building. In the reception area a middle-aged woman in a blue check pinafore was pushing a trolley of crockery off somewhere. Henry asked if Sarah O'Brien was around, she was expecting him. The woman said she was, and promised to go look for her. She returned a minute or so later, sans trolley.

"She says wait here 'n she'll be down in a minute, love."

Henry waited. The reception area was a kaleidoscope of posters and leaflets, for local drug rehabilitation programs, for Alcoholics Anonymous, for shelters, Citizen's advice... He was still contemplating all the myriad ways a human being could fall foul of life when he heard someone call his name.

"Henry White?"

A sturdy-looking, pinafore-clad woman with peroxide-blonde hair and a hard but not mean face stood in the corridor.

Henry moved to meet her. "For my sins. And you're Sarah O'Brien?"

"I am," she answered. "I understand you're curious about 65 Oakbourne road? That right?"

"It is."

"Why?"

There was nothing casual in the question, and Henry saw that even now after agreeing to meet him this woman could still decide she didn't like what she saw and keep whatever secrets she might have to herself. Unwilling to risk falling foul of her bullshit detector unless absolutely necessary, he told the truth.

"I have a friend; her mother was one of the people who died in the fire there. I think her name was Valerie."

"And what would your friend's name be?"

"Kate."

Sarah O'Brien pursed her lips, looked Henry up and down and finally said, "Come on, let's go grab a table in the canteen."

Henry accompanied Sarah O'Brien along the corridor into the room beyond. The canteen was half full, populated mostly with men. He guessed the majority of them were homeless. He and Sarah joined the queue and got two cups of tea, ten pence each. Henry scanned the chalk board menu. The day centre offered inexpensive meals and a few of the canteen's patrons looked like they could do with one. Alcohol was a powerful tonic for forgetting your troubles for a bit, but didn't score big in any of the five main food groups. Henry's mind wandered back to Dr William

Lockley. He wondered how far the doctor was from eating his lunch somewhere like this. According to its web page, apart from a cheap meal, the centre also offered its patrons showers, haircuts, and advice with claiming benefits, housing and clothing, all made possible by volunteers like Sarah O'Brien. Angels wore pinnies instead of wings around these parts.

Sarah guided Henry to a quiet table at the corner of the room. He pulled out a chair for her and was rewarded with a nod and a modest smile. He took a seat opposite.

"So you volunteer here?" he asked.

"I offer what help I can. I know first-hand, life can be tough. A good many of the people in this room have nothing. Well, save for problems, I suppose. They've no shortage of those." She sipped her tea, and held Henry's eye. "What are you hoping I can tell you Mr White?"

To the point, aren't we? Good, Henry thought.

"You stayed at 65 Oakbourne Road for a time, and if what Mathew Mears tells me is true you left because you grew uneasy with what was going on there. My friend Kate lived there too, and now she's got mixed up with the place again…"

"Mixed up how?"

"Someone's got her involved with a medium who claims her mother's spirit, Valerie, is trying to tell her something, send her some kind of message. Her father died recently, her adopted father, I mean, and naturally she's grieving, confused and vulnerable. She's lost a lot of people close to her, her birth mother, her adopted mother, her husband, her son… Not long ago she told me she felt cursed, and because she lost her birth mum first, for some reason she's come to believe that could be the key to it all. If I can give her answers as to what went on at 65 Oakbourne Road, then maybe she won't be so keen to mess around with mediums and séances to get them."

"A medium, eh?"

Henry waited.

"Alright, Mr White, I'll tell you what I can remember about what went on in that house on Oakbourne Road, although whether or not you choose to believe me is up to you. It was a long time ago now, and sometimes even I wonder if some of the things that happened really happened. Then again, I think perhaps I'd have slept better over the years if they hadn't."

—

"I came here from Belfast in 1989 for two reasons, to get myself an abortion and to escape my family, although the other way around works just as well.

"I'd got friendly with a boy. He was a little older than me, we fooled around some, and being young and silly I got to thinking I was in love with him. Worse still, I was daft enough to think he felt the same way about me. One time things went a bit further than usual, and… Well, I'm sure you can guess the next part. When I told him I was pregnant he changed from the charming rogue I'd fell in love with to a sneering stranger just like that, said the baby must be someone else's. When I told him it couldn't be because he was the only boy I'd ever slept with, he just laughed at me like I was crazy. He said I was a slag, and that I'd probably been with half the estate. It was when I told my mum and da that things really turned ugly, though.

"My da went straight over to his house and beat the tar out of both him, his da, and his two brothers. After about a week of feuding it was finally agreed I and the boy would get married; I don't recall taking a great part in these discussions. Everyone thought the problem had been sorted, but not me. The last thing on earth I was

335

going to do was marry that boy, which begged the question of what was going to be done about the child. I did some hard thinking, stole the savings from the tin my da kept at the back of his wardrobe and left for England.

"I found a cheap bedsit to rent, and I got an abortion. Unfortunately the money didn't go as far as I'd hoped. My landlord wasn't big on charity, so I found myself kicked out on the street. I tried a few hostels, but more often than not I ended up sleeping rough. It wasn't too bad to begin with, it was high summer, but winter rolled around soon enough."

"You never once thought of going home?"

"Never. Once they'd found out what I'd done they'd have turned me away in any case. I was never going to be able to go home. I had no family anymore. After a while I made a few friends, but their situation was no better than mine. Then, just as things were looking grim, one of them, a nice girl called Lisa, found herself somewhere to stay. She'd met some woman called Selene Cole, a New Age hippy type who Lisa said sometimes handed out sandwiches and blankets to rough sleepers. Anyway this Selene woman had a big house in Edgbaston and she offered Lisa a room for a while, to get herself back on her feet. Lisa took her up on the offer, and that was the last I saw of her, until she came looking for me a month or so later. She looked different, clean, healthy and happy. I asked her how things were and she started raving about Selene and her other half, a fella called Lawrence, and their house, about how great it was, about how there were other kids like us there. She said that was why she'd come to find me. She'd asked Selene and Lawrence if I could stay with them for a while too. They'd said maybe, and suggested I come see them. Well it was mid-November around then, so sick of sleeping rough and half-freezing

336

to death, and with Lisa telling me I'd be mad not to give it a try, I thought, why not?

"She took me to 65 Oakbourne Road and I met Selene and Lawrence. We talked. I was honest with them, told them why and how I'd wound up sleeping on the street. They seemed like a nice enough couple, genuinely interested and genuinely sympathetic. I remember Selene telling me life was full of hard choices and that I wasn't to feel guilty about doing what I'd done. They said if Lisa was willing to share her room with me that was okay with them, until I got back on my feet. With the alternative being November and December on the streets I didn't have to think too hard on it. I moved in there and then."

"What was it like in the house?"

"Great, to begin with. It was like Lisa said; there were others like us there. Lenny, whose da had thrown him out because he found out he was gay, Darren, who was a bit of a dope head, but sweet as anyone I'd ever met, Sandra, whose boyfriend had run off and left her with a bunch of debts and their son, Tim, to look after—"

"Timothy Lamb?

"That's right. How did you know that?"

"My friend. She doesn't remember much, but she remembered his name. He was the boy who also got out alive."

"He was."

"I'm sorry. I didn't mean to interrupt you. Please, go on."

"There were a few others at the house too, but I suppose it'll be Valerie you're interested in. I remember her well, Val and me, we became pretty good friends. Her little girl, your friend, Katie? Real sweetie she was, cute as a button. Val had already been living at 65 Oakbourne Road for a while when I arrived. Once I got to know her a bit she told me how she'd wound up there.

"Val might not have come from a 'good' Catholic family like me, but her da hadn't been any happier than mine when she'd told him she'd got pregnant. He threw her out on the spot, told her not to bother coming back. The difference between us was, where I'd run away to get rid of my baby, Val ran away because she wanted to keep hers. She got mixed up with a married man, you see, at fifteen years of age. As you might imagine, when she told him she was pregnant he wasn't exactly overjoyed." Sarah O'Brien turned a dour eye on Henry. "Your lot are a wonderful bunch sometimes."

Henry responded with an apologetic shrug, accepting his sex guilty as charged.

"Want to know how she got mixed up with him?" Sarah asked.

"Go on."

"She was his children's babysitter. He used to drive her home afterwards, sweet-talk her, compliment her on how pretty she was, how she could be a model if she wanted. Then came the old chestnut; he was lonely. He and his wife didn't love each other anymore. Their marriage was a sham, had been for years, and no doubt plenty more rubbish besides to get inside her drawers… He was handsome, Val said, and I've no doubt a proper charmer, right up until the moment she told him the result of the pregnancy test she bought from the local chemist. He said she would have to get rid of it, and quick. It was okay, he would help her arrange it and that would be that. The mistake would be fixed. They could go on with their lives, but maybe cool things off for a while. Val was devastated. She told him she'd keep him out of it, that she wouldn't tell anyone who the baby's father was, but she was keeping her child and that was that. She braced herself and shared the news with her mum and dad.

338

"Her dad didn't take it well. He went wild, called her all sorts, filled a couple of black bags with her clothes and threw her out. Her mum was a timid thing by all accounts, said nothing to support her and did nothing either. With nowhere else to go, Val went back to her married fella, said she needed money, to pay for the abortion and to disappear for a while afterwards. Our married chap stumped up. Val took her cash, jumped on a train, and headed somewhere nobody knew her, taking her unborn baby and leaving all the shame and scandal behind her. You look surprised, Mr White. True, this was the late eighties, and sure enough attitudes were changing. The shame of being a single mum was fading, but attitudes hadn't changed where I came from, or where Val came from it seemed.

"Still, she was just a kid. She couldn't have known how hard it would be. She kept her child, though, and tried to raise her right. She did her best, until she got mixed up with a fella who turned out to be worse than her da and her daughter's da rolled into one. Val said he had the temper of the first and was about as principled as the second. Years later, and poor Val's taste in men was still rotten. So she ran away again, spent time in a few homeless women hostels, fighting to keep Social Services from taking her daughter off her, then she bumped into Selene and Lawrence. They offered her a break and like me and the others there she took it."

"But...?"

"As nice as things were at 65 Oakbourne Road, they weren't what you would call normal. On the face of it I guess you could have taken us for a sort of weird happy family. Mum and Dad—Selene and Lawrence—and us kids, a family of misfits, and it was as nice as that sounds, for a while, before things got too weird."

"Too weird?

"Selene and Lawrence, they were kind of hippies, but without the tie-dye and flower power. They were spiritual, always going on about the power of positive thinking and chanting affirmations and the like, always telling us we had to believe something was possible before we could hope to make it happen. It was nothing heavy to begin with, but as we started to go along with it things steadily started pushing further. We were encouraged to gather and talk about what we wanted from life, and then to ask the universe to give us these things. I think we all felt a bit daft at first, but we were all grateful to Selene and Lawrence too. We wanted to keep them happy, so we went along with it, and to be honest in those early days it did seem to help. As things wore on, we stopped feeling daft and started to open up. All of us were messed up one way or another, and talking about it helped us see life wasn't just something that happened to you. You played your part too. And if it had just stopped there I wouldn't have had any problems with it."

"How did things change?"

"The affirmations changed, started to become something closer to rituals. They began to involve objects that were supposed to represent what each of us wanted. The use of drugs became more common; a bit of grass to begin with, which most of us used a bit of now and then, but soon other stuff most of us hadn't messed around with before. Hallucinogenic stuff, brewed up in tea, magic mushrooms, peyote... Unsurprisingly, it was around this time things really started to change. The gatherings stopped being just about helping us change our outlook, and started to include fooling around with other stuff. Selene encouraged it, 'experimenting' she called it, 'just a bit of fun'."

"What kind of stuff are we talking about, Sarah?"

"Trying to talk to each other without speaking, trying to see with your mind what was happening in another room, trying to light matchsticks just by focusing your mind on them, or move things without touching them. It seemed innocent enough at first, like Selene said, just a bit of fun. Only the problem with the drugs was it was impossible to know what you'd really done or seen. What was real, and what were hallucinations? I 'saw' people lift up off the carpet, saw someone make a marble spin off a book cover just by staring at it and concentrating, and more besides, but you could never be sure, you see? And Selene always insisted that it didn't really matter anyway. If we all *believed* something had happened, then it had. Some really got into it, but I just felt confused and more and more uneasy. I felt smothered too. No one really left the house very much. It had all got very inward-looking. I would make up reasons to sneak out, take walks... I struck up a friendship with a boy who lived down the road. It helped me see things clearly again, so that when things started going even further I knew it was time for me to move on."

"Further, how?"

"They started trying to talk to spirits, doing séances, using Ouija boards and the like... I was raised a good Catholic girl, and even after all that had happened to me there was still enough of that girl left to know fooling around with that stuff is plain wrong.

"I made excuses not to take part. Selene noticed, and although nothing was said outright, nothing aggressive, no shouting, somehow I knew not going along with it was causing a rift. Eventually it was going to come to a head.

"It was hard. I'd started to think of the place as my home, I'd made friends. I went to see the only other real friend I had outside the house, the boy up the road. I told him about what was going on, and that I wanted to leave, to move away, maybe somewhere up north. The problem was I had next to no money. He said he'd been saving for a racing bike, and offered to lend me what he had, said I could pay him back once I got on my feet." Sarah smiled. "It's funny isn't it? Only looking back years later did it occur to me that he was probably a bit sweet on me.

"So I took his money, got up one morning very early before everyone else, packed my stuff into a rucksack and left. I hitchhiked up here to Manchester, managed to get myself a room in a WMCA, and soon after that a job. I sent the boy's racing bike money back, every penny, along with a postcard or two, letting him know how I was getting on. The next time I thought about 65 Oakbourne Road was when that newspaper fella, our friend, Mathew Mears, turned up looking for me. He told me how he'd written a newspaper story about a house fire in Birmingham. Six people had died in the blaze, 65 Oakbourne Road. He asked a few questions, and for some reason I told him a bit about what had gone on there. I think I needed to get it off my chest. And then, I got on with my life.

"I won't say I've not thought about that house over the years, and what happened to the friends I made there, and maybe what spared me from sharing their fate." Sarah O'Brien paused, and then said, "My faith is the reason I'm still alive, Mr White. I believe that, I truly do. What they were fooling around with in that house was wrong. Don't misunderstand me, I'm not saying it was God himself who saved me, but it *was* my faith in him told me I shouldn't be taking part in that kind of business."

"And the children got out too, remember."

Sarah seemed to think about this, and smiled, "Yes, they did didn't they? The children got out too."

"And Lawrence."

The smile evaporated. Sarah O'Brien's brow became a puzzled frown. "Yes, that's true too." She looked slightly thrown.

"Did you know he was sick?" Henry added, "He died less than a year later, you know? He had cancer, a brain tumour."

"No, I knew he went crazy, but I didn't know he died so soon after. The tumour makes sense now though."

"How so?"

"He used to get headaches, really bad ones. Sometimes he wouldn't come out his room for a whole day they were so bad, and the day after he would look like death warmed up."

They talked for a while longer, but Sarah O'Brien's part in the story had come to an end. Henry thanked her and left the day centre.

He already knew his next move. He wanted to speak to Lawrence Hawley's ex-wife.

Chapter 56

Nadine lay on the bed, waiting for the phone to ring.

Sebastian had promised to call, but once again evening had slid into night without a word from him. Ever since Kate Bennett had arrived at The Retreat, Nadine had been forced to stay at Sebastian's apartment in the city. If the pretence of Nadine being a medium Sebastian had sought out was to be maintained then naturally she couldn't stay at The Retreat with him, not while Kate Bennett was there, and yet Sebastian said he had to be there to keep watch over Bennett.

This situation chafed. She had seen the way Kate Bennett caught his eye, and in her deepest moments of paranoia, times such as this when he neglected to call despite promising to, it was all too easy to imagine she had been forgotten. Anxiety gnawed at her, and for relief she had resorted to the old remedy. Crisscrossed along her pale forearms ran a series of fresh cuts, not deep, just enough to draw a little blood.

They had spent so long waiting, planning, and now they were so very close. Nadine wanted it done. The date was approaching quickly, but, for her, not nearly fast enough. She rolled over on her side, tried to ignore the twisting in her gut and sleep.

Beside her the phone remained silent.

Chapter 57

Scarcely five weeks had passed since her dad's funeral, but to Kate it felt longer, like a different season. In a literal sense it soon would be. Summer was drawing to a close; the greedy fingers of early autumn were already stealing rusty leaves from the trees, but inside the changes seemed to ring deeper still.

She had sought out Sebastian upon waking, and asked him if he would accompany her somewhere. He had asked where. She had told him, and he had said of course, in that 'nothing is too much trouble' way he did.

The cemetery was quiet. It was a mid-week afternoon and visitors were thin on the ground. She bought flowers from a stall outside the cemetery gates, now she laid them down, fussing with their arrangement, wanting them to look nice.

Sebastian had offered to wait in his car, but she had asked if he wouldn't mind coming into the cemetery with her. She didn't want to be alone, not just yet. They stood in silence for a time, in front of the graves of her father, her mother, her husband and son. Perhaps still concerned he was intruding, Sebastian had asked Kate if she would like him to take a stroll for a while. "Perhaps, in a few minutes?" she had replied, and he had nodded.

Kate looked over the plots. This would be her final resting place too. Her dad had arranged for it when he had helped her deal with Robert and Joel's funerals. There was a space for her here, although part of her felt like it was here already, had been for years.

"I thought I knew where my life was going. You know?" she heard herself say suddenly. "I'd made all these assumptions, and then in one fucked up afternoon everything changed. One afternoon was all it took for my son to never get his first day at school, never go off to university, never fall in love, get married, have children... My husband and I would never be grandparents, we'd never retire to the cottage we joked about somewhere sleepy, we'd never grow old together... One afternoon and they were both gone." Kate stopped, her throat suddenly too tight to speak.

"And you were left wondering how the hell you were supposed to go on without them?" Dahl responded. He met her eye and smiled. The smile was sorrowful, enough to be an explanation of sorts. "I lost someone too. We weren't married, but..."

"You loved her?"

Dahl nodded, his gaze shifting to the graves before them.

He nodded slowly. "Very, *very*, much."

"Is she... what happened?"

"She died, and there's not a single day passes she doesn't cross my mind."

"And if you could have her back, have things just the way they were?" Kate asked.

"I would give anything, everything. Wouldn't you?"

"In a heartbeat."

Dahl reached out and touched her hand.

"I really do think I should wait in the car now," he said. "Take as long as you need."

She watched him go. Take as long as she needed? She could wait until the earth tumbled into the sun and it wouldn't be long enough. Her mum was gone. Her dad was gone. Robert and Joel were gone. They would always be gone, and that meant she would always be broken. How could it ever be otherwise?

She knelt, fussed with the flowers some more, said a few things, first to Joel, then to Robert, and finally to her dad. Then, as always after such visits, she wondered if the whole exercise had helped or just

346

scratched at places within her that were still tender and sore.

And finally when there was nothing left to say, she bid her lost family goodbye and returned to Dahl, dutifully waiting in his car.

Chapter 58

Ray delivered the goods again. The former Mrs Lawrence Hawley, Margaret Hawley, was alive and well and living in a care home in Cheshire, but he had more. While conducting his search, Ray had discovered Margaret Hawley had co-authored a number of books during the late fifties and early sixties with her husband Lawrence Hawley. The Hawleys were academics, social anthropologists, whose field of expertise lay in travelling cultures, specifically gypsy travellers. Despite it being long out of print Ray had even managed to obtain a copy of one of their books from an online used book dealer who specialised in academic texts. Henry had spent a while leafing through it and found it surprisingly interesting.

Spying an angle, he called the care home where Margaret Hawley lived and presented himself as an amateur interested in Margaret and her past work. A short conversation with Margaret Hawley followed, and an arrangement to meet the following day.

The care home was clearly of the upmarket variety, a big detached house in a leafy area with well-kept gardens and a cosy ambiance. It reminded Henry of a guest house his family used to holiday at when he was a kid. Stepping into its entrance hallway was like stepping into another decade. One of the home's staff, Joan, a cheery middle-aged woman welcomed him in and had him sign the visitors' book. From here he was led through to the common room where Margaret and a group of other elderly folk were watching afternoon television.

Henry introduced himself and with the aid of a Zimmer frame Margaret got to her feet. She said they would be able to talk more freely in her room. They rode a small lift to the third floor where Margaret's room was.

Margaret lowered herself into one of a pair of armchairs positioned either side of a window overlooking the gardens. As Henry took up her invitation of the other armchair, Joan rapped on the door and enquired if either of them would like a drink. Margaret declined and Henry said he was fine too. Joan said to let her know if they changed their minds and took her leave.

Margaret Hawley was in her late eighties, but looked remarkably well for it. Impeccably groomed and wearing a salmon-coloured knitted cardigan with pearls, she surveyed Henry with intelligent eyes and a warm smile.

"So," asked Margaret when they were settled, "what exactly is it you'd like to discuss? Is there an area of my work that's of particular interest to you?"

"Ah... I should probably put my cards on the table," Henry answered. "It's not just your work I'm interested in, but your late husband, Lawrence Hawley."

The old woman stiffened, straightening in her chair. "I see. And what exactly were you hoping I might be able to tell you about him?"

"I was wondering if you might tell me what he was like. What sort of person he was, something about his background."

"What sort of person he was?" Margaret said, almost without expression. "That will be easy enough. Lawrence was a selfish cowardly cheat. He ran off with a girl half his age and never once looked back. Now if that will be all, Joan can show you out."

"I'm sorry, I never intended to upset you—"

Margaret Hawley's steely gaze held fast.

"I'd like to explain, if I can?" Henry said. "Please?"

The old woman waited.

"Lawrence Hawley was only one of three people to survive a house fire in 1989," Henry said. "My friend, Kate, was another and right now she's in trouble. I believe the key to helping her lies in understanding what happened in that house, maybe before the fire, maybe on the night of the fire itself."

"Go on."

Henry did. He explained about the show, about Sebastian Dahl and his house and everything else. Margaret Hawley listened patiently. When he had finished, he shrugged. It sounded insane when laid out, but if there was a chance Lawrence Hawley was a key to the puzzle... He needed answers, and Margaret Hawley might be one of the few people left who had them. On the up side, she hadn't started yelling for someone to eject the crazy man from her room, or at least not yet. In fact, she looked almost sympathetic.

Her first words were, "A spirit?"

"You don't believe in them?" Henry asked.

"I believe in a good many things, Mr White, but I understand you wanted me to tell you about Lawrence..."

Chapter 59

"Lawrence and I met at Oxford University in 1951. We were both students of social anthropology.

"It's fair to say I was attracted to Lawrence from the start. He was handsome, and in the most alluring way, by which I mean he was almost completely unaware he was. On top of this, he always seemed so unburdened and carefree, unlike most of my peers. Later, of course, I discovered the truth, that he was literally unburdened and carefree. His family were what you might call old money, minor aristocracy, land owners initially, until Lawrence's grandfather sold off much of these at the turn of the century and invested the capital in the financial markets. He chose wisely and the family did very well out of it. They were respectable, wealthy and extremely well-connected. There was never any question of Lawrence having to work for a living. He was inclined toward academia, and was drawn to the developing field of social anthropology. Perhaps because he belonged to a clan of sorts, social groups, tribes, cultures, clans were something that held a fascination for him.

"This is what initially brought us together. Lawrence and I shared an interest in the cultures of travelling peoples, gypsies in particular. Social anthropology, as you're perhaps aware, concerns itself with the study of how human beings behave in social groups, structures of family, economic interactions, politics, religion... Nomadic cultures such as gypsy clans are particularly intriguing because they operate outside of geographical constraints. Many are also very old, and as a rule very secretive.

"Lawrence and I began courting, and soon after were engaged. We earned our degrees and were married the year after we left university. I suspect there were eyebrows raised at Lawrence's choice among the Hawley family, but his parents rarely denied him what he wanted, even if that was to wed a girl from common stock. They always treated me courteously, and their wealth made it possible for Lawrence and me to pursue our shared passion. We began planning and researching our first book, an examination of Romany travellers. We were very happy, and keen to become parents. After two years our first book was published. A child, however, remained elusive.

"We resolved to stay optimistic. So long as we were patient, we told ourselves, children would come when they were good and ready. There was no rush, we were both still young. In the meantime we poured our energies into our work. We travelled widely, seeking out travelling peoples, talking with them, and studying them. When able, we would fight their corner when they met with prejudice or injustice. We made friends of many such groups, and during the course of our interactions with the most venerable of them we encountered a reoccurring myth with intriguingly common elements. It dealt with the origin of the travellers, the very first tribe of gypsies to roam the ancient world.

"According to the story the first travellers were Egyptians, led by an exiled lector priest. The tale differed marginally between tellings, but broadly it went thus:

"During the reign of King Ramses III, a lector priest led a group of his followers, courtiers, and harem ladies in a plot to bring down the pharaoh. The priest was a skilled magician, who had long experimented with sorcery and forbidden magic of the darkest kind, and using this knowledge he crafted a spell designed to destroy his king and all his bodyguards in one fell swoop.

"Using the ladies of the harem, the lector priest obtained hair, nail clippings and bodily fluids belonging to the king and his protectors, which he then fashioned into detailed effigies of his enemies, preparing them for the ritual that would bring about their demise.

"On the eve of the ritual, however, the priest and his conspirators were betrayed by one of their own. Furious, the king dispatched soldiers to seize the priest and his cohorts for execution. In the ensuing skirmish the priest and a number of his group somehow managed to escape, although not without cost. The priest was severely beaten and stabbed several times.

"Despite this, his faithful conspirators succeeded in smuggling his broken body beyond the city walls, where upon they fled the kingdom. Through the use of powerful magic the priest restored himself to health. He kept his life, but his plot had failed. He and his group were exiles, fugitives, branded traitors, imperilled everywhere the pharaoh's influence extended, forced to roam distant lands, never certain of their safety.

"The priest was alleged to have wandered the earth for the span of many mortal lifetimes, leaving Egypt far behind him, and after his passing his clan lived on, continuing to travel to all the distant corners of the earth. In later ages the clan, sometimes referred to as The Exiles, sometimes the Grey Road Clan, splintered, spawning other travelling clans, each of them retaining elements of the old culture, the Romani, Dom, Lom, Banjara, Leniche and others.

"This was to be the priest's legacy, his final victory. While Egypt's power waned the clan and its progeny endured, carrying all their knowledge and secrets with them throughout the centuries.

"Over the years we would occasionally hear whispers that the Grey Road Clan had been encountered by other wandering folk, a clan that could trace their lineage directly back to the mother tribe that left Egypt, the last true keepers of that tribe's ancient secrets."

Margaret smiled, a dry curl of the lips, and added, "Of course there was absolutely no evidence to support the existence of any actual Grey Road Clan, but that didn't prevent Lawrence falling in love with the legend, and becoming obsessed with tracking them down. As I said before, Lawrence came from a wealthy family, a family which was content for him to indulge whatever passion took his fancy, and because I loved him and shared his passion I was happy to indulge him too. We spent the next ten years travelling the world, searching for evidence of the clan. Many of our expeditions took us deep into Eastern Europe. This was back when the Iron Curtain still existed, and it was perhaps only because we were academics, and more specifically academics with money, that we were able to explore places where others often were not.

"Once or twice we arrived at places where the clan were alleged to have recently camped at or passed through. Lawrence was always thrilled on such occasions, convinced we were getting ever closer, I was, as they say, rather more sceptical.

"And then we found them."

Chapter 60

Margaret Hawley leant back in her armchair.

"It took a year of tracking them and much patient negotiation to even get them to talk to us. Perhaps understandably they were wary of us and our interest in them, as they were of all outsiders, but when one of the clan's elders finally agreed to grant us an audience Lawrence just charmed them. The key was knowledge. Lawrence had spent a good deal of his adult life studying not just their kind, but their tribe in particular. The sheer force of his enthusiasm, dedication and sincerity gained their trust, or as much as any outsider was able to—which wasn't all that far to be frank.

"He kept at it though, kept in contact, and helped them out whenever he could. Occasionally they would agree to let us meet with them. Lawrence and I would share our thoughts and our studies into their kind with them, and slowly their trust in us grew. They began to share small details of their tribe's history and beliefs. I have to confess, these were fascinating. Their outlook was intensely spiritual, extremely superstitious; the existence of sorcery and magic was deeply ingrained in their culture.

"Over the next few years we met periodically with them wherever they happened to be, continuing to glean what we could about their ways, their customs, culture and religion... not in view to publishing anything of an academic nature about them, but simply to satisfy our personal curiosity. We had earned this kind of access, not because we were academics but because we had become their friends, and we knew that to publish anything they shared with us would have meant an abrupt end to the relationship. It was a price we were content to pay.

"In the winter of 1967 we met with the clan after a break of some eighteen months. The invitation had been extended to us earlier in the year; we were welcome to meet with them when they planned to arrive in Kemer, Turkey, at the tail end of November.

"We found them camped on the outskirts of the village, but as soon as we approached them we knew something was wrong. We expected to be welcomed in the usual way, but instead we were told to leave immediately. After some wrangling, Lawrence managed to talk to one of the elders. If there was some sort of problem, he said, maybe we could help? The elder thanked him, but said no, we were to go. Lawrence asked if we could at least beg their hospitality until the next day; it was late and the weather was turning bad... With considerable reluctance the elder relented and we were taken in.

"It was a youth whom Lawrence teased the truth out of. The boy had been a small child when we first encountered the clan, and was now in his teens. He'd grown up accustomed to us, and so perhaps trusted us more than he should have.

"The crisis that had the clan in turmoil involved one of the elders, a matriarchal figure, and a young girl who had been caring for her. Both had been held under lock and key for several weeks. The boy claimed not to know why, all he knew was the matriarch was very sick, and seemingly deranged. As for the girl, she was withdrawn and all but mute.

"In an effort to find a solution to the crisis, and admittedly curious too, Lawrence waited until early morning and crept out to one of the caravans the two were being imprisoned in and spoke to the girl. He knew her. Like the boy she had grown up used to our visits. If she had been almost mute with her clan people, she was not so reserved with Lawrence. She told him the Matriarch had lost her mind, had accused

356

her of being possessed by an evil spirit. She was scared, she said, and told Lawrence her worst fear. She was terrified the clan would deal with the problem by putting her to death. When he tried to reassure her they surely would do no such thing, that he would talk to the elders, make them see sense, the girl only grew more agitated. He thought he knew the clan, she said, but he did not. She assured him similar crises had been dealt with this way in the past and would be again. If he truly wanted to help her then he should take a pair of bolt cutters from the blacksmith's caravan and help her to escape...

"Fearing what might transpire if we failed to intervene, we helped the girl escape. She was eighteen, scarcely a child, and the clan had no legal control over her. We took her with us, booking rooms for the three of us at the Istanbul Hilton. Our plan was to get the girl to safety, then attempt to mediate with the clan, deal with the issue, and perhaps even see her returned to the fold. The girl, however, had other ideas. When we told her our intentions, she became almost hysterical. She said she wanted nothing further to do with the clan. We assumed she would calm down, begin to miss her kin, and eventually come around.

"We stayed two months at the Istanbul Hilton. One afternoon I returned to find them gone: Lawrence, and the girl. The room had been emptied of all belongings but my own.

"I was in shock, I think. A part of me wanted to believe I'd got it wrong, that it was all some big misunderstanding. Something must have happened to force Lawrence to flee with the girl suddenly. They would come back, contact me and tell me where to join them.

"I stayed a further fortnight at the hotel, slowly and miserably coming to my senses. Devastated, I resolved to leave, return home, try to regain my equilibrium and work out what exactly had happened, but before I departed the clan found me.

"I arrived back at my room one evening to find someone in my room, one of the clan elders. I knew not to waste time asking how he had got in, and instead asked him what he wanted. He eyed me dispassionately. I told him Lawrence and the girl were gone; Lawrence had deserted me. The elder did not seem surprised, but unless I imagined it, he seemed to soften a little toward me. He told me the clan's crisis was over; the matriarch had passed away several days past. It was done, and so were we. He warned me never to attempt contacting the clan again. I was no longer welcome, I had betrayed them and this would never be forgotten.

"As for the girl, as far as the clan was concerned, she was free, but banished. Should she encounter them at any point in the future she would be certain to regret it. Lawrence too would be wise to never cross the clan's path again.

"And so, not really knowing what else to do, I returned home. What I found was the house emptied of all Lawrence's valued belongings, a lone sheet of writing paper in their place, a letter from my absent husband.

"I won't bore you with the details. Suffice to say the letter contained much in the way of self-justification, some nauseating drivel about 'being a slave to one's heart'… I found it worse than heart-breaking; I found it insulting and terribly inadequate. The only useful purpose it served was to confirm my worst suspicions. My husband had indeed run off with an eighteen-year-old girl and had no intention of returning to me.

"The letter closed with the news that the house was now mine, together with a not inconsiderable sum of money in a joint account we shared. I emptied the account. I sold the house. I did my best to get on with my life.

"In practice this did not prove as easy as I'd hoped. The speed with which my life had been dismantled ate away at me. Bitterness has a way of festering, and in an effort to disinfect the wound and put what had happened behind me I began to look for answers. Despite being warned not to, I sought out the clan.

"It took over a year and a half, targeting locations I knew they favoured, but eventually I found them. When I tried to engage with them, though, they faced me like strangers, demanded I leave. I refused to listen. I trailed them for weeks, and eventually, out of pity I think, the same elder who had come to me in Istanbul agreed to speak to me. I asked him, simply, what had happened? What had the girl done, and why had she been banished? I *needed* to understand. Not knowing was corrosive. Little by little it was destroying me.

"The elder listened to my plea, and seemed to reflect upon it. Then, to my surprise, he told me that if it was truly what I wanted he was willing to tell me what had brought about the crisis the clan were wrestling with prior to my and Lawrence's arrival in Turkey—but that he doubted it would bring me much comfort. I had studied his clan for many years, I knew something of their beliefs, but I did not share them. He would tell me the truth, but it wouldn't matter because I would not believe it. I told him I thought him an honourable man, and that I would take him at his word. With a look that suggested this had done nothing to change his view he nevertheless began to tell me what had happened.

"The events that led to the girl's imprisonment began with one of the clan's elders, a matriarch who commanded great respect and influence. She was viewed as the clan's spiritual mother, venerated for her intimate connection with the clan's ancestral spirits and her knowledge of the old secrets. A woman of advancing years, her health had been in decline for some time. Unbeknownst to the clan, she had been conducting 'workings'—the clan's euphemism for acts of magic or sorcery, in an effort to treat her illness."

At Margaret's mention of 'workings', Henry felt a shiver run though him, but said nothing. Margaret Hawley was in full flow and the last thing he wanted to do was interrupt her.

"The nature of these workings," Margaret Hawley continued, "involved acts that expressly broke the clan's laws, acts that were understood by all to be strictly forbidden. I asked exactly what this meant, but the elder refused to elaborate, instead he told me how he and the other elders had confronted the matriarch. United, they had demanded she cease performing these workings immediately. Contrite, she had agreed, but only days later she was discovered engaging in another.

"The matriarch was again confronted, and again she promised to refrain. This time, however, the elders needed reassurance. They arranged for a trusted younger member of the clan, an eighteen-year-old girl, *the* girl, to attend to the matriarch. The matriarch was frail, the other elders insisted, and was deserving of some assistance. Ultimately, though, they all knew what the girls' true purpose was, the matriarch perhaps most of all, to keep watch on her. The old woman would still be shown the respect she was due, but would be expressly denied anything she might seek to employ in a forbidden working.

"Several weeks passed without further incident. The girl was attentive and the matriarch appeared to grow to enjoy her company. It looked like the problem had been dealt with.

"Then, one night the clan was roused by hysterical screaming. The screams led those who rushed to investigate to the matriarch's caravan, where they found the old woman bound by the wrists and ankles, wearing a gag tugged down to her chin. The girl, however, was nowhere to be seen. When they tried to quiz the old woman as to what had happened she only grew more agitated. Eventually they calmed her sufficiently to make sense of what she was saying. The matriarch had stolen her body, overpowered her, bound her hands and feet, gagged her and fled.

"The clan immediately set out to track the girl down, or if the story was to be believed, the matriarch in the girl's body. They caught up with her a few miles away, and returned her to the camp by force. At first she tried to continue the pretence of being the girl, claiming the old woman had lost her mind. However, when the girl's parents were brought in the deception crumbled. A parent knows their child, and the girl's mother and father knew at once the spirit in the girl's body was not their daughter as surely as they were forced to accept the spirit in the old woman's body was.

"The clan resolved to reverse the matriarch's act of sorcery. They assured the girl and her parents that whatever it took they would find a way to set things right. In truth, though, this proved far from easy. The matriarch was learned and skilled, and when she had carried out the working she had been determined and desperate, a potent combination. Her body had been frail and her health faltering to begin with. After all that had happened, it was only frailer still. Where was the incentive to reverse what she had done and return to her ailing body?

"The clan elders attempted many workings in an attempt to reverse what had been done, but none succeeded. The girl remained trapped in the old woman's body. Without the matriarch's compliance, undoing the crime was beginning to look impossible. The clan tried to reason with the matriarch, and when this failed they resorted to threats. If the old woman's body died with the girl's spirit still trapped inside it, then they would destroy the girl's body and the matriarch would perish too, and the deed would not be carried out compassionately.

"This stalemate persisted until I and Lawrence intervened. The rest you know.

"Once the elder finished telling me what had happened before Lawrence and I arrived, he told me what happened after we left. The matriarch's escape was too much for the girl and the faltering body in which her spirit was trapped. She died only days later, and with no earthly vessel to contain it, her spirit's time on this plain came to an end too.

"Here the elder concluded. It appeared he had nothing more to say. I thanked him and we parted ways.

"I had asked for answers and he had supplied them. It was only some time later I began to wonder why, if perhaps they were intended as a brand of punishment, make me face the true cost of my complicity, see that in comparison to the clan girl and her parents I was a minor victim at best. Either way, I never sought to contact the clan again."

Margaret Hawley fell quiet in her armchair, regarding Henry with her sharp, watery blue eyes. Time may have thinned and creased her skin, weakened her bones, wasted her muscles and bent her back, but Henry saw it had not diminished her mind one bit.

"Do you believe the story the elder told you?" he asked, when it became clear she intended to add nothing more to the tale.

"No, not then, or at least there existed a comfortable corner of me that did not."

"But you changed your mind?"

"I did. In 1989 someone who had once been a mutual friend of Lawrence and I got in touch and informed me of a house fire he had read about, in Birmingham. Half a dozen people had perished in the blaze; there had been only three survivors, one adult and two children. The children were not named, but the adult was. It was Lawrence, and if there were any doubt the survivor was indeed my ex-husband, that was quashed by another detail the story contained. Among names of the dead listed was another I recognised immediately: Selene. It had been the matriarch's name.

"I'd not thought about my ex-husband for many years, a divorce petition had been sought and accepted a decade previously. I had moved on with my life, but the story incited an itch in me. I grew curious enough to make further enquiries. What I discovered was Lawrence had been committed to a mental institution. Due to trauma or perhaps grief he had suffered some sort of mental breakdown. After much internal debate, I eventually contacted the hospital where he was being treated and was able to arrange a visit."

"What did you find? When you saw him?"

"It would be more apposite to tell you what I did not find, and that was Lawrence. The man I encountered may have looked like my ex-husband, an older, greyer, heavier, sicker version, but it wasn't him. Not inside. I have no idea who the poor soul really was, but he was not the man who broke my heart."

"What are you saying?"

"I think you know what I'm saying Mr White, and I think that brings a close to anything I might be able to tell you about Lawrence Hawley. I will, however, offer you one piece of parting advice."

"You will?"

"When dealing with this Sebastian Dahl fellow, I would recommend you take nothing at face value."

Chapter 61

Kate woke to sunlight slicing through the bedroom drapes.

Bleary-eyed and dry-mouthed, she groped for the bedside clock and called upon her sludgy brain to decipher the arrangement of hands and roman numerals. Two p.m. Afternoon already. She'd woken late again.

She wasn't stupid. Recent events were catching up on her, her dad's death, Henry's betrayal. Her head felt stuck in gear, churning everything over and over, which made her feel anxious, which in turn left her exhausted. Mostly, though, she felt detached, numb, like someone had pulled a plug on the place she kept her emotions, allowing them to bleed slowly away, all the positive ones at least.

What she needed was momentum, purpose, an escape from the introspection that threatened to peel away her mental and emotional armour layer by layer, until she was raw and tender as an exposed nerve. She had to get back to the house, resume her dialogue with her mother, get past the seemingly endless series of delays. Nadine Smith's suddenly busy schedule had translated into days of inactivity, causing her to feel trapped in limbo. It had been more than a week since their last visit to the house, and the assurances of 'soon', 'soon', 'soon', were wearing frustratingly thin. After appearing as driven as she was at the outset, Sebastian suddenly seemed happier with a slower, more cautious, pace. Why, she wondered? Was he afraid she was losing it? Unravelling? Could she blame him, when she was beginning to wonder the same thing herself?

Only yesterday she had spent several worrisome minutes trying to work out exactly how long she had been staying at The Retreat. The answer turned out to be twenty-seven days. Including today that made... twenty-eight, now? Or had that been the day before yesterday?

Part of the problem was staying at The Retreat was too easy. Her meals were prepared for her, her clothes washed and dried, there were people around, even if she hadn't exactly been socialising much. It was enough to allow herself to feel she wasn't isolated. In a sense, The Retreat was the perfect dark corner in which to curl up, somewhere she didn't have to deal with the outside world, with all its tiresome obligations and complications. She quelled her conscience by telling herself this was what she needed right now, an oasis, somewhere she could concentrate on the past and her mother, because until these were dealt with nothing else mattered. Perhaps once they made sense she could move forward again.

When Sebastian returned this evening she would appeal to him to press Nadine, try to get her back to the house again soon.

Before the pull of the undertow grew too strong.

Chapter 62

Henry called Ray first. The serpentine edges of a puzzle were slotting together in his mind, a story was taking shape. What he needed now was to lay the story out, see if it sounded as crazy out loud as it did in his head.

Ray had listened patiently, never once interrupting. When he finished Henry asked, "So am I crazy?"

On the other end of the line Henry heard Ray blow air slowly through his lips. Then came a pause and his reply, "If you are then we should probably get them to measure me for a straitjacket too. It's hard to know what to think. There's a big part of me says this stuff is impossible, but... I know what I saw when we took part in that first séance. I saw Kate talking, and knew it wasn't her in charge for a while there. You need to speak to the rest of the crew. If Kate's in danger they'll want to help."

"I don't know, Ray. Charles might believe, but the others—"

"Trust you, and care about Kate."

—

They all met up at Ray's house. Every seat in his lounge was taken. Mark, Keith, Claire and Charles had all answered the call, and Henry loved each and every one of them for that alone.

Ray had primed them the best he could, but the story was the story. Either they would believe it or they wouldn't.

The story. Henry delivered it steadily and soberly, assembled from facts and anecdotes, gaffer-taped together with several swatches of guesswork. It went something like this.

In 1951 two students of social anthropology meet at university. They are united by an academic interest in travelling folk. They become lovers and, after graduation, husband and wife. They spend the next decade and a half fostering relationships with various gypsy groups, documenting their cultures and customs. During this period they encounter a reoccurring story, the legend of a gypsy clan who claim to trace their lineage back to the very first travellers who were believers in and practitioners of sorcery. Captivated by the tale, Lawrence is determined to find them, and after years of searching he does just this, and fosters a relationship with them.

In 1967, Lawrence and Margaret visit the clan, and find them in crisis. They are holding two of their number captive, a matriarch of the clan called Selene and an eighteen-year-old girl. The Hawleys help the girl escape. A short while after this Lawrence runs off with her, leaving Margaret devastated and confused.

In an effort to make sense of what happened, Margaret returns to the clan seeking answers and discovers the nature of the crisis she and her husband took it upon themselves to intervene in, and the subsequent repercussions. The elder clansman tells Margret how the old woman performed an act of forbidden sorcery, stealing the girl's body and driving the girl's spirit into her own sick and aging one. The clan was seeking to reverse the crime when Margaret and Lawrence helped the girl, or more accurately the old woman in the girl's body, escape. Without the girl this became impossible. Only days later the old woman's frail and ailing body expired, taking the young girl's soul with it. Haunted by the gypsy elder's tale,

Margaret returns to the ruins of her life and attempts to move on.

Some twenty-two years later, in 1989, Lawrence Hawley, by now in his late fifties, and the girl, now a grown woman in her middle years, buy a house in Edgbaston, Birmingham, 65 Oakbourne Road. They begin to offer shelter to waifs and strays, young people who have no one to ask awkward questions should anything happen to them. Valerie Jones is among them. She is mother to a seven-year-old girl, Kate.

Lawrence and Selene cultivate a free-thinking household, and their guests soon fall in with it. The couple begin by encouraging positive thinking, and 'tapping into the energies of the universe', but in time the experiments start. Stuff that doubtless seems like a bit of fun to begin with, just fooling around. There are attempts at telekinesis, mind reading, astral projection, pyrokinesis, Ouija boards, and all sorts of other paranormal/spiritualist/mystical thinking-type stuff. A good deal of drug use accompanies these experiments, rendering the results highly subjective, or to put it another way—how can you know what you've really seen when you're high as a kite and tripping balls?

One or two, like Sarah O'Brien, perhaps sensing something wrong is going on beneath the surface of Lawrence and Selene's altruistic refuge, grow uneasy enough to leave. Those who remain coalesce into a trusting, unquestioning group happy to engage in whatever experiments Lawrence and Selene guide them into.

They don't know Lawrence and Selene have a plan.

Lawrence is dying. There's a tumour growing in his brain. It gives him monster headaches, and some day in the not-too-distant future it will kill him. The house's guests are elements of a working Selene and Lawrence are carefully constructing, a way for Lawrence to escape his fate.

The evening arrives where the working is set in motion, only something goes awry. Somewhere between Lawrence successfully stealing the body of Timothy Lamb, and Selene attempting to steal the body of the girl who will grow into Kate Bennett, a fire starts. Only three people escape: Lawrence, Kate and Tim. Timothy Lamb, bewildered at finding himself trapped in the body of Lawrence Hawley, quickly finds himself confined to a mental institution. Lawrence (in Tim's body) and Kate are taken into care.

Kate is adopted. Lawrence bounces through a few foster homes before running away, emerging years later going by a new name, Sebastian Dahl. He acquires the house in Oakbourne road, demolishes it and rebuilds it halfway across the country on the coast, transporting Selene's spirit along with it, and begins to search for Kate, a task that can't have proved easy, hard enough to take years. Let's say somewhere around ten.

Here Henry stopped. Until now he had resisted the urge to study any of the faces before him. He had wanted to present his case first.

"What does Dahl want?" he said."If I'm honest, I think he wants to finish what he and Selene started back in the house on Oakbourne Road all those years ago. I think he wants to take Selene's spirit and put it into Kate's body. And who the hell knows where that will leave Kate."

There was a long pause, and then Keith simply said, "I'm in."

For a moment Henry was lost.

"You're in?"

"Yeah," said Keith. "We're going to snatch Kate back right? Like in America when one of those crazy cults gets their hooks into someone, the Moonies or whatnot, and their families kidnap them back."

"And you're prepared to help me do that?" Henry asked, trying to keep up with the direction Keith's response had steered things in.

"Me too," said Claire.

"And me," said Mark.

Ray nodded vigorously. "Let's do it."

"Of course you can count me in too," Charles said. He had waited until last to speak. Henry had the ominous feeling it was no accident. "But we need to be smart about this. Everything you just told us, Henry, I can't argue it doesn't fit together, but it also begs the question, what exactly are we up against?" Charles took out his phone. "Forewarned is forearmed. I think we should take another trip to see Eamonn."

Chapter 63

Simon stared out over the gardens. He watched Sebastian and Kate Bennett through one of the upper windows, strolling together across the grounds. From this vantage point one could be forgiven for thinking they were old friends.

Not for the first time recently, Simon felt a spear of guilt, and promptly made the effort to squash it. The Kate Bennett he looked out on now was a very different woman from the one he had encountered at the fund-raising day only months ago. Even from this distance the change was stark. It showed in her body language, the distinct shuffle in her walk, the way her head was always slightly bowed and the way her shoulders sagged forward as though the effort to keep them straight was just too great. The difference was ruder still when you saw her up close. The dull glaze of her eyes told their own story. She'd been wounded, they said, diminished. What wasn't so evident, maybe, was that the recent traumas in her personal life weren't the only things to have taken a toll on her mental and physical wellbeing. Unbeknownst to her, Kate had been systematically doped and sedated to a greater or lesser degree since the evening she had stepped through The Retreat's gates. Her drinks and meals laced with a selection of secret seasonings, a little diazepam, sometimes a pinch of Rohypnol, carefully chosen to make her more suggestible and agreeably docile.

Sebastian's plan had demanded Kate become fixated by the presence in the house on the cliff. Simon wasn't privy to every detail, but Sebastian had been sure to impress upon him how crucial it was to detach her from her regular life, her father, her friends and associates. Success, Sebastian had said, hinged upon drawing her toward a mystery she could not possibly ignore, while simultaneously gaining her trust and isolating her, sowing discord and friction between herself and anyone who might draw her away from it.

Sebastian had been very explicit concerning one detail of the plan: the day and date they had to be ready for. During the past few months Simon had nursed some serious doubts everything would come together. It had seemed impossible. There were just too many variables at play. Then something had happened that had made everything almost easy. Kate Bennett's father had died. In a single stroke her world had been upended. Her relationship with Henry White had been an unforeseen complication, but with a bit of scheming, luck and decisive action, White had been dealt with too. Now Kate Bennett was exactly where Sebastian wanted her, confused, isolated and alone. But then didn't things always seem to have a habit of settling just the way Sebastian wanted them to?

They had duped and damaged Kate Bennett. Simon took no pleasure in it, it was what Sebastian wanted, and he owed Sebastian. It was a question of priorities, of loyalty. Sebastian had saved him, had helped him rebuild a life, cared for him far more than either of his real parents ever had. He had only been ten when his mum had run off, leaving his dad to raise him alone—if you could call it that. They had muddled along for a year or so before his dad met Chrissie. She'd seemed okay enough at first, but then by accident or design (Simon suspected the latter) Chrissie became pregnant and everything suddenly changed.

By the time the baby came Simon had somehow become the spare screw or piece of plastic that always seems to be left over after assembling a piece of flat-pack furniture. There was a place he was supposed to fit, somewhere among his dad, his new partner and their new kid, but it seemed his dad no longer cared enough to take the effort to find where it was. Like Chrissie increasingly had, his dad began to treat Simon like he was always in the way, a problem. In response, he had done what kids often do when they crave attention, he started acting up, getting into trouble, disappearing for days, drinking, stealing... Of course, all this did was make things worse, and worse.

At fourteen he ran away. At eighteen he joined the army. At twenty-two he left the armed forces, got into a mess and wound up on the streets. He fell back into thieving again, sliding from drink to drugs to still harder drugs, swapping pills for needles. The streets were where Sebastian found him, teetering on the edge. He had been fucked, again.

Getting caught short without gear was not uncommon, only this time it wasn't his fault. This time he'd been turned over, robbed, and when he eventually caught up with Cardigan Pete he was going to kill the twitchy fucker, or make him wish he had.

The second he had found his things gone he knew exactly who had nicked them. His smokes, his works, his blankets... He would be lucky not to freeze to death, but that wasn't the worst of it, the worst thing was that he had been stupid enough to leave the last of his cash in his tobacco tin. Pete must have followed him back to the underpass where Simon was currently dossing. The sneaky fuck had been sniffing around. A blind man could see he was strung out and hurting for a fix. He'd even been as dumb as to try and cadge some gear. Simon had deflected him with some waffle and assumed he had given up and gone looking elsewhere. A mistake, because Pete must have been lurking. Somehow he had got to his stuff while he was napping. Now he had no money and no money meant no fix, and going without a fix didn't bear thinking about...

His first thought was shoplifting. It was a quick way to raise some cash. Steal high, sell low and all that, only he didn't need a mirror to know he must look in pretty shit shape. He could already feel sweat slick on his brow and the cramps acting up in his guts. The second he poked his head through a shop door some security wanker or store detective would be hovering closer than a seagull over a bag of chips. No, he was going to have to go for something a lot less subtle. As the darkness crept over the city he loitered in an alley between the shopping area and a nearby multi-story car park praying for an easy mark, a nice frail pensioner who would cave with a convincingly delivered threat, or some lone silly tart teetering on high heels, where he could just grab her handbag and run, but it just wasn't happening. The evening was getting colder and darker, and the shopping crowd quickly thinned to nothing, beginning to be replaced by happy hour pubbers and clubbers.

Finally he'd been hurting enough to try begging a small hit off a dealer he knew hung around near the station. The fucker was having none of it, though. Simon's plea had been met with a laugh that would almost have passed for a cough. Simon tried to conceal his desperation, determined not to give him the satisfaction. Who did the arsehole think he was anyway, acting like he wasn't a fucking junkie himself and didn't know going without was no joke? Less than ten minutes later, loathing himself, Simon slunk back and tried again, promising he would pay the dealer tomorrow, double, he swore. The wanker just laughed his shitty cough of a laugh again. When Simon pressed him a third time, the dealer quit laughing, reached into his long coat and pulled out the kind of knife you'd imagine Satan himself might carry. Simon got the message.

He slunk back to his underpass, feverish and cramping, every cell of his being begging him to deliver it a fix. The best he could do was to get out of the icy wind that had picked up. He huddled tight against the underpass wall, but that had been fuck knew how long ago. The gnawing for a hit was all he could think about now, the cold chewing away at his fingers and feet scarcely even registered.

He needed some gear. He needed money. He needed to make it happen, but the effort required was beyond him. His limbs felt like frozen cords of wood, and he couldn't even feel his hands and feet. He slid down, rolled on his side against the wall, burying his fingers deeper into his armpits as though, far enough in, there was still some warmth to be found, some tiny nugget of comfort. There wasn't. The cold and the grinding hunger—the sucking pull for a hit was eating him alive. He was sick, worse than he'd ever known.

He wanted to die; it would all go away then, the hunger and the cold and the pain...

He heard his name. The voice that said it echoed through the dank underpass, calm and even. It was an effort, but Simon opened his eyes. Someone was resting on his haunches in front of him, a dark-haired man wearing a smart grey woollen greatcoat with matching gloves. He had a thermos in one hand and the screw-on lid that doubled as a mug in the other. The mug was filled with liquid. Vapour curled off surface. Simon smelt chocolate.

"Do I know you?" he croaked.

The man smiled. It was big, wide and white. "No, Simon, but *I* know *you*. My name is Sebastian Dahl, and I'm here to help you. Would you like that, Simon? I can fix you, if you'd like."

Simon stirred. "You've got a fix?"

The man smiled patiently. "No. I said I could fix *you*," he said slowly, "so you won't need one."

Simon's small spark of hope was instantly crushed. "What?" he croaked bitterly, "with a mug of fucking cocoa?"

If he hadn't felt so wretched, so cataclysmically fucking ruined, Simon may even have laughed in the man's face. Who was this guy? A fucking weirdo, a pervert, a do-gooder, a religious twat come to save his soul? Whatever he was, he didn't look to be offering anything close to what he really needed.

Seemingly untroubled by Simon's response, the man responded, slowly, kindly, the way you might speak to someone who's a little slow on the uptake, "No, Simon, I can't fix you with a mug of cocoa, although if I were damp and cold and lying in an underpass I might be inclined to accept the offer of a hot drink while it still was hot."

Simon was about to tell the guy to stick his hot cocoa up his arse while it still was hot, when a thought occurred to him. Maybe this was just the weirdo's opening offer; what if he had something else in mind down the road? Perhaps this opening offer would be followed by another, one that might translate more readily into cash. Simon was hurting enough to be open-minded. He reached out and accepted the mug. Its heat spread into his numb fingers, causing them to tingle. He tried to return the guy's smile, look grateful, but given the way he felt fuck knew what the result looked like.

He put the mug to his lips and drank. The warmth of the cocoa felt even better in his throat than it did in his hands. The guy watched, still wearing his patient avuncular smile. Then he said it.

"Do you believe in magic, Simon?"

By now, Simon was short of the energy even to take the piss, so in lieu he simply answered honestly.

"No. There's no magic around here, mate. Not unless you count the kind that comes out of bottles, cans and needles."

The man smiled. "Ah, I'm sorry to hear that Simon, because I do believe. Are you a gambling man?"

"What?"

"A gambling man. You see, I'm prepared to bet you I can prove magic is real."

Still smiling calmly, the guy reached inside his greatcoat. Simon half expected the gloved hand to emerge holding a Bible, but instead he brought out a weird doll. It was a proper rough-and-ready thing, clearly handmade. It looked to be made out of an assortment of odds and ends. Simon saw that its head was a stuffed scrap of cloth, tied at the neck with string, with what looked actual human hair glued crudely on top. Its eyes were sewn-on buttons, its body a Zippo lighter of all things, and its arms appeared to be made of rolled up metal and its legs rolled up pieces of card. As Simon looked closer he saw that one of the legs had once been a photograph. He caught a snatch of face on the photograph that struck him as oddly familiar... then the familiarity of the other bits sank in. The lighter, the Zippo, was *his* lighter, there was a deep scratch across the surface he recognised. The buttons were from his shirt, the snatch of face belonged to one of his old army mates. The arms were clipped sections of his tobacco tin...

For an instant Simon was killing angry. The weird doll was made out of stuff that had been stolen from him that morning, but the anger was like the flare of a damp match, it didn't last long. Rage required fuel, and all his energy was gone. Ultimately, he was too tired to do much but state the obvious.

"You stole my stuff..."

"Yes, Simon, I did."

"Why? I don't understand. Why would you need—?"

"Do you want me to help you?" The man wasn't smiling anymore. Suddenly he looked different, deadly serious, maybe even dangerous.

"You got money?"

The man smiled again, but the sliver of quiet menace remained. "I can do better than that." He pulled a little polythene bag out of his pocket. "If you take my wager, and I lose, if I fail to fix you, I promise to give you this baggie of heroin I have here—if you want it."

Oh, I want it, thought Simon.

The man may have well read his mind, because he said, "Maybe you will, maybe you won't, and besides, you've not really much to lose have you? By the time our wager's done you'll either get your drugs, or you'll no longer need them."

The man smiled again, at the same time his gloved hand vanished back into his pocket, the baggie with it. When it remerged it was holding a small glass jar. The lid had holes punched into it. Simon saw why straight away. Inside was a mouse, small, white, pink-eyed, whiskers twitching. The man set the jar at Simon's feet, together with the doll.

"What say you, Simon? You going to take my bet? Time to make your mind up. I won't ask again. I'll just leave you here, do you understand, and you'll rot, whether you get a fix tomorrow or not, you'll rot."

Thinking only of the baggie, Simon nodded.

The man nodded, pleased, and said, "Give me your hand."

Simon did as he was told, offered up his hand. The man reached out, twisted it palm side up with a thumb and forefinger.

The small blade appeared as if from nowhere. It ran across Simon's palm far too fast for him to do anything to prevent it. The cut was actually quite shallow, but it produced blood, enough for it to soon be dripping onto the ground.

The man collected the doll and pressed it into Simon's bloody palm, folded his fingers around it. Then he picked up the jar and unscrewed the lid. He upended it, tipping the mouse into his waiting fist. He beckoned

378

to Simon to give him the doll. Dazed, Simon gave up the blood-stained effigy.

The man started to mutter, a low, rapid train of words. Simon tried to make them out, but it was hard, they ran together. Suddenly Simon didn't want to know what the words were; he wanted to tune them out altogether. They began to crowd his ears, make his head feel strange. Then his body started to feel weird too.

The sensation wasn't exactly unpleasant. Ironically, it felt curiously similar to a getting a hit, not as intense, nowhere near, but powerful in its own way... It felt like... it felt... *comfortable*? Even though the cold still clung to him, the tiredness, the *hunger*, that sucking black hole of *need* was evaporating. Almost before he was aware of it his craving for a fix was gone.

The man stared at him. He must have seen what he was looking for because an instant later he unfurled his hands. The doll and the mouse flopped onto the ground between them.

The blood-stained doll lay still, the mouse did not. The creature looked in pain. It was gripped by a succession of violent spasms, and the sounds it made, pitiful squeals and whistles, made Simon want to cringe. Something was badly wrong with the mouse. Wracked with successive spasms, it fluctuated between almost disappearing into a ball to arching so violently the opposite way that its spine practically formed a ring. Simon looked from the mouse to the man, but the man was already climbing to his feet.

Simon started to ask, "What the—"

The man's shoe came down hard, rocking from heel to toe. A slow muffled crunch accompanied the small creature's release from torment. The man looked down, from the mouse's split, crushed and twisted remains, to Simon's dazed face.

"How do you feel?"

Simon had to think for a moment.

"Normal."

The man rewarded him with a satisfied nod.

Chapter 64

Kate pulled her coat tighter. The day was what her dad would have called fresh. There was a marked chill in the air, and The Retreat's gardens were taking on an austere, bare look that confirmed summer was already handing the baton to autumn.

"Want to hear some good news?" said Sebastian.

Kate slowed her step. "Nadine?"

He nodded. "Despite her still being occupied with a more urgent case, I've managed to persuade her to free up a small window for us. She's agreed to meet us at the house this evening, a bit later than I'd have preferred, but..."

"Tonight?"

"Oh," Sebastian frowned, as though surprised, "if you'd rather wait until she can accommodate us during the day, or if you don't feel ready, we can postpone. I'm sure once she's dealt with this other case—"

Kate cut him off mid-sentence. "No. Really, tonight will be fine."

"You're sure?"

"Yes, definitely. I can't wait any longer. I want to know what my mother's trying to tell me. What time are we meeting her?"

"Nine thirty. We'll have a couple of hours before we need to set off. I've taken the liberty of asking a few people if they wouldn't mind coming along with us, it will be quite dark by the time we get there and I thought having some friendly faces around might prevent things from feeling too oppressive. I asked Simon, Helen, Carl, David, Leanne, and Adrian... Don't worry, while we're performing the séance they'll keep well out of our way."

Chapter 65

Eamonn's view on callers hadn't changed since Henry and Charles last visited, which was to say he preferred not to have any. Henry had overheard Charles's side of the call from Ray's kitchen. It sounded like it took some work, but eventually Charles managed to persuade him.

"He's agreed to see us, but strictly on the condition we keep it brief. He's finding things... tough at the moment."

"Then I guess we should get moving before he changes his mind, eh?"

Henry's first thought after Eamonn unlocked his door was that he looked terrible, like a man who had been kidnapped, locked in a cellar for a month, escaped and then promptly gone on a weekend stag do in Magaluf. His eyes were dark hollows. His pale, drawn face was scrubby and unshaven, and he appeared both agitated and distracted, even more so than he had on their previous meeting. Charles had said something about Eamonn finding things tough at the moment, but nothing could have prepared Henry for the wrung-out and twitching wreck Eamonn presented.

When they entered, the medium practically scuttled away down his hallway into the front room. Once there, he remained standing, directing a jittery hand at the cupboard where the deck chairs were kept. The ticks he had exhibited in their previous visit had bloomed into full on spasms. His jaw jutted out intermittently, usually accompanied by a violent spastic twist of his neck.

"Five m-m-m-mmm..."

"Minutes?" Charles said.

Eamonn nodded. "Th-th-th-that's a-all Ch-Charles."

"It's bad?" asked Charles.

"Vurgh-very," said Eamonn, absently scratching at a patch of skin on his forearm that was already livid and raw, "and you t-t-t-two being hur-hurgh-here is mmmm-making it w-wuh-worse. You're s-s-s-stirring them-mmmm up-up." Eamonn head swivelled violently, his eyes darting to a corner of the room where they seemed to track something for a few seconds. Henry followed his gaze, saw nothing.

"If you've gurgh-got s-s-something to ask, purgh-please g-get o-o-o-on wuh-with it."

"Okay Eamonn," said Henry, "we'll try to make this as brief as we can."

They caught Eamonn up on events. When they had finished, Eamonn was twitching worse than ever.

"Tuh-to exchange sss-s-souls wuh-with another puh-puh-person..." Eamonn seemed to retreat into himself, as though thinking, and then became distracted. Something in the corner of the room had snared his attention again. Henry wondered if they had lost him, but a moment later he was back. "Wuh-would it even buh-be p-p-p-possible..? Purgh-perhaps, if..." He turned his hollow eyes on them. "The wuh-working would be cuh-cuh-complex... The p-p-preparation and s-skills ruh-required, c-considerable... The ssss-symbolism and ritualistic elemmm-ents would likely be eh-extensive and eh-ehhh-extremely ihhh-intricate. The purgh-practitioner would need ih-immense..." Eamonn fought to get the word out, "buh-buh-buh-belief. Every s-single duh-detail would be cuh-crucial, the people, the t-t-time, the place, the duh-dates..."

Henry suddenly felt sick. His mind latched onto an awful fragment of information. He fumbled his phone from his pocket and doubled checked the date.

"Oh no."

Charles must have realised something was wrong. Henry found him staring at him, his expression a question mark.

"Oh shit, oh no, no—"

The date. Henry was already heading for the door. The date of the fire at Oakbourne Road, the date Kate's mother and the others perished in a blaze they failed to escape—the date upon which Henry was sure to his marrow Lawrence Hawley had stolen the body of young Timothy Lamb and exchanged it for his own was the 22nd of September, the same date it was today.

"What?" Charles yelled, fast on his heels.

"He's going to do it tonight, Charles. I even know what time. The Oakbourne Road house fire started at about ten o'clock."

–

Henry and Charles scrambled into Henry's car.

"Can't we just call the police," Charles argued, "tell them someone is breaking into Dahl's place?"

Henry reversed and screeched to a stop in front of the tower block's security gate, drumming his fingers impatiently on the steering wheel while the gate slowly wheezed open. "Too risky. If they got there and everything looked fine Dahl could just talk to them, reassure them everything was hunky dory and send them on their way. If they got there too late… No. I'm going to have to stop it. If I can just get there and throw a spanner in the works, interfere with Dahl performing his working that should be enough, right?"

"If *we* can throw a spanner in the works," Charles corrected him. "I'm coming with you."

"Are you sure? We don't know how far Dahl is prepared to go to see this through. It could be dangerous."

Charles took out his phone. "Then it's just as well we'll have strength in numbers. I'm calling Ray and the rest. They'll want to help too."

Henry checked his watch; it was 6.03 pm. It would take them at least four hours to get to Dahl's house, and even that would call for crossed fingers and no traffic cops. Ten o'clock. It was going to be tight.

Chapter 66

Simon turned in. A brief trundle and the headlights soon picked out the weed-choked gate. He pulled over, parking the people carrier beside the dirt track.

The rear doors slid open and the kids, Helen, Carl, David, Leanne, Sean and Adrian spilt out, chattering, surveying the house on the hilltop, behaving like they were on some grand adventure. They were part of it. Simon didn't know all the specifics, just enough to know they were important.

They'd been primed, like every youth who had enjoyed the hospitality of The Retreat. Each one had been carefully steered down a path leading to this house, fed a diet of free-thinking spiritualism, group meetings, positive affirmation rituals, insidiously gentle brainwashing to win their loyalty and unquestioning obedience… There had been many other Helens, Seans, Carls, Leannes and Adrians. Simon had watched them come and go over the years, kids whose absence wouldn't even be noted should they happen to vanish, but they had escaped their fates, due to nothing more fortuitous than timing. Sebastian had been preparing for this night for a long time, but the final, apparently crucial, piece, Kate Bennett, had only fallen into place eight months ago.

Simon got out of the people carrier and put his game face on. He joined the youths, engaged in a little banter, and led them through the gate and up the rise. By thin beams of torchlight they scaled the hill to the front porch where Simon unlocked the door and let them in, lambs to the slaughter.

Chapter 67

Nadine swung onto the dirt track and drove up towards the gate, stopping beside Simon's people carrier. She peered through the windscreen up the hill to where a light burned in the house's lounge window, collected her torch and left the car's warm interior for the cold autumn night.

The working was buried within her. She could feel it, coiled and powerful, waiting to unfold. She and Sebastian had crafted it together, and once it was done everything would be different. She would be different. Her past, all her regrets, all her mistakes, all her pain, the damage, abuse and self-loathing would be something that happened to somebody else. She would cast the old Nadine off like a butterfly its chrysalis, emerging transformed, born anew and yet at the same time so much more than she was before. The old Nadine would exist only in name and appearance. A new Nadine would walk in her shoes, a Nadine who would have Sebastian forever.

Chapter 68

Kate had expected to feel excited at the prospect of another séance, galvanised, but in truth she felt strangely detached. They had eaten before leaving The Retreat, and even though it had been little more than a snack she felt afflicted with the drowsy leaden feeling that usually follows a considerably heavier meal. Her thoughts felt slippery too, simple concentration seemed to demand more effort than it ought.

Sebastian was at the wheel of his Ferrari. She was in the passenger side, eyeing the darkening skyline. The sonorous hum of the car's wheels on the motorway's asphalt resonated up her spine, lulling her to sleep. After she had rested her eyes for the umpteenth time, Sebastian looked over at her and said, "Why don't you take a nap? We'll be a while yet. I can wake you when we get there."

She closed her eyes again, with no real intention of taking up his offer, but almost the moment they shut she must have gone. The next thing she knew she was being nudged gently awake. She blinked and rubbed her eyes, disoriented, until she looked across and found Sebastian smiling at her reassuringly. The car was stationary.

"Kate? We're here."

She tried to rouse herself, but despite the nap, the torpid sensation persisted. Sebastian was getting out of the car. Kate scraped together the effort to join him. From opposite sides of the Ferrari they stared up the hill. A light burned in one of the house's windows. Kate glanced back, and spotted a people carrier and Nadine Smith's car parked further down the track.

"Looks like we're the last to get here," she observed.

Sebastian checked his watch. "It's only nine thirty. I imagine they arrived just ahead of us. Come on. Let's go join them."

They squeezed through the gate, and made their way up the rise by the light of Sebastian's torch. Kate's leaden legs found the ascent tougher than usual. By the time they reached the porch she felt exhausted. Someone must have spied their approach, because Nadine was ready to greet them at the door. Kate spotted a few youths from The Retreat too, but they had obviously been asked to keep out of the way, because they quickly vanished into the back rooms, leaving her, Sebastian, and Nadine alone. Nadine took them through into the lounge. It was illuminated by a solitary battery-powered halogen lantern perched atop a corner dresser.

"You're both ready?" asked Nadine.

Sebastian and Kate agreed they were, Kate trying to appear more alert than she felt. It was hard, she just felt so tired. Her head felt woolly and slow. She joined Sebastian in the centre of the lounge where Nadine was waiting. A moment later the medium was orbiting them, pouring salt in a thick white cord, marking out a ring around them. This done, she reached into a pocket and handed Kate the same charm she had given her last time, with the same instructions. Hold it tight. It would help protect her.

They were ready. Nadine started.

"Spirit, come forward. Make contact with us, come forward..." She closed her eyes, tilted her head back.

Almost at once, Nadine's voice began to fade. To Kate's ear it sounded muffled, distant. The room shuddered, dimmed, swam out of focus.

Kate gripped the charm tightly as the world listed like a ship about to capsize. The last thing she saw, or imagined she saw, was the door to the lounge swing open. Several figures entered and took up positions on

Nadine's salt circle, like cardinal points on a compass. Nadine's voice burbled from a million miles away, and then they were gone, the room was gone.

There was only darkness.

Chapter 69

Henry screeched to a halt on a scrubby verge near the turn-off to Dahl's house. He and Charles jumped from the car and sprinted to the neck of the track. No one appeared to be around so they pushed forward and came upon three vehicles. Henry identified Nadine Smith's Polo and Dahl's Ferrari, the third was a mystery people carrier.

Henry cupped his hands to its side window. It was empty, but the track outside the vehicle's sliding door was lousy with footprints. How many people had Dahl brought with him, and who were they? Henry reckoned he could take a good guess: they were youths from The Retreat. Why? He took another stab—because there had been youths the first time, all of whom had wound up dead. Time really was running out.

"Charles, we've got to get up there."

Charles had seen the footprints too.

"Shouldn't we wait for the others?"

Henry looked up the hill to where the house's silhouette was broken by a single light burning in the lounge window. Ray and the rest of the crew might only be minutes away, but right now that could be time they didn't have to spare.

"It's nearly ten o'clock. We can't wait. For all we know they've already started."

"No, of course..." Charles agreed, looking less confident than he sounded. "You're right. So do we have a plan?"

"What are your views regarding improvisation?"

"Depends on the situation."

"Look, we just have to get in the way, disrupt anything that's going on. If everything has to be so meticulous, hopefully that should be enough, right?"

"Right," Charles responded. "Let's do this."

They slipped through the weed-choked gate and hurried up the rise. Several tracks had been freshly beaten through the long grass, snaking up in the direction of the house. They followed them. Henry knew if his suspicions were correct, Dahl had been planning this night for years. Years. So close to his goal, Henry reckoned he might need quite a bit of intervention to be stopped now, and judging from the tracks they were following, he and Charles looked to be outnumbered by at least three to one.

—

The room is gone, replaced by a swirling confusion of dark shapes. Amid the shapes Kate glimpses things, half-seen in the tempest, then the darkness lifts and—

She's running through a field of wheat, laughing. In the distance, in the next field, she can make out the tops of the tents her clan has pitched for the night.

The wheat is tall, ripe for harvest. It whips her dirty sun-browned legs while at the same time the spirits who follow the clan tug playfully at her long hair and dress. The spirits babble like running water in her head.

Selene knows she is special, knew it even before the elders told her so. They know the spirits seek her out. They know they talk to her and her to them. The elders say it has been a long time since someone with a gift as keen as hers has been born into the clan. They have promised to school her in the old ways, teach her how to control the spirits and direct them to carry out the clan's bidding—in time, when she is ready. When they promised her this, Selene had listened solemnly and nodded, thanked them, but kept her secrets, afraid to share with them the feats she had already carried out with the spirits' help.

As rapidly as it lifted, the darkness falls again. It swims, like ink tossed into swirling water, obscuring the vision. It curls its arms around her, and Kate is torn away again. It feels like falling, falling down into—

The girl is a girl no more. She is a woman now, leaning on the rail at the end of a caravan, watching the clan set camp. Some are raising tents, others are preparing the fire. Someone takes up a fiddle and the deepening twilight is filled with music. A girl skips forward, takes the hand of a young man, steals him away from his chores with a doe-eyed plea. The young man makes a half-hearted attempt to resist, but quickly yields. The couple begins to dance to the tune.

The woman knows the couple; she has grown into adulthood with them. What feels like such a brief time ago they were all children. Now they are men and women. These two are lovers. Watching them cleave to one another, moving to the music all can hear and the music that sings only between them, stirs an increasingly familiar melancholy.

Selene's talents have elevated her status within the clan, but they have carried unforeseen consequences too. They have set her apart. How was she to have known her gift came with a hidden price? As she and her girlfriends reached maturity it slowly revealed itself. While the others were courted, one after another going on to wed men from within their own clan or men from other venerable tribes, each learning what it was to be a woman, she remains alone. Respected, yes, revered even, but feared too.

It has been too long. Too many generations have passed since the clan has seen anyone with a gift like hers, someone with so strong an affinity with the spirits. While the clan elders tinker with tired and petty magic, she dares not reveal a fraction of what she is capable of...

Already she knows her fate. From girl, to woman, to matriarch, she is destined to be alone, wed to none but the clan. This is the price of her gift, and she is learning to accept it, even if there are times, like now, watching these two lovers dance, when the price seems painfully high.

The darkness swirls, implodes, blotting everything out, and Kate is tumbling again—

She sits in a caravan made into a makeshift prison at the centre of the camp. Another caravan stands a short distance away. Inside is an old woman with a girl's soul.

Selene knows she has done a terrible thing, and while she feels pity for her victim, one of the elders' daughters, it is diluted by her anger toward the clan. They drove her to do what she has done. All she had wanted was to slow the malignancy consuming her insides, find respite from the pain, and the clan had turned on her. They made ultimatums, then threats, and finally they made a prisoner of her. Under the pretence of care and compassion, they had sent a young girl to spy on her. This was how her life of sacrifice and service had been rewarded, to be treated like an old dog everyone fears has grown crazy enough to bite.

The slow realisation that the life she had led was worthless had almost been as agonising as the illness eating into her frail body. She had set aside her own happiness to devote herself to the clan, and for what? Only to discover she had been a fool.

She wanted the life she had forfeited back. Didn't she deserve that? Once the idea had taken root it was tenacious... There was old magic, dark magic... She had appealed to the spirits and they had guided her... and now she had this new vessel, a young, strong body, lithe and supple, free of pain...

The darkness returns. Kate tries to process what she has seen but it makes no sense, it—

She is on a train, in a sleeper cabin with Lawrence and Margaret Hawley. Outside the cabin's window it is dark as deceit. Inside, the train's motion rocks them like babes in cradles. Except, for Selene, sleep is impossible. Excitement runs through her like electricity. She can scarcely believe she is free, a young girl, with a life of infinite possibility stretching out ahead of her.

Her saviour lies in the bunk opposite. She has met Lawrence Hawley numerous times throughout the years during his periodic visits to her clan, but something fundamental has changed between them and she cannot help but view him differently now. She studies his sleeping form, trying to discern his face amongst the shadows. She is a different woman now, and because of that everything is different.

Until yesterday, Lawrence Hawley made scant impact upon her. Who had he been to her? A bookish inquisitive outsider? A man more than four decades her junior? Equally, what had she been to him? An aging sexless matriarch, wedded to her clan?

Her crime has recast them both. It has left her a young woman, and he a man in his prime.

The track bends and the train changes course, causing moonlight to spill between the window's drapes. It falls upon Lawrence's face and reveals she is not the only one still awake. It also reveals something else. In the darkness and shadow he has been studying her too. As his gaze meets hers she does not avert her eyes, on the contrary they meets his boldly; she tests the power and sway of the youth and beauty she now commands with a smile, and feels almost giddy when the smile is returned.

In the bunk above him, Lawrence's wife, Margaret, sleeps, snoring quietly. Had the decision been hers,

Selene is certain she would still be held captive while the clan elders fumbled to undo her crime. It was Lawrence who moved to free her. He alone was her liberator. Clever, inquisitive, handsome Lawrence Hawley. A long-buried hunger stirs.

She wants him.

And part of him wants her. The way his eyes catch on the curves of her now youthful body has not escaped her notice, and she likes it. Yes, she wants him, wants him to liberate her further, compound her enormous crime with a more modest one...

Darkness swirls, sweeps in again like the night drawing breath. It exhales and—

Selene is a girl no more. The youthful face has aged, but remains beautiful. She sits with an older version of Lawrence, mind reeling, in the back of a taxi cab. A hospital shrinks in the rear view mirror, years of happiness shattered by a devastating discovery. Lawrence is sick. Something is growing inside his head, a tumour. It is the cause of his crushing headaches, distant rumbles of a storm that will one day close in and tear their world apart.

Losing him is unimaginable. After knowing what it means to be loved she cannot go back to being alone. She always believed herself ready to embrace the end of this life when it came, but now she realises this was only because she had expected to reach those winter years by his side.

She has not communicated with spirits for so very long. They have shared an ordinary, a wonderfully ordinary life these past few decades, deliberately so, but the spirits are never far away. If she opens herself up to them she knows they will respond. Without even meaning to, she starts to plan.

Without the ancient spirits who followed the clan the working would prove tricky, but not impossible. There was another way. The powers of old spirits were equalled only by those of the freshly deceased... The implications are unthinkable, and yet so is the alternative. Already she finds herself contemplating committing the worst of crimes once again...

The darkness contracts, Kate tumbles, caught in the tempest, then it flexes, unfurls and—

In the room they now share, Valerie tucks her daughter into bed. The house is nice, big with lots of rooms, and the couple it belongs to, Lawrence and Selene, seem nice too, which is good because Valerie is in need of a little kindness. She's tired of running from bad boyfriends and bad debts, creepy landlords, her messy past, the family who erased her from their lives. Valerie makes a mental vow things will be different here, a fresh start for her and Kate...

The darkness swims, resolves into—

They sit in a circle in the lounge. Valerie has grown to love the people around her, they are the brothers and sisters she never had.

Lawrence and Selene urge her to see if she can do it again. The others join in and soon they are practically chanting in encouragement. She giggles. Selene's 'special tea' always makes her giggle. She surrenders to the group's wishes. She squeezes her eyes shut and in her mind's eye sees the twisted black candlewick burst into flame; she focuses on the picture, really focuses, makes it as vivid and solid as she can, and then gingerly opens one eye. For a second the wick does nothing. Then there is a faint shimmer of light and the flame ignites. The room erupts into claps and cheers of approval.

Valerie feels special, clever, powerful...

The darkness—

At first she had misgivings, but after speaking to Selene again she saw it was the right thing to do. Selene helped her put it all into the proper perspective and see things clearly. Valerie owed it to Kate to show her the way things really were. It was wrong to keep secrets, to hide truths and pretend the world was the way most people said it was when they knew different...

The gatherings, the rituals and the séances had made them a family, united them by something stronger than blood: truth. Their discoveries had changed the way they saw everything. Wasn't it only right that they should include the children?

If countless millions of Catholics were comfortable taking their children to church with them, said Selene, with all that faith's teachings, rituals and rites, some of which looked pretty strange from the outside, wafers and wine supposed to be the body of Christ, prayers to a god they could neither see nor hear, tales of resurrection and miracles, then what could be wrong in what they did? All most religions offered were books and blind faith, she argued, while in their house, they had communicated with spirits and performed feats most people would argue were impossible.

In place of wine and wafers they had their special tea made from the peyote plants Selene nurtured. She was well-practiced and the tea was always very mild, just potent enough to help them connect with a deeper, truer part of themselves.

Selene had given her a book. It was about the cultures of ancient tribes. The book talked about the practice of using roots, mushrooms and herbs to commune with gods and spirits. Three thousand years before Christ was even born, Native American Indians used peyote to speak with their gods and ancestors. According to the book, Siberian tribes used a type of mushroom, and South American tribes used yage and ayahuasca, the Scythians used cannabis... Using plants, herbs and fungi to unlock the human mind was as old as mankind itself. What they were doing wasn't new, it was something ancient, ways that had been lost and all but forgotten.

Sandra's son, Timothy, had already taken part in a ritual and a couple of séances. It was natural, Selene said, and unless Valerie had reason to lie to Kate then why should she? Didn't Valerie owe it to Kate to teach her the truth? Didn't she deserve to be enlightened, just as they were?

Darkness—

Chapter 70

Henry crested the hill and stood panting before the house, his lungs huffing great plumes of vapour. His legs burned and his chest was heaving from the effort of sprinting up the hill, its incline somehow seeming to have grown steeper, deliberately conspiring to be one more obstacle preventing from him reaching Kate before it was too late.

He couldn't know for sure what time the ritual back at Oakbourne Road in 1989 had taken place, but he feared he was already cutting it fine.

From his new vantage point he saw the lounge was painted by the harsh light of a halogen lantern, perched on the same dresser he had used to conceal the plaster he had smashed from the wall. Thankfully the halogen's glare was directed away from the window; in stark contrast to the figures populating the lounge, Henry would be all but invisible in the darkness outside. He moved quickly to the window and peeked in. The harsh planes of blue-white light and long black shadows carved out a chilling tableau.

A circle had been marked out in salt. Three figures stood just inside its perimeter. Six more lay at its boundary, cups scattered between them in pools of spilt liquid. The youths were clearly dead, curled into vaguely foetal positions, pop-eyed and blue-lipped. Henry knew without having to be told; they were kids from Dahl's Retreat. Sebastian Dahl, their benefactor, stood over them, his face etched with desperate intensity. Nadine Smith stood beside him, her lips moving, shaping rapid words through teeth bared in pain. A blade in her left hand scored a slow path through the fish-belly white skin of her right forearm. Blood dripped from her fingertips.

The sound of laboured breathing signalled Charles's approach. He had finally conquered the hill too. He rushed to Henry's side, stared through the window to share in the awful truth of it.

They were too late.

Henry's gaze was locked upon the third figure standing with Dahl and Nadine. Her face was bleached bone white in the unforgiving glare of the halogen light, and even though she possessed the physical appearance of the woman he loved, he knew he wasn't looking at the real Kate Bennett, not anymore.

Lawrence Hawley had finally finished what he had started over two decades ago, succeeded where Henry had spectacularly failed. His lover, Selene, was back.

Unlike Henry, Dahl had rescued the woman he loved from oblivion.

—

Kate is drowning. The darkness crashes over her, swells, unfurls—

The kitchen table buzzes with talk and activity. Selene is watching quietly, her face carefully arranged into a mask of motherly interest and encouragement. The crime lies in the near future, gnawing at her conscience. The five young adults and two children around this table believe themselves part of a family as caring and close-knit as any bound by blood. They are refugees from a harsh world that has hurt them, prostituted them, tried to break them, and finally they think they are safe. They couldn't be more wrong.

Lenny insisted upon cooking, a chicken casserole everyone appears to be enjoying, despite the overcooked vegetables and undercooked dumplings, hard-centred and chewy. Regardless, the meal earns

401

him no shortage of appreciative noises and compliments. *Why? Because Lenny is a fragile soul, sweet and easily hurt, so everyone gamely tucks in.*

Lisa is enthusing over a book Lawrence has loaned her about the Bedouin tribes of the Minaean Kingdom. Darren, whom she is in the process of teaching to read, hangs on every word. He is presently tackling The Fantastic Mr Fox *and enjoying it tremendously. Valerie is coaxing the girl, Kate, to eat some of the mushy vegetables. Tim, the boy, helps out by proposing a deal. He will eat all of his carrots, which he doesn't like, if Kate agrees to eat just half of the veggies on her plate. Tim's mum, Sandra, watches the exchange serenely, smiling vacantly. This is because she is stoned, again. If adulthood is defined by embracing one's responsibilities then her son could well lay stronger claim to the title than she.*

What none of them know is this will be the last meal they will ever eat.

Selene cannot afford to listen to the mewing of her conscience. Lawrence is sick and getting sicker. The death sentence growing in his skull gets bigger day by day, even now as they sit and eat it works tirelessly to steal him away from her.

Once the meal is eaten, the pots, pans, cutlery and dishes are washed up and put back in their drawers and cupboards. These mundane, routine chores are carried out as usual, the same as any other evening, until eventually the hour arrives and they retire to the lounge for the evening gathering. They are cocooned in a cosy haze of wellbeing, blinkered by the carefully cultivated unquestioning trust so core to life at Oakbourne Road. It makes the crime she and Lawrence are poised to commit so much simpler.

They form a ring. Selene circles them, encloses them in a boundary of salt, before taking her own place in the ring. She begins the working, calls out to the spirits.

The group take up her lead, lend her their energies. She welcomes the spirits to join them, part of a ritual so practiced now it has become routine.

The air takes on a strange quality. They are not alone. All feel it. Selene hands out the cups, pouring her special tea into each outstretched vessel, and returns to her place at Lawrence's side...

Chapter 71

He was too late. Henry gaped through the lounge window, the crushing weight of failure rooting him to the spot, staggered by the sheer injustice of it.

How could he be too late? After figuring it all out, the impossible logic of why and how, and getting here... How could he be too late? There had to be something he could do, even at this late juncture. There *had* to be...

He looked around. Beside the window a fist-sized half brick had fallen away from the wall, He reached down, scooped it up, took aim at the window—

"I wouldn't do that if I were you."

Henry and Charles spun around. Henry saw the gun first, its deadly eye trained on him. The gunman was a youngish guy, with cropped hair and a prematurely aged face. He seemed to have appeared from nowhere, although he must have rounded the house while they were both focused upon what was happening through the window.

The man took a slow step forward. His voice was calm, but strangely that much scarier for it. "So help me, if your hand moves so much as an inch, I'll shoot."

"I remember you," Henry said dumbly. "You're the guy I spoke to at the gates of that place Kate's been staying at, The Retreat." His arm was still raised, mind racing, weighing his options.

The man took a step forward, repeated his threat. "I mean it. Throw that and you're dead. Your friend too."

Chapter 72

Kate reels…

Valerie can feel the spirits in the room with them. The circle is alive with energy. It feels charged, heavy, like the air prior to a thunderstorm. They are ready to begin.

Selene urges them to drain their cups, and as she has done numerous times before, Valerie knocks back the bitter brew in a single gulp. Except tonight something is different, the tea tastes wrong.

Almost at once, her head feels light and her chest tight. Her hands fly to her gut as pain sinks in its teeth. Darkness begins to close in. She starts to convulse. Folding, she drops to her knees, gasping for breath. Her head pounds, and finally she keels over, her whole body shaking with violent spasms.

Valerie looks up from where she lies.

Selene still has Kate's hands and Lawrence has Timothy's, but the couple's usual tender countenance is nowhere to be seen. Each wears a mask of desperate determination. Gently clasped hands have become hard white-fingered grips. The children's eyes are wide, terrified as they take in the scene: their parents, friends, adopted aunts and uncles have crumpled as suddenly as puppets sheared of their strings, blue-faced and curled in agony, as they shake and thrash.

Some unseen force begins to travel through the four. Their hair and clothes ripple and flutter as though caught in a stiff breeze. Selene's lips move rapidly, forming words. She and Lawrence seem unsurprised by what has happened, and too late Valerie realises why. They were expecting this. It was planned. She and her friends have been tricked. There is hidden meaning to this horror, and the children are somehow part of it.

Valerie fights, clings to life. Her daughter needs her. She is all Kate has… but the air she sucks in doesn't seem to reach her lungs. A kaleidoscope of red and yellow, blue and purple spots bloom before her, crowd her vision…

Then there is simply darkness. For a moment there is nothing at all, nothing but the darkness and silence.

Then something happens. Brilliant ribbons of light begin to cut trails through the void. By their light, Valerie can see again. The light begins to dissect the space around Selene and Kate, Lawrence and Timothy. They etch a circle, then a web of searing arcs, like the after burn of tracers left by bonfire night sparklers. They whip and whirl, weaving a mesh between Kate and Tim, Lawrence and Selene.

Although she cannot say why, Valerie instinctively grasps what she is watching unfold. It is one of the rituals they have become used to performing in action. She is witnessing the crafting of spiritual energy. The ritual blazes like a diagram etched upon the shadowy facets of the room—what was once a simple circle marked in salt now burns like a filament, acting as both boundary and focal point. Her friends lie about its perimeter. Their bodies are dead, little more than crudely daubed shadows, but their spirits… Their spirits burn with the same brilliant light that circulates the ritual, each one a tiny sun. The four figures inside the ring radiate a light too, but theirs burn from within, like embers.

Selene is still mouthing words, but in this place they are something more; tendrils of light unfurl from her mouth like strands of molten gold. They snake out, make contact with the ribbons of light circulating the ritual. At once the web shifts, bends, converges upon the quartet still standing; Kate and Tim, Selene and Lawrence. Valerie feels a pull to move closer, to touch those brilliant ribbons of fire. The spirits of her friends

406

must feel the lure too because some are already drifting towards those brilliant currents of light. Valerie alone resists.

When the first of her friends' spirits nears the ribbons of light it is snared, swept into the serpentine geometry of the ritual, spun like white hot thread into a loom. Soon the rest are snared too; the ritual blazes, tracing a path between the two adults and children like magnetic poles. The path between Lawrence and Timothy begins to oscillate, burns impossibly bright. An instant later the light at their cores are ripped free of their shadowy bodies. Their tiny suns drift in the void momentarily, and then Lawrence's is swept up by the current of light and propelled into Timothy's body. Lawrence's body abruptly teeters, then slumps to the floor.

In the very same moment Valerie comes to a horrifying understanding.

Chapter 73

The darkness stutters. When it lifts Kate's perspective of the room has pivoted one eighty degrees. From observed to observer, from Valerie to—

Selene's eyes move over the youthful bodies curled on the salt boundary; their cups lie similarly scattered, remnants of poisoned peyote-infused tea pooling beneath them. The youths' newborn spirits circulate the working now. Confused and raw, they are for that very reason immensely powerful, but only for so long. Eventually they will realise what has been done to them and at that point the working will begin to spiral and collapse. Lawrence stands before her in his new guise. He stares at her in wonderment from the eyes of a boy, at a stroke spared the sickness and death that threatened their future.

And yet, if it is still to be a future they are to share, Selene must act quickly, finish the working while it still bends to her will.

She closes her eyes and allows the boy's spirit to drift away from the working. Once all this is done, he will join his mother's spirit in the beyond. It will be a painless death, free from suffering, a journey as simple as slipping from waking to sleep.

She takes up the reins of the working, guiding the energies so that they flow through her and the girl. She marshals her will, commands the working to tear their spirits from their bodies...

The darkness falls, and again the room blinks one eighty degrees, from Selene to—

Valerie sees the ribbons of energy blaze bright and shift again. The path between Kate and Selene begins to burn brighter, as it had with Lawrence and Timothy only moments before. Kate's and Selene's spirits are suddenly torn free, and Valerie watches helplessly as Selene readies to steal not just her daughter's body, but her future, her life.

It's torture. Kate needs her and she is powerless to act. Her impotence seems like a cruel judgement, designed to underscore everything she has always feared—that she has been left wanting as a mother, inadequate, too young, too naive, foolish, careless and irresponsible, so much less than her beautiful daughter deserves. That she loves her girl with all her heart hasn't been enough, not enough to give her the life she deserved and not enough to save her now. The knowledge crucifies her. She would do anything, give everything to save her daughter now—

Something happens, Valerie feels it, and an instant later sees it too. From somewhere inside her, what feels like her core, threads of light have emerged. They are reminiscent of the ones Selene produced, but this is where the similarity ends. Where Selene's were thin and smoky tendrils of gossamer-thin gold, Valerie's are thick as steel rope and shudder like high-voltage cables. They snap forward, whip and thrash crazily until they make contact with the ribbons of light flowing between Kate and Selene.

All at once the ritual collapses.

The circle shakes and dims, the ribbons of light begin to peel free, arcing violently searching for another focal point. They loop back toward Valerie, surge and whip around her, through her. Acting purely on instinct, she reaches out and steers them toward Kate's spirit. The bright sun of her spirit is immediately snared and spun back to Valerie. She seizes it, holds it tight, terrified, exhilarated, wishing she could hold her beautiful daughter close forever... Instead she focuses, drives Kate's spirit back where it belongs, into the smudgy indistinct form of her vacant body.

Selene's spirit hovers in the void, adrift. It wavers, as if wary of the searing ribbons of light whipping and lashing the space around it. No, not as if, Valerie thinks. Selene's spirit is wary. She is deliberately avoiding the light. It dances, keeping its distance... Then suddenly darts. Valerie sees why; Selene's spirit is making a beeline for the shadowy form of her recently abandoned body. Selene intends to return to her flesh, escape.

Viewing the blazing brilliant ball of light that is Selene's spirit, Valerie suddenly thinks of the candlewicks winking alight in her mind's eye, how purely by the force of her will she had made them catch fire. She directs the blazing ribbons of light on Selene's earthly body—

The darkness returns. Kate reels, lost memories slamming into her mind with the impact of a freight train.

Kate blinks. She is back in the lounge, back inside the ring of salt, where her mum and her aunts and uncles lie dead on the boundary. The room is bathed in a rippling orange light. The heat is so intense it tightens the skin on her face. She lifts her eyes and sees the origin of both.

A roaring column of flame rolls across the room, rears like a great snake and then falls upon the only adult left standing, Auntie Selene. The fire doesn't so much strike her down as swallow her whole. She erupts into flames like a bundle of petrol-soaked rags.

Kate shrinks in fear. Like any frightened child she looks to her mother, scrambles to where she lies, unmoving, and cries for her to get up. She tugs at her, and she rolls over, flops onto her back. There is nothing there behind the glassy eyes that stare blankly at the ceiling. Her mum is dead too. The knowledge is too colossal for her young mind. She crumples.

She is only dully aware of the fire snake now. It rears again, wavers in the air, and suddenly darts toward the doorway. It has identified a new target. Kate looks across the room and sees Tim at the doorway. He backs up, bumps into the door frame. Go Tim, she thinks. Go, before it gets you like it did Auntie Selene. Tim bolts and the fire follows, leaving a trail of flaming carpet in its wake. The room is filling with smoke, and Kate thinks maybe she might die too if she doesn't run like Tim, but she can't. She can't leave her mum.

Instead she lays her head on her mum's still chest and hugs her, screws up her eyes and prays it's all a bad dream, that she is really asleep upstairs, that she will wake up tomorrow and none of it will have happened. Her mum will still be alive, to kiss her and hug her and tell her it was just her naughty head making bad stuff up—

The darkness—

Valerie shoots out of the room, chasing down the shadowy figure that was once Timmy, but now holds the spirit of Lawrence Hawley. She has to be careful. Tim's body can't be harmed. If she can catch up to Lawrence, somehow drive his spirit out, then she might yet put Tim's spirit back where it belongs, as she did Kate's. She swoops through the doorway into the hall after the thief, cutting him off at the foot of the stairs. He ducks, wheels and doubles back, begins to scramble up the staircase. Valerie goes after him. In desperation she lashes out and catches his arm. He screams in pain. His shirt sleeve has burst into flames. He bats at them, stumbles, but maintains his footing and gains a further two steps. Valerie goes after him again, until something abruptly stops her.

She can feel herself losing control; the cords of light are fraying around her. They begin to spin out, disperse and she feels an irresistible pull. Its source is back in

411

the lounge. Somehow she is tethered to the salt circle, cannot stray far from it... She watches, impotent, as Tim, or rather Lawrence, bounds to the top of the landing and vanishes around the corner. She draws back, collects herself and the ribbons of light return and blaze bright again. She wheels and speeds back into the lounge, to find Kate hunched over a shadow. For a second she confused, and then she understands; the shadow is her, or what she used to be...

She scans the room, no longer viewing it with eyes. Kate is hunched over her dead body, the light in her small body burning. The bodies of her friends are scattered around the salt ring, they are dull shadows too, with one exception: Lawrence's body is different. Tendrils of thin golden light still cling to it. The body is soulless, but not spent, not yet. Valerie races to it, concentrates. In her mind's eye she sees the candle's flame extinguish, and almost at once feels a shift in whatever she is now. She focuses again, this time upon Lawrence's body, pushes, and drives her way in.

The change is abrupt and astonishing. Suddenly she is back in the room, but seeing it now through Lawrence's eyes. Through the smoke she can make out Kate clinging to her dead body, surrounded by flames. Slumped against the wall Selene's body is a blackened shapeless husk, licked by flames. The fire that destroyed her has spread quickly. Kate needs to get out of the house. Valerie tries to get Lawrence's body to climb to its feet, but the feat is beyond her. The body is strange, leaden. She can't operate it properly, not enough to rescue her daughter, and somehow she knows the fault lies not with it, but her.

She is different. The reason Lawrence was able to take charge of Tim's body was because, unlike her, his spirit had not passed on, but she had died while her body and spirit were still one. She couldn't explain how she knows this, she just does. It is another of the many

412

things she imagines she may come to learn about this new existence in time, unfortunately time is a luxury she presently cannot afford. For Kate to survive she must act quickly. She has an idea.

She abandons Lawrence's body; while she may not be able to make use of it, there is one present who might.

She focuses again, regroups, drawing the energies around her, and begins to search. She finds the brilliant ball of light drifting in the void just beyond the circle. She reaches for Timothy's spirit, sweeps him up and drives him into Lawrence's body, praying it will work...

The darkness—

Something causes Kate to look up from her mother's body. Through the flames and smoke someone is climbing to his feet. He staggers uncertainly and peers at her through the smoke. It is Uncle Lawrence. He blinks, taking her in. He looks bewildered, but begins to chart a path through the flames to where she lies. He grabs her hand, pulls her away from her mum's side, ignoring her protests and drags her through the eye-stinging smoke into the hallway and up the stairs.

They climb the steps to the landing. Above, the ceiling makes an ominous creaking noise. Lawrence picks up his pace, pulling her with him. The creaking builds to a splintering crack and the ceiling gives. They are doused with flaming debris. Kate screams in pain as the searing mess showers her neck and chest. She falls to her knees, may have remained there too, except Lawrence still has her hand. He hauls them from under the crumbling ceiling and along the landing, into a room where the moon shines through a shattered window—

Darkness sweeps Kate up in its inky black arms. Finally she knows everything, understands everything, not least that she is in trouble so deep she doesn't even know where the surface is anymore. Sebastian Dahl has

413

tricked her, and worse still she has aided and abetted him at every turn.

Oh, mum, she thinks, I'm sorry, so sorry.

Chapter 74

Simon advanced, his gun trained squarely on Henry White. White still had the half brick clutched in his hand and to Simon's eye he looked like he was itching to pitch.

"Drop it."

"No."

White looked scared, but not, thought Simon, as scared as someone with a gun pointed at him should.

"You want me to shoot you? I will, if you make me."

"You might want to think about that. If me bricking that window's enough to disturb what they're doing in there, I reckon that gun you have there going off right outside would too."

Simon didn't answer.

White and the medium bloke, Charles whatsisname, were both eyeing him. He wondered how much they knew, or thought they knew. That they were even present suggested they'd worked more than a few things out.

"You don't understand what's happening here," Simon said.

"I know full well what's happening here. They're trying to steal Kate's body to put some gypsy witch's fucking spirit in it."

Simon shook his head, "No, that's Nadine. Your friend Kate's just a..." he searched for the word Sebastian had used, "a *conduit*. Nadine's to be the host, but the spirit has to go *through* Kate."

Henry's fingers tightened around the brick, his eyes twitching to the events unfolding through the window. "Bullshit."

"It's true," Simon pressed. "The spirit can't remain in her for good without passing through Kate first, and about now I'd say they only look about half done. If you throw that brick, who knows what'll happen? You could lose Kate forever, but if you wait... They can finish it. It'll be over. You and Kate can walk away like none of it ever happened."

"*Like none of it happened?* Are you fucking serious? What about those kids there? They're dead. Take a look at them, because I'd say they're past walking anywhere."

Simon didn't look, he didn't want to. Time and again Sebastian had assured him there was no other way. Even after all the justifications, even after he weighed the cost against all the other kids they'd saved from rotten lives and given fresh starts, Simon knew taking their lives was wrong. And yet, he had gone along with it, done everything Sebastian had asked. Why? Because he owed Sebastian. When everyone else had left him to rot, Sebastian had found him, saved him, and cared for him more than his own flesh and blood ever had.

It was the very same reason Simon would do whatever it took to prevent White from getting in the way of the working.

–

Sebastian scarcely dared draw breath. A mixture of joy, hope and the hovering spectre of failure rooted him to the spot. They were close now, he could feel it. Nadine was doing it, holding the working together.

Just finding someone like her had taken years. After preparing all the ground work based on nothing but sheer blind hope, she was the first of the final two crucial pieces to fall into place. They had tested his faith those years. Suffering the frustration of possessing the knowledge to do what was required, but not the power, had been excruciating. After Selene's schooling he could perform some workings, but he would always be limited. Like an aspiring athlete damned by poor genes, he could strive all he pleased but he would never possess the raw talent a working of this magnitude demanded. To save Selene he needed someone with the gift, but under his control.

He found Nadine. Her talent was as obvious to him as it was opaque to her. You couldn't share half your life with someone like Selene and not recognise when you were in the presence of someone with that kind of power. Nadine had the gift alright, but it was unfocused. She was like a ferocious engine roaring away in neutral. For his purposes she couldn't have been any more perfect.

Slowly, step by step, he had taught her everything he needed her to know, and no more, testing his authority and influence over her at every step. This, her weakness, her reliance on him, was what would enable him to deal with her upon Selene's return. He had no doubt, his betrayal would destroy her, but then for Nadine destruction almost seemed her destiny.

When he had found her she had been teetering, riding the lip of a sheer drop. He had steered her from the edge, but once he stepped aside she would find it again soon enough, drawn to the abyss. His intervention had done little but postpone the inevitable.

And if she did not immediately tumble into the abyss, if she weathered his betrayal and entertained thoughts of reprisal? Well, by then Selene would be at his side, and Nadine would find out just how little she really knew.

Kate Bennett gazed into the middle distance, her lips shaping words too low to hear. He needed to be ready, be poised to act the moment Selene returned. Across from Kate, Nadine's face worked, betraying the effort it was taking to bend the spirits to her will. It was tragic really. She honestly believed he intended Selene to share her body, that she and Selene would blend together to become someone else, someone unique. Even if such a thing were possible, Sebastian wouldn't want it. He would never give Selene Nadine's body. Abused, prostituted and polluted, he would no more gift Nadine's body to Selene than he would a stray dog's. No, Selene's was to inhabit Kate Bennett's body. That was how it was supposed to have been, that was how it was going to be.

Suddenly Kate's lips stopped moving. Her eyes lost their distant glaze and she turned her head, found him, studied him. Kate Bennett's spirit was gone, a new spirit stood in its place. Sebastian felt almost giddy.

Her lips parted and the woman he loved, more than anything in this world or the next, spoke to him directly for the first time in nearly twenty years.

"Lawrence."

He tried to answer, but his throat was suddenly too tight. Instead he nodded, undiluted euphoria rushing through him. His soul-mate stood before him. He had done it, after all the years deprived of her... He fought to recover himself. The time had come to act, to finish it. He wheeled and drove a foot through the salt boundary, breaking it, scattering it. Advancing, he snatched the charm from Selene/Kate's hands and tore it open, spilling the contents wide.

Nadine stared, bewildered, but not for very long. She was naive, but far from stupid. She knew what his actions meant. Her expression charted her understanding, from baffled surprise moving quickly to wounded hysteria. The truth slid into her heart like a knife. He didn't want her, never had, not even part of her. She responded precisely as he had anticipated. The knowledge broke her. She literally staggered before him.

He dismissed her, took a step toward Selene, who appeared equally unmoved by Nadine's distress. She stared deep into his eyes, and when she spoke his heart sang.

"I knew you wouldn't give up," she said, simply. "I *knew*. Not if there was the smallest chance to finish what we started."

He nodded, overcome. He yearned to touch her, to feel her again, warm-blooded flesh and bone. His fingers reached out to touch her face. "It's been so long..."

She nodded.

—

On the hillside outside the window, something drew Simon's attention. Events were unfolding in the lounge, but they didn't appear to make any sense. Sebastian had just broken the salt circle around Nadine's working and snatched the charm from Kate Bennett's hands, tearing it to pieces... something, judging from her expression, Nadine had not been expecting.

Nadine's initial confusion soon evaporated, like Simon she quickly understood what Sebastian's actions meant. It seemed Sebastian had another plan, different in one fundamental aspect to the one he had shared with Simon and Nadine. The spirit Sebastian wanted to rescue was back, but its intended host was not Nadine, and likely never had been. One look was enough to see Kate Bennett was no longer really Kate Bennett at all.

All this had captured Simon's attention for mere seconds, but, like many mistakes, that was all it took for things to turn. A flash of movement in the corner of Simon's eye pulled him back, to find Henry White lunging for him, the rock in his hand hurtling for his head.

Simon's trigger finger knew what to do.

Chapter 75

Charles flinched as the gunshot barked into the night, shattering the silence. The report was nothing like the crack of action movie gunfire. It was closer to a firecracker going off an inch from your ear. When Charles reopened his eyes it was to find Henry and the gunman rolling around on the ground.

Charles girded himself to enter the fray. He circled, trying to identify where the gun was in the tussle. He saw it, and was about to lunge to seize it when another shot bellowed out.

Something hit him and he staggered back. His coat was wet, spattered with a mess of something. Shocked, he blinked and dabbed dumbly at the gunk peppering his chest. It was warm, gritty, sticky...

There was a grunt, and a shove, and the topmost of the two figures at his feet rolled onto his back, heavy and lifeless. Then Charles saw his head. A large chunk his skull was gone. The cavity glistened darkly in the light spilling from the window. Charles was frozen to the spot, unable to move.

"Well, don't just bloody stand there," Henry wheezed from the ground next to the man's lifeless body. "Give me a hand up."

Dazed, Charles reached out and pulled Henry to his feet. He was upright for maybe a second or two before he buckled and peered down at his leg.

"Oh. Fuck."

Charles followed his gaze. One of Henry's thighs sported a slowly expanding black splodge. In the centre of the splodge there was a neat little hole, pumping dark treacly liquid. Henry tried to stand straight again, and to Charles's surprise actually succeeded.

421

"Good god," said Charles, "you've been shot. Your leg's bleeding. Oh, I say, there's rather a lot of blood…"

They both stared at the wound.

"Um," Henry mumbled. "I can't really feel anything. Is that normal?"

"How the hell should I know?"

Henry, though, seemed to have moved on. He was staring through the window into the lounge. A moment after this he was peeling the gun from a dead man's fingers.

—

Sebastian reached out to touch her face, joy and relief rolling through him in delicious waves. He had done it. Selene was standing before him; they were together again, after so many years…

"You're back, oh, Selene, you're—"

The words withered in his throat.

She had slowly begun to shake her head, her lips curling into a thin smile, cold and hard as a mortician's slab.

"Selene?"

Too late, he understood. Joy and relief shrivelled, curdled into panic, panic bloomed into terror. *Oh no,* he thought, *oh, no, no, no—*

She advanced on him, but he was already backing away. From somewhere a shot rang out, and then moments later another. Sebastian scarcely noticed, not just because the woman in front of him wasn't Selene, and not just because she was no longer smiling, but because he feared he knew who actually was standing before him.

"I knew you wouldn't let her go," she said. "I knew you'd never give up, no matter how many innocent lives it cost. I *knew* you'd keep trying, so I held on."

He heard his response, small, afraid.

"You?"

She didn't even answer. Instead, she turned her gaze on Nadine. Something approaching pity crossed her face, although to Sebastian's mind it resembled the brand of sympathy one might express for a rabid animal about to be put down.

"And you?" she said softly. "I see it. All the hurt, all the pain. I see how brilliantly it burns. Do you feel foolish? You thought he loved you, cared for you?" She shook her head again. "He doesn't, never did. It was a lie. He always meant to use you and then cast you aside. Worse, he knew it would crush you." The woman's voice dropped to a hushed whisper. "Wouldn't you like to show him how wrong he is? Show him how it *hurts*, how it feels to burn as you burn?"

Nadine's wounded gaze moved from the woman's to his, and Sebastian saw something that gave him hope, only the barest glimpse, but it was there: Nadine didn't want to believe it. Even now he could see in her the longing to believe it was all some awful misunderstanding, that he did love her after all.

The woman moved to stand beside Nadine, whispered into her ear, working to turn his tool against him. Don't, he thought, don't listen to her...

He was about to open his mouth, the lie ready on his tongue, when Nadine closed her eyes and cast her arms wide. From beside her the woman smiled dangerously, but only for a second. Like her spirit, the smile slid from Kate Bennett's face to Nadine's in the blink of an eye.

Sebastian didn't waste a further second; he turned on his heel and sprinted for the door.

–

Henry and Charles crashed through the front door into the entrance hall. The lounge lay to the right. Henry seized the door handle and barrelled in. As he threw the door wide it collided with something; having entered with considerable commitment, whatever it was Henry hit was sent flying.

The thing turned out to be Sebastian Dahl, hurled him back into the room he had just been attempting to leave. He tumbled, lost his footing and crashed onto his back, skidding to a stop. Nadine Smith stood in the centre of the lounge, tear-streaked eyes closed, arms flung wide. A shudder ran through her, and Henry stopped dead in his tracks as in the same instant someone else took charge. He had seen the woman Nadine Smith became before, only this time she looked like she had come to do more than just talk.

The air around her began to ripple. To Henry it called to mind asphalt on a scorching summer day. Even from the doorway he felt the temperature begin to climb sharply. She closed in on Sebastian Dahl who lay sprawled on the floor, utterly petrified.

A short distance away, Kate blinked and raised a hand to her face. She looked, disoriented, around the lounge, at the dead youths littering the floor, at Henry and Charles in the doorway, and finally at the dangerously shimmering figure of Nadine Smith bearing down on Dahl.

Whoever presently commanded Nadine stood over his trembling figure. Dahl started to gibber, every ounce of the Dahl self-assured persona suddenly deserting him. The haze around Nadine pulsed ominously for a few seconds, then a white-hot pillar of flame ignited from out of nowhere like a serpent. It twisted, alive, conscious, and coiled a ring around Dahl, trapping him.

Henry couldn't say what he read in its mistress's face, whether it was anger, sorrow, regret or triumph. Perhaps all these and more besides. What he didn't doubt was her intent. Sebastian Dahl was about to get his.

Nadine turned her head, looked at Kate. Except Henry knew it wasn't Nadine, nor Selene either. It was Kate's mother standing over Dahl, Valerie. She had saved her daughter once before, and now she was back to finish the job.

Henry could only imagine the things she must have yearned to say to Kate, in the end, though, it came down to a single word. He saw her lips form it through the rippling haze and smoke.

"Go."

If Kate heard or saw, she took no heed. Quite the opposite, seemingly undeterred by the rapidly expanding ring of flames scorching the ceiling and floor boards around the terrified figure of Sebastian Dahl she actually started to advance.

Spurred back into action, Henry hobbled forward and grabbed hold of her before she met the flames. She fought him as he pulled her toward the doorway. They had barely reached the threshold when Nadine erupted like a phoenix. The flames around her exploded, rolling and cavorting like spiralling orange ribbons. She fell upon Dahl. His screams issued from the blazing white fire and heat. The conflagration ballooned, brilliant, rippling, licking the walls and ceiling. Henry continued to haul Kate back, the hairs crisping on his skin as he fought to drag her away from the two figures now blazing like gasoline-soaked mannequins.

Then Charles was at his side, and together they wrestled Kate into the hall and out of the front door.

425

They staggered out onto the rise, only to be immediately bowled like skittles to their faces as the ground shook and a blast of scorching heat and flying glass rushed over them. Henry pulled his face from the damp grass, twisting to look back. Great tongues of flame were rolling from the house's windows. Then a second thump followed the first, fire belching from the windows in great sheets. There was a momentary shriek of structural surrender before the house crumpled on one side. A third thump soon followed, bringing what remained of the edifice down. In little more than seconds the house was razed to a pile of fiery rubble.

Good riddance, thought Henry blearily. He felt light-headed, almost drunk, and so drained he could scarcely keep his eyes open. He rolled over and gazed into a star-shot sky daubed with blue-grey smoke and twirling embers. He had earned a rest, he reckoned. They'd done it. Kate was safe. Almost as if this thought had been enough to summon her, Kate's beautiful face, soot-smeared and tear-streaked, suddenly filled his field of vision. She swam in and out of focus, towering over him, Charles too. They were babbling about something, about a leg. His leg? They looked so agitated. Could he muster the energy, he would have told them both to chill out. They'd done it. It was over, done. He peered down to find Kate fussing with his leg. Black treacly liquid was pumping from the wound like an oil rig that had struck gold, dark and wet in the firelight. An old TV theme song popped into his head—he smiled to himself. Ha, black gold, Texas tea...

Kate wasn't smiling though.

He wanted to tell her to relax, that it couldn't be too serious, because he could hardly feel a thing. He shut his eyes—and just like that he was floating, looking down on himself, rising up amongst the embers swirling on the wind, although in his imagination he looked like some sort of a vampire sprawled on the damp grass, pale as porcelain. One leg of his jeans was stained dark as the night. Kate and Charles were both bent over it. He wanted to tell them not to worry.

Everything was okay.

Kate was safe.

It was over.

NINE FEARED DEAD IN BIZARRE TV 'HAUNTED HOUSE' TRAGEDY

The Devon and Cornwall police force launched a major investigation today into the bizarre events at a cliff-side Cornwall property last night which led to a house fire resulting in multiple deaths and two shootings.

A source claims crew members from cable ghost-hunting show 'Where The Dead Walk' are alleged to be involved, with the house having been slated to feature in a forthcoming episode of the show.

Detective heading the investigation, Inspector George Barry, declined to either confirm or deny if any of the show's crew members were among the dead or those brought in for questioning. It is believed, however, that at least on

429

Chapter 76

Kate stood at the foot of the rise.

The dark winter months had passed, spring had sprung, bringing with it longer days, welcome warmth and sunshine. Kate put her hand to the gate and pushed. It opened easily now. The weeds and bramble choking it had been cleared away and its hinges greased. The hedgerows bordering the rise had received similar attention and looked chocolate-box-picture neat. As for the workmen who had wrought these changes and others over the past couple of months, they had since moved on. The rise was again deserted. The most obvious vestige of the rise's occupation was the caterpillar tracks scarring the hill leading to where the house once stood. A plateau of raw earth was all that remained of it, ready for nature to reclaim.

Kate pulled the gate shut behind her and started to climb the hill.

Of the many queer turn of events to emerge from the aftermath of Sebastian Dahl's machinations, one was this: the house (or what was left of it) and the surrounding several acres now belonged to Kate. Dahl, it transpired, had amended his will a mere forty-eight hours prior to his death, naming Kate the sole beneficiary of his entire estate. Of course, the precise question of who Kate Bennett might soon be when he had done this was a considerably more fluid matter than the solicitor handling the matter could possibly have imagined, and afterwards it became something of a moot point. Kate had inherited the lot. After all she had lost, it was an odd legacy.

As soon as the police investigation had concluded, lines of enquiry exhausted, case suspended, white forensics tents and police tape taken down, she had arranged to have what was left of the house levelled. The debris had been thoroughly crushed and disposed of, dispersed around no fewer than a dozen different sites across the country. However unlikely the prospect, Kate had made damn sure no one would ever be in a position to reconstruct the house again. As for the rest of Dahl's considerable estate, save for the hillside she now scaled, she kept nothing. The remainder had been liquidated, the proceeds donated to the homeless charity *Shelter*.

If the inheritance was a strange and unexpected discovery, it was by no means the most bizarre to surface. That dubious prize went to the discovery of the skeletal remains of a middle-aged woman buried beneath the lounge floor. According to the police forensic team, the remains were estimated to be around twenty or more years old, and were yet to be identified, by the authorities at least. Kate, however, required no DNA evidence. She knew the remains belonged to the woman called Selene Cole. At some point Sebastian had made it his business to acquire them. Kate preferred not to dwell on the finer details of how exactly he had gone about this.

Actually, there were a good many things she tried not to think about after all that had happened, with varying success. Occasionally she found herself contemplating just how long and hard Dahl must have laboured in the hope of bringing his lover back from the dead, and how deeply he must have cared for her to have done so.

Was there a time she would have done as much to bring back Robert and Joel, if she'd believed such a thing were possible? It was an uncomfortable question, to which the answer was never as convincing as she would have liked. Kate knew only too well how blinding grief could be, how it could make any vision of the future seem impossible. She had also come to see that in order to live you have to retain the capacity to look forward. If you can't, then real life stops. Looking back, counting all you've lost, is a dead end, and wrong too; the pain that comes from loss is only possible if you were lucky enough to have had something valuable to begin with, and the harder the loss, the more fortunate you were, even if only for a while.

You have to accept that everything is borrowed, because whether it's the living obsessed with making contact with the spirits of loved ones they've lost, or spirits unwilling to let go of the living, refusing to cross over to wherever it is our essence ultimately goes, it becomes a distraction from the real business of living, looking and moving forward.

She crested the rise and stopped at the place where, amid wild grass and scrub, the plot of freshly turned clay and earth lay, Dahl's house had once stood. For months the police had pored over the ruins. The detectives had asked their questions, picked and pored over evidence, and come up empty-handed. While a tantalising buffet of strange acts and potential crimes presented themselves, including arson, assisted group suicide, multiple murders, kidnapping, fraud, a wealthy celebrity stalker and a bizarre cult seemingly attempting to practice acts of witchcraft, the hard facts available to piece together what had *actually* happened (as woefully inadequate a route as one could choose to divine the truth in this particular instance) were frustratingly sparse. And so, despite the whole affair exciting a mixture of intense curiosity amongst the press and the public and lingering suspicion amongst the authorities, the truth remained elusive, and with the remaining few individuals in a position to explain the whole crazy business not feeling remotely inclined to, it seemed destined to stay that way. Not that there wasn't speculation.

The tabloids favoured the following scenario: attractive television presenter Kate Bennett, unbalanced by the recent death of her father, fell under the influence of a celebrity stalker. Sebastian Dahl, a wealthy charismatic figure had, through manipulation and the use of surreptitiously administered drugs, drawn her into his cult, masquerading under the guise of a charity called *Doorways* that purported to help homeless youths. Dahl's witchcraft-obsessed devotees had, among other things, acquired the skeleton of a woman through means unknown (but one would imagine with the aid of a spade and a graveyard) to use in an occult ritual. Whatever the point of the rite, it appeared to culminate in an act of group suicide, with Dahl presumably intending to take the object of his obsession, Kate Bennett, with him. When some of Kate Bennett's friends, the crew of *Where the Dead Walk* attempted to intervene, a struggle with one of the cult's members ensued, resulting in a double shooting, the two victims being the cult member himself and *Where the Dead Walk*'s producer, Henry White. Like the police, though, the journalists had little concrete to work with, and their interest in the story quickly dwindled, overtaken by X-Factor love rats, footballer's wags, and occasionally honest to goodness real news.

Kate looked out over the swatch of dirt where the house had festered for a decade. A few slender shoots of grass were already peeking from the soil. She imagined the area covered with grass, all evidence of the house eradicated. The rise would be left to grow wild. Let the birds, bugs and animals have it.

Beyond the cliff's edge the ocean shone under a blue, cloud streaked sky. Kate lifted her face to the salty breeze, squinted her eyes against the sun.

A courteous cough prompted her to look over her shoulder. She smiled as he moved to join her. Even after all the physiotherapy he retained a slight limp, not that he grumbled. It had been scary for a while there, and in light of everything else that had happened they were both inclined to feel he had got off lightly. If Ray and the others hadn't arrived when they had, if the air ambulance hadn't been available, or got there in time...

Henry curled his arms around her, resting one hand lightly on the bump beneath her coat, and asked the question she knew was coming, even though they had been here before. Someone who didn't know him as well as she may not even have heard the trepidation in his voice.

"Anything?" he asked.

She shook her head.

"No. She's not here, not anymore."

"No one is, right?"

"We are."

She leaned into him, drew his arms tighter around her and gazed out over the ocean to the horizon.

Looking forward.

End.

Did you enjoy this book? Well don't keep it to yourself, let me and others who might like the book know about it.
How?
Glad you asked.

- Leave a review. I'm curious to know what you thought of the book, and honestly do read each and every one.

Get alerted to news of forthcoming books, content and deals by emailing 'news me' in the subject heading at:
johnybwritesnews@gmail.com

You're also welcome to contact me directly to talk books and writing at:
johnybwrites@gmail.com

or visit me on Facebook at:
www.facebook.com/JohnBowenWrites

John Bowen.

Acknowledgements

Many thanks to all who helped see this book to the finish line.

My wife Caroline, who I'm sure I don't deserve, my kids, Henry and Freya, my mom, dad and step-dad, Richard Daley, my iron man of draft readings, Sarah Wilson, Joanna Franklin Bell, Leanne Cook and Malorie my GoodReads pals who offered invaluable contributions to its editing, and everyone else who ever helped make me feel like I wasn't wasting my time.

Cheers guys.

Also by John Bowen,

VESSEL

Forget all you know.
History's biggest secret was hidden behind legends and
lies...

Running for her life, carrying a secret with the
potential to change what it means to be human, Holly
Reilly calls the only person she knows with the skills to
keep her alive: her estranged husband Gabriel.

Caught between two deadly adversaries, Holly and
Gabe are drawn into a centuries-old conflict, one poised
to spill into the modern world, threatening chaos and
bloodshed.

DEATH STALKS KETTLE STREET

Imagine your neighbours start to die in a series of
accidents, only they aren't accidents...

Someone is murdering Greg Unsworth's neighbours
and staging the deaths to look like accidents.

Greg knows the truth, but when he's grappling with
OCD and simply closing his front door and crossing the
road are a battle, how is he supposed to catch a serial
killer?

19841053R00247

Printed in Poland
by Amazon Fulfillment
Poland Sp. z o.o., Wrocław